The Ladies of Covington Send Their Love

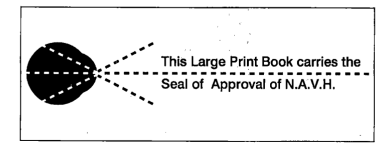

This Large Print Book carries the Seal of Approval of N.A.V.H.

The Ladies of Covington Send Their Love

Joan Medlicott

Thorndike Press • Thorndike, Maine

Published in 2000 by arrangement with St. Martin's Press, LLC.

Thorndike Press Large Print Americana Series.

The tree indicium is a trademark of Thorndike Press.

The text of this Large Print edition is unabridged.
Other aspects of the book may vary from the original edition.

Set in 16 pt. Plantin.

Printed in the United States on permanent paper.

Library of Congress Cataloging-in-Publication Data

Medlicott, Joan A. (Joan Ayna).
   The ladies of Covi███ ███ se███ ██ ██ ██ / by Joan
  Medlicott.
     p. cm.
   ISBN 0-7862-2976-4 ███ ██ ██ ██ ██ █aper)
   1. Aged women — Fic██ ██ ██ ██ ██ male friendship —
Fiction. 3. North Carolina — ██ ██ ██ 4. Boardinghouses
— Fiction. 5. Retirees — Fiction. 6. Large type books.
I. Title.
PS3563.E246 L33 2000b
  813'.54—dc21   00-064794

With love and thanks to my aunts,
Lina Kushner and Charlotte Paiewonsky,
to my good friend Jeanne Keck,
and to the memory of my mother-in-law,
Winifred Medlicott

Acknowledgments

✿ I would like to thank special friends who helped me with this book: Penny Aylor and Celia Miles for their faith in me, their encouragement, and excellent criticism; my cousin, Marcia Paiewonsky, for her meticulous editing of punctuation and spelling and her creative suggestions; and my agent, Nancy Coffey, for her enthusiasm, keen insights, superb editorial skills, and her wisdom.

1

A Gift of Love

Grace Singleton grasped the oak railing firmly and forced another step up the narrow wooden stairs. Beneath her palm the railing was smooth and cool and indifferent, a sharp contrast to her heated and agitated state. The fourth step creaked, but today the creak sounded less like the mere scurrying of a mouse than it did like the roar of a lion. Grace's legs trembled. She wanted to stop, to yell, "No, I won't do this," but after much discussion and argument, she had agreed that it must be done.

At the top, in the dimly lit hallway leading to the bedrooms, Grace paused and looked back down the stairs into the foyer with its faded floral wallpaper, its standing coatrack, and its long, narrow, wall mirror over a walnut table that had seen better days and now played host to three straw baskets that served as receptacles for their mail, and past all this to the doorway of the kitchen. Two women stood in that doorway, one tall, her face determined, one short, twisting her hands. The tall woman nodded encouragingly and waved Grace on.

Grace drew a deep breath, lifted her head, and started down the hallway feeling like a common thief as she slid the key into the door of Amelia's bedroom. Perspiration beaded her forehead, her upper lip. She tugged at the checkered bandanna tucked at her waist, wiped her face, and slipped one end back under her belt. The house, usually filled with kitchen clatter or chattering voices, was quiet now.

"How did I allow Hannah and Olive to badger me into sleuthing?" she muttered. Her mind raced. I'm about to commit a monstrous invasion of Amelia Declose's privacy, opening her drawers, riffling through her closet, I, who detest prying, snooping, meddling in someone else's business. This overriding sense of guilt left her nearly breathless.

"Someone has to do it and you know her best," Hannah Parrish, her strong-willed fellow boarder had insisted.

True, Grace was closer to Amelia than either Hannah or their meddlesome landlady, Olive Pruitt, but how close was that really? Anticipating entering Amelia's room, even under these circumstances, made Grace tremble.

But if I don't do it, Grace reasoned silently, that pushy Olive will, and she'll shove and yank and dump things from drawers without any respect for Amelia. I'll handle Amelia's belongings with care. Resolutely, Grace squared her shoulders, took a deep breath, and turned the knob.

Amelia's room was impeccable with white walls, white lace bedspread, lace-edged pillow shams, and no magazines strewn casually about as they were in Grace's room. Pink satin slippers were tucked neatly under the bed, and books were carefully stacked on the night table. Grace walked over and read the titles: Kahlil Gibran's *The Prophet*, a slim volume of Shakespeare's *Sonnets*, and a copy of *The Shell Seekers* by Rosamunde Pilcher. As she turned, the mirror over the bureau caught her eye. Why was it draped with a towel? Was it cracked or clouded? She peeked. The mirror was intact. Grace scrutinized the bureau, a model of fine handcrafting with its turned mahogany legs and trim. It bore the marks of time: a zigzag scratch on one side, a water stain on its surface, and behind the brass pulls were tiny nicks where fingernails had gouged the finish.

It seemed least intrusive to begin with the closet. Amelia's dozen or so white dresses and several white pantsuits filled the small space. The floor was bare. The round flowered box that Grace removed from the shelf above the clothes rod revealed no letters, no diary, no address book, no photographs. Nestled inside the box, wrapped in sheaves of white tissue paper, lay a wide-brimmed, white straw hat with a cluster of cherries securely fastened on one side. Grace smiled. The jaunty hat reminded her of those worn by women strolling the Boardwalk in Atlantic City in old 1920s photographs.

Standing on tiptoe, Grace shoved the hatbox back onto the shelf alongside several pairs of sturdy SAS shoes, a pair of New Balance walking shoes with the heels worn down on the inside edges, and a slim pair of white Capezios.

She could still hear Olive Pruitt's voice informing them about the new boarder just before Amelia arrived a few months ago. "I think Amelia Declose used to have money. She's been lots of places, like Europe. Fancy lady she is, you can tell to look at her. Prissy too, always wears white. Uses funny foreign words, too. I hope she don't put on airs." Olive had gibbered away in

10

her usual magpie fashion as she dished up their dinner of corned beef and cabbage. "I run a simple clean establishment." She set a blue crockery platter on the table. "Nothing fancy, and I don't take kindly to snooty folk."

Grace had tuned out her landlady's cigarette-strained voice, and when Amelia arrived, wearing a tailored white linen suit with a pale blue scarf tucked about her neck, Grace found her a pleasant, though rather reserved person, but not the least bit haughty, unless you counted — and Grace did not — the sprinkling of French expressions that slipped into her speech, especially when she was excited or pleased. Amelia's tentative smile, her soft voice, her unassuming ways, reminded Grace of friends back home in Dentry, Ohio, and Grace had gone out of her way to make Amelia feel welcome.

The bureau drawer was open. Had she opened it? No. Yes. She must have. Silk scarves of varying shades of blue, neatly folded and stacked one atop the other, lay alongside lacy white handkerchiefs, lace collars, and a striped gray-and-white stocking case. The second drawer held white cotton underwear, silk vests, full slips, and long silk bloomers and under the vests a small, unlocked, sandalwood case containing several fine pieces of sterling silver jewelry.

Increasingly uncomfortable, her hand shaking, Grace shut the drawer and took refuge in the upholstered rocking chair by the window. The rocking chair, the mahogany bureau, a Tiffany lamp, a battered steamer trunk, a watercolor of two girls sitting on a beach watching a sailboat race at sea, and two suitcases were all that Amelia Declose had brought.

How much did she really know about Amelia? Amelia spoke longingly of the latest Broadway production in New York, enjoyed the music of Mozart and Vivaldi, and worried about cars driving above the speed limit on Sugar Maple Road. She volunteered little information about her past, and Grace had never asked. Yet it puzzled her that Amelia received no phone calls or visitors, and Grace now realized that there were no photographs in Amelia's room, not on her walls, not on her bedside table, not on her bureau. What quirk of fate had brought this lovely, well-traveled woman to Olive Pruitt's drab boardinghouse at Number 16 Sugar Maple Road in Branston, Pennsylvania?

Grace raked her teeth across her lower

lip. Her mind drummed a constant reprimand. This is wrong. This is dishonest. I'm betraying Amelia's trust. How will I ever face her? Outside the window she could see all the way down Sugar Maple Road. Straight as a ruler's edge, the solid, redbrick houses with their squat, second-story roofs, redbrick steps, and square, stubby front porches lined the street. A dark-haired boy rode by on a shiny blue bicycle tooting its horn.

"What's taking you so long? Did you find anything?" Olive's deep, raspy voice coming from the stairwell jarred Grace.

"Not yet. Be down soon."

A moment of silence. Then the voice again, crackling with impatience. "Hurry up, it's almost lunchtime."

Grace shivered. The idea of food sickened her. Her head ached.

"Almost finished." Grace roused herself and hastened back to the bureau where she had found the Capezio shoe box in the bottom drawer. She carried the box with her to the rocker, for it would be disrespectful to sit on Amelia's fine lace bedspread. Under a linen handkerchief and a tan leather-covered address book with blank pages were three letters with a North Carolina post office box return address.

Grace wiped the perspiration from her upper lip. Her reading glasses hung about her neck on a grosgrain ribbon. Grace slipped them on and one by one, according to their dates, opened and read the letters.

November 29, 1995

Dear Mrs. Declose,

I hope this letter finds you well and that you will forgive my intrusion into your life. For the past year I have been researching my family's genealogy, searching not only for roots but for relatives. I myself am the last of my line, the Furrior line that is, an old man, bereft of children, who has outlived his family.

I enclose a genealogical tree to illustrate the connection between us. You will see that we had a great-great grandfather, William Austin Furrior, in common. Apparently our great-grandfathers went their separate ways and rarely communicated with one another after emigrating from France to America in the 1800s.

I am taking the liberty of enclosing a snapshot of myself that was taken recently. I look forward to hearing from

14

you, to sharing our family histories. It would be good to reconnect our two families through a friendship. I would appreciate having a photograph of you.

Sincerely,
Arthur Austin Furrior

The distinguished white-bearded man in the photo reminded Grace of pictures she had seen of General Robert E. Lee, only this man sat, not tall and proud on a horse as the general was often depicted, but tall and somber in a wheelchair.

The second letter was dated January 8, 1996.

Dear Amelia,

It is my hope that your holiday season was joyful and healthy. Receiving your letter blessed my Christmas and the New Year.

Amelia is a lovely name. Thank you for writing and thank you for the picture. Your lovely smile reminds me of my dear wife, Eleanor, whom I lost eight years ago to cancer, a dreadful end for a kind and gentle lady. I sigh and agree with you that when we are young freedom is everything and time moves too slowly. Growing old is another matter; it is then that time dashes by and old friends and family matter most.

I regret that my health makes it impossible for me to travel to see you and that you are unable to visit me in North Carolina. But it will be a pleasure to correspond with you, perhaps chat on the phone, and catch up on each other's lives.

His letter went on for several pages and included a story of a big game hunting expedition to Africa in the 1940s on which he had accompanied his father. He wrote of their guide's vigor and enthusiasm and how the man, a retired veterinarian, had inspired and later encouraged him to become a veterinarian.

Grace studied the photo of Arthur Furrior. Amelia, she knew, was sixty-seven. This man looked many years her senior. She picked up the third letter, dated February 2, 1996, five months ago, just after Amelia had come to live with them.

Dear Amelia,

It was a pleasure to receive your letter. Thank you for telling me about your life. I admire the good and important work you and your husband did with the Red Cross. You have seen more of the world than I have, and I've had a wanderlust all my life. Not only do we share a love of travel, but we share a love of music as well. I envy you hearing Maria Callas sing at La Scala Opera House in Milan. Music has been my solace in troubled times. Having been raised in Iowa, I have always longed to live near water, to go to sleep listening to the sound of the surf. How fortunate you were to be able to spend summers on the Rhode Island coast.

My health is deteriorating rapidly and soon I may be confined to bed. Not a happy prospect. Like my father, I am a man who thrives out-of-doors, and in my chair I can at least sit under my oak trees and feed the squirrels and birds. But confined to my bed? I don't know, cousin. I don't know.

But for this I am grateful, that my research led me to you, my own flesh and blood, my cousin. Your letters have brightened my life and made me happy. Thank you. You have given me, in my advanced years, a family. I remain faithfully,

Arthur

Grace felt a tug at her heart. The handwriting had changed with each letter, becoming more shaky, reflecting Arthur Furrior's failing health. A small rectangle of paper folded and tucked into the envelope caught her eye — a cable dated June 19, 1996.

WE REGRET TO INFORM YOU OF THE DEATH OF ARTHUR A. FURRIOR ON JUNE 16, 1996. J. B. PENNYSON, ATTORNEY-AT-LAW.

Saddened, Grace folded the cable and tucked it back into the envelope.

"You dead up there? I'm coming up." Olive's voice unsettled Grace.

"Nothing here, be right down," she called, playing for time to calm herself.

Grace slipped the letters and Arthur's picture into a deep pocket in her shirtwaist dress just as the doorknob turned.

"Nothing at all," Grace said, clutching the box. She willed her trembling hands to be still. The letters were so personal that she could not bear to think of Olive snickering over them. "Just more scarves. This is the last box. I've looked everywhere." Carrying the Capezio box to the bureau, Grace knelt and slipped it back into the bottom drawer. Then she pulled herself up, turned, and combed the room with her eyes, seeking telltale signs of her intrusion. Satisfied that there were none, she tucked her arm through Olive's, who guided her into the hallway and closed Amelia's bedroom door behind them.

Hannah, waiting at the bottom of the stairs, raised her eyebrows as her eyes met Grace's.

"Absolutely nothing," Grace called down. "I'll be right down." Needing time alone now to compose herself, she headed for her own room.

Grace's room was the largest of the three upstairs bedrooms, close to the bathroom she shared with Amelia. A bright room with a southern exposure, it had been painted a drab beige with faded, rust-colored curtains. Grace had transformed the room: painted the walls a pale shell-pink and placed a six-by-nine emerald-colored rug alongside her bed. Revitalizing an old chaise longue had been accomplished with a soft rose-and-white-striped cover, and she had hung new bright flowered chintz curtains. Olive had helped her shove the chaise longue to the low wide window that, like Amelia's window, overlooked Sugar Maple Road. And books,

books everywhere, including treasured volumes that had nourished her imagination, her soul as a young woman: Homer's *Odyssey*, an account of Schliemann's unearthing of ancient Troy, Lord Carnarvon's and Howard Carter's chronicle of their discovery and excavation of the tomb of Tutankhamun.

Bringing her hand to her chest, Grace moved it slowly around and around as one might rub a baby's tummy. Reaching the chaise, she eased herself down, pulled a small bottle of nitroglycerin pills from her pocket, and slipped two of the tiny tablets beneath her tongue.

It was a relief when the pressure in her chest eased. She took a deep breath, closed her eyes, and reminded herself that Olive and Hannah were waiting downstairs. "Get up, go down," she muttered, then shook her head. Just another minute. A car horn sounded below, jolting her, and she stared about as if surprised to find herself in this room in this house. Below her window on Sugar Maple Road, two young women strolled by chatting, toting shopping bags. Across the street Mr. Spooner, a retired Barnum and Bailey clown, sat dejectedly on his front porch. Alongside him on another chair were bright red-and-blue hoops, a bulbous clown nose, and a carrot-colored wig. She sensed Mr. Spooner's loneliness, perhaps, the same that she felt, a loneliness endemic to the loss of home and loved ones and, most virulent, the loss of meaning in one's life. But Sugar Maple Road was a street of primarily older folks with the occasional sprinkling of grandchildren, and only the seven-year-old twin grandsons of Mrs. Oglesby, two doors down, showed any interest in him. Grace watched the twins turn the corner and hasten toward Mr. Spooner, who smiled, perked up, jammed on his circus nose and hair, and began to juggle the hoops.

Grace eased herself out of the rocking chair and crossed the room. Stopping at her dresser, she picked up a recent photo of her son, her only child, Roger, and his English companion of ten years, Charles, in flowing Saudi garb, their arms about each other's shoulders, smiling self-consciously. Roger had visited his father, Ted, once in the six months of her husband's battle with cancer and of course he and Charles had come for Ted's funeral. A year later, she had been well on her way to full recovery from her little heart attack when Roger flew in again from Saudi Arabia. He had rushed about like one possessed, had refused to acknowledge that she was fine and content where she was, and had suggested, urged, then insisted that she sell her things and move. In so doing, he had turned her world topsy-turvy.

Grace sighed, set the picture back among the assemblage of family photographs, and tried to push the memories of those days out of her mind. What was done was done. Reliving them only depressed her. Taking a moment, she ran a brush through her still ash-brown hair, then straightened her shoulders and pulled open the door.

Olive scowled, shook her head, and wiped her hands on her apron. "Seems like Amelia's got no next of kin. How could I have taken her in my house without finding that out?" Still muttering, she busied herself at the kitchen sink, then turned as Grace came through the doorway. "The hospital called while you were upstairs, Grace. Amelia's one lucky woman. A tumor it was and not malignant."

"Thank heavens. That's wonderful news." Grace's heart lightened.

"Still, if Amelia comes back and can't climb stairs, she's got to go. I'm not serving food to no one in their room. In my house you take care of yourself or out you go."

"We'll help her, Olive. She won't be a trouble to you." Hannah's voice was firm yet unusually conciliatory as she pulled out her chair at the round kitchen table. Her salt and pepper hair was cut short and swept back from her face. Sporty dark gray cotton slacks and a black-and-white-checked long-sleeved shirt ordered from a catalog suited her casual yet efficient manner.

Hannah always sat facing the door. "It makes me nervous," she had told Grace, "to sit with my back to an entrance. I'm paranoid that someone will catch me off guard, come up behind me and grab my neck." Hannah had tossed the words into the air casually like snowflakes, but they had struck Grace's soul like hard-edged flints camouflaged in a snowball.

All meals at Olive Pruitt's were served in the cool, dim kitchen where the strong odors of beans simmering, fish frying, onions browning, and cabbage steaming often permeated the room. The houses were no more than fifteen feet apart and from the window one could peer into the kitchen of the house next door. Olive

23

picked up a glass and dried it vigorously. "I know about old people. Surgery's the beginning of the end. Amelia's frail. She'll never really recover. Come back for a couple of weeks, and just like that" — setting down the glass, Olive snapped her fingers — "she'll pop off."

"Heaven's sake, Olive," Hannah said, "Amelia's not old. Old is eighty or ninety. Amelia's sixty-seven. Her tumor wasn't malignant. She'll be fine."

Dinner at Olive's table reminded Grace of the dining room table of her childhood, dominated as it had been by her humorless inflexible father, primed to admonish or criticize. Now, Grace reached for the bowl heaped high with tuna pasta salad that Olive plunked on the table. "We'll take her food up to her if she can't come down."

Olive's eye narrowed. "No family, eh? Real secretive that Amelia. Now I'm responsible for her final arrangements? Not my job." She shook her head again and grimaced. "How'd I let that get by me when I interviewed her?"

Hannah focused on the pasta salad, separating the ingredients into small piles, pasta, green beans, tuna, celery. It was her habit to eat each item of food separately.

"Hate Chinese food," she had informed

them. "Stuff jumbled together. Can't tell the taste of a celery slice from a bamboo shoot."

Grace watched as Hannah heaped a bowl with salad. Incongruous, Grace thought, since Hannah didn't mind a mix when it was part of a fresh green salad.

"Greens," Hannah insisted, "are essential for good digestion and elimination. A meal without greens is lopsided," and Olive, who hated to chop vegetables, had grudgingly acceded to Hannah's demand and now served them fresh salad three times a week. Olive never served soup. Grace missed a bowl of thick, hot soup, but mostly she missed not being mistress of her own kitchen.

Hannah's room was the smallest of the three upstairs bedrooms. A two-year resident, Hannah, had chosen it purposely. She enjoyed resting on her bed, from where she was eye-to-eye with the mature red maple tree that shaded the rear of the house and the pocket-sized backyard. Hannah had gardened actively, had owned a plant nursery. Her daughter Miranda, an intense reticent woman, now owned the business and had expanded the nursery to include a flower shop. Every week, regular as clockwork, fresh flowers came and potted plants for the holidays: vibrant orange lilies at Easter, cheerful yellow chrysanthemums on Labor Day, flaming red poinsettias before Christmas. Today a lovely arrangement of bright white and yellow daisies mixed with blue ageratum sat on the night table beside Hannah's bed.

After kicking off her sturdy Naturalizer shoes, Hannah threw herself, fully clothed, on the bed and stuffed a firm pillow under her knees. That usually offered some relief from the nagging pain in her hip and back. At Grace's quiet knock, Hannah propped herself up on her elbows.

"Hannah, Olive's gone off on some errand."

"Good. So, tell me what you found, Grace."

"What makes you think I found something?"

"Your face is an open book. I'm surprised Olive didn't realize there was more to this than met the eye."

Grace set a large envelope on a chair, then hesitantly drew the letters from her pocket and handed them to Hannah, who reached for her reading glasses on the nearby table. While Hannah read, the silence was broken only by her intermittent comments. "Arthur must have been a fine-looking gentleman in his day. Husband with the International Red Cross, so that's why Amelia traveled so much."

Then Hannah read the cable. "This is sad. No one for Amelia now, is there?" She glanced at Grace, looked away, dangled her glasses between her fingers.

"Amelia deserves better than Olive Pruitt looking after her, after her . . . you know what . . ." Grace said.

"Her final disposition?" Hannah raised her hand. "Yes. We'd have to do it."

Grace sank into the chair near the bed. Her fingers trifled with the ends of the bandanna tucked into the belt of her dress. "I feel guilty enough invading her privacy." Her eyes sought Hannah's. "Imagine having to make those kinds of decisions for someone."

"She's alone, no children."

"Are we luckier for having children, Hannah?"

Hannah's eyes clouded. "I'm not sure. Can't recall when I last had a meaningful conversation with my Laura. Since she moved to Maine three years ago with what's his name, the boat fellow, it's as if she's fallen off the planet." A wistful smile tugged at the corners of her mouth, then a sense of satisfaction crept into her voice. "Laura's a computer programmer, you know. I saw to that. Why would she go off to live on a boat when she could get a good job anywhere? Miranda? The last time we sat down to really talk was when I signed the nursery over to her two years ago, after my knee surgery."

"But all the flowers? And she calls fairly regularly."

"It's easier to send flowers than to touch or talk. Her calls are always short and specifically about my health, nothing beyond that." Her face grew sober. "My knee surgery. With the boys away at prep school, Miranda and Philip had the extra room. They insisted I stay with them after my week at the convalescent center, then they pretty much left me on my own to fend for myself." She tossed her hands in the air. "Well, with taking over the business, Miranda was busy, but Laura . . . Laura didn't even call."

"I've given up trying to understand how my Roger got to be so distant. We used to be so close."

Hannah shook her head, as if to put away her thoughts, and gave Grace her full attention. "I thought gay men were sensitive, cried at the drop of a hat."

"They're like anyone. Some do, I guess, some don't." Grace rolled the edge of the bandanna between two fingers and looked intently at Hannah. "It seems to me as we grow older it's women friends our own age we really need." She sighed. "What do our children know about how it feels to tire more easily, or that our heels ache because they've lost a lot of their natural padding . . . ?"

"Dry, blotchy skin." Hannah rubbed her arm. "Spare me. I'm not that old." She scowled.

"I'm serious. I've been thinking. We need seasoned women in our lives, women who've coped with love and loss and survived life's disappointments and ironies. It's the support, the empathy of our peers we need more than we need our children. They're another generation with hectic lives. They see us from their childhood perspectives. They can't imagine that we might still have hopes or dreams or longings." Her voice trailed off.

Hannah waved one of the letters. "Having said all that, surely you agree that we needed to check Amelia's room?" She looked into Grace's serious, wide-set, doe-brown eyes. Grace's eyes and face never failed to amaze Hannah — a pretty face, very pretty if not beautiful, with a peaches-and-cream complexion that was smooth and unlined. And her voice, well, her voice was soft and soothing. Sometimes when Grace talked, Hannah closed her eyes and wished that she would read to her from one of those books she so often carried. And Grace was, how to put it? Grace was a good woman, honest and generous of spirit. Hannah's heart skipped a beat because this short, chunky, sweet-faced woman from a small town in Ohio — whose shirtwaist dresses, socks, and oxfords were old-fashioned, and whose checkered bandanna, dangling from her waist, was ludicrous until you fell down the front porch steps and needed something with which to bandage your bruised and bloodied hand — lived at Olive Pruitt's boardinghouse and was her friend.

"Have you any idea how ashamed I am for doing this, and now showing you the letters?" Grace rose and paced from one end of the narrow room to the other. The room was crammed with Hannah's furnishings: a double bed, one bedside table, a wing chair with an ottoman, a goose-necked reading lamp with a tassel shade, a coatrack draped in sweaters and jackets, a stuffed-full umbrella stand, a tired old maple desk and chair, and a tall, narrow, cluttered dresser. Pictures, mostly nature scenes and florals, covered the walls, and a small bookcase packed with books about plants and gardening stood within reach of the desk. "I'm going to put those letters back," she said, "and I'm going to tell Amelia."

"Stop pacing, will you, you're making me dizzy. Be sure to tell Amelia you weren't snooping, just trying to locate her family." She shifted her body to relieve the pressure on her hip. "Damn. I can't stay in one position more than ten minutes," she muttered. Then she turned determined eyes to Grace. "We all need someone to take charge of things for us now and then. Didn't your son come from Saudi Arabia when you were ill and help you close up your home and move?"

Before Hannah's resolute blue eyes, Grace's resolve wavered, but only momentarily. "Yes, he did, but . . ."

"Would you have wanted to do it alone?"

Grace walked to the window, leaned on the sill, and peered down over the fence into the neighbor's yard, where a small dog circled, chasing its tail. She sighed, then turned and walked slowly back to Hannah.

"I'd never have given up my home," she said, taking the chair she had vacated. "Roger wouldn't let up, he kept insisting that I sell everything and move here, closer to an airport, he kept saying." Grace could not hide the irritation in her voice or the pain it caused her to think about it. Looking down at her hands, she fingered the plain gold band she still wore. "I can't tell you how I felt watching strangers walk into my home and cart away what had been my life and Ted's. I loved our Ethan Allen dining room set. It took us two years to save up to buy it." Her eyes met Hannah's. Her shoulders drooped. "Roger deposited me here a year ago, on my sixty-seventh birthday. I took one look at this house and thought, it's so frayed-looking, and you know, that's just how I felt." She sighed deeply. "I never imagined life would reduce me to living in one room in someone else's house."

"Couldn't you have refused to move?"

"It was all so fast, so unexpected." She hesitated, looked away. "I've never been good at saying no." Then Grace came and stood at the side of the bed above Hannah. "No one likes a complainer, my mother always said. But, Hannah, sometimes, I feel so downhearted, don't you?" The room fell silent as Grace looked expectantly at her friend.

"Course I do. Times I wonder what it's all been for, working sixty-hour weeks struggling to raise, to educate my girls, to end up so unconnected to them, especially Laura, and in a place like this. Inside of me" — she tapped her chest with two fingers — "in here, in my heart, in my spirit, I feel young, forty years old. Do they care? Do they know?" She brought a fist down on the side of the bed. "And your Roger's not much better. That's why we have to help Amelia. Who else will?"

"Still, Roger's my son. We're not Amelia's family. We have no rights in this case."

"You just said we needed one another. Act on those words. Amelia's got no family. We have a moral as well as a personal obligation to help her."

Hannah had a point, yet Grace was troubled by the method. Still she knew one way or the other, arguing with Hannah was useless. Hannah would say and do whatever she wanted. Then Grace remembered why she had come upstairs, and she held up the Federal Express envelope that had arrived just after lunch. "This just came. I thought I'd go and take it to Amelia in a

33

bit. If I may borrow your car? I thought you might like to come."

"Sure, I'll go. Give me a minute to freshen up."

With Grace gone, Hannah reached down, groaned, then eased first one leg and then the other over the side of the bed. "Damned hip," she muttered, "where's my cane?" It was ludicrous that a woman, five feet ten inches tall, taller than her husband had been, taller than many men, and as active as she had always been, should need a cane. Other than her hip she was a healthy, strong, and proud seventy-three-year-old with all her faculties and totally chagrined that a bad hip could so harness her independence.

It took several steps to, as she called it, "oil her joints," before Hannah reached the window and eased herself into the chair at her desk. She straightened her wide shoulders and picked up a pencil. By this age and stage of their lives they'd all had more than their share of success and failure, joy and pain, love and loss. On a pad Hannah doodled her daughter's names, Miranda, Laura. Did they blame her for their father's death? It was so long ago. Leaning her elbows on the desk, she rocked slowly back and forth for several moments.

What Grace had said about needing each other more than they needed their children had touched her. Amelia had no children to worry about, or be hurt by. Hannah doodled the word right. Searching Amelia's room had been the right thing to do. Sometimes others had to take charge of things, and this was one of those times. For a moment Hannah indulged in daydreaming, imagining herself in her lush and lovely garden fragrant with roses and brilliant blue hydrangeas and the area she had set aside for cut flowers, zinnias, coneflowers, daisies, gladiolas, alive with color. Knee surgery had gotten her walking again, but with the caveat, don't kneel, don't squat, bad news for a gardener. What caveats would come with hip replacement surgery? She hated this enforced retirement. If she had one wish, it was to be as physically fit as she had been before her knee and hip had betrayed her, and to once again be in charge of her own plant business.

The leaves on the red maple shimmered in a quicksilver breeze. Hannah studied the tree. "Love you best in spring when the birds come back and your sticky little leaves unfold." She had always talked to flowers, plants, trees. They brought her more comfort than most people; they never betrayed her. She could love them, talk to them, feed them, water them, and they rewarded her with stunning flowers that gave only pleasure. She loved trees with their strong limbs that supported tree houses and children's swings and offered wonderful cooling shade in summer. Hannah ran her fingers through her thick short hair, then using both hands, shoved herself up from her desk and moved toward the door.

Grace drove Hannah's clunky old station wagon at twenty miles an hour down Sugar Maple Road. As a driver she felt inadequate and self-conscious. "I didn't learn to drive until Ted died, you know," she told Hannah.

"Really?"

"After Ted died, I had to depend on friends for transportation to the market, church, drugstore, even the cemetery. I took driver's education three times before I felt confident enough to take the driving test. Dentry's a small town, population five thousand, three hundred and two, according to the chamber of commerce, five stoplights, and almost all streets marked twenty-five miles an hour."

"You only drove in that town?"

"Yep. I've never driven on an interstate or a four-lane." She shivered. "The thought gives me the willies." Grace did not tell Hannah that sometimes she dreamed of speeding along a highway singing at the top of her lungs.

"Did you talk to her?" Hannah asked, changing the subject.

"Amelia? Yes, I called the hospital. She's feeling better, wants company." Grace eased the car around a curve and crept down a tree-lined street. Ahead of them loomed the Isaac Branston General Hospital, all glass and brick and named, as the town had been, for a Union captain, a local hero of the Battle of Gettysburg.

Grace found a place as close to the entrance as possible, and moving at a snail's pace, in deference to Hannah, proceeded across the parking lot toward the hospital entrance. "Dammit." Hannah stopped for a moment. "I used to be as swift and agile as a deer."

And stubborn as a mule, Grace thought, and sometimes a bit overbearing, my friend.

Amelia opened her eyes and for a moment wondered where she was. The cream-colored walls, the floral-patterned curtains, an oil painting of a waterfall on the wall across from her bed were not what she expected in a hospital room. Then she remembered doubling over in excruciating pain in Olive's kitchen, a sense of speed and crush and noise, and later a tall doctor with horn-rimmed glasses and a brush cut who called her by name.

"Mrs. Declose, Amelia," he'd said, "you're a very lucky lady. We've removed a benign growth from your colon. You're going to be just fine." And he had patted her hand.

She would recover. She had before, even when she would have preferred not to. Life then, and even now, seemed more of an effort than it was worth. Her hand moved to her neck and throat. The Pain. Dr. Spencer had said she would forget, in time. But in all these years, she never had. Relax, Amelia said to herself. This is Branston, not New York, and I'll be out of here soon.

Outside her window puffball clouds scooted by, a sure sign of a brisk wind. She tried to sit up straight, but the pull of stitches stopped her. Holding her stomach, she sank back onto the pillows. I've slept well here, she thought. With the help of pain pills and sleeping pills of course.

Before being discharged she must wangle as many sleeping pills as she could from the doctor. Without them, she sighed, more endless, sleepless nights.

"When do I go home?" she asked the nurse entering the room.

"When the catheter comes out, Mrs. Declose." The nurse plugged a thermometer in Amelia's mouth and began pumping up the blood pressure cuff.

Amelia was in no hurry to leave. She would have another good night's sleep tonight. "Ouch, my arm feels as if it's going to explode, young lady."

"Sorry about that. Please keep the thermometer in your mouth."

Amelia Declose seemed a gossamer creature. Startlingly blue eyes looked at the world from a pale oval face, unlined except for a crisscross of fine winkles near her eyes, which leaped into action when she smiled. Her hair, pulled back in a bun at the nape of her neck, was white, not the white of melting snow in city streets, not white tinged with yellow, but pure silver white that accentuated her remarkable eyes. All her life people had remarked on her eyes: magnificent, amazing, such eyes, blue as heaven, like sapphires. Thomas, her late husband, who had been raised in Montana and who, therefore, ought to have known, called them Montana sky blue, which had a romantic aura, and pleased her most of all. Slender and of average height, she had been a perfect fit with Thomas when they danced.

Then Amelia saw Grace and Hannah standing in the doorway. "Ah, *mes amies*," and with her free hand beckoned them to enter. As a companion Amelia preferred Grace, but she had developed great respect for Hannah, a single parent before it was acceptable, a woman who had owned and operated her own business. She's tough, doesn't let life beat her down; Amelia had thought it about Hannah before and she thought it about her now. Cane or not, Hannah had plenty of starch in her.

Amelia knew things about Grace's life, about Hannah's life, but they knew nothing of hers. It was still, after four long years, too painful to talk about.

The nurse folded the blood pressure cuff, accepted the thermometer Amelia handed her, wrote some notes on a chart, and left the room.

Grace stood at Amelia's bedside. "How are you, my friend?"

"Recovering."

From their initial meeting Amelia had been drawn by Grace's warm smile and trusting eyes. There was about Grace a serenity, a sense of slow and quiet deliberation. Grace considered things before voicing an opinion. Where she, Amelia, though she appeared friendly, was cautious of people, Grace had a welcoming, optimistic attitude toward all comers. Amelia liked Grace, and oddly, having had a mere smattering of female friends and having known Grace for only a short time, she trusted her. One evening, Grace had made a batch of her special sugar cookies, and the three of them settled on Olive's front porch to indulge themselves while the sweet sound of someone playing Gershwin on a piano drifted from somewhere down the street. That evening Grace had talked about her little heart attack, her one arterial angioplasty, and about her weight.

"First I had indigestion, but it got worse and then my arm went numb. I called my doctor — I'd known him all my life. He rode with me in the ambulance to the hospital in Dayton, a good hour's drive away, stayed right by my side all during the angiogram and the angioplasty. Talk about scared. I was so terrified I almost stopped breathing. They had to give me oxygen. Humiliating, but the nurses were wonderful. Dr. Frank said I was lucky, just one artery blocked, but he wanted me to take off weight. 'Add years to your life,' he said." Grace had crossed her hands over her chest. "Well, all my life I've gained and lost weight. I was fed up with it. One day I just stood in front of my full-length mirror and said, so my behind juts out, my hips sprawl, and that's how they're going to stay." Then in a burst of levity she waved her hands in the air. "I had the mirror taken down."

Now, reaching out both hands, Amelia clasped one each of theirs. "How good to see you both."

"We miss you at Number Sixteen. When do you come home?"

"Tomorrow. Day after tomorrow."

Amelia thought Grace's winsome face looked strained, her eyes anxious as she placed the envelope on the bed.

"What's this?"

"Don't know. It came today."

Amelia passed the Federal Express envelope back to Grace. "Do the honors, please."

Slipping her finger under the flap, Grace

extracted three items and handed them to Amelia.

Amelia read the letter to herself, exclaimed, "Oh, my," and then read it aloud.

Dear Mrs. Declose,

Your cousin, the late Arthur A. Furrior, has made you a gift of love. You are the beneficiary of a property near Asheville, North Carolina, in a town called Covington. The property is comprised of a farmhouse, twenty-eight acres of land, a year-round spring, and a stream. As Mr. Furrior was unable to visit this property in the last several years, it may need refurbishing. With this consideration in mind, Mr. Furrior has provided a sum of fifty-thousand dollars ($50,000), enclosed herewith, for repairs should they be necessary, or you are free to dispose of this money and the property in whatever manner you wish. A local farmer, Harold Tate, looks after the property and can be reached at 555-859-2567. If I can be of any further service, please let me know.

Sincerely,

J. B. Pennyson, Attorney-at-Law

Amelia stared at the check. "Unbelievable. Incredible. Fifty thousand dollars. It's been forever since I've seen this much money."

Wide-eyed, Grace gawked at the check. "I never have."

Amelia's eyes filled with tears. She held a slim blue-veined hand over her heart. "How generous, how kind and dear of Arthur." She looked at Grace, then at Hannah. "He was my cousin. I'll miss him. He found me, and now he's gone."

Grace nodded, feeling guilty and unable to stand the strain of her snooping. "I know about Arthur, Amelia."

"How? I never told anyone. I hope you don't feel offended, Grace, Hannah. His first letter was so unexpected, so special. I didn't want to share him with anyone for a little while, and now it's too late to share him with anyone." Her eyes brimmed with tears.

Hannah found herself explaining. "We felt if you had family, we had to let them know you were in the hospital. Grace didn't want to. Olive and I insisted that she go into your room to see if she could find an address book, a letter, someone we could contact on your behalf."

"I found Arthur's letters, picture." Grace

sunk to her knees alongside Amelia's bed. "Forgive me. I've betrayed your trust. I feel so guilty."

"Get up, Grace, please. I can't see you down there. I understand. It's natural you'd want to contact my family, if I had any." She fingered the check. "If I'd told you about Arthur, you wouldn't need to feel guilty. I'm the guilty one for keeping him from you. Understand? There's nothing to forgive."

Grace exhaled a sigh of relief. "Thank you, Amelia, thank you." It was then that Grace noticed the patchy discoloration of burn scars on the side of Amelia's neck and down onto her shoulder.

Amelia felt Grace's eyes on her neck and her hand flew to cover the scar. "It's so ugly, an awful reminder." She flushed. "That's why I wear a scarf."

"How did that happen to you?" Instantly Hannah regretted the words that had flown out of her mouth.

Amelia turned to Grace. The sheet she pulled to her shoulders did not quite cover the crumpled white scars. "Hand me my scarf, please, Grace." She pointed to a hook on the wall near the door. "I meant to ask the nurse for it. Thanks." Amelia took the silky, blue scarf and

45

wound it about her neck. "I feel quite naked without a scarf. It's not something I can talk about easily. At least not now."

2

The Call to Adventure

✿ "Here's Asheville." Amelia's finger jabbed the creased map of North Carolina spread out on the kitchen table. "But where's Covington?"

"Covington's probably a crossroad, a speck. Too small for the map." Hannah sprawled in a chair pushed away from the table, right leg extended, cane propped against her thigh. From the middle of her back down to her feet, everything ached. Damn rain, she thought, shifting position.

The Asheville Chamber of Commerce had mailed them sheaves of brochures about the Biltmore House, motels, bed-and-breakfasts, antique shops, river rafting, trail rides, outlet malls; their sole interest was locating Covington.

Grace stepped back from the table. "I agree, it's a very small place. We do have the right name, Covington? C-o-v-i-n-g-t-o-n."

Reflecting her growing sense of agitation

and urgency, Amelia's fingers strummed the smooth wooden surface of the table. "We need to go down there."

"You mean go to North Carolina?" Grace's heartbeat quickened. "How? When?"

"I think we should just pile into Hannah's station wagon, what's her name, Nelly? all three of us, drive down and have a look at this farmhouse." With eager eyes Amelia looked from one to the other of her friends. "Maybe it's wonderful. Maybe it has a big porch with lots of gingerbread trim." Then she turned to them with a worried look. "You can't drive, Hannah, not with your back giving you so much trouble. I gave up driving years ago. Will you do it, Grace?"

Before Grace could reply, Hannah said, "Old Nelly'll need a tune-up, rotate tires, need to join AAA." She longed to be away from Branston, away from this house and the droning voice of their landlady. She longed for the country, longed to sink her teeth into the crunchy flesh of an apple fresh from a tree, perhaps to slowly browse in a country flea market.

Grace's throat tightened. "No," she managed. "I can't do that."

"Why not?" Hannah challenged.

"For one thing, it's too sudden. I need to think about it and, well, I've . . . I told you, I've never driven on an interstate."

"You've never driven on an interstate?" Amelia looked at Grace with disbelieving eyes.

Grace bridled. Just because she hadn't traveled like Amelia or been a single, independent working woman like Hannah didn't mean she was stupid. "Of course I've driven on interstates, who hasn't? I just haven't been the person behind the wheel. Never needed to."

"Driving is driving, Grace," Hannah said definitively. "You can do it."

"It's only seven weeks since your surgery," Grace appealed to Amelia. "You can't be ready for such a long trip."

But Amelia was ready. Nothing had excited her in years the way the prospect of this trip did. She busied herself with folding the map, using the time to plan a strategy. Hannah was a go. Grace would require bolstering and gentle persuading. "I feel great," she said. It was irrelevant that she tired in the afternoons, all that mattered now was getting to Covington, to the farmhouse Arthur Furrior had left her. Grace must go. Besides the fact that she was the only driver among them, Amelia

49

had come to depend on Grace for comfort and companionship and couldn't conceive of the trip without her.

"You can hardly make it up the stairs, how will you sit in a car all day long?" Grace asked Hannah.

"Doctor'll prescribe pain pills. I'll stretch out in the backseat." Hannah raised her eyebrows. "You're slow as molasses, but I trust your driving."

Amelia said, "We'll stop often to eat, use the bathroom, maybe do a little exploring. Must be some nice little towns along the way."

"I won't do it." But even as she said it, Grace realized she was echoing Ted's convictions about how dangerous the world was beyond Dentry, Ohio, and its environs.

"Treacherous driving on a four-lane, much less an interstate. Wild, reckless drivers, drunk drivers. Here read this." He'd shoved the newspaper at her. "A twenty-car pileup on the interstate, truck jackknifed, killed four people."

Having no experience with which to refute him, Grace had accepted his judgment, and now, faced with the challenge and responsibility of driving them to North Carolina, she found herself automatically falling back on Ted's opinions. But there was another part of her that hankered for the thrill of adventure.

Amelia's hand rested lightly, reassuringly, on Grace's shoulder. Her voice softened. "I can understand how the speed on an interstate would make you nervous, but don't say no just like that. Think about it. Hannah and I could take a plane, I guess, and take cabs, but I don't want to go without you. This is very important to me. You're my dearest friends." She looked from one to the other. "I need you to go with me. I want you both to see it. It might be a great old house in a wonderful place, or it might be a huge disappointment. One way or the other, I need your support." She paused, aware that Grace listened attentively, and Amelia was certain she detected a mix of caution and excitement in her friend's eyes. "Tell, me, Grace, what speed are you comfortable driving?"

"Thirty-five, forty," Grace replied. "I've always been uneasy with speed."

"Minimum speed on an interstate's forty miles an hour. Sure, cars will seem to fly by, but we can stay in the right-hand lane and drive forty. Please, please do it for me."

"Ted hated interstates. The news is full

of accidents, pileups, drunk drivers smashing into cars, killing innocent people." She shivered and shook her head.

Amelia tried another tack. "There's less traffic on the roads after Labor Day. We won't go until then." Then her eyes grew dreamy. "The Shenandoah Valley's so beautiful. Have you ever seen it, Grace? We could stay at motels with inside rooms."

Grace looked puzzled. "Inside rooms?"

"You go in the lobby, like in a hotel. Ramada Inns, Hampton Inns, lots of motels have inside hallways now instead of having to enter the room from the parking lot. It's safer."

"Didn't you ever travel, go on vacation?" Hannah asked, disbelief in her voice.

"No. We stayed home. There were lots of things to do near Dentry and Ted preferred going fishing at Lake Bixby, just up the road," she said defensively.

"Didn't you want to go anywhere else, do something different?"

"We were satisfied right at home. And travel is so expensive." Grace's voice went flat; she felt stodgy and unsophisticated. No, she didn't know about inside and outside rooms. She didn't know how much to tip a porter or if her clothes were right. For a moment she felt ashamed to admit, even to herself, that her life had been so restricted.

Amelia moved around the table, pulled out a chair, and motioned for Grace to sit. Then kneeling, she placed her hands gently on Grace's knees and spoke in a low soothing voice. "There are wonderful places to visit in this country. Please say you'll do it. I want so much for you to go."

Amelia's eyes, so lovely, so pleading, touched Grace. Still she vacillated: torn between her desire to please, her own deep longing for change and adventure, and her deeply ingrained fears about driving Hannah's big station wagon on the open road. The whole escapade stirred a long dormant yearning for things and places that had been available to her only in books and movies. "I can't read a road map," she said.

"I can," Hannah said.

"What will I tell Roger?"

"That we're all three of us going on a short trip."

"He worries about me. I've never done anything like this, just gone off, in my whole life." She strained the ends of the bandanna between two hands, in a tug-of-war between deep-seated anxiety and wanting to support Amelia.

"But it's okay for Roger to live in Saudi Arabia?"

"It's his work." Grace turned to Amelia. "What if I start out and then find I can't go on?"

"That's not going to happen, Grace," Hannah said, trying to control her impatience with her friend. "Once you start, you'll become more, not less, confident. That's how these things work."

"How do you know that? You just sit there, Hannah, and say that's how these things work. How can you say that?" Grace's face reddened as she spoke.

Hannah drew a deep breath and shifted in her chair. "I know because I had to confront an upbringing that instilled in me the belief that 'marriage is for better or worse' and that you 'stick with a man no matter what.'" Distress covered Hannah's face. "Bill was a lousy drunk and abusive, and I stayed for far too many years. Can you imagine what it was like for me, scared to death of him, taking my girls and running away from Bill, away from Sault Sainte Marie? But I did. Made it over the Canadian border into Michigan to a truck stop." Closing her eyes, Hannah bit down on her lower lip. "Bill found us, pulled out a gun, threatened to shoot me."

Grace could find no words to express her horror. She recalled that day in the kitchen when Hannah explained why she must sit facing the door. Hannah had spoken so casually that Grace had dismissed it, preferring not to dwell on the implications, but today she could not help but think that it had been her husband who made her fearful.

"My God. What happened?" Amelia asked.

"He shot holes in the car's radiator."

"What'd you do?"

"I froze, just like those sprays of water that arced from the radiator and froze in midair. I was so scared I wet my pants," Hannah confided, looking them square in their faces. "I couldn't move, couldn't think. Then this big hulking truck driver came out of the gas station, knocked the gun out of Bill's hand, and offered us a ride. He took my arm. I grabbed both girls by the hand and shoved them into the cab of his truck, and off we went. I can't even remember his name, but thank God for him, a stranger. He saved us that night."

"Oh God, Hannah. I knew you raised the kids alone, but I thought you were widowed," Amelia said. "I'm so sorry. What a terrifying thing to happen. Why didn't you tell us?"

"It was the worse thing that ever happened to me. I hardly ever think about it anymore."

"I'm so sorry," Grace said.

Hannah straightened her shoulders and shrugged. "He's dead. Whole other story. It's a long time ago." She took a sip of coffee, then plunked the mug on the kitchen table. "Some things hide in the recesses of your brain, I guess. Then something happens or someone says something and pop, like a jack-in-the-box, the whole darn thing's up and out again."

"It's my fault you're even thinking, talking about it now," Grace said, hugging herself with both arms.

"It's life," Hannah said. "It's in the past. I learned a great deal and I'm telling you, Grace, just drive that car. Fear's a box we grow used to, convince ourselves it's all the space we need, that we like its color, its smell, its protection. Comes a time to stop hiding, stop being afraid. If we don't break free of our boxes, our spirits shrink, we shrink in every way imaginable. Oh, Grace, my friend, don't let fear, especially someone else's fear, prevent you from living your life. I promise, if you step out of that box, you won't fall off the edge of the earth." Hannah's facial expression softened and her eyes filled with tears. "You'll fly," she said. "I did."

Amelia moved behind Hannah and gave her shoulder a firm squeeze. "We've had a lot going on here. I'm sorry we stirred up such painful memories for you. Listen, we need a diversion. How about all of us going to a movie?"

They chose *The Little Mermaid* and came out annoyed at the way Disney distorted the fairy tale they had all read and loved as children.

"I used to cry every time I read it," Grace said. "The Little Mermaid gave up so much for love, and it's so unfair how it turned out for her."

"It's all the pizzazz they add that bothers me," Hannah said. "With that Calypso singing crustacean and that huge octopus witch."

A coffee shop across the street attracted them and they ambled over for pastries and café au lait. Caught up in myriad worries about traveling, Grace sat silent, stirring her coffee with added milk and topped with whipped cream as she debated sharing her concerns. Would they laugh? Compared to Hannah standing there in the freezing cold night staring into the barrel of a gun, her fears seemed trivial. She took a deep breath. "You see," Grace wiped whipped cream from above her lip, "I can't share a room with anyone. I'm up several times a night to go to the bathroom, and I have trouble falling asleep again."

No one laughed. Instead, they both nodded, and Amelia realized that by not pressuring Grace, by seeming to let it go, she had won. Grace would hesitate, vacillate, offer excuses, and continue to express anxieties, but in the end she would go and she would drive. Amelia pressed her hands tightly together in her lap to control the sense of victory that flooded her. "We all have our own sleeping habits," she said. "We'll take separate rooms. That way we'll all be comfortable yet close enough if we need one another." Her eyes shone.

"We'll be like *The Three Musketeers*. One for all; all for one," Hannah, feeling her old self, chimed in.

"What clothes would we take for a trip like this?" Grace asked.

"Everyday, comfortable clothes and shoes. No one dresses for a road trip."

"Not even for dinner?"

"Heck no," Hannah said, thinking that

this was a conversation she might be having with a visitor from overseas, not with an American woman in her sixties whom she had lived with in the same house for over a year. "We'll fall out of the car into a Howard Johnson's, an Olive Garden, a Shoney's restaurant" — she waved her hand at their surroundings — "a Starbucks." Hannah considered, for the first time, that perhaps there was a need beyond corporate greed for restaurant chains. The repetitive styles and signature colors of their buildings, their identical menus, and even their reliably clean bathrooms were responses to a craving for comfort and familiarity in the marrow of a mobile and rootless people.

And it was that very image of restaurants and motels with familiar names that helped ease Grace's apprehensions. That, and the fact that Amelia had unwittingly tapped the slumbering gypsy within her. "Doesn't sound quite so scary anymore," she said. "I'll think about it."

Later as they said good night in the hallway outside their rooms, Grace knew she didn't want to think about it anymore. Anxious still but no longer scared, she wanted very much to be part of this adventure. "I'll have to drive slowly." A mischievous look flickered in her soft brown eyes. "Take my time, go slow, don't get frazzled." She brought the knuckles of one hand to her mouth, suppressing a grin. "You know," she confided, "I've really always wanted to do something like this."

At this Amelia shot Hannah a triumphant glance.

At dinner the next evening Olive Pruitt stared at them aghast. "You're what?" She scowled at Hannah. "I'll have to let your daughters know." She turned to Grace. "I'll have to telegraph your son."

They could not restrain quick conspiratorial glances. "We're not children, Olive," Hannah said. "We pay rent here; you don't own us."

"I have responsibilities. I'm licensed as a retirement home. There are rules."

"Rules?" Grace's salad fork stalled in midair. Tipping her head, she looked with amazement at Olive. "What kinds of rules?"

Olive shrugged. "I feed you three nutritious meals a day. I must pass sanitation and kitchen inspections. I'm responsible for calling nine-one-one in an emergency and notifying your next of kin when . . ." She stopped, set the platter on the table, and stood with her hands on her hips before turning back to the stove. "Can't just go off like that. I'll have to notify your people."

Olive wasn't going to put a damper on their plans. They exchanged knowing smiles, and Hannah assumed the role of spokeswoman. "Is it because we're over sixty-five that we need a keeper? Medicare's the cutoff point for what, intelligence, judgment, or just living in general? Is that how you see it?"

Olive's features contorted, her face turned red. Grace considered it expedient to change the subject. "Dinner looks great, Olive. I'd love to just pour on the gravy." She sighed and set the gravy bowl back on the table. "Doctor's orders."

"You use that as an excuse when you don't want to eat something," Olive snapped at her before she stomped from the room still muttering, "Going to notify your people."

Olive must have made things sound pretty dire because two days later a cable arrived from Roger from Saudi Arabia:

CHARLES AND I RETURNING TO THE STATES TO LIVE. URGENT YOU STAY PUT. ARRIVING SOON

61

This announcement shocked Grace. They had never lived close by, and it had never seemed to matter to them before. Grace sat on the edge of her bed and reread the cable. Urgent she stay put? Why? For a moment old habits reasserted themselves, and she considered telling the others she could not go. But it had been a difficult decision for her. She was excited now and looking forward to the trip. Roger had not even said when they were coming. She'd probably be back before they got here. Grace folded the cable and laid it on her night table.

And from Hannah's daughter Laura, who lived with her longtime companion, Captain Haines, on a charter boat moored in Rockport, Maine, came a phone call.

"Olive called. She sounded hysterical. What's going on, Mother?"

"What's going on? Before hello, how are you?"

"Sorry, how are you, Mother?"

"I'm fine."

"Now, what's Olive so upset about? What's going on?"

"One of the women I live with here has inherited property in North Carolina, and the three of us girls are going to pile into old Nelly, my station wagon, and go see it."

"Girls? You're hardly a girl, Mother."

"I feel like one tonight."

"Is it wise?"

"Is what wise? Feeling like a girl and not an old bag of bones?"

The exasperation in Laura's voice was clear. "You're toying with me, Mother."

Her daughter was humorless. Hannah kept forgetting. "Listen, Laura, Amelia's my friend, and she's inherited a farmhouse and some land. We're taking a few days and going to North Carolina to see the place. We'll let Olive know where we are. Don't worry about us, between us we have . . ." She calculated on her fingers. She had always been good with numbers. ". . . two hundred and seven years of experience. Good-bye now, Laura." She hung up. Seconds later the phone rang.

"Mother." It was Laura again. "It's raining here, and I had to row to shore in order to make this call, so don't hang up again."

"Fine, Laura." Hannah strummed the side of the phone. "What is it?"

"Who's driving?"

"Grace, a solid citizen, drives about fifteen miles an hour."

"But that's too slow on the interstate; that's as bad as going too fast."

63

Hannah rolled her eyes. "I'm kidding, Laura. Grace drives cautiously, not dangerously."

"Can't I say anything to dissuade you, Mother?"

"No."

"You'll be sure to let Olive . . ." she hesitated, ". . . and Miranda, know exactly where you are?"

"Certainly. Good-bye now, Laura. My best to the captain. I can never remember his name, I'm sorry." Clear and strident, Laura's voice traveled the lines from Maine to Pennsylvania.

"Marvin, Mother. His name is Marvin."

"Marvin then, my best to Marvin."

Hannah hung up and stood there shaking her head. "How did I ever raise such a stick? And why, suddenly, all the fuss?"

"At least she called. Roger cabled an order," Grace, standing nearby, said.

Hannah's eldest daughter, Miranda, arrived early on Sunday morning just as Grace and Amelia hefted the last of their suitcases into the spacious rear section of the Chrysler station wagon. Tall and thin with the stoop-shouldered stance sometimes assumed by slender, small-chested women, Miranda's dark eyes skittered from her mother to Amelia, to Grace, to the station wagon, and back to Hannah.

Grace missed not having a daughter, and it saddened her that Miranda and Hannah were not closer and that Hannah hardly saw her grandsons, even when they came home for holidays from their Massachusetts prep school. She listened carefully to the exchange between the two now, hoping that Miranda would not scold or be cold or indifferent.

"I'm worried, Mother, your car's so old. What if it breaks down?"

"We joined AAA." Hannah's smile was meant to reassure Miranda. It failed.

"You're often in pain, and you need that cane. Won't this trip be too much for you?"

"Think not." She sighed. "I need the change, try to understand."

Miranda peered into the car, walked to the house, then back to the car. She shook her head, slid her hands up and down the sides of her gray corduroy slacks, then her eyes shifted to Amelia, who had risen from the step and begun to tug the ice chest closer to the edge of the stoop.

"Let me do that." With two long strides she was at the porch and had grabbed the chest, filled with ice and drinks and sandwiches for their journey, carried it to the open back of the station wagon, and secured it between two suitcases.

"Thank you, Miranda." Slamming the back shut, Hannah leaned against the car. "Spoke to Laura. Rowed in from the boat to phone me. Told her we'd be in touch with you and Olive."

"Laura's a fool. Never satisfied with anything, lives in her head, disillusioned with modern civilization, she claims. Maybe living on that charter boat and working with Marvin she's found a sense of meaning, who knows? Meanwhile I'm the one who'll handle everything if anything were to happen to you, God forbid. When was the last time Laura came to see you, us?"

"Long time, Miranda." What Miranda said about Laura rang true, but hearing it made Hannah feel guilty, responsible. She preferred not to think about it. Now her eyes met those of her daughter's. "I know you're worried about me, and I do appreciate your concern, but I'll be just fine. I think Olive may have worked everyone up unnecessarily. You're such a worrier, Miranda. Remember that time we drove from Kalamazoo to Philadelphia, just you two girls and me, and you fretted all day every day about whether we'd find a place to sleep that night? What were you, nine, ten?"

"Ten. No. Yes. I don't remember that part, just that Laura wanted the windows open. I wanted them closed. It was awful. But that's beside the point. Do you have an itinerary?"

"Actually, we don't. We'll get down into the Shenandoah Valley tonight. Way past Labor Day, so there's bound to be plenty of available motels." She turned to Grace. "You remember the umbrellas? They get sixty-six inches of rainfall in the Asheville area every year. Bet most of it's in the fall."

Grace nodded, held up a neatly packaged new umbrella.

Hannah reached out to her daughter. They had never been a hugging family, but suddenly she wanted to hold Miranda. She patted Miranda on the shoulder. Miranda turned and for a moment seemed about to hug her mother, but then retreated with an embarrassed look. She reciprocated Hannah's gesture with a touch to her mother's arm.

Hannah's face flushed. "It's going to be all right. This little trip will do me a world of good. I've got pain pills. I'll be fine.

Only a day and a half drive. I'll call you."

The pale yellow light of the morning sun struck the porch steps as the station wagon lumbered away, leaving a concerned yet resigned Miranda and a fretting Olive standing side by side in the driveway watching until it turned the corner out of sight. At that moment, twenty minutes away at the Branston airport, Roger and Charles stepped from a 727.

3

Amelia's Story

Buffeted at times by wind whipped up by the force of a sixteen-wheeler tunneling past, old Nelly wavered, and Grace, responding to a rush of adrenaline, clutched the steering wheel with sweaty hands. They cruised along slowly and easily enough to appreciate the lush sprawling countryside while cars and trucks tailgated, then zoomed by, their impatient drivers shaking their fists and glaring at them. At Winchester they entered the Shenandoah Valley, a place of charming hillside towns, of livestock grazing in pastures, of meandering streams, of red barns and bright white farmhouses, of tobacco cut, staked, and drying in the autumn sun, of dogwoods tipped reddish-yellow, and orange-berry pyracantha foreshadowing winter.

In one of her more relaxed moments, Grace said, "I'm feeling quite proud of myself."

"And you should be," Hannah chimed,

from the backseat.

"I shouldn't be. 'Pride cometh before the fall' was hammered into me by my father. One time when I was in eighth grade I brought home an all 'A' report card. He wouldn't even look at it. 'Pride's the devil's work,' is what he said."

"What'd you feel like, the devil's hand-maid?" Hannah laughed, but the thought of her father had sobered Grace.

"Why, yes, sort of." She was quiet for a moment. "I didn't much like my father, then and for a long time after. Years later, when he got cancer, I helped my mother take care of him at home. He'd been a bookkeeper for a small handbag manufac-turing company, and being around their house as an adult gave me insight into how much he hated his work and how insecure he was, too insecure to change his job, or move, take any risks."

"The old fear thing," Hannah said. "Sounds like he bequeathed some of his insecurity to you."

It hurt to hear it so bluntly stated. "Why, yes, probably. And his rigidity certainly left no room in his life, or the family's, for pride, laughter, joy, certainly not adven-ture."

"What was it like living in a small town

like Dentry, Grace?" Hannah asked. "Weren't you bored?"

"Bored? Hardly. I was a full-time wife and mother, baked for church suppers, volunteered at the school clinic, collected for the March of Dimes, then the United Way. Early on, I was busy chauffeuring Roger. I gardened a bit, had lots of friends. Ted liked bowling, so we did that twice a week. No, I wasn't bored."

"Were you happy with Ted?" Hannah asked.

The question surprised Grace, but then, Hannah had been amazingly frank about her own life. "Happy? Yes, I was, most of the time. Near the end, after they stopped the chemotherapy, Ted asked me if I'd been happy as his wife. Of course I said yes." Grace turned her head slightly, directing her answer to Hannah. "Ted and I were high school sweethearts, married after graduation. I was taught, if you start something you finish it. It never occurred to me to question whether I was happy with Ted. He worked hard at the steel mill, took care of us. I took care of him and our son."

"No regrets then?" This from Amelia, who had been staring out the window, seeming a million miles away.

For a few moments Grace focused on an old rattletrap of a truck loaded with squalling pigs that clattered past. "I wanted a large family. I miscarried twice, a girl and a boy. I was depressed for a long time, until Roger was born."

Amelia turned back to the window. "I understand," she said softly.

Once in the Shenandoah Valley they chose the town of Staunton, population twenty-five thousand, to stay the night. Hannah, who had been reading the tour book, explained to them that Staunton was one of the oldest cities west of the Blue Ridge Mountains.

"Settled in 1732," she informed them. "Staunton survived the Civil War un-scathed. It's got beautiful nineteenth-century houses and churches, a Museum of American Frontier Culture. Let's take a day and see some of it before we get back on the interstate."

And they decided that in the morning they would do some sight-seeing.

They were surprised to discover that the tiny three-bedroom suite they took at Frederick House was accessed by a winding staircase from a private foyer. It felt as if they were ascending the turret of a tower. Grasping the iron railing tightly with their right hands and pressing their left hands against the smooth, white, curving wall on the left for support, slowly and carefully they climbed the steep stairs.

Halfway up, Hannah stopped to catch her breath. "I can't go up and down these steps again tonight. Let's order in."

Once inside the suite, Amelia chose the large multiwindowed bedroom, Hannah the room closest to the hall bathroom, and Grace placed her overnight case and purse in the smallest but coziest bedroom. With its canopied single bed it reminded Grace of a little girl's room. "It's charming," she told her friends. "I'll sleep fine in here tonight."

Between Hannah's and Grace's rooms was a small undistinguished den with 1950s forest green faux leather chairs and a thirteen-inch television set and inadequate reading lights. Hannah ordered dinner from a nearby Pizza Hut, and it reassured them that the delivery boy was as winded as they had been after negotiating the narrow twisting stairs. In robes and slippers they ate pizza in the den sitting on the floor around the coffee table, where true to form, Hannah picked the pepperoni, mushrooms, and peppers from her slice, eating each separately.

Later, lying in bed, Grace's mind turned to Hannah's question, had she been happy with Ted? What would I have done differently, she asked herself. I was a good student, and probably could have gotten a scholarship to college, could have become a history teacher. She took a deep breath. Rarely did she think about the future, or what she would like to do with the ten or fifteen years or more her doctor said could lie ahead, and she certainly was not about to do so now. Grace yawned. What does it matter anyway? Ted's gone. Regretting's a waste of time, Grace thought as she reached over and snapped off the light.

Driving around the following morning, they wandered into a neighborhood of small clapboard houses, many in the process of being refurbished, and on past them to an area of well-preserved Victorian homes set back behind tall wrought-iron fences. Hannah's guidebook directed them to historic Trinity Episcopal Church.

"Built in 1855," Hannah said as they started up the steps. A plaque read:

74

THIS CHURCH IS BUILT ON THE SITE OF
THE BUILDING WHERE THE VIRGINIA
ASSEMBLY TOOK REFUGE IN 1781.

They sat for a few minutes in one of the
wooden pews and when the others rose
and went outside, Grace lingered awhile
before joining them in the parking lot. It
was peaceful sitting there. Closing her
eyes, she imagined the rustle of women's
long skirts, the tread of boots on the wood
floor, soft whispers, and in that moment
Grace felt connected to the hundreds of
parishioners who had come here to worship or perhaps for town meetings. "Ted,"
she said softly, "I'm glad I came. I'm
driving very carefully, so don't you
worry."

In the car again, Hannah said, "Now,
let's go explore the Frontier Museum."

At the museum they fell into step with
Hannah, who was determined not to let
her slow movements or her reliance on
her cane stop her. And so they ambled
along, stopping often so Hannah could
sit a moment and rest and chat with the
costumed interpreters who explained and
depicted life in Germany, Ireland, and
England before they had immigrated to
America, and then their lives on an

eighteenth-century working farm.

"Bet they're exhausted at the end of the day," Hannah said as they moseyed back to the station wagon.

Grace's heart brimmed with appreciation and admiration for the actors — men, women, and children — who so enthusiastically depicted the daily lives of their ancestors. "The immigrants," Grace said. "They traveled so far, faced such hardships in a strange land." She cupped her cheeks in her palms. "My face still feels hot just from watching that woman bending over, stirring her food in that pot over that open fire in the hearth."

"Long dangerous trek across the mountains," Hannah said. "Full-time job felling trees, chopping wood, cooking, washing clothes, trying to keep warm in winter, hauling water in buckets . . ."

Grace chimed in. "Hunting for food and at night no privacy, everyone sleeping in the one wood-heated room."

Amelia made a wry face as she opened the door of old Nelly for Hannah. "*Mon Dieu*, I'd never have made it, probably would have lain down on the trail and died."

Lexington, the small, historic, hilly town — home to Washington and Lee University and Virginia Military Institute and the burial place of Thomas J. "Stonewall" Jackson and Robert E. Lee, Grace informed them — was their next stop.

"Please," Grace pleaded, "I want to see Stonewall Jackson's horse, Little Sorrel."

"Why?" Amelia asked.

"Where's Little Sorrel?" Hannah was curious.

"He's stuffed and mounted in the museum at Virginia Military Institute," Grace informed her.

Amelia said, "I cannot believe anyone would do that to an animal."

"Roy Rogers has Trigger in his museum," Grace informed them.

Grudgingly Amelia trooped after Grace and Hannah into the museum. "The general loved Little Sorrel. It was his favorite battle horse. Even though he was a small horse, he was gentle and dependable under fire and very sturdy." Grace moved close to the glass case that protected the horse and walked slowly around it. "Imagine loving your horse so much."

Amelia would not go near the horse, but hung out near the exit, urging them to hurry. "It's creepy, let's get out of here." Taking Grace's arm, she pulled her along even as Grace continued to offer a history lesson. "Jackson got the name 'Stonewall' at the first Battle of Bull Run because he stood like a stone wall against Union forces, did you know that?"

"Can't say I care," Amelia said with little emotion as they exited the building.

"He taught military tactics at this institute. He was shot and killed accidentally by one of his own men after winning the Battle of Chancellorsville here in Virginia. Friendly fire it's called today."

"Get in. Let's go, Grace," Amelia urged as she held open the driver's side door of the station wagon. "If I wasn't so anxious to see the farmhouse, I'd enjoy these little sight-seeing side trips much more."

Grace and Hannah exchanged knowing glances. It was quite clear that Amelia would never voluntarily visit Little Sorrel under any circumstances.

Grace slid behind the wheel, Hannah eased into the backseat and stretched out her legs, Amelia pulled the visor on her hat low over her eyes. It was not far, then, past the mountain city of Roanoke and up and out of the Shenandoah Valley onto the plateau where Interstate 81 turns west toward Johnson City, Tennessee. It was a day of fast food and pit stops, and as Grace grew increasingly confident and cheerful, her foot grew heavier on the gas pedal. She revved the station wagon to forty-five miles an hour. Cars and trucks still zipped past them, but they no longer fazed Grace. She was driving faster than she ever had in her life, and it felt good.

" 'Oh, I went down south for to see my gal, singing polly-wolly doodle all day,' " Hannah sang, and the others joined in. In voices that would never qualify for a choir, and with Amelia often off-key, they sang every verse they could remember of songs from the 1940s and 1950s as they started up the new four-lane highway from Tennessee into North Carolina.

Awed into silence by the majesty of bold mountains, dark now against the lingering pink and orange of sunset, they were unprepared for the nerve-jangling descent into North Carolina on a winding, narrow road in the encroaching darkness. Stiff-shouldered, Grace leaned forward, clutching the wheel as she braked old Nelly down into the bowl surrounded by mountains where Asheville nestled.

"Thomas Wolfe set his book *Look Homeward Angel* in Asheville. He was born in Asheville. The mountains, he felt, shut out creativity, confined him, fostered narrow-mindedness."

"So he fled to New York City," Amelia said.

"I never liked his work, too long-winded," Hannah said.

Once down the mountain they followed signs to the small college town of Mars Hill, thirty minutes from Asheville, and found Hillside House, an antique-filled bed-and-breakfast, where, the following morning the affable proprietor, Margaret Olsen, gave them directions to Covington.

"It's about twelve miles northwest of here," she said, handing them the paid receipts for their bills. "Covington's a blink of an eye, farmhouses, a gas station, a hardware store, a church, lots of cows and tobacco fields." She held the front door open for them. "Do you want to reserve rooms for tonight?"

"We'll spend tonight in Asheville," Amelia said. "It's been lovely here though and thank you."

A graduate backseat driver, Hannah now sat in the front with Grace and issued directions while Amelia squirmed and twisted in the backseat. "Oh, stop, stop. Look at that wonderful house with all that gingerbread trim. Oh, I hope Cousin Arthur's house looks like that."

"Stop yelling, or we'll end up in some

field or ditch," Hannah half-rebuked her.

"Everything's so quaint, and so beautiful. Don't you love to see cows grazing in a pasture? We just passed some. Did you see them?" Refusing to be hushed, Amelia went on and on exclaiming over every field, hillside, and stream.

Covington, the rusty sign read. Grace braked.

"For goodness' sake, don't do that," Amelia called from the backseat, as her hand came down hard on the rear of the front seat.

"I'm sorry. It came up so suddenly that sign. Covington. Where?"

"Remember, Margaret Olsen said not to expect much. Let's go on a bit."

Slowly, they followed the curving road and pulled into a seedy-looking gas station that appeared on their left. Piling out of Nelly, they stood looking around. There were no other buildings, just the gas station with one dilapidated-looking pump. Filled with excitement and anticipation they pushed open the torn screen door, stepped inside, and found a general store from out of the past, where they could buy chewing tobacco, worms for fish bait, tin buckets and pans of every size, grass seed, nails and paint as well as milk, butter, sodas, potatoes, onions, and detergents — and they could rent videos. The sullen young clerk eyed them with curiosity and gave them directions to the "old Furrior place."

"Y'all can't miss it. Yonder down the road a piece and turn back right. Big old oak." He lit a cigarette. Amelia thought him gross for blowing smoke rings in their direction, Hannah didn't care, and Grace found his speech interesting.

There were no neighbors on either side of the weather-worn two-story farmhouse that sat approximately a hundred feet back from the road across an overgrown grass and bramble-covered lawn. The driveway leading to the house was nearly indiscernible under its blanket of flowering goldenrod and white Queen Anne's lace. No gingerbread graced Arthur Furrior's farmhouse. Instead, several shutters in front hung askew, and the entire house needed scraping and painting. A wide wraparound porch, one end in need of jacking up, stood eerily empty. There were sad dogwood trees flanking the porch. Overhead an impossibly blue sky formed the backdrop for towering cumulus clouds that rode the backs of hills in the near distance.

Halfway to the house a huge, solitary oak spread a canopy of leaves across a wide circle of scraggly weeds and bare earth and shaded a rough-hewn bench that had collapsed to one side. The women clambered from the car and stood for a time just looking, allowing their reactions to settle. Amelia's heart sank.

"This whole place looks like a set for a Tennessee Williams play," Grace said. Depressing, she thought, just like Tennessee Williams's plays, focused as they were on the decadence of the Deep South. She had read *The Night of the Iguana* and had enjoyed *Cat on a Hot Tin Roof* as a movie, with Elizabeth Taylor as Maggie, but disliked the book.

"Reminds me of a haunted house I used to take the girls to at Halloween when they were little," Hannah said.

Amelia's voice quavered. "It's not what I expected, *mes amies*. It's so run-down and overgrown, look how dilapidated everything is." Suddenly she was overcome with disappointment at not finding something she scarcely realized she had hoped would give her someplace to belong. What had she expected? A charming, homey, shiny white house, neat as a pin? Big white rockers beckoning to them from a vine-draped porch?

Grace's arm circled her friend's shoulders. Compared to her own rounded shoulders and arms, Amelia's bones seemed barely layered with flesh. "It's amazing what a coat of paint and a lawn mower can do," Grace said.

"Lawn mower won't do it. Needs bush-hogging," Hannah said unequivocally.

"You're such good friends to come here with me." Amelia hung back, reluctant to move toward the farmhouse.

"Well, no sense standing here, let's have a closer look," Grace said.

"Not sure I can make it through the grass with this cane."

"Over here." Grace walked to one edge of the driveway, where the grasses appeared to have been walked on recently. "I'll go ahead and tramp it down a bit more. Just take it slow." Ignoring the burrs and thistles that snatched at her skirt and snagged her stockings, Grace started through the overgrowth, stomping hard, making it easier for Hannah. Amelia walked alongside Hannah, lending her arm for support, but Hannah shrugged her off and head high moved gingerly along behind Grace with Amelia bringing up the rear.

It was obvious that Amelia could hardly look at the house, much less go near it, and they sought the dim, cool shade of the huge oak. "I forgot to call about the keys," Amelia said. "Maybe it's just as well. I'm not sure I even want to see the inside."

"Why don't we just sit here and get the feel of the place?" Grace suggested.

With Grace and Amelia's help Hannah lowered herself to the ground and propped her back against the oak trunk. Grace arranged herself cross-legged nearby, and Amelia leaned back on her arms, stretched out her legs, and made herself as comfortable as she could.

Overhead the shrill caw of a crow on a branch shattered the silence. Another crow zoomed into sight, and with a loud ruckus a territorial struggle ensued. Amelia's eyes followed the crows, one demanding ingress, another protecting his home from the intruder. The look of the farmhouse had quite unsettled her, evoked a crush of emotions that left her disheartened and thwarted, vulnerable and adrift and utterly sad. "I had a house once, two blocks from the ocean," she said, her voice a low monotone. "I had a beautiful daughter, Caroline. She got sick in India, some rare intestinal disease. We used every connection

Thomas had to get her back to a hospital in the States. Caroline died in my arms on the plane. She was only nine."

It was so unexpected that both Grace and Hannah gasped. Grace's eyes fastened on Amelia's anguished face with a look of love and empathy that further disarmed Amelia. She had loathed the look of pity in people's eyes when she spoke of Caroline's and Thomas's deaths, and for years had assiduously avoided telling anyone. But now, to her amazement, she found herself willing, even eager, to share her stories with Grace and Hannah.

"Thomas, my husband, was an executive with the Red Cross. He was twenty-one years my senior, but we had a good marriage. Caroline was totally unexpected, a change-of-life baby. We were so worried. I was forty-nine when she was born, but I did fine." Fishing a Kleenex from her purse, Amelia blew her nose. "I'm sorry." A vein at her temple throbbed. Swaying branches cast filtered shadows across her face.

Then Amelia's vision tunneled. The car on the road disappeared, the oak vanished, the farmhouse evaporated. Memory swept her away from her friends, through time and down into a black pit of anguish.

Fighting her way back, out of the pain, she threw back her head and brushed a long strand of hair from glazed and misty eyes. "When we lost Caroline, Thomas withdrew from me, from life. He simply dried up. Still had a few years with the Red Cross, but I watched him literally shrink in stature and barely make it day to day. When he retired, we bought our first and only home near the beach at Silver Lake, in New Jersey." Amelia's voice quavered. "It was just a house, not really a home, not without Caroline. With her gone, the light went out of our lives. We existed in a kind of suspended animation, two lonely people sharing space, hardly talking."

She seemed to collect herself then, for she straightened her shoulders, wiped her eyes. "Thomas made foolish investments, lost a great deal of our money in the stock market. We'd always had money and spent it quite casually." A hint of a smile, almost apologetic, creased the corners of her mouth. "People adjust to living on whatever their income is, I guess." She swiped at the tiny gnats circling her face. "Six months later we were driving home from a movie. It was drizzling. Thomas was going at a normal speed." Amelia's eyes were huge and despairing in her pale, drawn face. "It happened so fast. An enormous sedan with darkened windows came from Thomas's side and ran a red light. I saw it coming. I remember crying out, as if that would stop it. Hit-and-run. The police never caught him. There was a fire." Almost fiercely, she wiped away tears with the ball of her hand. "My God, I still can't talk about it without crying. I'm sorry."

"You've every right to cry." Grace edged closer to Amelia and touched her hand.

Amelia lifted her left arm to show them. "This arm was broken, also my collarbone, and there were burns on my neck and shoulder." Amelia's fingertips flittered across her shoulder and arm. "The pain, the skin grafts, were horrible. When they told me that Thomas had died, I wanted to die."

Knees drawn tight against her chest now, Grace ignored the tears streaming down her face. Across from her Hannah pressed hard against the tree, every muscle and nerve taut. Her jaw and neck ached from struggling to suppress tears.

Amelia blew her nose again, smoothed back her hair, shifted her legs, attempted a feeble smile. Then her shoulders rose slightly in a gesture of resignation. "So now you see me," she said. "I smile. I behave appropriately most of the time. How else shall I act? But inside I'm empty." Her graceful hand, the long slim fingers clenched now and pressed against her lips.

Grace and Hannah hardly breathed. The three women sat close, almost in a circle. Hannah reached over and touched Grace's shoulder, and with a swish Grace let out a breath she didn't realize she was holding. "Dear God," Grace whispered. "You've been through hell."

"I feel like a hollow reed," Amelia said softly, and then she fell silent.

Odd thoughts raced through Grace's mind. Hollow reeds make beautiful music. With all her suffering, Amelia's still beautiful; her appearance seemingly untouched by the slings and arrows of her life. Genes, it's probably her genes that keep her eyes so lustrous, her skin so unblemished after all she's been through. One would never guess her inner turmoil.

Suddenly the earth seemed unbearably hard. Stones and tiny acorns poked Grace's bottom and twigs scratched her legs. Hannah struggled to get up, and Grace scrambled to help her, then Amelia. Slipping her arms gently about Amelia, Grace hugged her. "I am so sorry. I'm glad you didn't die. I love you."

Hannah found speech, even condolence, difficult; strong emotions discomfited her. She assiduously avoided them. Now she simply felt inadequate. "So sorry," she managed.

As they walked back to the car, Amelia turned, paused a moment to look at the farmhouse. "Guess we ought to get the keys tomorrow, at least go inside."

For a while they drove aimlessly, silently up one road and down another, each absorbed in her own remembrances, unstirred by the soft rolling countryside, the bright red of sweet gum trees, before they returned to Mars Hill and found the highway into Asheville.

4

A Question of Mind Over Matter

�֍ Settled for the night in an inside room of a Hampton Inn in Asheville, Hannah picked up the phone and reversed the charges. On the other end Miranda made no effort to hide her annoyance. "Mother? Where are you? I expected you to call last night."

"I was exhausted last night, but we're all fine, Miranda."

"Grace's son and his friend, Charles, arrived. They're staying at Olive's for the night. She's homophobic. Stupid woman. She put Roger in Grace's room and Charles in your room — said she hoped you wouldn't mind."

"I don't mind. Listen, Miranda. We found the farmhouse. Going to inspect it tomorrow. Need another day or so, won't be back tomorrow."

"Mother. Mother, don't hang up. I know

that tone of voice. You're about to hang up, right?"

"There's nothing else to say. We're well. We're safe. We're busy. I'm tired. It's been a long drive, and we stopped several times to see the sights."

"Mother, where are you now? How can Roger reach Grace? He says he must talk to her."

"Roger will see Grace in a few days. Do us all a favor, will you? Please entertain Roger and Charles."

"I guess I can do that, but tell Grace she needs to phone him."

"I'll tell her. You take care, now. Good night, Miranda." Hannah set the phone on its cradle and leaned back on the bed against the hard foam pillows. Tonight she ached all over.

"You need hip replacement surgery," the orthopedic surgeon had said matter-of-factly. "Pretty routine surgery and very successful. You'll be walking pain-free in a few months."

"And during those months?"

"You'll need someone to clean, cook, and generally do for you. Special equipment, like a motorized chair, would make it easier for you to get up and down. Then there'll be physical therapy."

"How long altogether?"

"Six weeks, two months, I'd say."

Hannah's spirit spiraled downward. She had spent eight depressing days in a rehabilitation/convalescent place after her knee surgery. All those people in wheelchairs; she couldn't look at them. And hip surgery carried a longer recovery period.

"Ambulatory only. I don't do assisted living or home care." Olive Pruitt had been adamant.

The possibility of losing her place at Sugar Maple Road filled Hannah with consternation. She knew of no other place close enough from where she could take an inexpensive cab to the plant nursery. Talking with customers about the plants, doing a bit of pruning, a bit of transplanting made her feel useful. So, she had dismissed the hip surgery, though every increasingly uncomfortable step she took confirmed the inevitable.

Now, lying there on the firm motel mattress, Hannah closed her eyes and thought about Miranda and Laura. Financially, it had been touch and go all those years making sure both girls had bicycles, Nike's like their friends wore, soccer clothes and equipment, the occasional weekend at the beach, and most important, an education:

Miranda a degree in horticulture, Laura in computer technology, though you'd never know it, living out on a boat like that without even a phone. Breadwinning had left little or no time for fun, for travel, for listening. Now the daughters she had spent every waking moment providing for, nurturing in the only ways she knew how: insisting their homework be top priority, demanding good grades, holding them to a strict curfew when they started dating, were independent women. And almost strangers. What she had failed to do, Hannah realized, was talk to them, listen to them. But then, Hannah thought, they had never shared their problems or concerns and had merely shrugged her off when she'd asked, "What's the matter?"

Out of ignorance and uncertainty she had ignored Laura's tantrums when she was fourteen and Miranda's dark moods during her last year of high school. Hormones, she had thought. Just hormones. They'll grow out of it, and indeed they seemed to do just that. They had both done well in college.

Hannah's jaw tightened. Swore I'd never raise my children as I was raised. Ironic to think how like my own upbringing theirs was, my father gone, my mother struggling to make ends meet. She never had time, either. Hannah sighed. But how could I have done it differently? I had no models, no one to suggest alternatives. If I could only change things, make us a close family. She inhaled in short jerky breaths. I don't know how. I do love them. Wish they loved me.

Easing herself from the motel bed, Hannah walked into the bathroom and studied the tub — deep and wide, with grab bars on either side, and a vertical security bar on the wall. Impulsively, for it had been a year since she had taken any-thing but showers, Hannah lowered herself onto the edge of the tub, turned on the faucet, and felt with pleasure the gush of warm water over her hand.

The prospect of a bath was irresistible. Undressing, maneuvering one leg and then the other into the tub required an act of determination. The moment she began to ease into the inviting warm water, pain cinched her hips and back and Hannah knew it was a mistake. Briefly, she ago-nized over how she was ever going to get out, but soon the soothing water closed about her, the pain dulled, and toe to shoulder the strain lessened and her mis-givings abated.

Hannah allowed her arms to float, and when water covered her chin and trickled into her ears, she scooped up handfuls and splashed her face and neck. "This is what being watered must feel like to a thirsty plant," she whispered as she settled into an unaccustomed state of bliss.

The flow of water became suddenly hot, and involuntarily she yanked her legs back, her feet away from under the faucet. The jerk sent a slash of pain up her thigh, taking her breath away, and pleasure gave way to a growing sense of panic as every nerve and muscle in Hannah's body, utterly relaxed a moment ago, tightened.

"Dammit. Dammit." The flat of her palm struck the water, splattering droplets on her face and into her eyes. "I'll be scalded red as a boiled lobster if I don't shut this water off." She wiped her eyes with the ball of her hand. "Get a grip, Hannah," she admonished. It was an unusually long tub, and water covered her mouth as she slid down, stretched her foot, reached the faucet, and with her toes pushed the lever to off.

Hannah rested, annoyed at the predicament she had so foolishly foisted on herself. She lifted her arms and shoulders out of the water, then sunk back, and holding her hands up to her face, she studied them. Fingers all wrinkled already. Can't just lie here, but I'm just dead weight. My legs will never support me. I'll fall, break a leg, arm, hip. Can't get out without help.

"Help," Hannah called, then realized that her cries would not be heard outside the room. I'll beat on the wall. Tears came. She could beat all night on the high, white, tiled wall and no one would hear. Feeling as trapped and desperate as she had during those last years with Bill, Hannah rested her head on the back of the tub and stared at the ceiling. Tears came, and memories, and that old paralyzing fear dating back to the night he struck her for the first time.

"Bill," she had asked, "did you withdraw five thousand dollars from our savings account?"

"You're always snooping around my money. I'll do what I want. It's my money. I earned it. Leave me alone."

"We have the girls to educate."

"Stop bitching at me."

"We have to talk about this, Bill."

"Out of my way. I'm sick of talking." He had staggered to his feet, and as Hannah tried to bar his way from the kitchen, he hit her.

She iced her forehead, told the butcher

and her neighbor that she had tripped on the stairs.

Bill had apologized, crying. "I don't know what came over me."

Worst was a blow that sent her reeling as his belt buckle drew blood across her neck and raised huge welts on her breast. Involuntarily, now, Hannah's hands moved through the water to cover her chest. That day she had vowed to leave. How much do the girls know? she wondered. What do they recall of that terrifying, freezing February night? We've never talked about any of it.

She had never seen Bill again; the girls had never seen their father again. Another memory jumped to mind. Months after she had fled with the girls she contacted an attorney in Sault Sainte Marie about a divorce and he had mailed a clipping from the local newspaper. AMERICAN RETIREE, WILLIAM PARRISH, DIES FROM STROKE. WIFE AND CHILDREN MISSING. Hannah showed the clipping to the girls.

"We're not missing." Laura stamped her feet.

"We should have stayed, been there to help him." Miranda's voice had been hard and hostile. At that moment, the girls turned to one another and shut her out.

They had been united against her then. Now they hardly communicated with one another. Hannah sighed. That had been years ago. The breach between herself and her children, sadly, had widened and deepened. For a moment Hannah covered her face with her hands. Should I have tried to close that distance? Should I even think of trying now? What would I need to do?

Hannah shivered. How long had she been in this tub? The water had cooled. Rolling to the left, she reached for the safety bar on the wall and attempted again to get up. Pain reduced her legs, thighs, buttocks, to rubber. Her heart crimped. The prospect of falling terrified her. Then suddenly, behind closed eyelids, Hannah revisited the office of the chiropractor where she had worked for many years. There was the receptionist's cluttered desk, the pale green walls, the gold-framed prints of hunting dogs hung along the hallway, and women with arthritis lying on foam mats on the hardwood floor of what had become the exercise room, their slow deliberate movements guided by Dr. Hansen's confident yet gentle voice.

"Think it first, then do it. No sweat. No strain in it. Visualize the movement. Then let your body follow your mind."

She had paid little attention then, considered his mind over matter technique a New Age fad, though his patients raved about it. She would try it. Remembering his admonitions to his patients Hannah pictured her hands grasping the tub bars, her right hand reaching across her chest to clutch the vertical safety bar, her thighs tensing to provide the lift she needed, her body stiffening, shifting, thrusting as she eased up and out of the water, then stood and turned to sit on the edge of the tub.

Over and over Hannah repeated the visualization until she felt ready. Resolved to succeed, she reached for the short bars on the side of the tub, wrenched herself to a sitting position, and gasped as the familiar, punishing presence of pain circled her hips. Forcing her consciousness from the pain, she clenched her teeth, swung her right arm across her chest, and wrapped her hand around the cold metal of the vertical safety bar. She could feel the strain in her arms, her shoulders, her chest. She hurt so much, wanted to let go, to crumple and slump back into the soothing water. The water fell away, delivering her tall angular body to the air. For a moment she tottered, bit her lip, screwed her eyes shut, and held fast, determined not to tumble. A chill blanketed her. Slowly, like a robot, Hannah rotated her torso and lowered her stiff body onto the side of the tub. She balanced precariously for a moment, hoisted one leg, then the other, to station both feet firmly on the bathroom floor. A sigh of relief exploded from her chest. She hurt like the devil, but she was safely out and wrapping a towel around her shivering body. On the bathroom counter sat her bottle of Tylenol with Codeine pills the doctor had given her. She reached for them. Thank God I've got these. They'll be a blessing tonight.

In the adjoining room, Grace unpacked her hairbrush and face cream, brushed her teeth, washed her face, and pulled on her flannel nightgown. Once in bed she stared heavy-hearted into the darkness, until it grew intolerable. Then she switched on the light. For the tenth time tonight, Grace burst into tears. What can I do for Amelia? she wondered.

"Pray for Amelia," a voice in her head seemed to say. Pray?

"Isn't there something more concrete I can do?" she whispered. Church prayer groups, her own prayers, had not healed Ted. She didn't believe any longer in the efficacy of prayers. These days her philosophy could be boiled down to a simple, "What's to be will be," but now something was urging her to pray.

"How does one pray?" she whispered.

"Thank and ask." The answer floated into her mind.

Grace closed her eyes. It seemed proper to clasp her hands. "Help Amelia, dear God." And then she whispered, "Help me. Help Hannah. Thank you."

Amelia brushed her teeth, then stared into the mirror above the sink. Slowly she raised her arm, and with two fingers of her right hand tugged the scarf until it slid free. Amelia gasped as if seeing the offending scars for the first time. She never brushed her hair or put on makeup or earrings without securing the scarf about her neck, and she covered her bedroom mirror to avoid any encounter with a sight that still pierced her heart and affronted her vanity.

Tentatively, with her fingertips, Amelia touched the patches of taut, discolored graft closest to her ear and neck and winced with remembered suffering. Unanswerable questions plagued her. Why didn't I die, instead of Thomas? His work was important. I had, have, no work, no real life without him. What will I do? Spend the remainder of my life waiting blandly for death in some cheerless retirement home in Pennsylvania?

Back in Branston, Amelia's imagination had recast the farmhouse from a house to a home, an alternative to Olive's, but it had proven to be weather-beaten and dilapidated. Living in it was out of the question, and living in it alone was even further out of the question. Alone was terrifying.

Immediately an image took shape in her mind of herself, clutching the marble urn with Thomas's ashes, sitting rigidly in the taxi that took her back to Silver Lake from the hospital. Seemingly endless, lonely, and frightening months followed as the icy blasts of winter, powerful Atlantic Ocean winds, echoed her pain and devastation as they sighed and moaned and beat upon her walls, upon her very soul. She would never forget the spring morning, the rowboat, the old man in his yellow parka straining over the oars as he rowed her out to sea. Thomas's ashes scarred the ocean with a long, murky wake that trailed the little boat before dissolving into the deep, dark ocean.

I did the right thing to sell the house in

Silver Lake and its furnishings, Amelia assured herself. I couldn't bear to look at pictures of Caroline or Thomas. I had to pack them away. She had been impractical, she knew, but no one could have stopped her when feeling parched as bones in the desert, she had taken some of her savings and fled to Europe on a mad, impetuous, unrealistic escape, visiting old acquaintances in Madrid, Rome, Vienna, London, Dublin, and finally back to America: to nothing, no home, no family, no friends.

Deploying all her inner forces now, Amelia willed these unsought bits of memory away, but not before revisiting, in her mind, the hotel in Philadelphia where management had found her curled in a ball on the floor of her room. The private clinic, her home for nine months, absorbed most of her savings, leaving her with only part of the proceeds from the sale of the Silver Lake house. Any ideas for an upscale retirement community vanished. A concerned doctor suggested Olive Pruitt's boardinghouse.

"You won't be alone," he said. "There are two other ladies living there. Olive's a gruff woman, but she's clean and conscientious."

Adrift, desperate for a safe haven, Amelia had taken his counsel.

Heavy-hearted now she pulled back the sheets and collapsed into bed. Turning on her side, Amelia's hand slid onto the empty space on the king-size bed. For a moment her heart constricted, as it had for four years whenever her hand accidentally slipped onto the cold, bare side, Thomas's side of the bed. At Olive's she had downsized to a twin. There were no memories attached to a twin bed.

5

A Challenge to Renovate

✻ The next morning after arranging for Harold Tate to bring the keys, the women drove slowly up to the farmhouse, got out, and stood staring at the dilapidated building.

"Look, Amelia," Hannah said, "imagine red geraniums in big clay pots on the steps, and pink roses trained along the railing." Hannah's eyes devoured the landscape: the lay of the land, flat about the house, then rolling gently behind, while in the distance hovered the mountains layered in haze, mysterious and beautiful. Hannah's eyes shifted to the upstairs rooms, the dangling shutters. "I wonder how many bedrooms there are?" She pointed to the right. "If I lived here, I'd plant a corn patch over there. I'd set up wire fences between the rows for beans to climb on and I'd have lots of tomatoes. Can almost taste a fresh-picked tomato." Hannah licked her lips. "Plenty of space for an orchard, cherries maybe or apples, maybe both, a garden for cutting-flowers and an herb garden and a shade garden under the oak."

At that instant, the morning sun hurled itself over the mountain behind the farmhouse, outlining the house in its golden glow. Quickly Grace brought her hand to cover her eyes. Long forgotten memories of an old friend's, Freda Harris's, farmyard flashed into her mind, and she heard again the squawking hens, saw herself ducking to avoid the swirl of flying feathers stirred by Freda's hand plundering their nests for warm fresh eggs. Grace brushed a strand of hair away from her forehead. "I used to buy fresh eggs from a friend, Freda Harris, to make Mexican omelets for Ted's and Roger's Sunday brunch. Freda had a wonderful porch, kind of like the one on this old farmhouse. Sometimes we'd sit at a little round wicker table, look out over the pasture and down to their pond, and drink tea and just chitchat about nothing." She sighed. "It was so peaceful, so safe, so simple, just sitting there believing that life would go on and on as secure and certain as on that particular day." Grace shifted her weight from one leg to the other and looked first at Hannah, then Amelia. "There's such a mystique about porches that makes me feel all warm and nostalgic: wicker rockers, swings, hanging baskets, vines, lace curtains you see hints of through the windows, and friends, families gathered together. Happy families of course." She smiled.

"All I see are sagging windows, a listing porch, tilting steps, and grimy clapboard," Amelia said. "The place is pathetic." Fixing it up would be so much work — finding workmen, getting appraisals, choosing colors, fabrics, appliances, furniture. Too much to cope with. Behind her back Amelia clenched her fists and pictured the photograph for the month of July on her wall calendar. If only this porch looked like that picture, painted white with lavender wisteria trailing from its fretwork, potted ferns on tall stands, wicker rockers, an American flag. Amelia brought her arms forward and crossed them over her chest. "If I were younger. If Thomas was here. But he's not, and I can't do it alone."

A blue GMC pickup truck with a bumper sticker that read I, a heart for love, and the word Covington, pulled in front of the station wagon. A short, wiry, middle-aged man with a brush cut, a lined and deeply tanned face, and friendly blue eyes got out, slammed the truck door, and walked toward them. A wad of tobacco caused his left jaw to slightly protrude. His hands were shoved casually into the pockets of his faded overalls.

Amelia extended her hand and took his warm and callused palm. "I'm Amelia Declose, Mr. Furrior's cousin, and these are my friends, Mrs. Singleton and Mrs. Parrish."

"Well, good," he said. "Howdy, ladies. I'm Harold Covington Tate." He waved his arm toward the farmhouse. "Might could look better, sure needs a bit of work. Sad to see a place go down like that." He shook his head. "Ready for a look around?" Turning, he started up the overgrown driveway. They followed in his tracks, Grace tromping behind him, further flattening the weeds to allow for Hannah's passage. Amelia followed, and this time Hannah took the supporting arm.

Past the sheltering oak, up the tilting front steps, and onto the porch they went. Harold inserted the key in the front door, stood aside, and motioned them through. The hinges protested. "Oil will fix that," he said. Beneath their feet the scruffed pine floorboards of the hallway scrunched with accumulated grit. Dust charged the air. Cobwebs dripped from corners. They heard the sound of a scurrying creature.

"Possum, maybe," Harold Tate said.

"Possum?"

"You never know when a place's been shut up as long as this has." He leaned against a wall and reminisced. "Sure miss Arthur. Now that man could spin a fine yarn, about huntin' in Africa, explorin' the Amazon. In the fall we'd get us a raft and head on down the French Broad River, hit a few rapids. Sometimes we'd be a-sittin' out on that porch talkin' until my wife Brenda'd phone to say 'send Harold home.' " He chuckled. "Sure do miss old Arthur."

He removed his cap, scratched his head, and headed for the kitchen, explaining that the pump often needed priming, that the stream to the south of the house routinely overflowed after a heavy rain, that the chimney of the wood-burning fireplace in the living room was a fire hazard and its flue needed cleaning, and that the place needed a new heating system. "When Arthur took ill and stopped comin', well things just went downhill." Harold's Adam's apple bobbed. He smiled at them, plowed his hands into his pockets. "Well, ladies, you probably want to stay a bit, look about. I'll be gettin' along now."

Amelia extended her hand. "Thank you for telling us about my cousin. I never knew him, and I regret that. We'll stay awhile, lock up when we leave."

"Your keys, ma'am." He handed her a key ring made of thick leather in the form of a bull, nodded to them and turned to leave. "Fifth step's loose," he said pointing to a narrow stairway at the end of a hall.

"We'll be careful. Thank you. I'll see you have a set of keys before we leave for Pennsylvania."

Then Hannah asked, "Mr. Tate, is Covington named for your family?"

"Sure is, ma'am. Covingtons moved up here from the coast back in 1877. Figured they'd grow cotton. But this country's too rocky and steep for cotton. My daddy turned to raisin' cattle and tobacco. Just me and my brother and our kin's left of the Covingtons." He nodded, smiled, and tipped his hat. "Be goin' now."

From the kitchen window they watched Harold stride across the grass jungle that had been lawn. Once he turned and spat tobacco juice on the ground before climbing into his truck. His head popped out of the window as he started the engine.

111

"Now y'all, holler if I can help." He smiled and waved with a quick lift of a finger, a motion they would come to recognize as a common North Carolina country driver's greeting. Then the GMC, noisy and lumbering as a slow freight train, pulled away.

A long hallway divided the downstairs: kitchen, pantry, and small bathroom on the right, dining room and living room on the left. In what Grace considered a futile attempt to upgrade the kitchen, a gas stove had been installed next to a dust-and-grime-crusted, wood-burning cookstove. Yellow linoleum, buckling in spots, worn in others, would need replacing as would several soft boards underneath it. A motley variety of chairs kept company with a scarred and pitted pine table that sat in the center of the room, and dotted swiss curtains of questionable vintage hung limp at the window over the chipped porcelain sink. The bare lightbulb dangling from the center of the ceiling seemed both harmless and threatening and added to the feeling of decay, as if the room, the house itself, were indeed an old movie set gone to seed. In the pantry a half dozen rusting cans of pork and beans needed to be thrown away.

Together, they explored the musty old house. Across the hall in the square high-ceilinged living room, double-hung windows were slick with grime. A quick swipe of Grace's bandanna and they took turns peering through a space as big as a dinner plate at a view of an unkempt lawn, a solitary oak, and across the road white cows grazing on a verdant stretch of undulating pastureland. Beyond the pasture lay a white farmhouse with a red roof and beyond that the famous, mist-shrouded Blue Ridge Mountains looped and dipped along the western horizon. Then Amelia flitted through the room, pulling the protective sheets off the furniture. Moments later they were all laughing as Amelia all but disappeared into a threadbare, oversized armchair. Grace gave her a boost up on her feet.

At the end of the hallway the stairs, covered with a dark green, worn carpet fastened tightly at the edge of each step with a dull brass strip, led to the second floor. "Remember," Hannah said, "Mr. Tate said the fifth step's loose."

Four bedrooms, two on either side, sprouted like branches from the narrow upstairs hallway. Hannah pushed open the door of one room, walked in, wrapped her hand around a knob of the brass headboard and lowered herself onto the springy bed. The mattress was sunken in the middle, suggesting that it had been molded by a great weight over time. A Winslow Homer print of a man and boy at sea hung askew, exposing a tear in the faded striped wallpaper. The room oozed with an unpleasant, stale mildew odor. Amelia threw open the closet door and screeched in alarm as a mouse sprinted across the room. Three moth-eaten plaid flannel shirts and a pair of stiff, paint-stained khaki pants hung inside. "Surely these didn't belong to Cousin Arthur," she said. Slamming the closet door, Amelia sank onto the bed beside Hannah. "Do you feel all right? You look peaked."

"Overdid it last night taking a bath," Hannah said. "Quite a struggle getting out of that tub. Thought you'd find me lying there butt-naked this morning, but I got out. Sheer willpower. Miranda's been after me to get a cellular phone. Would have been useful."

"What an awful experience," Amelia said.

"Sounds painful," Grace said.

"It hurt like Hades."

Grace struggled unsuccessfully with the window latch, then wiped a section of dusty pane with her bandanna and peered out. To the left, about a mile down the road, solidly planted in green patches of grass, sat seven well-maintained white clapboard houses with gable roofs and dormers extending out over covered front porches. Across the street from the houses stood a trim white church, serene behind its white picket fence.

They moved on to another room where the window slid open easily, and as there was no screen, Grace poked her head out. "I like this room. Hear the stream? We had a stream in our backyard in Dentry. I've missed the sound of gurgling water." She leaned farther out. "On this side of the house, the stream's close, maybe thirty feet and narrow. One good long stretch and I could step over it." She leaned even farther out, craning her neck to the right, eager to see as far and wide as possible from this contorted vantage point. "The grass is really high. The stream goes on and on, seems to curve in a wide arc around the house." Grace pushed back from the window. "Some of it's narrow and some places you'd need a footbridge. Maybe there's even a bridge there. I couldn't tell for sure."

Unable to contain her delight Grace danced a little jig over to Amelia and hugged her, then bent and hugged Hannah. "Thank you both so much for insisting I come with you. It's a gorgeous piece of property you have here, Amelia."

The land surrounding the house — pastureland, flat and fertile — extended for over two hundred feet before, in the back, rolling gently up to meet the trees. Bisecting the land, the stream curved widely and beyond it lay an ancient orchard. Above the trees the land grew increasingly steep as it rose to the crest of the hills that formed a protective semi-circle about the property, sheltering the house from winter winds and storms. It was indeed, as Grace said, a gorgeous piece of property.

But for now the women's exploration of the house continued. There were two bath-rooms on the second floor, one with a pull-chain toilet and a claw-foot, free-standing tub, and a smaller bathroom with sixties' era pink and aqua tiles and a stall shower in which the tiles seemed glued together by blackened strips of mildew. The double-hung windows in all the upstairs rooms had been replaced with sliders. The floors were scruffed, unfin-ished pine.

In one of the two bedrooms that faced

the north side of the house Hannah motioned them to the window. "There's a mare and her foal at the split-rail fence over there." About fifty yards from the farmhouse, a split-rail fence started in the woods far above and staggered past the house to the road. Beyond it lay a weathered, sagging gray barn with a rusting tin roof. A large tawny mare rubbed her jaw against the fence while her foal nuzzled her broad chest. "Wonder who owns those horses? Don't see a house," Hannah said.

"Arthur told me he had owned a horse and boarded it next door, but I got the feeling that was long ago."

Something scurried by. "Did he tell you he had guests, maybe possums?" Hannah used the wall for support as she retreated toward the door.

"Or mice?" Grace said. They laughed. A lightness, a sense of optimism flooded Amelia. The house didn't seem so impossibly awful anymore.

Making their way downstairs, the women stepped out onto the bare front porch, where Hannah and Grace settled at the top of the weather-beaten steps. Amelia walked the length of the porch, stopping occasionally to touch a worn clapboard, a dusty shutter, the slim, stained-glass panel in the front door. She ran her finger along the cracked putty that held the glass in place. "It's almost as if I hear Arthur saying, 'Fix it up.' "

Hannah pounced on the idea. "He left you the funds to do it. So do it. We'll help you."

Amelia stopped walking and snapped about to face them. "Oh, I couldn't, not really."

"I can see in your eyes, Amelia, you want to. Grace and I'll help you, won't we, Grace?" Hannah's cane went rat-a-tat on the wooden steps.

"I could never stay here. I could never do this by myself. If you two would help . . ." Amelia's shoulders lifted, her eyes brightened. "Next summer, maybe we could do it next summer."

"Next summer?" Hannah asked, her voice deceptively calm. "Why not get it started now? Why do we have to rush back to Branston? If we stay down here until December, I bet we could get a lot of it done."

"Not go back to Branston?" Grace's heart flipped. "But Roger's there. I have to go back."

"We'll be back in Branston before Christmas."

Amelia folded her arms. The blue of her scarf matched her eyes. Staring at the misty mountains in the distance, she seemed miles away, but her heart raced, and she felt energized. Had she been secretly hoping for this and been too frightened to broach it herself? Probably, yes. Ah, but would Grace agree to stay?

"Three months? That's crazy. I'm almost out of money. I can't afford to be gone much longer. I talked to Roger. He's very eager for me to come back," Grace sputtered.

"*Mes amies,* why not let Cousin Arthur treat us all to rooms at Hillside House, to food, gas, other expenses? The money is there, and I decree it's for our use."

"Bet Harold Tate could find us carpenters, plumbers, painters, whatever we need," Hannah piped in.

A growing excitement, the kind of delight Amelia assumed she would never feel again, swept over her, leaving her almost breathless. "This is what Arthur wanted. I just know it."

"Or is it what Amelia wants?" Hannah smiled up at Amelia.

Grace held up both hands. "Wait a minute, now. You're going too fast for me. You're saying we should tell Olive we're

119

not coming back until December? And Roger? Charles? They've come from Saudi Arabia."

"Didn't Roger say he's back to stay?" Hannah asked.

Grace remembered her brief conversation with her son. Roger had been insistent. "Charles and I have something very important to discuss with you."

"Can't you tell me on the phone?"

"No," he had replied firmly. "We need time to catch you up on things."

"Sounds serious."

"Not serious, important."

Grace looked at Hannah. "He sounded sincere. He's got something important to discuss with me."

"You going to let him dictate everything you do for the rest of your life?" Hannah's eyes, firm and unwaveringly, held Grace's.

Grace hugged her shoulders. "I have to get back to Roger. I can't do this renovation thing."

"Like you couldn't drive on the interstate?"

"That was different."

"No," Hannah said. "That was Grace making a choice, doing what you really wanted to do. Think about it, my friend. How could our staying here longer hurt

anyone, even your Roger? If it's so important it can't wait, he can tell you on the
phone. He deserves to wait. How much
notice did he give you when he decided he
was coming back to the States?"

Grace's mind raced. The thought of
driving had terrified her, but she had done
it and felt great about it. Yet guilt nagged
at her. She felt as if she were abandoning
Roger. She shook her head. "I just can't do
this." She'd go back to Branston by herself,
but how? Neither of the others could drive,
and if she took the car, they'd be left
without transportation. Grace ran her fingers through her hair. She'd been happier
these past days than she'd been in years
and the thought of living at Olive's without
Hannah and Amelia invited depression.

Grace's eyes narrowed. Her fingers circled the porch railing and her brow furrowed like an old-fashioned scrub board.
"Roger'll be furious."

"But it wouldn't hurt him to wait for
you."

"You're right of course, so many times
I've waited for him."

Unspoken but very much on Grace's
mind was the painful truth that all her
interactions with Roger over these past
several years when she needed him at

home, when Ted needed him, he had not been available for either of them. Straightening her shoulders, Grace tipped her chin up and looked to her friends as if for reassurance. "Well maybe," she said.

Amelia made a circle, right on, with her thumb and first finger, but it was Hannah's words, back in Olive's kitchen, that sounded in Grace's head now. "One for all, all for one." In her mind she played that old childhood game, pluck the daisy. Stay. Go. Stay. Go. She noted that "Stay" made her feel lighthearted while "Go" saddened her. Another adventure loomed. Who would it hurt and how could she walk away from it? Grace swallowed hard. A low-grade headache lay in wait at the back of her head. She would stay. Grace looked into Amelia's hopeful eyes and said, "Okay."

"*Merveilleux.*"

Then Hannah grasped the post at the top step and hauled herself to her feet. With faltering steps she moved toward the front door. "Friends, I suggest we conduct a grand tour of this place and make a list of everything that needs to be done."

Margaret Olsen's small living room at Hillside House served many purposes, as a family room, for entertaining guests, and as her dining room, where she ate at a low table before the TV. Margaret Olsen had dabbled at interior decorating and the walls were a bright canary yellow, with magenta-, blue-, and yellow-striped slipcovers on chairs and couch. Since the ladies occupied three of her four guest rooms, she had opened her private quarters to them for relaxing, reading, listening to music. It was from this room that Hannah reversed the charges and phoned Olive.

"So, where are you now?" Olive's imperious voice demanded after reluctantly accepting the charges.

"North Carolina," Hannah said into the phone. "Calling to say we won't be back until probably December."

Silence.

"Do you hear me, Olive?"

"Miranda, Roger know about this?"

"Of course they do. Our rent checks are in the mail to you."

Olive was silent, then she said, "Roger's ready to split a gut with Grace acting so foolish. Lemme talk to her."

Hannah rolled her eyes. "She wants to talk to you."

Grace took the phone. Under her shirtwaist dress her knees quivered. Heartbeat at a trot, she wondered if she could talk to Olive without feeling guilty, or getting teary. "Hello, Olive, how are you?"

"What's going on down there? That's what I want to know," Olive said huffily. There was no mistaking her sulking anger. "Everyone's worried sick, and now I have your son and his, whatever you call him . . ."

"Companion," Grace said coolly. "Charles is Roger's companion."

"Well one of 'em's calling me every other day."

Grace swallowed. Hannah stood close, her eyes reassuring. Grace twisted her bandanna, and when she spoke the words in her mouth felt like hard little pebbles in a dry streambed. She managed to get them out. "I'm sure they won't be bothering you anymore. We've given them a phone number and an address."

"Well," Olive persisted. "They're driving me nuts."

"I'm sorry about that."

"What the devil you doing down there?" she asked again.

Not skilled at lying, Grace got off the phone, fast. "See you in a couple of months. Good-bye now." Hanging up, she collapsed into a chair.

"Well done," Hannah said.

Amelia responded with, "Bravo," and a silently mouthed, thank you.

6

A Place of Their Own

⚘ September greens bowed to October's soft sepia, peach, and yellow tones with a sprinkling of red. The ladies clambered into layers of clothing, vests and T-shirts under long-sleeved shirts and sometimes sweat-shirts as well as sweatpants every morning, and stripped the layers off during the day as the temperature climbed thirty degrees by noon. Arthur's money paid for their rooms at Hillside House in Mars Hill, their food, gas for Nelly, incidentals, and Amelia insisted they each have twelve hundred dollars, "A gift from Uncle Arthur," for bedroom furniture.

Harold Tate had taken the ladies under his wing, introduced them to a local plumber, electrician, and air-conditioning man. But best of all he introduced them to a young carpenter, Tom Findley, who had come from Indiana to homestead in the mountains.

On the day Tom arrived, they waited on

the porch as the stocky young blond stepped from his truck and strode up the driveway. A leather tool belt with a wrench, a hammer, and a screwdriver hung about his waist; his shoulders and upper arms swelled from years of manual work and he exuded an air of quiet confidence.

"*Mon Dieu*," Amelia whispered, "he looks strong."

"Hi," Tom Findley said. "Mrs. Declose?" He looked from Amelia to Hannah.

Amelia extended her hand. "You must be Tom."

"Sure am, ma'am." He stepped back, surveyed the porch, stepped back again, and scrutinized the house. "Corner over there needs a bit of jacking up." He stood on a step and pressed his weight down. "Needs new steps." He smiled up at them. "No big thing."

Amelia nudged Hannah. "My friend Mrs. Parrish knows more about houses than I do."

"Tell ya anything ya wanna know. Just ask," he said, standing there, thumbs in his pockets.

"Well," Amelia said, "it's so run-down looking. Is it safe to live in?"

Hannah cleared her throat. "We want to know if the foundation's sound. This farmhouse was built about 1930. What about termites? We're concerned about the roof. Will it leak the first heavy rain we get? Are the floorboards sound? How about insulation? How much is cosmetic and how much is structural repairwork?" Suddenly Hannah realized how much she had learned driving old Dr. Hansen to inspect the house he was having built for his son. The chiropractor had depended on her to verify work completed before he paid a single subcontractor. Hannah smiled, thought to herself, nothing's ever wasted. Never imagined I'd remember so much about building.

"Yes," Amelia nodded, "and what will it cost?"

"Well, ladies." Tom joined them on the porch. He shoved one hand into a back pocket and stared into space, a stance they would come to chuckle over as Tom's thinking pose. "I kin start in the attic, check everything room by room, then I'll let ya know. These old places are built outta solid, well-aged pine and oak and they can take a beating."

That day Tom Findley climbed in and out of the attic, clomped from room to room opening and closing windows and tapping walls, tramped across the galvanized tin roof, and crawled under the house. At two in the afternoon, he handed Amelia a list.

Repair and jack up porch — new front and back steps.
Replace rotted kitchen floorboards — upgrade kitchen.
Upgrade bathrooms.
Fix fifth step and replace stairway carpeting.
Oil door hinges.
New screens on doors and windows.
Rehang shutters up and down.
Replace oil furnace with heat pump and A/C.
Replace fireplace with sealed gas unit.
Paint everything in and out.
Install new closets.

"Great old place ya got here," he said. "Bit of rot here and there." He tapped a soft board on the kitchen floor with the toe of his boot. "Electric's okay. Roof's sound. Not too long ago, looks like, someone put on a new roof, added insulation, and had the place rewired. Work's mostly cosmetic." He stood in the kitchen doorway, one thumb tucked into the tool belt, the other hand jammed into a back pocket. "Cost ya, maybe twenty-five thousand dollars."

Amelia looked at Hannah, then Grace, then nodded. "That'll be just fine."

"Come on outside." Tom said, shifting his weight from one leg to another. "Wanna show ya ladies something."

They followed him, feeling young as they marched across the foyer and the front porch, down the steps, and around the corner of the house to a nearly leafless lilac bush half hidden by tall weeds. "Watcha think? Wrens?" He held up a round bird's nest made of fine twigs, empty now except for a sad little egg that had not hatched. "Watch for 'um next year."

Grace cradled the nest in her hands. "Poor baby didn't hatch," she murmured. "Should we put back the nest?"

Tom shrugged. "Don't know. They might use it again, or build a new one."

The next day a Salvation Army truck belched into the driveway and belched away carting off the old furnishings, even the old wood-burning stove.

On Monday morning, Tom Findley and two helpers carried table saws, sawhorses, staple guns, sanders, and assorted small power tools into the house, and the work that would turn a disappointment into a celebration began. During the next two weeks, boards were torn out and new ones placed on the kitchen floor, the old fireplace in the living room was boarded up permanently — a sealed gas unit would take its place — all the shutters were removed for scraping, sanding, and painting, and jacks were inserted under the porch as the first step to leveling. One of the men started preparing the exterior walls for painting.

Amelia purchased a video camera and recorded the progress: the spackling of nail and other holes in the walls, replacing a window sash and screen, installing the new gas fireplace and mantel in the living room, repairing steps, building new front steps. During the third week, new grout, applied to all the tile in both bathrooms, produced amazing results.

"Look at this bathroom," Hannah called to the others. "Like new."

"You're an absolute genius, Tom," Amelia said.

"You really didn't replace the tiles?" Grace wanted to know.

Tom stood in the doorway of the bathroom, trowel in hand, patches of white grout clumped on his shirt. "Not a one, ma'am," Tom assured her. "Just the right cleaning products and elbow grease."

Tom Findley's wife, Marie, a dark-haired slender woman in T-shirt, jeans, and out-at-the-seams sneakers, was a painter, and she sent them off to Sears in Asheville to pick out the interior paint.

The Asheville Mall was situated east of the city on Tunnel Road. From its parking lot, turning one's head 180 degrees, you could see a lovely view of mountains. Sears anchored the mall on one end, J. C. Penney on the other, and in between were the usual chains.

In the paint department at Sears, Grace and Amelia spent almost an hour studying color strips, inside under fluorescent lights and outside in natural light, deciding and undeciding and deciding again. A beige-colored carpet had been ordered for throughout the house, and all three women agreed on white with a hint of beige paint for the halls and foyer, the dining room, and the guest bedroom. For the kitchen Grace opted for bright yellow walls. There would be new white Formica cabinets, and marbleized gray-white countertops.

"The living room should make a dramatic statement," Hannah said.

"I'd like the walls white like the hall," Amelia said.

They were standing in the paint section. Hannah stood her ground. "No, they should be teal, accented with terra-cotta-color moldings, baseboard, and fireplace trim."

Amelia grimaced. "Sounds so garish."

"Not garish, interesting with the beige carpets and furniture. You'll see, it'll be stunning."

"Garish." Amelia crossed her arms over her chest.

"Now you two stop this." Grace handed each a slender color chart. "Look at all the teals, dark to light. How about a shade somewhere in the middle?"

Amelia studied the line of colors, bent the card, and placed one color after the other against a white wall. "Well, if you two insist, this one, then." She handed them the color card. Number 722 was a cool mix of Caribbean green and blue.

"Darker would be more dramatic," Hannah grumbled.

"This'll be gorgeous. Once it's on the walls, we'll never remember the rest of these shades," Grace said.

Selecting bedroom colors took longer. "I've always had a white bedroom," Amelia said. "This time I'm going to be, what is that word? Ah, yes." She cocked her head. "Brazen." After puckering her lips and scowling over slightly different shades of white, Amelia chose a color she called, "a tad deeper than white," and which Grace considered to be light cream. "Beautiful," Grace said. "Soft and light."

"I know it's light, but it's a big change from my usual bright white."

Grace vacillated between pale pink and pale peach. "It's got to be a warm color," she said, rejecting shade after shade. Then she decided on a soft, light apricot. "This, I love," she said.

Once the living room had been settled on, Hannah watched them patiently from a high stool at the counter. A bright clear shade of spring green had been her immediate choice for her room and the can sat on the counter near her elbow

"*Mon amie.* You're Mrs. Green Thumb, or better yet, Queen of Green. You'd paint the whole world green given the chance," Amelia kidded her as the store clerk loaded the ten gallons of interior paint into the rear of the station wagon.

As they drove back to Covington, they

improvised on nursery rhymes in their own outrageous manner.

"A tiskit, a tasket, Hannah's got a green room," Amelia sang.

"Little Miss Muffet chose a cream-colored tuffet." Grace pointed to Amelia. "Say, how come nobody calls a footstool a tuffet these days?"

"You two are nuts," Hannah said. "Actually we're like the old woman who lived in a shoe." She put her fingers to lips and lowered her voice. "Only our shoe looks to all the world like an old farm-house." Then more loudly. "Our children are our plans and dreams." And so it went, singing, poking fun, laughing all the way home.

During all those weeks, concerned that Miranda with her knack for worrying would fly down to North Carolina, Hannah phoned her daughter every few days with a progress report.

"We took Margaret Olsen out to see the house last Saturday," Hannah reported. "When the men cleaned out the attic they found four old cane seat chairs, so we took them to be recaned, and we were amazed to discover that under the black paint put on them by heaven knows who, they're the most beautiful walnut with burl veneer decorations. They'll be perfect in the dining room."

"They sound lovely. But, Mother, we miss you. When are you coming home?"

"Soon. Just don't worry. We're having a great time."

With her bandanna bunched into a tight wad in her fist, Grace spoke to Roger weekly, and used all her willpower to resist giving in to his pleas that she come home now.

"Charles and I've decided to live in Branston," he informed her one evening. "If you were here, we'd learn about the city so much faster."

"I'll help in whatever way I can when I get back," she replied.

"Get back soon, then. We've got something very important to discuss with you."

How many more times would he tell her that? She would have liked to tell him how solid the old farmhouse looked now with the porch propped up straight and new steps, or that they had bought three wicker rocking chairs and that they sat on them on the porch every evening to watch exquisite flame and gold sunsets over the mountains. She would have liked to laugh with him, as they had done when he was young, about how careless she could be. As a child he had chided her for never looking down, and she wanted to share her story with him about how she would have fallen into a hole where boards had been removed in the kitchen floor of the farmhouse had Tom Findley not pulled her back with his big strong hands, but clearly Roger was not interested.

"I'm beginning to worry. What could be so important that Roger can't tell me, even give me a hint on the phone? Is he sick, I wonder?" Grace said the next morning at breakfast.

"Probably wants money," Hannah said cryptically.

Grace sat back from the table. "Ridiculous. What money do I have?"

"House in Dentry."

"Don't be facetious, Hannah. Roger would never ask for that." And they dropped the matter.

Each day, things at the farmhouse improved and like clockwork every day at five, when the men had left, they drove to Covington to tally up another day's progress. Soon they were congratulating themselves on their choice of cove lighting for both bathrooms and the large bevel-edged mirrors that reflected new white pedestal sinks and other bathroom fixtures: sleek, clean-lined, modern. They watched Tom's wife, Marie, measure, cut, and paste wallpaper in one of the bathrooms — bouquets of forget-me-nots and lilies-of-the-valley on a pale green background, and in the other bathroom they held the folded pasted sheets for her as she climbed her ladder to match up row after row of lovely multistripe paper.

Two days later, they found Marie in Amelia's bedroom scraping away the crusted and peeled paint and gray mold on the windowsills and frames and they returned the following afternoon to find them transformed, glossy white and impeccable.

They ran from the hammering and pounding as workmen ripped away the dank, musty tiny bedroom closets; they praised the eight-foot closets built in their place and watched the carpenters install the white louver fold-back doors. Everything sparkled. Everything shone. "*Magnifique.*" Amelia's face glowed with happiness as she reached for the closet knob, then quickly drew back, her hand smeared with fresh white paint.

Five weeks into the renovations, they arrived one afternoon to hear a radio blaring from the kitchen along with the shrill whir of a drill.

At first he didn't hear them, but then he looked up and smiled. "Hi, ladies," Tom said. "Wanted to surprise you. Just installed the fronts of the Formica cabinets. Like them?"

They stood back. "Oh, indeed," Hannah said.

"They're lovely." Grace stepped forward and ran her hand lovingly across the smooth glossy white surfaces. "Easy to clean."

Amelia clapped her hands. "You are a marvel, Tom Findley."

Then on a Friday morning of the sixth week, Amelia opened the front door and the ladies stepped into a structurally completed house. Sunlight streamed through spotless windows across scoured floors awaiting carpet. The three stood in the hallway and looked around, absolutely delighted.

Tom welcomed them and led them to the kitchen. "Tomorrow we'll lay the vinyl floor in here, so you can call Sears for delivery of the kitchen and laundry appliances, Mrs. Declose, for Thursday the latest. Another week and we're out of here."

And then the day came when Grace and Hannah and Amelia parked Old Nelly on Cove Road, as they had that first day. Silently they sat and stared at the house, the white rocking chairs that now awaited them. Slowly Hannah started up the driveway and within minutes Amelia and Grace carried into the house the comforters and pillows and bedspreads they had bought. They had promised themselves that when the work was done and before they left for Branston, they would walk as much of the twenty-eight acres as they could. Now, Grace said, "Amelia, let's get into our grungies and go for a walk up the hill behind the house. You don't mind do you, Hannah?"

"It's fine. I'll just relax on one of our new lounge chairs." Hannah started toward the great oak with several gardening books in her arms. Ten minutes later, she was so engrossed in marking pages and making notes in a small pad that she did not see Amelia and Grace approach in their high-topped boots and long-sleeved shirts, shouldering sturdy sticks cut for them by Harold Tate to warn off snakes, until they stood at the foot of the lounge.

"We're off now," Grace said, waving her stick. Harold had told them, "You just swoosh these sticks about in front of you, and that'll send any old snake lyin' about runnin'." He had chuckled and scratched his chin. "They're more scared of you than you are of them. Footsteps rattle the leaves, they're gone."

An hour passed unnoticed by Hannah, who read and daydreamed and dozed and was dozing when, breathless and flushed, Grace and Amelia returned. "Wake up, oh, great earth woman." Amelia prodded her gently on the shoulder. "The explorers have returned." She unbuttoned the top two buttons of her shirt — after making sure that her scarf, a turquoise and white polka-dot, was spread wide and tucked in securely — threw her stick on the ground, and pointed. "We'll now tell you about the lay of the land. Behind the house there's a gentle slope, then a hill. We climbed all the way to the top.

"It was a hike believe me, Hannah, but we found this beautiful little glen circled by trees. Very shady, like here, but the ground was thick with this small-leafed ground cover. I brought you a piece.

Maybe it'll grow under this oak." She handed the trailing stem with its rounded, fleshy green leaves to Hannah.

"European wild ginger, *Asarum europaeum*," Hannah said, running her fingers over the leaves. "Must be moist where you found this."

"Yes, there's a spring that spouts right up out of the ground all fresh and gurgly, then it spills over some rocks and becomes a little stream," Amelia said. "Halfway down someone's built a reservoir. That's where our water comes from, gravity-fed."

Grace leaned her stick against the trunk of the oak, and patted its bark, only to catch herself as she did. "Gosh, Hannah, I'm getting as bad as you, treating the tree like it's a person."

"It's a living breathing thing," Hannah replied, smiling.

Grace sank into one of the oak-stained, wide-planked wood chairs, much like the Adirondack chairs that they had bought at a summer's-end sale in Asheville and placed beneath the tree along with two small round tables. "I'm smitten by the beauty of these North Carolina mountains. Harold says folks around here call people from the Piedmont or the coastal areas of the state or further south flatlanders. They feel

142

sorry for them because they don't live in the mountains, but they aren't eager for them to move up here, either." Unbuttoning the cuffs of her shirt, she rolled up the sleeves. "Did you ladies know that these mountains are the oldest in the United States and that they break up the wind so the area doesn't get hurricanes or tornadoes? Isn't that interesting?"

"I didn't know that, but it's certainly a bonus." Amelia nodded.

A soft breeze stirred the branches of the big oak, sending yellow leaves fluttering to the ground, onto Hannah's lap, onto Amelia's and Grace's hair and arms. "Never thought about hurricanes or tornadoes," Hannah replied, making a circle out of the leaves that had landed in her lap. "What's beyond the stream?" She pointed to where the land angled out of view.

"Must be a hundred feet of meadow, then a once-upon-a-time apple orchard, in such sad condition." Amelia slipped into a chair near Grace. "I said to Grace, Hannah will know just what to do with these apple trees. We'll have a crop next year."

"Are there apples on the trees now?"

"I don't think they're good, Hannah. Most of them are on the ground, mushy, small, smelly," Grace skinned up her nose.

"That's too bad," Hannah said. "By the way, Harold stopped by. He's found someone to bush-hog all the brambles and overgrowth right up to the edge of the forest." She leaned over, placed her books on the ground, and her eyes turned serious. "Been thinking. Turned out splendidly, didn't it?" She nodded toward the farmhouse.

It had turned out beyond their wildest expectations.

"Winters are much harsher in Pennsylvania than they are here," Hannah continued. "Harold says they get one maybe two light snows a year. Melts in days. Heavy snowfall every couple of years but then everything shuts down, schools, work, banks. Not enough equipment to plow, like in Branston. Been thinking, if we pooled our financial resources, we could move here, live here year-round." Hannah held her breath and waited for their reactions.

"I've been thinking much the same." Amelia leaned forward in her chair, placed her elbows on her knees and her chin on her hands.

Aghast, Grace looked at each of her friends in turn. "What are you saying? I thought this was to be a summer place?" Escalating anxiety caused Grace's voice to quiver. She had the sense of free-falling or plunging through white water in a raft without oars or a guide. Her fingers drummed the arm of her chair. "What's next? I can't handle any more changes. I don't know how to explain all these weeks to Roger, much less tell him I'm moving down here."

Hannah turned to her. "Let me ask you, Grace, what does Olive Pruitt do for us that we can't do for ourselves, and for each other? We can even dial nine-one-one, imagine that." Hannah punched the air with a finger. "Think about it. If we pooled our financial resources, we could live nicely here. My income's fifteen hundred a month." She ticked her costs off on her fingers. "Olive, seven hundred; Medigap policy's ninety-seven dollars and fifty cents; car's four hundred a year in insurance; there's life insurance, few things I need from the drugstore." She paused. "Little enough left. Here we could share food, electric, gas, repairs, lawn maintenance, things like that. I'd probably have enough to hire a pair of knees to weed for me."

Springing from her chair, Grace flung her arms into the air. "I barely adjust to one thing and you two want to go even farther. This is too much for me. Too many changes! Too many . . ."

"You're tougher, more adaptable than you think," Hannah retorted. "Things are different now; you own your own life. Time you initiated change."

These same thoughts, seditious and confusing, had begun to creep into Grace's mind of late, but she was not ready to admit to having them. Pausing, Grace looked out at the hazy blue layers of the Blue Ridge Mountains that reached to the edge of sight. As always they took her breath away. "So beautiful," she murmured, then shook her head.

Amelia was silent, watching and listening to this interchange.

"What do you really want, Grace?" Hannah asked. "What's right for you? The three of us sharing a home, helping one another seems very right to me."

"But I'm sure Roger decided to live in Branston because I'm there."

"Maybe. Maybe not," Hannah challenged. "Sounds more like he wants something from you. Aren't you the one who said we need the support and understanding of our peers more than our children at this stage in our lives?" Hannah sat very still, hands folded in her lap, all her attention on Grace. "Sure, we can go back, waste our lives at Sugar Maple Road, or we can grab this opportunity Amelia's offered."

Anticipating angina, Grace's hand eased to her chest and moved about tentatively. One hand sought her pocket and closed over the bottle of nitroglycerin, but there was no tightness, no distress, no need for medication. She brushed a leaf out of her hair. She seemed to be the only one functioning in slow motion; the others were traveling at high speed. Another leaf landed on her shoulder. This one she held and studied the dark veins staining its bright yellow color. *I really love it here,* she admitted to herself. *Every day that farmhouse feels more cozy, more of a home, my home.*

Amelia sensed the struggle taking place within her friend, recognized the mix of hope and conflict in Grace's eyes. Amelia rose. "Look at me," she said, walking over to where Grace now stood staring out at the pasture across the road, seemingly absorbed in the perambulations of cows heading for a feeding trough piled with fresh hay. Gently, Amelia touched Grace's arm, her sapphire eyes entreating. *"Mon amie,"* she said softly. "Perhaps this is the time to make a change. We don't have aeons of time. We're all unhappy at Olive's. I'm happy here. Hannah's happy. You're happy, yes?"

Grace nodded.

"This place," Amelia waved her arm toward the farmhouse, "is better in every way than living at Olive's. When I think of Number Sixteen, dreary is the word that comes to mind." Amelia's hands fell to her sides.

Grace's brows furrowed. She closed her eyes for a moment, saw the uninspiring sameness of Sugar Maple Road. Then her mind shifted to the stirring loveliness of stream and hills visible from her window here. "My father said no to life. Ted never took risks." Her voice was low; concern and yearning were written across her face. "I don't want to be like either of them." Her arms hung free at her sides. The ends of the bandanna that she had tucked into the waistband of her slacks blew gently in the breeze. "But it's so hard to change one's view of things."

"But you have changed, don't you see? You drove us here. You're not afraid any longer to drive more than twenty-five miles an hour and —"

Hannah interrupted. "You decided, under incredible pressure from Roger, to

148

stay here, you helped turn this dilapidated farmhouse into a lovely home. Didn't you ever, in all these weeks, think maybe . . . ?"

"I hardly dared." Grace's eyes sought the skeleton branches above them, lingered on the last golden leaves and beyond to the pale blue sky. "I'm so happy here. Yesterday, I stood at my bedroom window and cried, I wanted so much not to leave. But when you blurted it out, the old way of thinking rose up like a ghost demanding an audience. It is too wonderful to give up."

Then Grace's face grew serious as she moved toward the great oak. Sitting, she clasped her hands on the small table before her. "Ted's pension, Social Security, and the rent from my home in Dentry is twenty-one hundred a month." She paused. An impish grin painted itself on her face. "They'll think we're outrageous, my son, your daughters."

"So?"

Grace brushed her hair back from her face. They meant so much to her, these two women. After the wrenching business of leaving lifelong friends behind in Dentry, she had been sure she would never have true, dependable friends again, but she was so blessed. When had she come to love them? Out here, under this tree, when

Amelia had shared her life? In the car when, usually so private, she had felt safe and comfortable answering their questions about her life with Ted? Or had her feeling grown slowly as they planned, shopped for paint, furniture, linens, kitchen pots and pans, and watched the old farmhouse come back to life? Grace smiled, knowing suddenly that it was all those reasons and more. Hannah and Amelia accepted her, listened to her opinions, encouraged her, applauded her. What did it matter when, or how, or why she loved them. She simply did, and not once since she had been here had she been lonely, or agitated, or fearful, or anxious, or ill.

Hannah interrupted her musing. "We'll plant an herb garden and a flower garden and a vegetable garden. We'll have so many vegetables next fall we'll be hard-pressed to get all the canning and freezing done." A radiance flooded her square jaw and her face and in that moment Hannah glowed, a truly handsome woman.

"Tom will build raised beds for vegetables and wooden planters along the porch for flowers so you can garden without kneeling," Amelia said.

"I'll make you my special dishes, meatballs with prunes, stuffed cabbage cooked in gravy with raisins, sugar cookies."

"No vegetables?" Hannah asked.

"Yes, that, too. Ted loved my cauliflower casserole."

"I adore *le choufleur.*"

Grace clapped her hands and smiled broadly. "I cook, Hannah plants, what will you do, Amelia?"

Amelia clasped her hands behind her head. "Photography. I've always wanted to do photography."

Reaching from her chair, Hannah touched the rough bark of the oak with her fingertips. "Well, old girl," she murmured, "we're going to be calling the same yard home." Then Hannah turned a worried face to them. "About my hip. I've refused, for a long time, to admit that I must have hip replacement surgery. There's a long recovery period, months."

"*Cherie,* we won't put you out, like Olive would. You can have it done here, if it can wait until we come back in the spring," Amelia said. "We'll convert the dining room into a bedroom for you so you don't have to deal with steps."

"I nursed my father and my husband, I'll take care of you."

Hannah gave her friends a grateful smile, and then went a step farther. "The house is painted, our bedroom furniture arrived yesterday, why not check out of Hillside House, spend our last week here in the farmhouse?"

Grace shrugged. "What's one more change?"

A squirrel startled by their hearty laughter scurried up the oak and sat on a branch, head cocked, beady black eyes watching them warily. Amelia got up and hugged Grace, and uncharacteristically Hannah reached out her arms to hug both Amelia and Grace. They no longer felt like three women of a certain age concerned with an aching hip, a tenuous heart, or a fear of being alone. They were pioneers, driven by hopes and dreams, they were visionaries with sweeping goals.

It was a clear crisp day when the ladies said good-bye to Margaret Olsen, loaded their suitcases into the wagon, and drove the narrow roads to Covington.

In October, Harold Tate had harvested his tobacco and hung it in his barn, and in November when the long leaves were brown and desiccated, he had bundled them much as he bundled hay, and they had seen his pickup lumber past the farmhouse several times, piled high with bales of the crinkly brown leaves. The rich dark fertile earth, newly plowed of corn and tobacco stalks, rested now. Crows pecking at carrion on the road rose in a swirl of black, cawing shrilly in reproach as the station wagon drew near. A curve to the right, to the left, and right again into the driveway of the funky convenience store with its single gas pump. They had won over the sullen young man behind the counter, and he smiled at them as they bought milk and other groceries.

Supplies in hand, Grace turned the wagon into the freshly graveled driveway, past the great oak. Now its limbs and branches created calligraphic shapes and forms against the sky. Looming tall and proud, the farmhouse welcomed them. With great excitement they hastened up the steps onto the porch, transformed now into each woman's fantasy: wicker chairs with thick rust-colored cushions, low wicker tables alongside which stood tall clay pots that Hannah had filled with drying hydrangea clusters and rust-red sweet gum branches. Propelled by the wind, a hanging swing swayed gently. Gardening magazines spilled from a straw basket near one of the chairs. In the spring, Hannah envisioned baskets of ferns, pots of geraniums and marigolds, vines and roses making their porch so glorious that passersby would point, exclaim, and feast their eyes.

Leaving their suitcases in the wagon, they stepped into the foyer and for a time stood silently, seeing it as if for the first time, the long sweep of hallway leading to the stairs, the teal-colored living room with its terra-cotta molding and baseboard, the light beige carpet, the soft-cushioned beige canvas-covered couch and chairs. "Ah, *c'est magnifique.*"

"Yes indeed," Grace said.

They wandered upstairs and in and out of each bedroom. Amelia had decided on white wicker furniture and, as she tolerated no mirror, had bought a copy of a Chagall print for the space above her dresser. The headboard in Grace's room was wrought iron with a traditional scroll design, while Hannah's room looked like a flower shop: a nosegay of pink and yellow and purple strawflowers on her dresser, rust and gold potted mums on a table near the window, and in one corner a tall vase filled with wheat-colored grasses, goldenrod, and blood-red sumac gathered from the side of a road. A new mahogany armoire housed her television set. Everything sparkled. Everything delighted. Tom and Marie had gone to great lengths to make certain that everything looked beautiful.

Later that day while the others unpacked or rested, Grace moved contentedly about the kitchen humming "If I were a Rich Man" from *Fiddler on the Roof* as she stuffed a pitted prune into the center of a meatball she held in her hand. Then she sprinkled the meatball on all sides with seasoned bread crumbs. When she had made about fifteen meatballs stuffed with prunes, she browned them in olive oil, then transferred them to a deep skillet, added tomato paste, plenty of water, sautéed onions, and half a box more of pitted prunes, and covered the pot. It would simmer for several hours. The result would be her special treat, meatballs with prunes. As it cooked, the liquid would turn to thick brown gravy, without the use of flour or other thickeners. Grace cooked a pot of rice to go with it and made a salad. They ate that night at the round oak table in the kitchen on new white plates by the light of tall dark blue candles and short white candles in glass holders, on a blue tablecloth that, along with pots and pans and utensils, had been purchased at Kmart.

"This is delicious," Amelia said. "I never imagined prunes used like this."

"An old East European recipe given me by a good friend. Roger loves it." Grace looked about her. "He and Charles would really appreciate the work that's been done in this farmhouse. I hope they come to see it soon."

Hannah nodded. "I hope Miranda will visit."

"Wouldn't that be nice? Maybe all our children will come — like a family reunion." Grace's brows puckered. "Do you think we should have gotten a king-size bed rather than two singles for the guest room?"

"No, singles can always be pushed together." Hannah laughed lightly. "Maybe even my two grandsons will come. They haven't shared a bed since they were three and five when Sammy kicked Philip out of their bed."

As they loaded the dishwasher, they heard the crunch of tires. From the kitchen window they watched Harold step from his truck, walk to the other side, open the door, and extend his hand to a trim woman of medium height who followed him up the steps of the porch. Amelia opened the door to Harold and the

156

woman, about fifty-five, with short auburn hair, a broad open face, high cheekbones, and serious brown eyes.

"We saw lights. Worried maybe it was prowlers. Glad there's no trouble. This is my wife, Brenda."

Brenda shook hands with each of them. "Glad to meet you. Welcome to Covington, ladies."

"Would you like to come in for a cup of tea or coffee?"

"No thanks. Just finished supper at the Athens Restaurant in Weaverville, 'bout twenty minutes from here."

Amelia felt awkward standing in the doorway, but the Tates seemed comfortable.

"How good of you to stop. We couldn't resist moving in."

"Well good. If we'd a known you were here, we'd have brought you over some pickled beets and one of Brenda's mama's fine old apple pies." He turned to his wife, pride written all over his face. "Brenda here's principal of the elementary school in Caster, next town down the road a piece. Got to be up bright and early. Mighty glad y'all are just fine."

Brenda nodded. "Harold's right." Her laugh came easily. "I'm no morning person, and he's got the job of rousting me at five A.M. Can we take a rain check?" She slipped her arm through her husband's.

"I used to do a story hour for second graders at our school library back in Dentry, Ohio, my hometown," Grace remarked, as Harold and Brenda started down the porch steps.

Brenda turned. Her intelligent, clear eyes studied Grace. Her voice was soft but to the point. "We'd be mighty pleased if you'd come over to our school and read with our children."

"We're going back to Pennsylvania the end of next week, but we're coming back in the spring." Straightening her shoulders, Grace looked from Hannah to Amelia, her eyes radiant and satisfied. "Can we talk about it then?"

"Certainly," Brenda replied.

The Tates waved good-bye, and the ladies stood on the porch watching the tail-lights of the pickup truck grow fainter as it moved down the road a mile or so, then turned right into a driveway. Grace rubbed her arms and turned to go inside.

Amelia followed her into the house. "Nice neighbors."

"Like folks back in Dentry." Grace locked the door, flicked off the porch light, and took a deep satisfied breath.

"Good friendly folk," Hannah said.

They said good night at the top of the stairs. Unfortunately, not everything would be as smooth as their first weeks in Covington. Later that night a water pipe in the upstairs bathroom broke, initiating them into their new, more challenging, and more complex life in the country.

7

The Flood

Grace's feet squished in her slippers. She flipped on the bathroom light. "My heavens, the floor's sopping wet." Confused by the situation, she stood for a moment looking down, then stepped out of her slippers and wiggled her toes, which grew colder by the second. Where's the water coming from? Gathering up the increasingly wet bottom of her flannel nightgown, Grace snatched two bathroom towels from their racks, lobbed them onto the floor, and stepping out of her soggy slippers stomped on the towels as if sopping up the water would fix the problem. She could see at once that the water was not coming from the bathtub or shower and the sink was dry.

She and Ted had had a leak like this in their downstairs bathroom once. What was it Ted had done? Think, Grace, think, she told herself. Ted had found their leak coming from the knob behind the toilet. Kneeling by the toilet, she peered behind it. Sure enough, there it was, a small but steady drip from the juncture of knob and pipe. Without further ado, and with a sense of being in control of the situation, Grace's fingers circled the knob, and twisted as Ted had done. "This should stop it," she muttered.

But the knob was old and rusted, and it turned only halfway so that the leak, though slowed, continued. I've made it worse, she thought. The knob feels loose, as if it might break off completely, and we'd have a flood in here, down the hall. Self-confidence waning fast, Grace sat back on her haunches.

Eyes puffy with sleep, Amelia appeared in the doorway, holding her white silk robe and nightgown above her ankles. "It's two in the morning, what's going on?"

"Leak."

Hannah, in green pajamas, appeared behind Amelia. "Leaking from where?"

"Behind the toilet. I tried to turn off the water, but the knob and pipe are rusted. How did Tom's men miss this?"

In her dismay, Amelia stepped into the bathroom, letting the bottom of her lovely robe trail on the wet floor. Her eyes grew helpless and frightened, and increasingly agitated, she instinctively tightened the

161

sash about her waist. This drew her attention to the hem of her nightgown, now thoroughly wet and cold and clinging to her ankles. "Oh no," she whispered, and yet she made no move to help. "What are we going to do? How could we think we could manage in this old house, just the three of us with no man around?"

"Worry about that later," Hannah said. "We've got to get downstairs, find the master water valve, and shut it off."

"Our new carpet's going to be soaked. The whole house will flood." A high-pitched, inappropriate laugh was quickly buried as Amelia suppressed both laughter and tears. Clutching her nightgown and robe, Amelia drew them up to her knees with one hand, then with the other wiped her eyes with her sleeve. "My feet are freezing," she said.

Aware that Amelia was about to come apart, Hannah took her firmly by the shoulders and gently guided her out of the bathroom and into the hallway. "Look at me, Amelia. It's going to be all right. Trust me. We need your help, now. First, find every towel we own and bring them here."

Amelia's eyes registered bewilderment. She didn't move.

"After you get the towels, get out of your

wet things. Get dressed warmly." And when Amelia nodded, Hannah released her and started toward the stairs.

"Where are you going?" Amelia asked, her eyes anxious and scared.

From three steps down, Hannah turned. "To the basement. There's a pump down there. I'll try to find the master water valve and shut it off."

"Bring me towels, hurry," Grace called from the bathroom.

"Amelia, get Grace the towels, now," Hannah said.

Amelia nodded blankly but made her way to the hall closet, and Hannah continued down the stairs. A door below opened and slammed shut.

Picking up the wet, soppy towels from the floor, Grace threw them into the tub. Then she covered the entire floor with dry towels and stifled the drip with another towel. "That should hold it for a while."

"You're shivering," Amelia said from the doorway.

"My nightgown's sopping wet up to my thighs. I'm cold. Once we solve this we've both got to change into something warm and dry."

Minutes later they emerged from their rooms in dry clothes. Amelia looked blankly at Grace. "What shall we do?"

"Let's go down and see if Hannah needs us." As she spoke, Grace pulled her dress up through her legs in front and tucked it under her belt, creating the effect of ballooning knee-high pants. "Ready?" Grace asked.

"I'm ready," Amelia said timidly.

Funny, Grace thought, the way some people stop functioning in an emergency and others go into overdrive. A sense of pride washed over her. She too had been flustered and shaken, her immediate reaction that they could not handle it, but then she had tried to do something about it. Grace shook her head. Amelia was not used to having a home, having things break, or having a husband who could fix things. And now this possible flood, however contained, in her newly renovated house must seem overwhelming to her. When this crisis is over, I'll try to reassure her, Grace decided.

Grace sniffed the basement air as she descended the plank steps that led down from the mudroom. It was dry and slightly sour. Temperatures fell into the low forties at night now, and the basement retained a permanent chill. One bare bulb suspended by a cord from the ceiling revealed the hot water heater, a half-wall that hid the pump, a roll of insulation, and a stack of empty cardboard boxes in a corner. Over the steady chug of the pump she heard Amelia, three steps behind her, cough. Hannah was obviously on the far side of the wall. "Find the valve?" Grace called.

Hannah emerged, wrench in hand, a grease stain smearing her cheek. "Over here, Grace, Amelia." She waved her arm. "I can't find a valve on his pump."

"There must be a valve." But when she looked, Grace could not find one, either.

"Must be outside," Hannah said. "Let's get out of here." They came out of the basement into the mudroom, and immediately Hannah started for the door leading outside onto the back stoop.

"Don't go out there, Hannah. It's so dark outside." Amelia's bottom lip was red from chewing on it. She looked nervously about, reached for Hannah's arm, and drew her into the kitchen, which seemed so bright compared to the dark beyond the walls of the house. Amelia lowered the shades of the window above the sink. "No one can see in here now," she said almost apologetically.

"Who's out there at three in the

165

morning?" Hannah muttered.

Opening the Formica cabinet above and closest to the sink, Amelia took down a glass, filled it with water from the tap, sipped it, and set the glass on the counter. At that moment all she could think of was that fresh springwater tasted so much better than the chlorinated stuff in cities.

Before going to bed, Grace had set the table for breakfast. Hannah pulled out two chairs. "Come here and sit down, Amelia." She fixed her eyes on Amelia's troubled face. "Listen to me, Amelia. This kind of thing could happen anytime, even in a newer house. We can handle this, all we have to do is find the valve."

"Or we could just shut off the electricity to the pump," Grace suggested. "Once the pump's off, the water'll stop running." She scratched her cheek. How did she know that? Osmosis, from living with Ted, a terrific handyman. The pain of missing Ted, vastly reduced after two years of grieving, intensified, and suddenly Grace longed for him the way she had those first few months after his death. To hide the tears brimming in her eyes, Grace busied herself wiping water splashes from about the sink.

Amelia pounced on that bit of information. "Grace, how do you shut off the electric?"

"We find the fuse box," Hannah said as she got up. "It's a metal box, probably gray, either on the wall or set inside the wall. Amelia, check the pantry. I'll look in the mudroom. Grace, you check in here."

A moment later, Grace called, "Here it is." On a narrow wall between the refrigerator and the door to the mudroom was the gray metal box. "It's so obvious against the yellow wall, how come we never noticed it?"

Hannah yanked it open, then stared with trepidation at the unlabeled rows of black switches staring at her. "Damn. Nothing's labeled."

For a moment it seemed to Grace that Hannah would slam shut the metal door and walk away; instead she straightened her shoulders. "Turn on the faucet in the sink, Grace. I'm going to click off each of these fuses. When the water stops running in the sink, we'll know we have the right one."

"I'm ready."

"What can I do?" Amelia asked.

"Sit down and pray we get it turned off before water soaks everything upstairs."

"Here goes." Hannah snapped a switch.

167

The refrigerator stopped. She shoved the switch back, and with a soft whir it started up again. Another fuse brought darkness to the kitchen. "Why didn't I think of a flashlight?" Hannah said, as the lights came back on.

"I've got one right here." Amelia pulled a flashlight from one of the kitchen drawers and handed it to Hannah. She felt so helpless, but now producing the flashlight made Amelia feel a trifle more useful.

Across one row, then the other, Hannah flipped fuses back and forth. Lights went off and on in the hallway, then the outside lights flared and darkened and then, at last, Grace said, "The water's off."

"There's no water anywhere in the house now. Won't be until we get a plumber." Hannah snapped the metal door of the fuse box shut, moved to the kitchen table, placed her arms on the table, and lowered her head onto her arms.

"We should have filled containers with water for brushing our teeth, flushing toilets. Back in Silver Lake whenever we had a hurricane warning we'd stock up on bottled water, fill the tub and buckets with water," Amelia said.

Hannah lifted her head, her face a study

in annoyance and resignation. Wearily she pushed up from the chair. "Okay, get some buckets. I'll flip the fuse back on and we can fill up."

"We have buckets?" Hair askew, and with her dress tucked up into her belt, Grace could have played the part of a tired and slightly befuddled butcher or baker from the *Arabian Nights*.

"Buckets weren't on our list," Amelia said apologetically, again feeling that she had failed them.

"What can we put water in?" Hannah's voice sounded like she felt, edgy. She rubbed her hip.

"I've got four glass canisters I was going to put beans, rice, stuff like that in. They'll give us enough water to brush our teeth, make a pot of tea, coffee for you, Hannah, in the morning." Amelia scrambled up and helped carry the canisters from the pantry to the kitchen sink. In less than a minute Grace said, "All full, ready to go."

Back at the metal box, Hannah flipped a fuse. The room went black. "Damn. Wrong fuse. Flashlight, Amelia."

Then came a thud and Amelia's stifled cry. They heard the snap of the fuse and light flooded the kitchen. Amelia lay on the floor, unhurt as it turned out, with one leg over a fallen chair, arms spread wide on the floor, her toes with their brightly polished nails wiggling in the air. She was laughing, a full, absolutely marvelous laugh, and it set them all laughing until tears rolled down their cheeks.

Then Hannah pushed the correct fuse, and the water in the sink stopped running.

"We've survived our first crisis," Grace said gleefully as she helped Amelia to her feet.

"I'm afraid I wasn't much use. I'm sorry, really." Amelia looked ruefully from one to the other of her friends.

"You helped with the towels upstairs, and you found the flashlight," Grace said, remembering her intention to make Amelia feel better.

"Come." Hannah put her arm around Amelia's shoulders. "Let's have ice cream." Moving to the refrigerator, Hannah took a gallon of Tom and Jerry's Rocky Road from the freezer. "Let's enjoy."

8

Three's a Crowd

✣ With air-conditioning and heat in place and the new gas fireplace installed, they arranged with Tom and Marie Findley to look after the house all winter, and along with taking care of a few odds and ends, Tom would build new steps into the basement with a sturdy handrail on either side, install shelves for storage, and hang better lighting. They would return to take up permanent residence in the spring, but for now, light-hearted and happy, they felt like migratory birds who, flying out of their past, had alighted and discovered a far better present.

On their last afternoon, while Hannah perused seed catalogs for spring, Grace and Amelia strolled down the road for the last time this year, past rolling pastures with grazing cattle and stands of mixed evergreen and bare-branched deciduous trees. The day was crisp and cool, but not cold. The sky a clear hydrangea blue and cloudless.

They had taken this walk many times and, as usual, were filled with wonder at the beauty of the countryside. Amelia's farmhouse was situated along a paved road, Cove Road, that ran through a long wide valley. On either side of the road, fields stretched sometimes a few hundred feet, sometimes considerably farther before the pastures ended and the woods began. Beyond the trees, taller more dramatic mountains guarded and sheltered the lower hills.

They had walked about a half a mile when a straggle of orange daylilies clinging to the low bank of a small stream drew their attention, and they stopped to rest on a grassy knoll close to the water.

"You seem very sober, my friend," Amelia said.

Grace sent a pebble skipping across the water. "I'm just nervous about facing Roger, I guess. I've never put myself first in anything."

"Seems to me you've put in enough time taking care of others."

"Why is it so hard for me to break old ways of thinking?"

"Takes practice, time, and patience with yourself."

Picking up a flaccid, wrinkled daylily

from the grass, Amelia cradled it in her palm and held it toward Grace. "Hannah says they last only one day, like their name. Did you know that?" Her fingers closed around the flower. Reaching over, Amelia slipped the crushed and faded blossom gently into the stream. Eddies of swirling water bore it away. Grace's eyes followed the crumbled flower as it swept downstream past an old willow tree whose dipping branches bore an occasional yellowed leaf.

"I feel like I've been bending and swaying all my life, like that willow tree," Grace said. She smiled at Amelia.

"Me too. You and I, Grace, have lived with rigid oaks. We needed to be able to bend. Now, maybe we can stand more erect, like Hannah. I see her as an evergreen, reliable, a tree for all seasons."

Grace tipped her face up toward her friend. "Yes, Hannah's certainly solid, dependable."

Amelia's face grew serious. "Do you feel old, Grace?"

Grace shrugged. "What's old? I've always thought age had to do with health. Ted was a vibrant active man, a young man, until . . . he got sick. All those trips up and down stairs taking care of him wore me out. I'd collapse at night, sometimes in my clothes. And all the worry, his dying at only sixty-seven. That's when I felt old, from all the worry and the caretaking. Did you know, Amelia, that seventy percent of caretakers become ill themselves? They wear out, I guess."

"I didn't know that," Amelia said. "I've always thought of age as a mind-set. Think old, feel old. Haven't you known people who seem old at forty-five?"

Grace nodded. "I have. I had an eighty-year-old aunt who could shop all day and party all night. When she was eighty-one, she took a train from Ontario to Vancouver. Said she'd always wanted to do that. I never had quite that kind of energy, but I never felt old until Ted's illness and death."

Amelia listened.

"When Ted died, for a while I felt like a used down pillow someone kicked into the air with its feathers scattered to the wind. Meeting you and Hannah, I began to stuff the pillowcase. Friends, being cared about, it means so much."

Amelia shifted, tucked her legs under her. "Since we decided to live together here I feel so much more alive, energetic."

"So do I. It's only some nights lately I

don't sleep well worrying about Roger."

"We'll get back, you'll settle all that with him. It's going to be fine."

"You're probably right, but making changes, even happy changes, takes getting used to. Ted made the big decisions in our household, and then Roger took over."

"Having to make your own decisions is hard when you've had everything decided for you. Thomas set the pace, the tone of our lives. I went along. When he died I felt like a zombie. Sometimes, I still do. Thomas once showed me a chart some therapist or researcher developed that rated stress, good and bad. Even happy things like births and weddings had points. It seems that it's the number of stress points in a short period of time that causes damage to your health."

"Easier to handle things in small doses, I guess. It's been scary being on my own and exhilarating too, like my driving here. If not for you and Hannah, I'd have spent my life driving twenty-five miles an hour." They laughed.

"All those years being an executive's wife, what a marvelous act I put on. My doctor at the hospital once asked, 'Who is Amelia?' I didn't know. Still don't, but I'd adore finding out. Olive's place was a devastating comedown for me. The only good thing was that it brought you and Hannah into my life."

"Yes, it's been a blessing for all three of us." The grass was damp. Grace brought her knees up and clasped them to her chest. "One thing, Amelia. I feel uncomfortable accepting money from your cousin Arthur's estate to pay my bill at Hilltop House and furnish my bedroom."

"It's not a loan."

"I like to pay my own way."

"When we come back, I'm going to put the house in all our names."

"You can't do that."

"Oh yes I can. I'm committed to us. Money, a house, what good are they, Grace, if fear keeps me from enjoying them? Look how hard it's been for you to break with old patterns, to take a risk; well, I'm afraid, terrified to tell the truth, of living alone. Yet, I was suffocating at Olive's. Then Arthur came into my life and gave me this miracle, but it was you and Hannah. By agreeing to live together here, you two gave me back my life; you owe me nothing."

Grace reached for her companion's hand and squeezed it. "You're special, Amelia, like a breath of sunshine."

The air grew cool. Amelia stood, brushed off her slacks, and extended her hand to Grace. After wiping her hands on her ever-present bandanna, Grace took the proffered hand and got up, and they walked leisurely back to the farmhouse.

Standing on the porch, one arm wrapped lightly about a post, one hand shading her eyes against the afternoon sun, Hannah watched them stroll along. They looked so chummy, like old friends, smiling and laughing. She scratched her chin. The usual threesome thing. Balancing relationships in a threesome was never easy. Damn, she hated being jealous, yet at this moment and for the first time since they had been in North Carolina, jealousy pricked and poked at Hannah's heart. Repressing it, she smiled at them as they drew near and waved toward the chairs into which they sank to sit and silently, reverentially, watch the magical quality of a lavender sky that hovered over the mountains.

Hannah broke the silence. "That must be what the song means by 'purple mountains majesty across the fruited plains.' I've never seen hills turn that color before."

Darkness came. The heavens exploded with stars.

"No light pollution," Amelia said. "How incredibly clear and bright. See, there's the Milky Way. The Big Dipper's my favorite constellation, or I should say the one I can easily pick out."

"Mine's Orion's Belt," Grace said.

"Mine too." Hannah leaned forward for a better view, pleased that she and Grace had Orion in common. "Ever wonder what primitive man felt seeing the stars glide across the sky?"

"He worshiped them," Grace said simply, as if stating an undisputed fact. "In ancient Egypt at one time the constellation of Orion, the hunter, represented their god Osiris." She spoke with energy and enthusiasm. "There's a theory that the great pyramid at Giza isn't a burial chamber at all. It served as a sacred place from where a dead pharaoh's soul departed to join the god Osiris as Orion, in the heavens. Most traditional Egyptologists reject this idea, but they never explain why there are no hieroglyphics anywhere in that pyramid when they cover the walls of other tombs."

Hannah craned her neck for a better view of the Orion constellation. "Not a tomb, eh? Interesting. As an old iconoclast, I love theories that shoot holes in traditional beliefs."

178

"I've got some books back at Olive's, if you're interested," Grace said, getting up and leading the way inside.

"I'm interested," Hannah replied, following her. She and Grace were connecting again and that felt good.

Amelia looked back down the road at the lights glowing in farmhouse kitchens and at the kaleidoscope of trees, fences, and hedges slipping in and out of a passing car's headlights.

It was with heavy hearts — for they dreaded, each for her own reason, going back to Branston — that they handed the house keys to Marie and Tom Findley the next morning, hugged them good-bye, and piled into old Nelly.

"I hate to leave." Amelia pulled the seat belt across her chest.

"So let's stay," Hannah chimed in, half in earnest.

"We can't do that," Grace insisted, her voice rising. Then she buckled up and adjusted the rearview mirror. "I don't want to leave, either. It's been wonderful being here. But we can't just walk out on Olive, all three of us, without giving her a few months' notice. She's got to replace three of us at the same time."

"And we have to help the children adjust and we have to pack," Amelia said.

They settled back then, and as Grace drove down the driveway she caught a glimpse of the house in the rearview mirror. The house would wait for them. It was Amelia's house, only now it seemed to belong to all of them.

They made a quick stop at the convenience store to say good-bye to the clerk, whose name it turned out was Roger, although everyone, he had told them, called him Buddy. Another stop at Hillside House. Margaret Olsen was not at home, and Amelia left a note on the erasable message board tacked to the wall of the porch alongside her front door. "See you soon. G. H. A."

Once on the four-lane highway, Grace drove old Nelly at fifty, then fifty-five miles an hour, and later in the afternoon, when they passed a car on the interstate, Grace muttered, "Slowpoke," and Hannah and Amelia burst out laughing.

How wonderful to laugh, Grace thought. Heaven knows what we'll have to deal with once we get back to Olive's place.

9

Mother Singleton
Speaks Her Mind

🐝 Sugar Maple Road bustled with activity; neighbors sat on their front porches soaking up the remains of an exceptionally mild December day. Mrs. Oglesby waved, as did the twins and Mr. Spooner, the retired clown, who were playing croquette on his miniature front lawn. The Finnigan sisters, bent, elderly ladies and longtime residents of Sugar Maple Road, ambled along pushing shopping carts borrowed from the nearby grocery. Two middle-aged men in shirtsleeves, their arms streaked with grease, leaned under the hood of a gray Buick. The smell of barbecue smoke floated in the air.

On the porch of Number 16, Charles, a short compact man with a round pleasant face and graying hair pulled back in a neat ponytail, sat rocking. Roger, tall and handsome, with wavy blond hair and a neatly trimmed beard — and obviously younger

— paced. Roger stopped pacing, crossed his arms over his chest, and glowered as the station wagon came to a halt in the driveway.

Flushed and feeling increasingly anxious, Grace started from the car, her arms flung wide to embrace the tall blond man. Roger welcomed her stiffly with a perfunctory peck on the cheek. At their last meeting in Dentry, and again when he left for Saudi Arabia, embracing Roger had been like hugging an ice sculpture; Grace came away chilled. If she had hoped for a thaw, she was disappointed. Charles, however, smiled and sprang from his chair to hug her and place a fluttery kiss on her cheek. "Welcome home, Mother Singleton," he said, his deep blue eyes warm and welcoming. He had always reminded Grace of the kind of man who would stop to help a child or an elderly person across the street.

"Well, you were gone long enough," Roger censured her. He stood apart from her, his shoulders stiff.

"I'm sorry," she began, then caught Hannah's eye and immediately felt irritated with herself for reacting as if she were guilty of some misdeed.

"I cabled you to wait here." Roger glared at Grace.

"Roger, Roger." Grace shook her head, thinking how when she'd last seen him it had been only about what Roger needed, wanted, thought, felt, and it still was. "It's wonderful to see you. How well you look."

Pink plastic hair rollers bobbed and jiggled on Olive's head as she rushed from the house waving her arms and yelling. "Back, eh? I haven't any supper, you know." She took the porch steps two at a time to help with the luggage, and Charles ran down to help unload the station wagon.

"You look utterly knackered, love." He put an arm around Grace's shoulders.

"I am tired. It's a long drive, but well worth it."

Hands shoved into the pockets of his gray front-pleated slacks, Roger followed Charles to the car.

"These are your mother's." Olive handed Roger two suitcases, passed Amelia's overnight case and a bag to Charles, slung Hannah's loose canvas bag over her shoulder, and headed for the house.

"Set those suitcases down, Roger." Grace stopped him on the porch. "It's so pleasant out here. Let me rest a minute." As she sat on the porch swing, she looked from her son to Charles, who had placed

Amelia's bags in the foyer and returned to join them. "It's so good to see you both. Charles, you've lost some weight. These are my very good friends, Hannah Parrish, Amelia Declose."

Charles shook hands, smiled. With an indifferent air Roger nodded toward the women, who then proceeded into the house, leaving Grace alone with her son and his companion. Charles settled alongside Grace on the swing. He was not much taller than she was, and companionably their feet shoved the swing back and forth. "Oh, Mother Singleton," he said, clasping his hands. "I wanted to ring you in North Carolina, but Roger put me off it, kept us busy hunting for a flat and all that. We've come to stay, you know."

Charles was thirteen years younger than herself. How many times had she asked him to call her Grace?

"No can do," he had replied. "Mother Singleton it is. It just feels right."

"What happened that you left your jobs in Saudi Arabia?"

"Why would something have happened? Maybe we were tired of the heat," Roger snapped, leaving her to wonder why her son sounded so defensive.

"Oh, Roger, don't be huffy." Charles

waved his wrist in a way that belied his full baritone voice and masculine appearance. "We have so much to tell you," he said, giving Grace his brightest smile.

"And I have something to tell you," Grace managed. She was exhausted and certain that she must rest before getting into any further conversation with Roger. "But it will have to wait. I drove. I'm worn out. Before we visit, I need to shower and rest. Could we have dinner later in some quiet restaurant?"

"Certainly. Right, Roger?"

Roger nodded.

As she walked into the house and hung her coat on the coatrack, the low ceiling and dimly lit foyer oppressed her, and Grace wondered how she had ever allowed Roger to leave her as a boarder in this house. Alone in her room, tears welled in Grace's eyes, tears of gratitude for Covington, the farmhouse, a new life looming. Soon this room would not represent her future. Grace pulled off the worn maroon cable-knit sweater of Ted's she sometimes wore and buried her head in it, though his smell had long been replaced by the odor of her own light floral cologne. She held the sweater up in front of her. "We had a good life, but you're gone now, and I need to make a life for myself." Her voice faltered. "I'm not going to let Roger intimidate me this time." Grace folded the sweater and returned it to its place in her closet.

The sign above and on the canopy read: THE GARDEN GRILL.

"This is a great restaurant," Charles said as Roger held the door open for Grace and she stepped into a foyerlike room filled with potted ferns and ficus trees. "We like it because it's got several small dining rooms and, of course, the food's good. We asked for a table in the Peony Room."

From a desk buried amid greenery a pert dark-haired young woman extended her hands to check their coats. The maître d', a tan, athletic man in a blue sports jacket and a tie with a bold floral design, stepped forward.

"Welcome, Mr. Singleton, Mr. Spensley," and to her a slight bow. "Madam, welcome. Right this way, please." He waved his arm and escorted them past a congested, smoke-filled bar, through one crowded dining room and then another. Grace was acutely aware of the hum of voices raised in conversation above the music, something with a drumbeat that she found irritating, and she hoped, as they made their way farther into the depths of the restaurant, that the sound would diminish. This, of course, did not happen, for speakers blared from the corners of each room. It's not forever, she reminded herself. Roger seems happy. Don't make a fuss.

The room was charming. Loud but charming. Glass-paneled walls expanded the space, doubling the number of tall potted palms and huge bowls of lush rose-colored peonies set on pedestals about the room. Grace tried to shut out the music and relax. She thought about Hannah using mind over matter to get out of the bathtub, and she said to herself, I can do that. I can concentrate on Roger and Charles and the food and this lovely room and forget about the music.

"Feeling a bit more rested?" Charles asked.

"I cannot believe they made you drive all that way and back," Roger said.

"No one made me." The music faded into the background of her consciousness. "I did it because I wanted to. It's a lovely drive. North Carolina's beautiful. I felt like forty again."

"But you're not forty. You're sixty-what, six — seven?"

"Sixty-something and young at heart," she said, troubled at the direction the talk was taking and determined to keep it light while she caught up on their lives. The music seemed louder.

"You've had a heart attack, and anyway, it's not like you to just go roaming about."

Ah, she thought, concentrating on her son, so that's it. Roger's uncomfortable with the change he senses in me. She smiled. He smiled back, a crooked uneasy smile it seemed to her. She was hungry and reached for the menu, but even as her eyes scanned the page, her heart beat faster, sensing that a confrontation, limited necessarily by the public setting, was brewing.

Roger ordered wine, then set down the wine list and picked up the dinner menu.

"Let's see." Charles ran a finger down the menu. "Salmon. Chicken. Veal piccata." Then Charles looked up at the waiter. "Ask Mr. Rickels, will you, Fred, if he could turn the music down, please." He put his hands over his ears. "It's a bit loud."

"Thank you, Charles." Grace sipped her water and looked closely at Charles over the tilted glass. His skin looks sallow.

Maybe it's the lighting in this restaurant. His hair's thinner too and his nails shorter, more brittle. He always kept them so well manicured. Charles caught her studying him. She smiled, reached over and patted his hand.

Roger sat across from his mother. Initially, he avoided looking directly at her and when he did, his deep-set dark brown eyes were intense and piercing. He gave her a quick distracted smile. "You know, Mother, I feel responsible for you. I like it that you're living here."

Grace stiffened. She could hear Hannah coaching her, "Speak up for yourself, Grace. Don't let him bully you." Swallowing hard, Grace looked into Roger's eyes. "I feel like an artifact you keep in the attic. Every now and then you take me down, brush me off, look at me, then out of sight, out of mind, for another year."

"God, Mother, don't be facetious. I haven't lived close enough to visit more often. But all that'll be different now." Roger glanced knowingly at Charles. The music had been lowered and was quite tolerable. Grace felt the old ache in her soul. She liked Charles. He was, as ever, kind, gentle, and considerate. But — and her heart caught in her throat — there would be no grandchildren, and that hurt.

At a table across the room and out of earshot a smartly dressed young couple with angry faces gesticulated wildly, drawing the attention of people at other tables. Grace felt embarrassed for them. She couldn't imagine such behavior in a restaurant. Suddenly the woman's arm hit her wineglass, and the red liquid stained the tablecloth and dripped onto her dress. The couple rose and after a brief exchange with the waiter left the restaurant.

At that moment their waiter arrived with the wine and poured a half inch into a glass. Charles swished the red liquid, tasted it, and nodded. Positioning her palm over her wineglass, Grace shook her head. The waiter filled Roger's and Charles's glasses, and Roger ordered veal piccata for himself and Charles. Grace chose grilled chicken topped with mushrooms.

She sat silently, her hands in her lap, and studied the two men. She could feel the vibration from Roger's leg jiggling the table. He cracked his knuckles. He's a wreck tonight, she thought. Charles, on the other hand, appeared relaxed, though at moments she thought his smile was forced. Something was troubling them both, of that she was certain.

"So, tell me," she said, keeping her voice soft and caring, "why did you leave Saudi Arabia?"

Roger's eyes darted to Charles, then away. His voice wavered, and immediately Grace felt a flutter of concern for him. "It seemed a good time to make a fresh start."

"We've always dreamed of having our own business," Charles said.

"What kind of business?"

"An entertainment shop." Charles leaned toward her, eyes alert and eager, his face flushed with excitement.

Her eyes widened. "Where people play video games?"

Charles looked appalled. "Heavens no, Mother Singleton."

Grace warmed to his broad grin and eager wide blue eyes. "Well, tell me. What's an entertainment shop?"

"A gift emporium, fine china, crystal, silver, linens, everything to turn an ordinary social event into a gala event, only we won't sell, we'll rent. We'll transform unimaginative parties into splendid entertainments." Charles's hands danced in the air. "Ordinary rooms will sparkle, like Versailles."

"We'll book the entertainment, too: pianists, string quartets, singers, dancers, poets, the reading of plays," Roger explained. His leg stopped nudging the table and instead he dangled his fork over his wineglass.

"That sounds exciting. Where will you do this?"

"That's where Miranda comes in."

"Miranda?"

"You tell her." Charles tapped Roger's shoulder.

"We got to know Miranda and Paul quite well, and we all get along. Paul's quiet, but he's intelligent and he's got a wry sense of humor and Miranda's very bright. She's smart and funny."

Grace raised an eyebrow. Miranda, she knew from Hannah, was a good business woman, but funny? An interesting concept.

"She adores our idea and she knows this area well," Charles piped in.

"We're talking partnership." Roger's eyes grew guarded "We'd like to open a shop here in Branston. Rent's cheaper than in Philadelphia. Branston's population's what . . . ?" He looked at Charles. "A hundred thousand? A lot of new money here, upwardly mobile types, you know."

"It's less than an hour to Philadelphia for expansion," Charles said.

"Paul's in marketing. He works at home.

He'll do our brochures, lay out an advertising plan."

Miracles never cease, Grace thought.

"The possibilities are endless, don't you think, Mother Singleton?"

"Yes, I do." A small voice inside urged her to take advantage of their enthusiasm to share her own plans, and Grace focused her attention on her son. "I have news also. Hannah, Amelia, and I plan to pool our financial resources and move to Amelia's farmhouse in North Carolina."

Roger's hand went to his face as if she had slapped him. "What? You're kidding?"

"No."

"But your heart."

"Listen to me, Roger. I had a 'little' heart attack. I had angioplasty to open one, only one, artery. My heart's fine. I feel better than I did before. Dr. Frank said I've got another good ten, fifteen, maybe twenty years ahead of me. Try to understand. I felt old before we went to Covington. Now, for the first time since your father died, I'm excited about my future." She read the skepticism in his eyes and plowed on. "Today, people in good health aren't old even at seventy-five or eighty. Slower maybe, but we've still got ideas, interests, dreams. We need a reason to get up in the morning, just like you do."

Scarlet patches spread across his handsome face, and he regarded her with a look of complete disbelief.

Grace reached across the table, intending to place her hand on his, but he retracted his and, rebuffed, she pulled back. "Would you prefer that I sit at Olive Pruitt's house and spend the rest of my life wallowing in depression?" Emphatically, she shook her head. "I hope you'd prefer that I be happy, even if it means moving to Covington, making a new life with good friends. It's a little town, no more than a thousand population, a few streets, a post office, gas station/convenience store, and of all things an old-time hardware store where you can even buy dog muzzles and thread, clocks, old iron cookware, and . . ."

"Covington," Charles murmured. "Reminds me of home."

"But, Mother," Roger said.

Grace lifted her hand to stop him. "You see, my son, we have something in common. We're both starting over."

"I'm flabbergasted. I had no idea you were unhappy at Olive's."

"You've spent the night at her place. Would you want to live there permanently?" She waved her hand, did not wait for him to answer. "It doesn't matter anymore." She leaned toward him but refrained from touching him. "Now, what did you have to tell me that was so important?"

"I can hardly talk about it. It's going to take me time to get used to this new mother I have."

"I love you, as I always have," Grace said, looking for signs that he might overtly reject her there and then.

Charles and Roger exchanged dubious looks. Then Roger straightened in his chair. "I know that, Mother." He shrugged. "Guess I'll just go ahead and tell you." He remained quiet for a moment as if collecting his thoughts, then said, "We need your help in order to start this business."

"My help? How?"

"The house in Dentry." He spoke quickly, firmly.

"What about my home in Dentry?" A prickling sensation skyrocketed up her spine. Her neck, cheeks, grew uncomfortably warm, and she hooked her fingers around the arms of her chair, trying to keep her voice low and her emotions in check.

"There's no mortgage on the house. It's worth about a hundred and forty-five thousand. I checked with a realtor. If we split it, that's approximately seventy thousand for each of us after the realtor's commission."

She waited, unbelieving, remembering Hannah's prophetic comment.

When she did not reply, he said, "You've always said the house is my inheritance, Mother."

"I'm not dead yet." She slapped her napkin on the table. Stunned, struggling unsuccessfully to curb her indignation, her sense of betrayal, Grace snapped at him. "You checked with a realtor behind my back? You want me to sell my home, the one thing I have to fall back on, God forbid? I can't believe I'm hearing right." Easy now, she reminded herself. You don't want to be a spectacle like that young couple.

"Don't get so riled up. If you're so averse to selling, you could take a mortgage." The demand in his voice angered her. Her face grew red and smarted as if she had been slapped. Grace choked back tears and as her anger mounted she cared less and less who knew it. Her voice rose. "This is outrageous. Mortgage the home your father worked so hard to pay off?"

"Not so loud, Mother." Clearly piqued

by her reaction, Roger glared at her, leaned toward her, his voice low, controlled, and determined. "We need the money. We can't open the business without it."

"Oil companies pay well when you work overseas. Didn't you save anything?"

"We traveled a great deal, bought antiques." Roger sat back and shook his head. "You've changed. I don't know this person."

"I have changed," she said, then fell silent as the waiter arrived with their dinners. The last thing she wanted now was food. Her stomach ached as if drummers were busy practicing inside her. I'll get right up and walk out of here, she thought. But pride and training stopped her. "I don't want to talk about this anymore." Picking up her fork, Grace shoved at the rice, ate a mushroom, cut a small piece of chicken, and took a nibble. The men ate heartily. Like Ted, she thought, who ate regardless of what was happening around him. She cut another small piece of chicken and considered how life can suddenly shift, spin out of control, take off in a new direction. This was one of those times. Her mind clouded. The constrictions of being in a public place, the frustration at her inability to stamp her foot or vent her anger, burdened her spirit and she felt suddenly exhausted.

Back in Hannah's bedroom Miranda and Hannah talked openly and honestly, as they had not talked in years. Miranda paced, swinging her long arms, then folding them across her chest. Stepping around her mother's outstretched leg, she looked down into Hannah's sober face.

"Mother, in order for me to go into business with Charles and Roger, I need to sell the nursery, but I can't do it unless you agree."

Hannah looked away. In the last hour they had been around and around this. It was as if her decision to move to Covington was being challenged, the past seeking to bind her, forcing her to choose, to decide again and then again.

Miranda slipped down on her knees in front of the desk chair where Hannah sat staring glumly out of the window. "Please, I truly need your help." Tears spilled from Miranda's eyes. "I've never told you this before." She hesitated. "I admire you more than anyone in the world."

The words stunned and at the same time thrilled Hannah. Turning from the window, she reached forward and slowly, tentatively, brought her daughter's face toward her. "Miranda, thank you. But you needn't say that to get me to do what you want."

Miranda recoiled. "My God, Mother. I'm not saying this because I want you to sell. You've explained about Covington, and I accept that you're going to live there. I know we don't see much of each other, but we've always lived close to one another, and in all these years I've never told you how I feel." She tucked her long legs beneath her. "You were always so strong, so sure. You intimidated me. I felt that I had to maintain distance to assure my own sense of self."

"I thought you blamed me for ruining your life when I left your father."

Miranda leaned close and placed her hands on her mother's knees. Her eyes narrowed and her voice hardened. "I was coming down the stairs. I saw him hit you with that belt. I saw the welts. I heard you crying. I hated him." She bit her lip. "And at the same time I wondered what you'd done to deserve it. After his death it was easy to remember the good things about him: how he'd tickle me when he helped me with my math homework, and how he'd take Laura and me swimming in the lake. For a long time I blamed you for his death and hated you, because I kept telling myself it was your fault that I'd never be able to thank him for the good things, or even to chastise him for the way he treated you."

Miranda relaxed back onto her haunches, brushed a long, dark strand of hair back behind her ear. "I'm grown up now. I know that men who beat women don't stop with once. It took courage to leave. I've wanted to tell you, you did the right thing, even dragging us into that truck with that big old trucker."

"So, you remember all that?"

Miranda nodded. Her eyes misted. "Laura remembers too, how that man hit Dad's gun into the snow and how you grabbed our hands and shoved us into his huge truck, and we were gone."

"My poor baby," Hannah said. "I'm so sorry. That truck was so hot, but you were shivering and shaking as if you had a fever."

"Those were terrible, frightening years for Laura and me. You hardly had time for us. Now, of course, I understand that you had to go to school, learn a skill you could support us with. You worked very hard to take care of us. You're my hero, Mother."

"I'm so sorry for all your pain." Hannah reached forward and stroked her daughter's thick, black hair. "My dear child."

Before Hannah could say any more, Miranda continued. "You've come home from North Carolina so happy. Maybe Covington's the right place for you. But I need a change too, and my boys are getting older. Next September Sammy'll be ready for college. Philip has two more years. It's been a struggle for us to keep them in prep school, but Paul and I feel that it'll give them a solid foundation and open doors for them with grants or scholarships for college."

Miranda's eyes lit up. "And, Mother, Paul's been up and down, depressed for years. Suddenly he's excited about something. He's working on the ads and drawing up a marketing plan for me and the boys."

"The boys?" Hannah laughed.

"Roger and Charles. I like them, especially Charles."

Mother and daughter reached for one another and this time they hugged hard. Then Miranda untangled her legs and got up. Reaching over, she plucked a Kleenex from a box on her mother's desk and gently wiped Hannah's cheeks. "Whatever you decide about the business, when you're ready to have surgery I'll make a room for you downstairs in my house, be there for you."

"Surgery? You know?" Laughter bubbled up from somewhere deep inside Hannah. It was good to laugh, to connect with Miranda. "Grace and Amelia want me to have the hip replacement surgery after we get back to North Carolina. They're longing to mother me."

Miranda smiled. "They're good women. I've come to like them. They're probably quite adept at mothering, especially Grace."

Hannah studied Miranda. Her gangly, self-conscious daughter, whom Hannah had so often harangued to "stand up straight," and "hold your head up," was gone, and in her place stood Miranda, self-possessed, strong and capable, a woman with dreams and aspirations of her own. Hannah was proud but suddenly she found herself totally drained; her arms, legs, back, her whole body screamed for rest.

"Now, give me a hand up, will you?" Hannah felt the strength in Miranda's upper arms as she pulled her to her feet, and Hannah felt cared for and loved in a way she had not known from either daughter since before . . . well, long ago. Leaning against Miranda, she walked with stiff, short steps to the bed. Swinging her legs up, she lay back and closed her eyes.

"Sell the business, Miranda. Take what you need. I'll need some money for what insurance doesn't cover when I have the surgery, and I'd like to have a small nest egg in the bank."

"Of course, Mother. Whatever I take will be a loan, and I'll pay you back a bit at a time."

"No. You've worked hard, you deserve compensation; you figure out what you need, give me the rest." Love for her daughter filled her heart, yet hovering at the edges, anxiety and grave doubt screamed, how can you leave now, when you and Miranda have at last connected in a meaningful way? If she left, would it all vanish?

"Roger what?" Amelia was livid. "That's some nerve after how he's treated you."

They were sitting in Grace's bedroom. Outside, in startling contrast to yesterday, the first snowfall of the winter season reached out its arms to tuck Sugar Maple Road under a soft white blanket. Hannah stretched out her legs on the chaise. Grace, propped up on her bed, said nothing. Then Hannah's voice filled the empty space about them.

"I've agreed to sell the nursery so Miranda and Paul can go into business with the boys, as she so fondly calls them. I think they've got an idea that'll fly." For now, Hannah kept her growing misgivings to herself.

"You too?" Amelia said.

"Do you really think it's a good idea for a business, Hannah?" Feeling increasingly guilty about refusing Roger, Grace too had begun to question her decision, and had even awakened at three in the morning with stomach cramps. Now Grace needed reassurance.

"We're more and more a service-oriented society. If you've got the means, and many people do, you pick up the phone, say the magic words, and someone else makes the party," Hannah said. "Yes, I think this business is a good idea."

"Then, you think I should sell my home in Dentry, give Roger the money?" She wanted to add, reassure me, remind me of how good it was in Covington, how much we all want to live there, and that it'll turn out all right. But she said nothing.

"I'm going to help Miranda, so if I say I think you should it'll sound like I have a vested interest. Think of it this way. We could do with a bit of cash ourselves, and they need to try something new. Why not help them?"

"Well, I think he's got colossal nerve asking you to sell your home in Dentry," Amelia fumed.

"That's how I felt at first," Grace said. "My first reaction was an emphatic 'no,' but I've been thinking. I've been reading and I've learned so much. There's money to be made in mutual funds, and I've worried that if I ever did need cash, it would all be tied up in my old home, could take months to sell or even to mortgage." And that's true whether I go to North Carolina with them or not, she thought. "Wouldn't I be better off putting half that money into a money market fund and the rest into a good solid mutual fund?"

Amelia's hand clasped across her chest. Her eyes looked as if they might pop right out of her head. "Sell your house? Invest in the stock market? My God, no. Thomas lost our money that way."

"But he bought and sold on his own, right?"

"Yes."

"I wouldn't trust myself to do that. Money market funds invest in government bonds and Treasury notes. For a mutual fund, stocks, I'd use a Fidelity Fund or a Vanguard Fund. They're spoken of as being reliable funds."

Grace's decision to sell her home in Dentry was made easier later that day when Roger called. "Mother, I want to apologize. Charles really let me have it, and he's right. I've been thoughtless and inconsiderate and I'm sorry. I've been a nervous wreck, totally off the wall since we got back from Saudi Arabia. My behavior last night was sullen, rude, and inexcusable. Can you forgive me?"

"It was very difficult for me last night. You caught me totally off guard, and in a public place."

"I'm very sorry."

"Of course I forgive you. I love you, Roger." She did love him, had always loved him, would always love him. So why, she wondered, now that he had come to live in Branston, was she leaving him?

"Again, I'm sorry. We won't talk about the house again."

"The rent from that house is part of my income. If I sell the house . . ." She stopped, realizing that for the first time she had referred to "the" house and not "my" home.

"We wouldn't expect you to draw on your principal, Mother. We'd pay you the amount you get for rent each month."

"Give me a few days to think about it. Good night, Roger." Grace set down the receiver and sighed. She knew that North Carolina or not, the time had come to let go of the past, to set Dentry and that part of her life behind her.

And there was Olive, cruel and fierce in her rejection. "Never in all my life," she declared when they told her, "have I heard such childish stupidity from supposedly mature women. Are you crazy? Do this stupid thing and you'll all end up miserable and alone, far from your children, from anyone you know. It's asinine and you're . . ."

"That's enough, Olive." Hannah was enraged. "You seem to forget we're mature women of sound mind, and we deem it best to pool our resources and share a home. You're out of step with the times. We're trying to change our lives, something different . . . alternative housing."

"Alternative housing? Sounds like a rest

home brochure," Olive snapped.

"Well, it's not," Hannah replied. "It's just another way to live our lives. To live, Olive. You're the immature, stupid one, stuck in the past, trying to control everyone's lives when we want to do things for ourselves: make a home, cook, garden, or . . . or . . . even meet new people. We have many productive years ahead of us."

Olive turned on Hannah. "You're talking. You, a crippled old woman."

Olive turned to Grace. "You could drop dead from your heart any minute. And you, Amelia, silly woman, neurotic, scared of everything. What's going to happen to the lot of you way out in some godforsaken piece of bush?"

"We'll take care of one another," Grace said.

"Well, you're the worst boarders I've ever had, selfish and inconsiderate. Good riddance. Why not leave now?"

"Because we need time to pack and ship our things, and there are still repairs going on at the farmhouse," Amelia said firmly.

10

The Church of
Our Lady

✿ Olive's attack shook Amelia to the core.
Was Olive right? Was she silly, stupid, and
immature? Were their plans too impulsive
and foolish and doomed to failure? A fitful
and restless night followed. Covington and
all their hopes and plans suddenly seemed
questionable. Amelia teetered on the edge
of a chasm, fearful that sharing her fears
with Grace and Hannah would open a
floodgate of doubt. Early the next morning,
she slipped from the house and walked,
briskly at first for it was cold, and the sidewalks bore patches of snow, then slower as
she rounded a corner. She went down the
street, turning unwittingly at this stoplight,
at that street sign, until unexpectedly she
found herself facing a small gray church
with a lofty spire. Church of Our Lady was
carved into the gray stone facade near the
entrance door.

As if drawn by a magnetic force, Amelia started up the steps. At the door she hesitated a moment before grasping the brass pull. The tall heavy door swung open and as she stepped into the deep, powerful silence, a sense of awe came over her.

The interior of the church stunned her with its loveliness: a replica of a Gothic cathedral with vertical lines of tall pillars supporting pointed arches, flying buttresses, ribbed vaults, and beautiful stained-glass windows. From somewhere deep at the rear of the church, powerful transcendent chords of an organ flooded the air, swirling and soaring to the lofty ceiling. Amelia walked to a pew in the center aisle and sat. In time a fine tranquillity seeped into her pores and with each breath filled her soul. The hair along her spine and arms prickled. She seemed to expand, to grow taller, and to be filled, amazingly, with a deep and boundless exquisiteness of spirit. And when at last the chords faded and stopped, the message-bearer of the indwelling spirit departed. So this is bliss, Amelia thought.

Having no will to move, she sat there, her face dampened with tears, and for one brief instant, she understood the meaning of mankind's joys and blessings and mangled hopes and unfulfilled dreams.

Then Amelia rose and walked toward the votive candles. Unsure, she stood a long moment and finally reached for a taper and lit a candle. She hesitated, then bowed her head. "My beloved Caroline, how I miss you." Amelia lit a second candle. "For you, Thomas." She spoke now, unaccustomed prayers, in a very soft whisper. "What shall I do? I was so sure, we all were, about moving to Covington. Will it be a disaster like Olive says? I'm frightened. Will it work out, the three of us living together, dividing chores, funds? Help me, please, help me." She hesitated. "Help me, God."

Organ music swelled then softened and a voice, a lone rich and beautiful baritone, began to sing. Amelia did not know the song or the melody but somehow from it she gleaned an answer.

"Thank you," she whispered. Amelia turned and walked from the Church of Our Lady.

Later, at Amelia's request, the ladies gathered in Grace's room and settled on her bed like schoolgirls. "I think we should talk about Olive's outburst, how we felt," Amelia said.

"Absolutely," Hannah muttered. "I've been thinking a lot these past few days." She sat propped against the headboard, and now Grace slipped a pillow beneath her knees. "Thanks, Grace," Hannah said.

Grace released a deep sigh. The tension that had been building in her body, and which had required her to use nitroglycerin twice that day, began to slip away. "Olive was awful. She was so mean. Why?"

"Jealousy, I think, that we have the freedom, the means, the will to do this," Hannah said.

"Well, how do each of you feel about our plans, now?" Grace asked. "I've been worrying myself sick about moving away just when Roger's come here to live, and then Olive makes me feel selfish and irresponsible."

"I've started to question whether we're just cockeyed dreamers," Hannah said. "I've even stopped looking at my seed catalogs."

"*Mes amies,*" Amelia began, "think about it. Isn't it logical that after all the excitement in Covington, we're having a letdown? I think we're all depressed just being back here, stuck in our rooms. I think we'd feel this way even if Olive had

212

smiled and wished us well." Amelia looked from Grace to Hannah. "Perhaps?"

"Probably," Grace said.

"Let's try an exercise I learned to do back in the hospital before I came here. Close your eyes." Amelia waited, the way the therapist had, glad now for that particular experience. "Think about Covington, see the house, your favorite rooms, the view. How does it feel?"

It seemed long minutes before Grace said, "Happy, relieved, free." She drew a deep breath and a huge smile spread across her face. "I miss it."

Hannah nodded. "I see myself as being totally well and creating a garden. When I can do that, I'll be able to put having to give up my nursery behind me."

"Now change the scene. We're not going. We're staying here at Olive's."

Hannah and Grace scowled, quickly shook their heads. "How utterly sad I feel," Grace whispered.

"Same here." Hannah opened her eyes, her voice was unwavering. "Depressing to the extreme. Our plans, the farmhouse, Covington, they're right for us."

"I haven't slept with worrying," Amelia said, letting out a sigh of relief. "This morning I found myself in a church praying."

"You, in a church?" Hannah said.

"Years ago, I rejected God because bad things happened to me. Well, I couldn't sleep, so early this morning I went walking, and I literally stumbled into this church. The oddest thing happened."

Grace leaned forward. "What happened?"

"You know, rejecting any kind of a spiritual life left me figuratively walking the plank alone."

Grace nodded. "Roger just said something like that to me; he said he wished he had religion, life would be easier."

Amelia struggled for the right words to explain what had happened to her in the church. Finally she said simply, "I felt God's presence."

"How?" Hannah looked at her with skepticism.

"There was wonderful music. I lit candles for Caroline, Thomas. Quite simply, a sense of awe overwhelmed me."

"So, that's it?" Hannah asked.

"The point is, God's accessible. . . ." She laid both hands across her heart. "Sort of waiting patiently for us to call him or it, energy, whatever." It had been so clear when she had been in the church, and now the whole concept was muddled.

"Like God sits there patiently waiting for your phone call?" Hannah asked.

"Well," Amelia shrugged. "Forget about all that. I feel better. Whatever happened helped me to understand that what's going on for us now is normal. After all, we're leaving familiar, though unpleasant, surroundings, uprooting ourselves and moving to a new place. It was like a vacation all those weeks in Covington. When we get back there we'll have to get down to the business of making new lives."

"I understand what you're saying." Grace nodded. "I look forward to it, even though it's going to take time finding new doctors, a good bakery, nonsmoking restaurants, bookstores. I do want to be a part of the community."

"You're right about the depression," Hannah said. "But I feel plenty better just talking about it. Thought I was the only one worrying."

"Obviously we all were." Grace patted Amelia's arm. "You're asking us to imagine life in Covington and then here helped immensely, Amelia. And I agree about God. It's comforting to think I can turn to Him at any time and He's there for me." In the silence that followed, Grace reached out and squeezed Amelia's hand, then reached for Hannah's. "Why, this commitment we're making to blend our lives, to take care of one another, is somewhat like a marriage, isn't it?"

"With all the adjustments, I'm sure." Hannah drew her shoulders up. "Be that as it may. Time to get out the garden catalogs again. Spring's not that far off."

11

Settling In

*They returned in April to a farmhouse whose white walls and yellow shutters gleamed in the sunshine, attracting the attention of passersby: men and women on their way to work, farmers in pickup trucks hauling fertilizer, or cattle or hay, and school buses brimming with children. All slowed or stopped to survey or marvel at the changes that had transpired at the old Furrior place.

They would have been even more impressed had they seen the inside. Arthur's money had covered all the repairs. The ancient kitchen was no more, its place taken by a shiny hardwood floor, white Formica cabinets, and modern appliances. Heeding the advice of Harold Tate, an attractive blue porcelain wood-burning heater now stood in the kitchen, in case the electricity should go off during a winter storm.

In the living room the dilapidated fireplace had been replaced by self-vented gas logs, and Marie Findley had located, stripped, and refinished an 1850s English pine mantel to surround the new gas fireplace. On either side of it, Tom had built floor to ceiling bookcases. A small powder room had been tucked under the stairs, and with the carpeting and the new living and dining room furniture, the downstairs of the house looked beautiful.

"Home," Grace said under her breath. "Home, at last."

Spring danced in. Purple and white crocuses leaped from the grass about the farmhouse, butter-yellow daffodils rambled along the length of the porch. Behind the stream dazzling purple irises dipped and swayed in the breeze. Each week brought new delights as the fecund earth offered its treasures. Ruddy-cheeked May ushered in red tulips, white blossoms dressed the dogwoods, and a single weeping cherry tree outside the kitchen bowed low beneath its cape of soft pink blooms. Spring rains sent a crystal gush of water spilling over the banks of the stream. Hannah sang the praises of that man or woman who at some time in the past had planted dogwoods in a wide swag at either end of the porch to shade meandering beds of pink and rose and white azaleas. The effect was stunning.

It had taken less than a week after their return to Covington to find an orthopedic surgeon in Asheville, and hip replacement surgery had gone off without complications. Hannah objected to coming home in an ambulance, but had finally acquiesced and adjusted to being temporarily dependent, especially on Grace, who cared for her as one would a child. Somewhat grudgingly, Hannah adapted to the equipment the doctor recommended.

"Options," the doctor said, as he urged her to rent a mechanized chair that would lift and lower her and ease the discomfort of getting up and down. He had insisted she have a walker and a cane.

Now, four weeks after surgery, she was enormously thankful to be well on her way to recovery. On this glorious May day Hannah had been tempted to sit out on the porch, but she would need assistance to get out of a porch chair, and besides, Grace had brought her several new plant nursery catalogs from the mailbox. Hannah settled down in her mechanized chair and lost herself in the Wayside Garden summer catalog, which offered a lush banquet of perennials, annuals, roses, trees. It was not until Grace coughed that Hannah realized she was not alone.

Grace stood in the doorway of the dining room they had turned into a bedroom, an apron over her dress, soup ladle in hand. "Sorry to disturb you. I've made a fresh pot of asparagus soup, want some?"

Hannah set the catalog down and consulted her watch. "Not quite noon, yet. Grace, you're a dear, but no more soup, please. I'm going to float away."

Unwittingly Grace brought the back of her hand to her mouth, and for a moment a hurt look flashed through her eyes. "I'm sorry, Hannah. I get carried away. Soup's what I've always made when anyone's been sick."

"I'm doing fine. Be up and about on my own soon." She closed the catalog. "I've hurt your feelings. I'm sorry. Here —" Hannah pointed to a nearby chair. "I think I'm so tough and self-sufficient. Fact is" — she crossed her hands in her lap — "I get lonely. Come sit with me a minute."

Grace wiped her hands on her apron, raked her fingers through her hair, and sank into the leather wing chair that had been brought down along with the bed from Hannah's room upstairs. "You haven't hurt my feelings." Her lower lip trembled, belying her words. "I've just fallen back into an old pattern from taking care of Ted, cooking and trying to feed him many times a day." Then she stood. "You'll be sending back that chair and using only the cane pretty soon."

"Please don't go." In an unaccustomed gesture of affection, Hannah leaned forward and reached for Grace's hand. "I've been wanting to tell you how much I appreciate everything you've done for me. In the hospital, here, I've been a cranky old biddy."

"You were in pain. It's understandable."

"Please sit with me. Now you know my secret — act like a stoic, but I'm really a coward when it comes to pain."

"Many of us can't handle pain."

"Well, I'm sorry about all my whining." She squeezed Grace's hand, smiled up at her. "I have enjoyed your soups."

Placated, Grace returned to the wing chair, sighed deeply, and folded her hands in her lap. "You know how certain smells remind you of one thing or another, carry you back to childhood sometimes?"

Hannah nodded, though soup smells brought back no particular olfactory pleasure.

"When I was ten my mother, brother,

and I spent two weeks in a rented cottage on a lake in the Poconos one summer. At home my mother only cooked soup when we were sick. But for those two weeks, she cooked one meal a day, a rich thick soup, and we'd carry bowls out to the lawn and eat sitting on the grass near the lake, telling jokes, laughing. It's the happiest memory of my childhood."

"What happened to your brother?"

"Amos? He never married, lived with our mother, took care of her until she died. He died of a heart attack three months after we buried her."

"I'm sorry."

"We weren't close after we grew up and I married Ted. Not much in common."

"How long have I known you, nearly two years?" Hannah asked. "You've become my family." If she had had a sister she could not care for her more than she cared for Grace. But for Hannah such feelings were so unfamiliar that they confused her and she blamed them for the twinges of jealousy she felt whenever Grace and Amelia seemed involved in something together — even simple things like planning meals or making a shopping list. Hannah flushed and looked away. "I'll have soup today, but could I have a ham and cheese sandwich tomorrow?"

"You can have a ham and cheese sandwich today."

A week later, Brenda Tate, the school principal, dropped by with a large jar of pickled cucumbers and a bouquet of early-blooming, sweet-smelling, pink peonies from her garden. Leaning on her walker, Hannah opened the front door.

"I've dipped them in water and given them a good shaking," she said as she handed the lovely blooms to Grace. "Hope I got all the ants off."

"Few ants won't hurt us. Can't blame the ants for enjoying the nectar," Hannah said, waving Brenda in.

"It's good to see you up and about, Mrs. Parrish. My mother had hip replacement surgery, and she can do anything and everything now," Brenda said.

"Call me Hannah. I'm getting there. Therapist comes twice a week. Itching to get down in that yard."

"If you need some help, Hannah, I have a sixteen-year-old son who's looking for a Saturday job." Brenda looked about her. "You ladies have turned this place into a lovely home."

Amelia, camera in hand, appeared in the

doorway. Warming up for her photography classes that would begin in four days, Amelia had been snapping this and that, a passing car, trees, cows, the stream. "We've had fun fixing the old place up," she said. "Would you like a tour?"

"I'd like that, but not now. Tell you the truth I've come on a mission." Brenda turned to Grace. "School's out the end of May, and we're starting a summer session in June for kids who need a bit more help before going into the next grade. Mrs. Janson, our second-grade teacher, has several youngsters who have trouble reading. She'd appreciate it if you could help her with a couple of her kids."

"What would I have to do?"

"Sit with a child, read to him or her, help sound out the words when they read."

Grace hesitated. "Do you think I can?"

"Of course you can, Grace. You're intelligent and kind, have an incredible reading voice, and you care about children," Hannah said.

"Why not give it a try?" Amelia urged.

Things, both scary and exciting, seemed to be coming at Grace from all directions. What she needed was a good long rest with time to stare at the wall. No. Plenty of time to rest when I'm dead, she thought. "When does your teacher want me?"

"Well, truth is, she needs your help now. Tomorrow or Thursday would be wonderful."

"Tomorrow?" Grace's brows furrowed. "What time? I won't leave Hannah until Mrs. Frankle, the therapist, comes."

"Any time you can make it."

"I'll stay home," Amelia said. "I'll be here with Hannah."

"Listen to the two of you, talking as if I'm not here, or as if I'm glass and might shatter." With one hand she shooed at them like so many chickens. "Go. Do what you need to do. I'm a big girl." But inside Hannah was flattered that they considered her welfare.

Grace's smile lit her face. "Then I'll do it."

Two weeks later on a bright and cloudless May day, Hannah planted Chrysler Imperial red roses. That is, she hired Brenda Tate's son, Rick, to plant the roses. As she prepared to supervise the process, a red pickup truck caught her attention. It drove slowly past the house, turned halfway to the little white church, and drove slowly back. The driver pulled to the far side of the road and shut off the engine.

No one got out. Hannah noted a deep dent and long scratches on the passenger side. Finally the motor started, and it drove away. Probably admiring the house, Hannah thought, and gave her full attention to Rick.

"I want a nice big hole," she said. There was only a twinge left when she walked, and Hannah had replaced the walker with the cane. She had called the rental people to come for their chair and soon she would donate her other paraphernalia of illness, the cane and the walker, to Goodwill.

The stocky, sandy-haired, sixteen-year-old slammed his foot down on the edge of the shovel, and the dirt flew.

"Easy, now," Hannah said, stepping back.

Rick grinned and began to work with less gusto.

"No. Not deep enough. Here's a ruler, measure it. Go down another six inches and at least six inches wider." God, she longed to get down on her knees and plunge her hands in the soil. Just holding soil she could diagnose its quality, if it needed more sand for drainage or peat for retaining water. Harold had tested the rose bed for acidity and alkalinity for her yesterday and assured her that the soil was a neutral six.

"Soil's pretty darn acid this part of the country," he said, handing her back her test meter. "This here ground's been worked, and it's gonna be just fine for roses."

Hannah stood over Rick, shaking her head as he worked. When he had widened and deepened the hole, she took a handful of fertilizer pellets and dribbled them into it. "Okay, now water it."

"Water a hole, ma'am?" Rick stared at her as if she were crazy.

One of these days, she thought, I'm going to write out simple instructions for anyone planting a bush for the first time. "Don't you ever help your dad? Fertilizer needs water to break it down so that it's usable to the plant's roots."

"I help with the animals. I don't much like farmin'," he said, and turned on the hose with such force that mud splattered his face and arms and splotched Hannah's shoes and legs.

Hannah started back gasping. Her first instinct was to snatch the hose and turn it full force on Rick.

"Sorry."

"Are you rushing to go somewhere?" she asked somewhat testily.

"No, ma'am. Mom said to do whatever you said and be quick about it."

"I could do with a little less quick. Now, come over here and let me explain how to plant a rosebush." He followed her to the steps and she sat. Hannah selected one of the bare-root rosebushes that had just arrived in the mail, and holding it sideways pointed out to Rick the thickened area about four inches above the roots. "Roses are pretty ancient," she told the boy. "Fossils have been found that are at least thirty-two million years old. There are about one hundred to two hundred species."

Rick yawned, his eyes glazed.

"This knot," she continued, placing her finger on the bulging part of the stem, "must be above the ground. These are hybrid tea roses, you see, and they've been grafted on hearty root stock. The knot here's where the graft was made. If we bury the knot, the bush'll revert to the original root stock, so we have to be very careful how we plant."

Rick stared at her with a bored look and nodded.

Hannah felt both annoyed and sorry for the boy. People who garden can always turn to the earth for solace, as she had so many times in her life. She thought about her own grandsons and how alienated she was from them and how she had failed as a grandmother to teach them about the earth and gardening. There was so much regarding her daughters and grandsons she would do differently given the chance.

"This okay?" Rick asked once he had set the roots in the hole and filled them with soil.

Hannah nodded. After much pacing, muttering, measuring, setting, and resetting the plants, fourteen fragrant Chrysler Imperial red roses in four-feet wide, well-mulched beds lined each side of the driveway from the porch to the main road. "Fragrance alone's well worth the work, sonny," she said to Rick as she paid him. "Can I count on you to help me again?"

He hung his head. "I'm hopin' to get a job at Burger King over at Weaverville after school."

"Isn't that far?"

"Only about twenty minutes. I gotta car."

"Well fine, then. Thanks for today." And he was off.

The next afternoon Grace and Hannah planted the new planter boxes that Tom

229

Findley had made, painted white, and attached to the porch railing. Grace brought a straight-back chair from the foyer and set it near the railing so Hannah could sit if she grew tired of standing. Then she ran down the steps of the porch to Hannah's wagon, returning with both arms loaded with flats of deep pink petunias and dwarf white daisies. Hannah sat, took a flat of petunias onto her lap, and Grace set the daisies on the floor at Hannah's feet. Suddenly there it was again, the red pickup crawling past their house, then turning and crawling back, this time not stopping.

"Who do you think that is?" Grace asked.

"Don't know. Yesterday, when Rick was planting the roses, I saw it for the first time, doing the same thing, and it stopped too but no one got out."

Grace waved a shiny new green-handled shovel at Hannah. "Probably house shopping. Look, Hannah, I prepared the dirt just like you said, equal parts potting soil, sand, peat moss, and Nature's Helper." Her eyes grew pensive. She sank to the top step.

"What's the matter, Grace. Are you all right?"

"Roger called. We have an offer for the

house in Dentry."

"How do you feel about it?"

"Strangely detached, even from Roger. You know, Hannah, he's a different person when I talk to him on the phone. I don't sense that uptightness, that anger in him anymore." She looked up at Hannah and smiled. "I'm ready to let it go. I'm excited about having cash and opening a mutual fund." She laid down the shovel. "You know, I used to think I'd never feel at home anywhere again and now look at me here." She threw wide her arms and her eyes shone. "Covington of all places, living in this wonderful old farmhouse, and it really feels like home." Grace rose then and planted a tiny plant with soil dripping from its roots.

Hannah stopped punching out petunias and thought about the red pickup. For a moment she felt a sense of uneasiness, then pushed the feeling away and tapped the edge of the chair with her fingernails. "Home. So many years I've perched, not nested, in this or that room, a half furnished apartment or rented houses, and finally that little place I sold to buy the nursery." She tilted her chin in the air. "I'm glad to be here, too." She handed Grace another plant and looked pleased

231

when Grace shoveled a hole, set the plant into it, then pressed the earth firmly about its roots. "You're a natural gardener, Grace."

From the parlor came the sound of Gregorian chants. Amelia loved their modal harmonies: their slow, elegant cadence and the satiny, rounded melodies never failed to lift her spirits and calm her. "It's going to be beautiful when you're done," Amelia said as she let the front door swing shut behind her and joined them on the porch. Her hair was pulled snugly into a bun at the nape of her neck, and Grace noted the delicate line of her cheeks and chin. At twenty she must have been so beautiful, Grace thought. Hannah's resolute, Amelia's charming and lovely, and I, what am I? Dependable? We do make a good team, she reflected, feeling tranquil. Moving a rocker closer to Hannah, she nodded for Amelia to join them.

Hannah with plants was akin to a child with candy, messy and delighted. With a broad smile she turned to Amelia. "This land, the house, the trees, they really satisfy my soul. Thank you, Amelia." Then she turned back to nudging rooted plants from their container and handing them to Grace.

Moving along the porch, Grace planted flower boxes, then stood nearby, leaning against the railing. "I lie in bed at night listening to the stream and loving the sound. I'm grateful for the turn my life's taken," Grace said.

Amelia held up her hands. "Now stop this, both of you. Without you two, I'd have had to sell this place." But they had touched a chord in her, and Amelia loosened the scarf about her neck, hooked a finger over one edge, and stared into space. "Sometimes I dream of my home in Silver Lake: just snatches of a wall, a color, a fireplace, a painting, just bits and pieces."

Grace dug a bit of soil from under her fingernail. She wondered whether Amelia had ever put the house in all their names. Amelia had never mentioned it since that day by the stream. Impossible to broach so sensitive a topic. If Amelia had, it would assure her that she and Hannah would have a home, no matter what.

"I'm going down on the lawn to see how our planters look," Grace said and hurried down the steps to stand below, hands on her hips, looking up. "I think it needs another daisy, there." She pointed, and Hannah stood. Holding the rail with one hand, she walked over to the end planter box and added the daisy.

"Good. That does it. Looks great. And you'll be walking good as new soon."

Amelia looked at Hannah. Yes, she'd be taking long loping gaits, as Amelia imagined Hannah's normal gait to be. For a moment Amelia wished she liked gardening, but she didn't. She hated getting her hands, her fingernails, dirty. That reminded her of her mother, who had gardened in planters just like these, and how she had nagged Amelia to help her, but Amelia would run away to the garage where she was sure to find her father woodworking. He would smile at her, give her a piece of wood to sand. She sighed. She should have been kinder to her mother. Well, it was too late for that.

There was an unspoken oneness among the women now that allowed for streams of consciousness and for shifting subjects without any of them feeling interrupted or discounted by the other. Moments later Amelia was telling them about her childhood. "My parents' home stood on a bluff overlooking the Atlantic, huge, with a wraparound porch, much too big for one little girl to ramble about on. I was lonely. My mother and her social activist ladies held their meetings on the porch. They brought me candy." Amelia laughed lightly. "I haven't thought about this in years." Sliding her hands up and down her arms, she swatted tiny gnats that seemed to relish her sensitive, fair skin while ignoring the other women.

The flat of plants she had held on her lap left a dark water-made stain on Hannah's slacks. She brushed at it. "You know, when a house is being built, some builders tie a tree to the top after the roof goes on."

"I read somewhere that in ancient times people buried a skull in the corner of a new village site for good luck," Grace said, coming to sit on the top step.

"Miranda buried crystals at the four corners of her house in Branston. Maybe we should have a ceremony of some kind for this house," Hannah said.

"We could bury a time capsule." Grace had given up the slacks, purchased for their early trip down, for her shirtwaist dresses, and now she stood and brushed sprinkles of dirt from her skirt. "We could each choose special things that represent us and bury them in a metal box."

Amelia gave her rocker a kick back. "Years from now a treasure hunter or an archaeologist might find it, and it would tell him something about us. Let's do it. Let's have a ceremony. Tell the land, this house, that we're grateful to be here."

"Great idea," Hannah agreed.

12

Tyler

Like students who choose the same seats in a classroom, or people whose instinct it is to sit in the same chairs at the dining room table, the ladies quickly established a placement on the front porch for their rocking chairs, with Grace in the middle flanked by Hannah to the right and Amelia to her left. It delighted them to sit there, warm and dry, breathing the moist air while the warm spring rain nourished the earth and dripped from the leaves of the great oak. It was for them a sensory delight to live part of their lives out-of-doors, whether listening to the patter of rain on the tin roof, or on fine sunny days swapping stories, drinking tea, and nibbling on Grace's sugar cookies while waving to passing cars and pickups on Cove Road.

Grace cooked and baked and kept a pink cookie jar full, which meant baking every third day, especially for Mike, Amelia's photography instructor. Mike had become a friend to Amelia and was a frequent visitor and a devotee of Grace's cookies.

Amelia antiqued with Mike. He drove her to town, pointed out the best shops, and introduced her to their proprietors. As a result, the bookshelves in the living room now shared space with a growing collection of porcelain pieces: a Meissen sauceboat, a Wedgwood vase with mythological figures in white on a deep blue background, and a tall green and yellow and white Tiffany goblet.

Hannah mothered the land, all twenty-eight acres, and every growing thing upon its soil. Although their days took them in different directions, every afternoon they sat on the porch to reminisce, to drink tea, to share their day's activities, and often merely to savor the strikingly beautiful sunsets.

Hannah took her tea in a mug, half-and-half, with cream, and three spoons of sugar, while the others enjoyed the delicate, translucent china cups Amelia had found in yet another antique shop in Asheville.

Grace told them about Tyler. "I read to a little boy at the school today. His name's Tyler, Tyler Richardson, a little redheaded fellow with big ears, dark coffee-bean eyes, freckles, and the sniffles. I gave him my bandanna for his sniffles."

"Let's hope you don't get the flu or something," Hannah said. "Little kids are always getting sick."

"We both washed our hands several times."

Amelia hardly heard Grace. She had no interest in children anymore, did not want them around her since she had lost Caroline.

Grace's brow furrowed as she continued. "He wouldn't read or say any of his letters. I tried with *A, B, C,* and then I read to him. His mother's dead, killed by a drunk driver five months ago."

"Oh, how awful." Amelia's eyes filled with tears. When she finally spoke, her voice was first aggrieved, then angry. "So sad, so many people losing their children. When I was young, I don't remember ever hearing about any of my parents' friends losing their children. But nowadays . . ." Her chin quivered, and struggling for control Amelia pressed a cupped hand against her chin.

Grace and Hannah were touched by Amelia's response. She had appeared so detached, indifferent, a moment ago. They were silent a long while, and it seemed that their silence found its counterpart in the increasing gray, low-lying clouds that seemed to hover above them listening.

Grace nodded agreement. "It's very sad. His mother's death has devastated Tyler. Mrs. Janson, Tyler's teacher, says he's very smart, but he's become withdrawn. She can't place him in third grade in the fall unless he can demonstrate that he knows the work. The last few weeks, especially, he's just scribbled on his paper, won't let anyone see what he's scribbled, and scratches it out with a black crayon. She's sent him to the school counselor, but he just sits there, won't open his mouth. She thinks that if Tyler has individual attention, one person he sees often and comes to trust, he might open up."

"Try getting him to draw." Memory carried Amelia back to a time long before Caroline. "Once in Italy, after a horrendous earthquake, I helped a therapist do art therapy with children whose parents had been killed. Drawing helped them face their fears, cope better."

"How do you do that?"

Why had she opened her mouth? Amelia wanted to get up and walk away, but Thomas would have wanted her to share what she remembered with Grace. "Give

240

him paper and crayons and ask him to draw something for you."

"And that helps?"

"I guess it does." She shrugged. "One child drew a head sticking out from under a pile of rocks, and another drew himself with tears almost as big as he was. The therapist said it was very healing for them." Amelia rocked slowly now, lost in memories.

"You've had such an interesting life, Amelia," Grace said. "Helping people must have been very satisfying. I feel like I've led a real stick-in-the-mud life."

"I did what Thomas said to do. I wouldn't have chosen a career in that kind of work, but yes, at the time it was generally satisfying. The Red Cross does make a difference in the world, you know."

"The Red Cross is an organization. It's people, you and other people, that make the difference," Hannah said almost fiercely. She blew into her mug, then sipped her tea.

"Thomas thought I was good with the children, but I never saw myself as very effective." Amelia sighed and fingered the silk scarf about her neck. Why were they going on and on talking about children, the past? It only triggered increasing sadness that threatened to divest her heart of peace. Her life had been very good lately. Was that why this had come up, to punish her for forgetting, even temporarily, Thomas and Caroline?

"Well, I'm sure Thomas was right," Grace said, her mind already back with Tyler. "Thanks, Amelia, for telling me about art therapy. I'll go into Mars Hill early tomorrow and get crayons, a big box with all the new colors, and paper." Grace leaned over and rested her hand on Amelia's arm. "You know so much more than I do. Why not come to the school with me? You'd be wonderful with the children."

Amelia stiffened. "There's a time for everything." She made no effort to disguise the edge in her voice, or the fact that tears were gathering just below her eyelids. "I've done that kind of work."

Raindrops slanted by a rush of wind splattered the porch, nearly reaching their feet. Hannah rose and pushed her chair back close to the wall of the house, and the others followed suit. The rain battered the tin roof of the porch and curtained their view of the road, and when Hannah looked at Amelia she saw a face pale and sad, a mouth drawn taut, and Hannah considered it best to introduce a lighter, happier subject. "How's your photography class going, Amelia?"

Giving the rocker a shove that sent it back against the house, Amelia snatched at the change of topic. She turned to Hannah. "Oh, harder than I imagined. Sometimes I wonder what I'm doing there. I'm the oldest student, and Mike insists we use manual cameras. All that stuff about f-stops and depth of field drives me crazy, and Mike keeps talking about the craft of photography."

"Craft first, art later," Hannah said. "It'll come to you, just hang in there." She took another sip of her tea, hesitating for a minute. She had wanted for some time now to ask Amelia about Caroline, and now she wondered whether it would be good or bad for Amelia to talk about her daughter. She realized it would be painful, but like children drawing their feelings it would probably help Amelia to talk about her child. Hannah decided now was as good a time as ever.

"I've thought a great deal about your family, your daughter, about the things you shared with us that day under the oak. I've been wanting to know more about your Caroline. What was she like? What was it like having a child so late in life?"

Suppressing her initial reaction to get up and run inside, Amelia sat quietly and stared at the sheets of water pouring from the porch roof. She had lived an unspoken vow of silence regarding her family, but why now? These were her friends, the best she had ever had; she lived with them, trusted them. Amelia's breath settled back into a steady rhythm and she smiled, glancing at Hannah.

"Caroline." The name was barely audible above the sound of rain.

The others leaned toward Amelia.

"I always wanted a little girl. I always knew if I were so blessed I'd name her Caroline." Amelia rose and, mindless of the rain, stood at the railing of the porch and lifted the face of a daisy blossom between two fingers. Even on this gray afternoon, the magic of springtime was everywhere: in the bright green lawn, the budding roses, these sturdy little flowers. "She was bright, like this daisy," Amelia said softly, wiping her arms with her hands as she turned and walked back to sink again into the rocking chair.

"I was embarrassed at first, being so old, and I tried to hide my pregnancy." Her brows drew closer together as she frowned.

"I worried people would ridicule me, but everyone seemed genuinely excited. We'd been in Japan and we returned to the States, to San Francisco, for the birth. It was a long labor. Twenty-nine hours. When they lay that tiny bundle at my breast," Amelia's face glowed, "I never knew such pleasure, such joy." Hugging her shoulders, Amelia remained silent for a time. The other women waited.

Then Amelia drew a deep breath. "After Caroline was born, our lives changed. We took a flat in London and I didn't travel with Thomas all the time, only on longer assignments and to cities where we could have a nice home and household help, like New Delhi in India or Kyoto in Japan. All his working life Thomas had been dedicated to the welfare of others. Now Caroline took first priority in both our lives." Suddenly Amelia looked from one to the other, her eyes wide and curious as if she was speculating for the first time on what she was about to say. "It's odd; Thomas and I stopped sleeping together. Not out of hostility," she hastened to assure them. "It started when Caroline had the mumps, and I moved into her room. He said he slept so much better alone in our bed. I slept better when he was gone also, so I just moved into another bedroom. It was all right, really. We were totally devoted to one another and to our child."

"What was Caroline like?" Grace asked. It embarrassed her to hear about Amelia's and Thomas's sleeping arrangements, which sent her mind dashing down corridors of sexual questions she would never ask.

"Ah, *mon petit chou*," she explained, smiling at them. "It's a term of endearment, my little cabbage. Caroline was beautiful: green eyes, curly blond hair like mine was when I was little. Very intelligent. Precocious. Spoke before she was sixteen months. Walked at eight months. Asked amazing questions for her age." She raised her hands by way of exclamation. "At seven she wanted to know what animals lived in Australia, and then we had to make a scrapbook with their pictures in it and something about their lives. She wanted to know about God and Jesus and about Shiva and the Buddha and how they were different, and if they weren't, then why were there so many names and different faces for the same person. She kept us hopping looking things up, explaining." Now Amelia's eyes grew angry and her rocking ceased. "Why would any

246

God take a child so bright, with so much potential and so young?"

"I don't believe God takes anyone," Grace said. "Life's arbitrary. Things happen."

"Or from the point of view of reincarnation, everyone chooses their body and family before birth," Hannah said. "They know what's going to happen, only at birth they forget. What are those lines from Wordsworth's poem *Ode: Intimations of Immortality*?" She turned to Grace.

" 'Our birth is but a sleep and a forgetting'?"

"Yes. That's it."

"That's mumbo jumbo to me, reincarnation. I care that Caroline's gone, Thomas is gone, and I'm alone." Amelia's voice exploded. "Sometimes I wish I were dead and with them." Amelia's fists came down hard on the arms of her chair, then her whole body seemed to crumble, and she lowered her face into her hands and keened a long low lamentation. "I cannot even sustain the one transcendent moment I had in that church, the only such moment I've had in my whole life." Her shoulders shook and she sobbed uncontrollably.

Grace was at her side in a moment. "I

247

know, I know. It's all right to cry," she said again and again until gradually the sobbing slowed and the rocker began to move slowly back and forth. Grace stepped away, and in time Amelia lifted her head.

"I apologize for my outburst. I hate to lose control like that. I'm ashamed to slip back to the far end where I understand nothing, feel as if I'm going to tumble headfirst over a precipice." As she dried her eyes on her scarf a wry smile crossed her lips. "Crying is good. I should be embarrassed, but I'm not. Would you like to see a picture of Caroline?" She hesitated then, remembering that she had stored away all mementos of her life and wondering if she was prepared to confront them.

"We'd love to, when you're ready, Amelia," Grace said softly.

"Maybe soon," Amelia replied. "Look," she said, pointing to the road. "This is making me crazy. Who's in that red pickup, what do they want? I've felt safe here, maybe we should install an alarm system."

Caster Elementary School, a small, two-story building made of weathered red brick, sat two blocks back from the main street of Caster and a block from the roiling river that sometimes flooded the town. Several years ago the school had been abandoned and the children bused to other schools. But the parents, upset at the long hours their children spent on the bus, raised a ruckus and volunteered their labor to renovate the school. A year ago it reopened.

Grace found the interior bright, cheerful, and completely charming. Outside the first- and second-grade classrooms the concrete block walls were painted in a rainbow of primary colors, and two pigs led two mice and two frogs and other animals dancing along the ribbons of color.

Uncertain about trying art therapy with Tyler, Grace set her deep canvas bag down on the pint-size desk that Mrs. Janson had placed in the hallway outside her classroom. The hum of children murmuring and Mrs. Janson's warm, rich voice drifted from classroom *A*. Grace poked her head inside.

"Here's Mrs. Grace. Say, Good morning, Mrs. Grace."

The "Good mornin', Mrs. Grace," had a singsong quality, welcome like a warm wind on a chilly day.

"Do come in." Mrs. Janson waved Grace inside. "Timmy was just reading to us.

Please continue, Timmy."

"The cat ran by the t-t-" Timmy hesitated.

A dark-haired elf of a girl in the middle row of desks squirmed in her chair and waved her hand wildly. "I know, Mrs. Janson."

"Let's give Timmy time to sound the word out. Go ahead, Timmy." Mrs. Janson walked slowly to Timmy's chair and knelt alongside it so that their eyes met. She touched his shoulder lightly. "T-ay-ble. You try, Timmy."

"T-ay-ble. Table." Timmy grinned at her.

"See you did it. When you feel like you can't do something, just take a minute, take a breath like I showed you all, and try again."

"I knew it was that all the time," the dark-haired girl said.

"I know you did, Cynthia, but when you get stuck on a word, you like for us to give you time, don't you?"

"Yes, ma'am," Cynthia said, never taking her eyes from Mrs. Janson's face. Her teacher smiled at her. The respect and caring between students and teacher was obvious, and Grace was happy to be here.

"Tyler, get your paper and pencil and

your book. You may go with Mrs. Grace into the hall."

Tyler sat in the back of the room shuffling his feet. Grudgingly, he picked up his book, a sheet of paper, and a pencil and headed for the door.

"I wanna read with Mrs. Grace," another boy said.

"Mrs. Grace looks like Mrs. Santa Claus," someone said, and several children giggled.

"All right. Sandi, Ellis, Robert, back to work."

Grace settled her solid frame on the small chair across from Tyler at the low table that had been placed in the hall for their use, and wondered if the chair would hold her weight. She could see herself sprawled on the shiny vinyl floor, and the children streaming from their classrooms giggling at her. *Humpty Dumpty had a great fall.* The old nursery rhyme came to mind.

A cowlick of red hair stuck straight up on top of Tyler's head. He pulled her bandanna from his pocket and offered it to her.

"You can keep that, Tyler. It's a present. It comes in mighty handy sometimes."

"I wiped my dog Fluffy's paws with it." His eyes held a challenge.

"I'm glad it was useful to you." Grace tugged at the bandanna tucked into her waist. "I have another one, see. When I cut up onions in the kitchen I use it to wipe my eyes 'cause the onions make me cry."

Tyler looked down and fidgeted with his pencil.

How stupid of her to mention crying. Reaching into the canvas bag, Grace pulled out sheets of colored paper and a fat box of Crayola crayons and set them on the table. Spreading the sheets of paper — green, yellow, white, brown, blue, pink, tan — she shook out the crayons. "What's your favorite color?"

A thump from Tyler's feet under the desk let her know how he felt.

Grace hesitated. It sounded so simple, the art therapy concept, and she had anticipated his cooperation. Instead it was clear he didn't want to do this. Foolish of her to try to do art therapy when she had no training. She should just focus on his reading. Yet, even as she considered this, Grace pulled a pale, pink sheet of paper toward herself, reached for a bright purple crayon, and drew three stick figures with bosoms and skirts and big floppy shoes and hats. Over their heads, Grace drew circles like you see in comic books and wrote,

Mrs. Grace in red, Mrs. Hannah in blue, and Mrs. Amelia in yellow. She studied the picture and then held it up toward Tyler.

"They need grass to stand on," he said, and she scratched squiggles of green spikes all along the bottom around their shoes.

"This is me," Grace pointed to the fullest stick figure, "and these are my friends, Mrs. Hannah and Mrs. Amelia."

Tyler slipped a thin finger, with dirt embedded under its nail, across the page and touched it lightly to the *A* in Amelia's name. "*A*. Like in my momma's name."

"You're absolutely correct. An 'A.' What was your momma's name?"

He shrugged, then said, "You draw funny."

"I do draw funny." Grace laughed. Tyler glanced at her shyly, gave her a crooked little smile, and a fleeting look of understanding passed between them before Tyler lowered his eyes.

"Will you draw something?"

He shook his head. Stared into space.

"Sometime, when you feel like it, maybe you'll draw me a picture."

They spent the rest of their time going over words, *child, mitten, laugh,* and Grace read aloud the entire story from his school-book, but he seemed bored and was inattentive.

This went on for another two weeks. Then for a week Tyler was sick.

Tyler returned, but Grace felt she was making little progress with him and often, while making her bed, or walking by the stream, or picking lettuce from the kitchen garden Hannah had planted, she thought about Tyler, silent and withdrawn, and her heart ached for him.

Mrs. Janson had filled her in. "Tyler's an only child. Lives with his dad and now his grandfather's come from Florida to live with them. Tyler's smart, but he's taking it hard. Your time with him's important, even if he acts like it isn't. I'd hate to see him held back."

"What can I do for Tyler?"

She smiled. "Be a friend. You don't know how much I value your coming in, Mrs. Singleton." A flurry of activity from the other side of the room drew her attention, and with a smile and a raised eyebrow, Mrs. Janson hastened to separate two boys who were arguing about a car one had brought to class.

Grace could not get Tyler out of her mind. His sad dark eyes haunted her. She dreamed of him running, playing, then turning those eyes, so full of pain, to her. Even as she knelt in the kitchen garden, gathering their dinner salad, she worried about Tyler, wondered how she could help him. Hannah's voice interrupted her.

"Grace, you're pulling that lettuce out by the roots." Hannah stood on the steps. Her hands gripped the railings. She gave Grace first a look of mild annoyance, and then, relenting, a look of pity.

"Goodness. Where's my mind? I came out to pick lettuce and radishes for a salad."

Now Hannah walked gingerly down the steps, gripping the railing with one hand. She had given the walker to Goodwill and hardly used the cane. Steps were still a bit difficult. "You're stewing about that little boy, aren't you? Takes time to walk again, but old or young, in time and with good friends or family, one heals. Little Tyler's got a caring father and grandfather and now he's got you. He'll make it."

13

What's It All for Anyway?

Amelia could not take her eyes from the family photograph. Finally she had unpacked the memorabilia box stored in this or that attic for over four years and the mustiness of it had brought on a coughing fit. For a moment, as she studied the photograph, she took pleasure in her daughter's sunny smile. Hand on hip, her head coyly tilted, dressed in a delicate handcrafted lilac organdy with a white lace collar, the child exhibited a poise one would hardly expect from an eight-year-old. "You would have been a beauty," Amelia whispered, bringing the frame to her lips.

Amelia studied the wide brimmed hat with the cluster of cherries that she wore in the picture. Bought in an antique clothing shop somewhere in London, it had been a gift from Thomas. She had loved it, worn it often. Sentiment dictated that she save the hat, and she had moved it again and again, stored it in every closet, in every room she had lived in since his death.

Though it was beautifully furnished in warm colonial maple and decorated with lace-edged pillows and bedspread, just a couple of weeks ago Amelia had noted how her room had begun to feel somehow unfinished, and as she lay in bed at night struggling to recapture Caroline's and Thomas's faces, Amelia knew she must find the picture. It took several days rummaging in the attic before she identified the box. Stricken by memories of the past, she had been unable to open it at once and shoved it under her bed until a week ago when she retrieved this photograph. How right the treasured picture looked sitting on her night table. How could she have lived without it for so long?

Her gaze lingered on Thomas, smiling and dashingly young for his age and smart in English tweeds. He had been so proud of them, his "special ladies." Drawn back now to the feeling of safety and happiness she had experienced as the photographer positioned them close together, Amelia closed her eyes and allowed herself to remember. Afterward, Thomas had treated them to ice cream, and they had strolled through a bazaar in Calcutta, buying trinkets, content and safe. Then her eyes jerked open. "Safe?" The word tore from deep in her throat with almost a snarl. Money, position, connections, location, nothing guarantees safety in this world. Nothing. She had certainly learned that the hard way.

"Time heals," people counsel.

On the surface perhaps, but would she ever really heal? Would she ever feel safe in the world again? "Terrible things happen to people all the time," she muttered. "Terrible things that make me so mad and so miserable that sometimes I think I could destroy myself just thinking about them." Destroy herself. That had been her first reaction to Caroline's death, but there had been Thomas. After his death, what had stopped her?

Amelia fingered the silver frame of the picture, then set it back on the table. What had stopped her? Her own upbringing had taught that suicide was a sin punished by eternal damnation. Eastern religions, to which she had been exposed for years, maintained that suicide was useless, for you would have to come back and repeat the suffering or the learning, as they called it, until you mastered it.

Amelia shook her head, shook the thoughts from her mind, rose, walked to her closet, and lifted down the hatbox. Holding it stiffly before her, the way a butler might hold a tray of canapés, she carried it to the bed and lowered it onto the coverlet. Tentatively she removed the lid, separated the sheets of white tissue paper, and lifted the hat from its box. At the mirror, Amelia positioned it on her head. It was huge, the white yellowed, the brim wider and floppier than she remembered. The cluster of cherries on the side looked silly. Her hair, light brown and soft to the touch when last she wore it, was now white, the texture coarser. Her eyes, however, were as wide and deep and as Montana sky blue as they had ever been. Everything changed. Nothing changed.

Tossing back her head, Amelia laughed, swayed and broke into movement. She began to dance, slowly at first, then faster and faster around and around the room, partnering with the hat until a loud knocking on her door brought her to a halt and silenced her laughter.

"Amelia, are you all right?" Hannah asked.

"Heaven, yes." Opening the door, she waved Hannah and Grace in. "Meet my

259

glorious hat. Hat, say hello to my dearest friends." She dipped the brim toward them.

Grace had wondered about that hat from the time she first saw it last summer. Seeing it again sent a slight shiver of guilt through her.

Amelia's exaltation had been intense, more than she could bear, and in the next instant she was sobbing. Grace moved to hold, to comfort her. Hannah noticed the framed photograph lying on the bed, and taking Grace's arm, ushered her from the room. "Amelia needs to cry. Needs to deal with her grief. Give her time to compose herself," she said.

Later, after returning the hat in its box to the shelf, Amelia walked calmly down the stairs and made her announcement. "Ladies, tomorrow I shall do my still life assignment. I will photograph my hat."

The hat with its gauzy ties and cluster of cherries teetered from a hook Amelia had screwed to the wall alongside the front door. Then she pulled over a chair, studied her composition, and fixed it in the lens of her Pentax K-1000 camera.

"It's going to look flat in that shade," Hannah said as she walked down the front steps. "Broken stem on that rosebush, there." She waved her clippers at Amelia.

Amelia jerked around. "How do you know that?"

"I can see it's bent over."

"Not the rosebush. About the picture coming out flat."

"Took a class once. Wasn't very good, but one thing I remember. No sunlight, no shadows equals flat-looking pictures."

"What does that mean, flat-looking pictures?"

"Dull, lifeless. Little or no differentiation of light or shadow."

She waved a dismissive hand. "Our assignment is inanimate objects."

"Nothing wrong with the hat, just move it into the light." Hannah snipped off the torn stem, stepped back, and nodded in satisfaction.

"I thought it would stand out against the teal door." Amelia jerked the hat off the wall and laid it on the top step. "There. It's in the sun now and not nearly as interesting."

"And it's noon. Too much glare. Makes your shot look washed out."

Hannah knew about plants and the environment, and about plumbing valves and fuses, and now about photography, and that really annoyed Amelia. "If you know so much about it, you take the pictures." Grabbing the hat, Amelia stormed into the house, and Hannah realized just how large a *faux pas* she had committed. It required immediate fixing.

Hannah found Amelia in her room. The hat lay on the floor, next to the bed, and Amelia sat in a small upholstered chair nursing her wounded pride. Mike had talked about not shooting between noon and two o'clock, but she had been too busy fiddling with the camera to pay attention. Annoying as it was, she had to admit that Hannah was right.

"For your best shots take them early in the morning or in the last few hours of the afternoon." Mike had said that in class and she had chosen to ignore it.

"My big mouth again," Hannah began, but Amelia interrupted her.

"What's it all for anyway? I'm no good at this. I'm not going back. I'll sell my camera."

"Don't do that."

"Why not? I'll never get it."

"You will get it. I've looked at some of your pictures. Clearly you have an eye for composition. Technical jargon is just that at first, jargon, and then suddenly one day it'll be clear as a bell."

"Why'd you stop taking pictures?"

"Took it up hoping to supplement my income. Could memorize technical details all right, f-stops, lighting, but my shots included extraneous items, branches, light poles, a passing dog's tail. Started gardening. I could do that. Don't give it up, Amelia. Could be one of the most satisfying things you've ever done."

Later with the sun at an angle, casting long shafts of light against the house, Amelia took the hat, walked to the south side of the house, and tacked it to the wall. She strolled about it, considering it from every angle. Then metering the light carefully, Amelia focused on a horizontal triad, white hat framed by yellow shutters. Satisfied, she snapped several shots, then moved to the front of the house where the western sun now bathed the porch in pale golden light.

From her room she brought a white cotton nightgown on a white satin-wrapped hanger and hung it on the hook against the wall. Moving the camera to exclude the teal door, she focused on the white-on-white composition. Then Amelia secured the hat to the wall above it and arranged the cherries into a pattern, more sprawling than clustered. There, she thought, that added touch of red cherries really sets the whole picture off. Amelia finished the roll of film and removed it from the camera just as Grace came out on the porch, purse in hand.

"Going to Mars Hill?"

"No, to Asheville. My weekly trip to Malaprop's Bookstore/Café and the library."

"I'll go with you. I need to drop off this film at Iris Photography. They do a great job developing and printing."

From the front yard garden Hannah watched them leave chatting and laughing and felt again that twinge of jealousy she hated. "Dammit," she muttered, forcing her eyes away from the two women in the world who she felt were truly her friends. She scratched her cheek where something had just bitten her. I wonder if either of them feel the way I do when they're not part of what's going on at that moment? I bet they do. Absentmindedly, she dabbed at the spot on her cheek where she had drawn a bit of blood. Two may be company, but we three will just have to rise above that old cliché, starting with me, here and now. With that, she reached for a stem on a top-heavy hydrangea bush and snapped hard with her clippers.

14

The Meeting of Bob and Grace

Grace had come to love the sad, somber, dark-eyed Tyler Richardson. His melancholy eyes haunted her, and she longed to hold and soothe him. But rules were rules, and she had been instructed not to touch the children. The special summer session was underway, and on Mondays and Thursdays Grace met with Tyler for an hour in the library of Caster Elementary.

It seemed to Grace she was getting nowhere with the child, yet she continued to tote crayons and paper in her deep canvas bag, and after a time spent going over the alphabet, sounding out words and dealing with his indifference, Grace would lay out her art supplies, including a portfolio of her own stick drawings: the farmhouse, bright yellow with globs of red and purple flowers, lollipop trees hung with red balls for apples, the stream, set in wide squiggly green lines with brown willowy trees drooping over it. Her drawing of orange carrots dancing on the clothesline brought a smile from Tyler and gave Grace hope.

One day, Grace found a children's book about angels in a bookstore she frequented in Asheville. She read it to Tyler.

"High in the clouds there lived a little angel. His name was Freddy. Freddy spent a great deal of time looking out at a great big blue and silver planet in the sky named Earth. In angel school he learned that those who lived on Earth are called people. He learned that many people on Earth needed help from angels. Freddy was unhappy because all his friends had been sent to help people on Earth, while he was told, 'Freddy, you're too young. You'll have to wait a bit longer.'

"One sunny day as Freddy sat watching the Earth spin around the sun, he heard his name. 'Freddy.' The chief angel called Freddy to his side. 'Freddy,' he said, 'we have a job for you.'

"Freddy was very excited.

" 'There's a little boy on Earth who needs a friend. It's going to be your job to help him.' "

266

The story paralleled Tyler's life. The child the little angel had been assigned to help was a boy named Kirk, who had lost, not a mother, but beloved grandparents. Kirk had shut out his parents, his friends, the world, for he believed that his grandparents had died because he had not seen the big wave at the beach that washed them out to sea. Kirk was certain they would still be alive if he had been watching, if he had warned them. Grace read on.

"Freddy ran to the edge of the cloud, but the chief angel grabbed him, and just in time. He removed Freddy's wings from his shoulders. 'You won't wear these on Earth. Let me explain your job. You are to help Kirk understand that he is not responsible for his grandparents' death. But there are things you need to know about Earth. Now, Freddy. Come, sit here.' He pointed to a lumpy gray cloud nearby. Freddy sat on the gray cloud while the chief angel explained.

" 'Earth is a school. People go to Earth to learn lessons. When they learn their lessons, they return to heaven.'

" 'They die, you mean?' Freddy asked.

" 'Yes, they die. A very wise Earth-man

once wrote: "There is a time for everything. There is a time to be born, a time to die. A time for all things." Your job is to teach Kirk this lesson. You must help him to see that his grandparents died because they had finished their Earth jobs, and it was time for them to do what Earth people call 'die.' They are angel spirits now, and they love him. They will watch over him all of his life. You must teach Kirk that by sitting quietly, shutting his eyes, and thinking about them, he can feel them close.'

"Freddy was excited about going to Earth. 'I can teach Kirk?'

" 'Yes. He needs to know how much his grandparents loved him, and how close they still are to him.'

"Freddy knew that this was a very important job.

"The chief angel put his hands on Freddy's shoulders. 'And you, little angel, also have things to learn: think before you speak. Look before you leap.' "

The library grew silent as Grace's well-modulated voice rose and fell. The librarian's hands lay idle on the papers spread before her on her desk. Children, squirming in their seats or whispering to one another, stopped and peered at Grace's and Tyler's table. Then the most unexpected thing happened. Tyler reached for a crayon and paper. He drew a long line, then huge wings, like butterfly wings, on either side. He added a round, smiling face with brown hair puffed out about it. "My momma's an angel, too," he said. His lower lip trembled as he slid the picture toward Grace.

"Yes, I'm sure she is."

"Maybe Freddy took her to heaven."

"Or some other angel just like him." The lump in Grace's throat threatened to bar speech.

"I didn't want Momma to go to the store."

"You didn't want her to go." Grace was stunned at the change in Tyler's behavior and uncertain how to reply until this gift of insight, astonishing in its simplicity and accuracy, informed her to listen carefully.

"I could have made her stay home. If I'd said I was sick, she'd have stayed home."

"If she had stayed home, then she wouldn't have been in the car accident?"

He nodded. "Yes. It's all my fault."

The tears spilled over, and Tyler's skinny little body shook. He put his head on the table and sobbed. Grace's own tears ran freely. Then Tyler slipped off his chair and ran around the table, flung his arms about her, and held tight. Ignoring prescribed rules, and oblivious of the librarian at her desk or of the other children, Grace gathered Tyler into her arms and rocked back and forth.

"Tyler."

Tyler looked up. "Grandpa. Grandpa." A tall, broad-shouldered gentleman with thick, wavy white hair, bushy white eyebrows over deep-set dark eyes towered over them, blocking the light from the window beyond. The man sank onto his knees, and in that moment before Tyler turned and flung himself into his grandfather's arms, Grace noted the tufts of hair on the man's thick knuckles, the sprinkle of freckles across his nose. Holding his grandson in one arm, Tyler's grandfather pulled out a chair and sat. With a big white handkerchief, he wiped Tyler's eyes and kissed his cheeks. Watching them touched Grace deeply, and she looked away.

"Grandpa," Tyler said in a ragged little voice, half-muffled by his grandfather's big shoulder. "My momma's an angel in heaven." He reached across the table and pulled the picture to him. "See, this is Momma."

Grandpa looked at the picture and nodded sagely. His eyes clouded.

"Tyler's a wonderful boy. I've enjoyed working with him," Grace said.

"I'm Bob Richardson." He extended his hand. "Came up to live with my son, Russell, and Tyler here, after, well, after we lost Amy."

Children shoved back chairs, a book fell on the carpet and was retrieved, someone giggled, the librarian coughed. This is a good man, reliable, self-assured, Grace thought as she laid her small hand into Tyler's grandfather's warm thick palm.

"Amy's my momma, Miss Grace," Tyler whispered.

"Been awful worried about this little fellow." Bob Richardson rested his hand lightly on Tyler's mop of red hair.

"Tyler's very smart, Mr. Richardson. I'm sure by the time summer session's over, he'll be ready for third grade."

Tyler climbed onto a chair and leaning over pulled the angel book closer to himself. "You didn't finish the last page, Mrs. Grace," he said, and he read: *"The chief angel kissed Freddy, first on one cheek, then on the other cheek. Then with a gentle shove, he pushed Freddy off the cloud. Freddy floated gently down to—"* Tyler hesitated. *". . . ward, toward the spinning blue . . .*" He sounded out the next word. *"P-la-en-et, planet. Freddy had an important job to do. He was a very happy angel."*

"Why you little scamp." Grace's face glowed with pleasure. She clapped her hands. "You can read as well as I do."

"This little fellow's been hiding his light under a bushel, as the old hymn goes." Tyler's grandfather's kind, intelligent eyes met Grace's and lingered, and mortified, she felt herself blushing. An energy, an aura of well-being, radiated from the man and unwittingly she responded to him with a quickened heartbeat. Grace turned away, startled by the effect he had on her.

A horn sounded twice from the street below. "My son, Tyler's dad, Russell, is waiting for us in the car. We've heard so much about you from Tyler. I'm sure he'd like to meet you." Bob Richardson offered Grace his hand, helped her to her feet. An odd little tingle passed from his hand up through her arm. He waved the way, and though a bit nervous, she preceded him from the library.

15

For All the Right Reasons

June 26, 1997

Dear Mother,

Enclosed is a check for $44,900. Let me know if you think this is fair.

At the end I hardly slept, worrying if I was doing the right thing, frightened to take a risk. Then I thought about the risk you took leaving Dad and moving us to Pennsylvania, finding a decent place for us to live near a school, and how you worked your way up to manager, keeper really, of old Dr. Hansen. I remembered that when anyone had a problem you'd ask, "What's the worst thing that can happen?" God, how that annoyed me at the time. I wanted yes, no, black or white answers. This time I settled for gray.

Roger, Charles, and I have found a

great space for the business in an area downtown that's been renovated. It's large enough for our stock, plus several intimate display dining rooms. People like to see what they're getting. There's been a write-up about us in the paper, and they're going to do a spread on us when we open.

Sammy and Philip are home for the summer. Mother, would you consider having them down for a week or two sometime next month, if you're well enough? It'll be over three months since your surgery. Philip's worked in the nursery. Sammy's in that horrific late teen stage, lazy, likes rap music. If you feel it's too much for you, of course I'll understand. Give my best to the other two ladies of Covington, Grace and Amelia.

Love, Miranda
P.S. Paul sends his best.

A sense of satisfaction swept over Hannah. Deciding to sell had been right for both Miranda and herself. She tapped the check against her open palm. With this money she was determined to reestablish her plant nursery but on a much smaller scale. Soon she would tell the others about the idea stewing about in her head.

Later that afternoon, Hannah and Grace sat on the front porch with a bushel basket of pea pods and a tin bowl of shelled peas between them. Grace was telling Hannah about meeting Tyler's grandfather. "He's got an energy that draws people to him."

"Has he moved here permanently? Is he retired?"

"Mrs. Janson says he's retired military. Hard to believe. I think of military as autocratic, dogmatic. He's seems like a gentle, caring man."

"I take it you like him. What's his name?"

"Bob Richardson." Absentmindedly, Grace's fingers caressed the length of a pea pod she had picked up from the pile on her lap. "Like him? I hardly know him. It's just that I've never met anyone like him."

Hannah's fingernails were stained greenish-yellow. Miranda's letter, which she had read to Grace, fluttered to the floor, its edges stained the same greenish-yellow. Hannah smiled, took the pod from Grace's hands, split and shelled it, then selected and handed Grace another pod from the basket. Suddenly self-conscious, Grace focused on the pods, snapping them apart, popping the shiny hard green nuggets with a ping into the metal bowl. She directed the talk away from Tyler's grandfather. "The tone of Miranda's letter's so warm and easy. I'm glad you two are closer now."

"Since that day in Branston when we talked, it's been better. Actually, we find it easier to write to one another than to speak on the phone. It's never quite as it is talking in person, is it, talking on the phone I mean? I've never liked doing it. But, yes," Hannah's top teeth raked her lower lip. "It's much better than before. But the boys." She shook her head. "I hardly know them. Didn't see much of either of them when they were small kids. Don't see much of them, now."

"Don't you want to know your grandchildren? I can't imagine not reaching out to these boys."

"They were rowdy, fought incessantly. I hadn't the patience."

"How old are they now?"

"Sammy'll be eighteen next March. Philip must be sixteen."

"They'll need a car."

As if that were the end of the conversation, Grace reached into the bowl and grasped a handful of peas that resembled oversized green beebees, then dribbled them into a glass jar and held it up to the light. "What color green would you say these peas are?"

"Lighter than spring grass, darker than light green," Hannah replied, peering intently at the jar.

"Beautiful, aren't they?" Grace shook the jar gently and set it on the floor. "I think you should let the boys come."

"What if they're still rowdy? What if they still squabble all the time?"

Grace laughed. "I doubt boys that age fight like they did when they were little kids." She grinned impishly. "How about telling them they can come if they tote and carry for us, mow the lawn, and, let's see, pick apples when it's pie-making time, and . . ." She stopped and tapped her fingers on the edge of her chair. "They should come. There are lots of reasons why. You need to know them, they need to know their terrific grandma, and they could help with a lot of things around here."

"I see you've decided for me."

Grace touched Hannah's knee. "Well, as you always say, sometimes someone else has to make the decision. Think about it. I miss not having grandchildren. It'd be nice having young people around."

"Need Amelia's okay. She's so darn busy, gone so much."

"She obviously loves photography, and Mike's become a good friend." Grace brushed bits of pea pods from her lap. "Sometimes she looks so melancholy."

"She's always been like that, even back at Olive's. Don't you remember how she'd just leave us, go off to her room alone?"

"True. Maybe she's thinking about Caroline. It must be devastating to lose a child, your only child."

Later, when Hannah asked Amelia how she would feel about having two teenage boys for ten days, Amelia put her arm about Hannah's shoulder. "You needn't ask me. This is your home as much as it is mine."

That night Hannah wrote Miranda.

Dear Miranda,

Thank you for the check. It's fair. Wonderful you've found the right space for the business. I knew you would. All luck. Send Sammy and Philip for two weeks. They'll need a car. What dates?

Best to Paul, and "the boys" at work.

> The ladies of Covington send
> their love.
> Mother

16

Lost in the Forest at Graveyard Fields

✿ It happened as Hannah predicted. One day in class the fog in Amelia's brain lifted, and she understood f-stops, aperture, and focus. Now, when she stepped outside she could judge the quality of the light.

"You've got a real aptitude for this medium," Mike Lester, her instructor, had said recently, inspiring her to redouble both time and effort. Selecting a subject and the challenge of visualizing the finished image captured her imagination. In the intensity and involvement of a shoot Amelia would lose herself. Photography, she discovered, was energy intensive. It required long walks to rivers, waterfalls, and other out-of-the-way but beautiful and peaceful places. On the downside were the nighttime leg cramps.

"Maybe you need more potassium. Try eating bananas, they're full of potassium," Mike said.

Amelia ate bananas and gritted her teeth against the grip of pain as she lay in bed rubbing the cramping muscles of her calves.

"I had cramps when I was pregnant with Roger. Hot baths helped."

Amelia soaked until her skin wrinkled.

"Drink Gatorade," Hannah advised. "Keeps athletes fit." Amelia drank Gatorade, thinking all the while that the real culprit was poor muscle tone and that in time her leg muscles would strengthen.

The mountains and the pastoral landscape delighted her, and photographing them absorbed her. It seemed to Amelia that she had found at last her own true vocation. She was meeting new and interesting people. Mike Lester, a transplant himself, had come from New England fifteen years ago and was now a popular photographer of the local scene. He was of medium height, agile as a mountain goat, and somewhere in his late forties or early fifties. On a shoot, he tied back his long brown hair thus accentuating his square jaw and the cleft in his chin. He was openly gay, but seemed to have no partner, and as their friendship grew he began to escort Amelia to the occasional museum, art exhibit, movie, or to the theater in Asheville. There were days now when Amelia hardly thought about Thomas or Caroline but this realization was inevitably accompanied by stabs of guilt. It was as if she had signed a pact never to forget them, never to allow a single day to pass without thinking of them.

Today their photography field trip would take them to a place called Graveyard Fields, high in the mountains off the Blue Ridge Parkway. There, Mike told them, fallen trees had, over time, been sprinkled with fallen pine needles and taken on the look of tombstones.

On a recent shopping trip to the mall in Asheville, Amelia had deviated from white and the occasional blue and bought finely woven flannel scarves in pale rose and mustard yellow and a pair of tan cotton slacks. Because she chilled easily, and their field trip would take them to a much higher elevation than Covington, Amelia wore the slacks with a new long-sleeved striped brown-and-white cotton T-shirt over a sleeveless shell that held the warmth to her body. She had borrowed from Hannah a long-sleeved khaki jacket, which hung low, providing good cover-up for all the bending and crouching that photography demanded.

A crackle of gravel in the driveway signaled Mike's van. From her window she could see the van filled with other students, and Amelia hurried downstairs. No time for a chat or breakfast with Hannah and Grace. "Don't hold lunch for me," she called as she dashed past Grace in the hallway.

The ride, south and west of Asheville, took fifty minutes on the Blue Ridge Parkway. Once they pulled into an overlook, but the morning haze shrouded the sea of mountains. The air was nippy. No one wanted to climb from the warm van.

"Easy does it. Ground's uneven down there," Mike said when they reached Graveyard Fields and his seven students climbed from the bus and started down the grassy incline.

Feeling exhilarated and capable of any challenge, Amelia's spirits soared. Talking avidly and waving his hands, Mike led them to a cluster of mummified trees, where they spent a half hour discussing their size, shape, and color. Shooting the petrified trees held no interest for Amelia; she was drawn instead to the ring of trees, part of Pisgah Forest, about one hundred feet away.

"I'll stay in this area," Amelia said when Mike indicated it was time to move on.

"If you decide to join us, just follow that trail. We'll be down in the gorge where the river is." He headed away from her, warning the others to "Walk carefully. Be alert for holes and rock outcroppings."

A mid-aged fellow student named Mary left the group and headed back up the slope. "I don't like it here. It's creepy," she declared as she passed Amelia. "I'll wait in the van."

Amelia watched Mary climb into the van and wind down the windows. The voices of Mike and the other students were no longer audible. In a lazy mood Amelia let her camera bag slip onto the grass, then flopped beside it. Mary must have stretched out in the van, for Amelia no longer saw her head of dark, curly hair in the window.

There was a pleasure in working alone, and Amelia had developed a process for "seeing," as she called it. By sitting quietly she could, in special moments, experience first a lightness, a tingly sensation, then a warm shiver that swept over her neck and shoulders, followed by a starburst of peace that radiated from the very center of her being, blending all her senses. It was as if she was tuned to a powerful antenna. The aftermath was a clarity of sight and hearing. Amelia waited, but *it* did not happen. She looked about her.

"There are interesting things to photograph within twelve feet of wherever you stand," Mike often told them.

"So let's see." She challenged this instruction. Hands on hips Amelia turned slowly, surveying an area approximately twelve feet in diameter. Grass. Weeds. Pebbles. Rocks. Nothing. The air grew warmer. Amelia looked up. A Montana blue sky. She had never seen one, but surely the dome of clear deep blue breaking through the morning haze could be no handmaid to a Montana, or any other, sky.

Her eyes fell on a minuscule bell-shaped, vivid orange flower that rose in relief above its bed of velvet-smooth green grass. The hairs on her arms bristled. She would use her macrolens, perfect for close shots. Intent on capturing the delicate, lustrous blossom framed, amazingly, by slivers of dark wood, Amelia lay on her stomach, sighted the orange flower high in the frame of one shot, low in another, until she had finished the roll of film. Using her body to shade her camera, she unloaded, reloaded, and returned it to its niche in the camera bag.

Her stomach growled. A packet of trail mix and a can of Snapple ice tea that she always carried on field trips took the edge off her hunger. She considered returning to the van and Mary, but instead she thought of wandering down to the shade of the forest below. Gathering up her things, Amelia headed toward the forest.

Amelia faced a world of towering trees. The light in the forest was luminous and green, all other color filtered out. "A green world," she whispered, remembering a book she had read, a long time ago, about people who had stumbled through an opening in a mountain and entered an enchanted world in which the light, water, soil, animals, everything was green. "Magnificent," Amelia whispered into the stillness that cloaked the forest. It felt good to be alive. Setting her equipment on the spongy green moss surrounding a tree's enormous, protruding roots, Amelia ambled into the forest. Soaring branches formed an arched canopy and the leaf-strewn earth, free as it was of brambles and undergrowth, made for easy exploration. Mesmerized by the suggestion of holiness that permeated the forest, she meandered farther and farther away from Graveyard Fields.

A ray of sunlight slashed through a break in the trees, creating the illusion of a clearing just ahead, and Amelia moved toward it, descending deeper into Pisgah Forest. Feeling lighthearted and free, she wandered on. A sound, of some forest creature perhaps, startled her. Amelia stopped. Looked about. The ground, so deceptively moderate on the descent, was steeper than she remembered. "Time to go back," she said.

But walking uphill was strenuous and caused her legs to ache. Sinking onto a patch of soft moss at the base of a tree, she massaged her calves with long pressing strokes, then stretched out her legs. "Everything's fine," she said, trying to reassure herself. "Graveyard Fields is just" — she looked about — "over there. No." She pointed. "Over there." The trees around here were so close together, so huge. Amelia thought it would take three men with long arms to encircle a single tree trunk.

Something rustled the dry leaves close by and Amelia froze. A sob hooked in her throat. How long had she been in this forest? Her stomach cramped with hunger.

She would give anything for a drink of water. It terrified her to think that she had no wilderness skills, would not recognize an edible berry. Never, not even as a child, had she roughed it, not even camped out in her own backyard.

"Mike," she called. "Mike." Her heart constricting with fear, Amelia started uphill in an effort to retrace her steps among the now sinister, looming tree trunks until, overcome by exhaustion, she sank to the ground.

The forest had grown darker, colder, more somber, as if a storm was brewing. Don't be a baby, she chided herself. You walked down. All you have to do is walk up. Yet when she looked about her it seemed as if a nightmare of trails too numerous to count radiated in all directions between the giant trees. Choose one, she urged herself. Decide.

Amelia forced herself onto her feet. It hurt to move. Her legs ached. Her back ached. She was dizzy. Reaching out, she supported herself against a tree. Go left? Go right? Her legs seemed cast in concrete. Struggling mightily, she managed to shuffle a few steps.

After an hour spent searching the area,

and after twisting his ankle, Mike had finally given up trying to find Amelia. Frantically, at the point of tears, he had called 911 on his cell phone and then had called Grace and Hannah. Now, he waited impatiently with Grace, Hannah, and Sheriff Max Hopkins in the parking lot above Graveyard Fields, his swollen ankle having been iced and bandaged by the EMT people.

"She's lost. In there." Hannah stopped pacing long enough to point to the seemingly endless stretch of forest below. "No food. No water. You've got to find her and fast."

"We're gettin' up a search party to go after her, ma'am," Sheriff Hopkins said. His cell phone rang. "'Scuse me, ma'am." He turned from them and moved a bit away while he talked on his phone. Then the sheriff walked back to Hannah and Grace.

"Volunteers 'er on the way. We've got 'bout another hour to dark. Now don't you ladies fret. We'll find her. She can't have gone far."

"If anything happens to Amelia," Mike said. There were tears in his eyes.

"Nothing better happen to her," Hannah muttered between clenched teeth. Being so totally out of control made her anxious to do something, take charge, issue orders, go down there and search for Amelia herself.

Grace's jaw quivered. She pressed her fist against her chin; she would not break down now. "Snakes? Are there snakes in there?" she asked, her voice trembling.

"Maybe. Maybe not. Snakes 'er more scared of people than folks realize. But you never know, comin' on 'em unexpected." He forced a smile.

The sheriff's deputy — the name on his shiny nameplate read, Jay Snider — shrugged. His big square jaw worked furiously, chewing gum. The way he slouched against the sheriff's car, seemingly bored, infuriated Hannah. "Why don't you send him down there now?"

Sheriff Hopkins touched Grace lightly on the shoulder. "Gotta have a search party, ma'am. Now, ma'am, we're gonna find your friend. How far could she of got?"

Unable to control her shivering in the growing chill and darkness, Amelia dissolved into tears. Her teeth chattered. Her feet were numb. Her hands, without gloves, were starting to quiver from cold and she jammed them into her armpits.

She was lost, a terrifying prospect. "Mike," she called. Oh, where is Mike? Doesn't he realize I'm lost? Overcome with self-pity and fear, Amelia wept. Thomas. If only Thomas were here. He had always taken care of her, made certain she was comfortable and safe.

Somewhere close by an owl hooted, causing her to jerk back and lose her balance. Dried leaves cushioned her fall. "Mike," she called again. Too cold, too tired, too frightened to move, Amelia simply lay where she had landed and pulled Hannah's long-sleeved khaki shirt close about her and wound her scarf more tightly about her neck. Her eyes darted about. Were there snakes? Were there bears? Between chattering teeth and desiccated lips, Amelia, in order to distract herself, began to whisper an old English ballad her father sometimes sang at family picnics when he brought out his guitar. She closed her eyes, saw his bent head, heard the strum of his guitar as he sang "The Golden Vanity."

> "There was a ship that sailed
> upon the lowland sea.
> And the name of the ship
> was the Golden Vanity.

And they feared it would be
    taken by the Spanish enemy.
And sunken in the lowland,
    lowland sea,
and sunken in the lowland sea."

My God, she thought, when she reached the end, I never paid attention to the meaning of that song. It's tragic, a sailor risks his life to sink the enemy vessel and is left to drift away on the tide by a captain who promised him the hand of his daughter in marriage. It's about betrayal and dying. She clamped her hand over her mouth to keep from screaming and struggled unsuccessfully to shake the crushing weight of loneliness, the intensifying panic that threatened to engulf her. Turning her eyes to the darkening canopy above, she prayed. "I'm scared. Cold. Please, help me, God."

Sirens blared. A Buncombe County EMS ambulance and a fire truck, followed by two pickups crammed with people, pulled up behind the sheriff's car. The volunteers wore high boots, thick jackets, and some carried rifles.

Harold Tate jumped from one truck and ran to Grace and Hannah. "My Lord, I came as soon as I heard." The sky had turned murky and he studied the darkening forest below with anxious eyes. "Amelia down there?" He shook his head, then squared his shoulders. "Hikers get lost all the time. We find 'em. We'll find Amelia."

"Before dark?" Grace asked.

"Why don't you people use flares, spotlights, airplanes, loudspeakers?" Hannah demanded of the sheriff, but by then he was walking away.

Grace's heart flip-flopped when she spotted Bob and Russell Richardson among the men. Bob started toward her with an air of confidence that reassured her. But Harold Tate intercepted him. "Sheriff's got vests, headgear, first aid kits." He pointed Bob back toward the cluster of men and several women, and Grace watched Bob and Russell slip on orange vests, secure hard hats with lights in front, and hitch on thick belts from which dangled water bottles, flashlights, and a few other items she couldn't make out.

"It's gettin' pretty raw out here," Harold said. "Why don't you ladies sit in your car . . . I'll have Jake" — he beckoned to a teenage boy — "stay here with you."

Hannah took Grace's arm and propelled her toward the station wagon. "I should feel more confident. They're trained for this." Nearby the EMS crew distributed Red Cross emergency medical kits. Within moments nearly two dozen men and several women, including Marie Findley, formed lines and started down into Graveyard Fields, their wavering flashlights simulating fireflies. Grace looked for Bob, but with their hats and gear she could not distinguish one man from another.

Hunger and cold were beginning to affect Amelia's mind, which felt as if it were drifting in slow motion upstream against a heavy current. Voices of children sounded from somewhere deep within the forest. A blond green-eyed girl bounded from the trees and raced toward her, arms outstretched. "Caroline." Amelia struggled to rise. The child vanished. "Oh, Caroline," Amelia moaned, sinking back. She was going to die, she knew it. Like the angel she was, Caroline had come to lead the way. It was better this way. Resignation coupled with a comforting tranquillity settled over Amelia.

Pawing at dry leaves, Amelia raked them close about her, piled them on her lap, then spread the leaves over her prone body like a shroud. She was ready. Would there be a judgment? If so, would she be judged worthy? Events of her life drifted through her mind. She saw herself sitting beside Thomas at a rickety metal table on the island of Martinique in the Caribbean writing the names of hurricane victims into Red Cross records. An instant later, she was holding a screaming, squirming baby in Liberia and trying to comfort mother and child as both were vaccinated against polio and malaria. Then she was lying in a hospital bed in San Francisco with Caroline, precious infant, in her arms and tears of joy cascading down her cheeks. She then saw herself with Thomas and Caroline walking beside the Ganges River in India, each holding firmly to one of their daughter's chubby little hands as she tugged to be free to jump and play in the slow drifting water.

A golden scale appeared and Amelia sat cross-legged on it, and opposite her a man dressed in white placed one by one on a matching scale the events of her life. They seemed feather light, hardly tipping the scale. Had her life been so insignificant? A sense of failure mingled with regret wound its way from the pit of her stomach and coiled about her heart. Would God discount her work because she had not determined it herself?

In Amelia's muddled brain random thoughts held sway only for a moment, then faded. Oddly disembodied, she floated up and hung midway between the forest canopy and the woman with white, disheveled hair covered with a smattering of forest floor debris. With a jolt Amelia realized that the woman below was herself, and in that instant the experience ended. Leaves weighted her body now like a suit of armor, and she felt again the inhospitable, cold earth beneath her shoulders and hips. Everything grew dark.

Harold Tate moved carefully through the forest. "Amelia," he called, and again, "Amelia."

Small creatures of the forest darkness scurried before his heavy-booted steps. The yellow eyes of an owl, caught by his flashlight, glared at him. Muffled voices sounded to his left and right. "Amelia," they called.

"God," he prayed aloud, "let one of us find her. Poor thing. The frailest-looking of the three of 'em." He would never have told the other women, but he was certain that Amelia could never make it through a night alone in the forest. At an elevation of fifty-five hundred feet, even in summer, the nights grew cold and frost settled with alarming speed.

Now and then, here and there through the trees, he caught a glimpse of another searcher's light. So many people had come out to help. Frank, the janitor from his wife's school was there, and Buddy, the morose young clerk from the local gas station.

"They're right friendly ladies. Always asking 'bout my ole dog, Hank, when they comes in to get milk 'er anythin'," Buddy said.

Tim from Prancer's Hardware had been one of the first to arrive. "Right good people those ladies," he'd said.

The carpenter, Tom Findley, and his wife, Marie, had rounded up the oddest long-haired, hippie-looking bunch of folks. Didn't realize so many folks like them live around here, Harold thought. I've been wrong about a lot of things. Like he'd told his wife, Brenda, when he'd first met the three ladies, "Not much chance they'll stay in that drafty old farmhouse." But they'd cleaned it up, fixed it up pretty, put in heat, and settled in, and folks liked them.

For half an hour or more Harold trudged along, using his compass to direct his course as he cautiously ducked branches and stepped carefully over fallen tree trunks that seemed to mushroom from the darkness. The forest was dreary and still, the ominous silence broken only by owls screeching and the sounds of unidentifiable night animals skittering away.

He stumbled, clutched a tree trunk to steady himself, readjusted his headlight, and set off again. Anxiety was building. It was a huge forest. How far had Amelia wandered? Suddenly his boot hit something soft. Instinctively he drew back. Soft in the forest could mean maybe a bear cub and a mother bear close at hand. Harold stopped, waited a moment, listening for the sound of leaves crunching. Hearing nothing, he dipped his head, and his light fell on a rectangular gray object which he knelt to inspect. Amelia's camera bag. Harold set down his gun, examined the damp bag, then slung it across his shoulder and resumed his search.

She couldn't be far, he assured himself. Any moment now he would hear a shout from one or another member of the search party. Someone would find her. But another half an hour passed, and no one signaled. Harold squinted at his watch. The lighted dial gleamed in the winter dark — six-thirty. Amelia had been in the forest for hours. He wondered if she was wearing warm clothing. Sheriff Hopkins had told him that no one from Amelia's photography class could recall if she had a jacket with her. He shuddered. With every passing moment, time was running out for Amelia.

For what seemed to him to be an interminable period of time Harold pushed on into the forest. Suddenly, through the trees, a light bobbed toward him.

"Wondering if maybe we ought to go back, call in the Guard?" Tim said.

"Can't go back," Harold replied. "We give up now, she's a dead woman. I found her camera bag a few hundred feet back."

That news energized the several dark forms that now surrounded him, their lights clustered like stars. "I agree with Harold. We can't go back," Bob Richardson said. "Come on, people, let's find her," and he turned away and headed into the darkness.

Harold clutched his gun tightly, and grateful for his light moved on into the dark forest. Again his boot struck something soft. This time, surely, it was a bear cub. His hands tightened about his gun. He froze. Nothing stirred. Then the thing made an odd moaning sound, and Harold lowered his light to identify the object. As the area about his boots brightened, Harold gasped and sank to his knees. Then he set his gun on the ground. "I've got her," he shouted. "I've found her."

From a distance shouts echoed and bounced from tree to tree. He called again and within moments heard the crunch of boots on the forest floor.

"Is she alive?" someone asked.

Someone checked Amelia's wrist. "Pulse slow, but it's there."

Tenderly, carefully, refusing anyone's assistance, Harold gathered Amelia into his arms. Someone draped a jacket over her. Someone took the camera bag and Harold's gun. Framed by the glow of other searchers' lamps, Harold Tate lifted the limp Amelia and carried her from the forest.

17

To Rest and Recover

Amelia awoke with a start. A tall man clothed all in white looked down at her. His eyes were blue and kind, his hair thick and silvery. A glow, the result of afternoon sunlight streaming in the wide windows, framed his head and shoulders.

Her whispered, "God?" sprung from muddled memories of her ordeal.

"Dr. Granell," he said. "You're doing fine. Be home soon."

"I'm not dead?" Her palms felt sweaty. A lump was rising in her throat.

"Couple more hours, hypothermia, you would have been."

"But I saw." Her voice trailed off. She pressed her fingers against her temples. "I don't remember. Who found me?"

"Ambulance brought you in." Dr. Granell flipped through Amelia's chart and made several notations. "You're going to be just fine," he repeated.

The last thing she remembered was the

sense of peace and relief that soon she
would be with Thomas and Caroline.
Instead she had wound up in yet another
hospital.

"You awake?" Grace and Hannah walked
into the room. "Meeting in hospitals like
this has got to stop." Hannah patted
Amelia's hand. "How you feeling, old
girl?"

"Fuzzy. Confused."

"We were frantic. The search and rescue
people took so long to get organized,"
Grace said.

"Search and rescue? Who found me?"
She could feel her heart thumping.
Somehow she had to know.

"Harold Tate. He carried you out. We
thought you weren't going to make it."

"Seemed as if all of Covington turned
out to help," Hannah said.

"I caused so much trouble. I'm so
ashamed." Amelia's anxious eyes misted.

"You're safe, nothing else matters."
Grace bent and kissed her forehead.

An unsought memory from her childhood drifted into Amelia's mind. Water.
Swimming had terrified her when she was
six or so. One day at the beach her father
had grabbed her, tucked her kicking and
screaming under his arm, and headed for

the end of the pier. "Shut up," he demanded, and trying to appease him and forestall what she anticipated was coming, she had complied. Before dumping her into the ocean he had said, "Fear is something you've got to overcome. Life's not for cowards." She hit the cold water and went down, down without a struggle, resigned to the inevitable, and came to, spread eagle on warm sand, hacking and coughing and spitting up water.

"I'm a coward," she said, taking Grace's hand. "If I hadn't been so frightened, maybe I could have found my way out." Tears trailed down her cheeks. Grace wiped them gently with her bandanna.

"Hush now. Stop blaming yourself. It's all right, all right."

Once home Amelia felt like a specimen. People she hardly knew, new friends like Margaret Olsen from Hillside House, Tom and Marie, members of her photography class, and strangers from the rescue party stopped by to visit her. Grace bustled about filling lemonade and ice tea glasses and passing trays of her increasingly famous sugar cookies. Amelia suspected that half the people came out of curiosity, and this further embarrassed her. When she was alone, Amelia spent hours carefully composing individual thank-you notes. The one to Harold Tate was the most difficult.

My Dear Harold,
I owe you my life and cannot find the words to express my gratitude.

She stopped, bit the end of the pen. Was she glad he had found her? Saved from death twice, once from drowning and now from hypothermia, why? So many times after losing Caroline and Thomas life had not seemed worth living. Amelia's eyes traveled to the mountains, so clear today that it appeared that if she reached out her fingers she could touch them. On the other hand, she considered, coming to Covington, living with Grace and Hannah, her photography — why she'd been quite happy lately, at times even joyful. Yet, if Harold had not stumbled upon her when he did, she would have passed quietly into the good night and would never have had to face a difficult death, like Thomas or Caroline, or her father, who had suffered with cancer. She continued the letter.

You, especially, and people of Covington, have made me welcome beyond my expectations, and I am embarrassed to have caused so much trouble. From the bottom of my heart, thank you, for all the many kindnesses you have extended to me from the day I arrived in your town. With deep appreciation,

Amelia

The envelope sealed, Amelia rocked slowly back and forth. A sense of failure beset her when she thought about her travail in the forest. She had panicked so easily. Yellow-bellied, her father would say. If she had remained calm, controlled her fear, she could have been coolheaded and able to retrace her steps. Instead she had crumpled under pressure and relinquished her power. The result? At six years old, and now again, she had been carried out half dead, a spectacle for others.

Amelia turned her mind to legal matters, to the deed of the farmhouse and land she had never changed to include Grace and Hannah, and she had no will. Upon her return she had made an appointment with an attorney Mrs. Olsen recommended, and Mike, his ankle better, would be here soon to pick her up and drive her to the attorney's office. The farmhouse and land would be put in their three names, and all her assets would go to Grace and Hannah with instructions that she be cremated and her ashes sprinkled into the wind near Graveyard Fields, where she had seen her child and where, to her astonishment and wonder, she had drifted easily out of her body. Was that what death was like, a rapid, peaceful drifting away?

A car turned into the driveway. Mike waved. Badly shaken and feeling totally responsible for her ordeal, Mike visited almost every day. She liked him more all the time and was beginning to depend on him, for he was a man able to comfort others and who was comfortable with himself and his life. And he made her laugh, entertained her with amusing stories in which he was, often, the butt of his own jokes. Rising, Amelia hastened down the steps toward his car. In a moment, Mike was out of the car and holding open the door of the passenger side for her.

Minutes later Grace brought a tray of ice tea onto the porch and Hannah soon joined her. Hannah had chosen this time, when she and Grace were alone, to discuss a plan that would inevitably turn her own life upside down.

18

Hannah Decides on a Greenhouse

✿ "You seem edgy, distracted lately." Grace poured ice tea into tall glasses and handed one to Hannah.

"I'm bored." Hannah pointed to the big oak. "I've finished planting and mulching our new shade garden." Easing off her gritty, damp gloves, Hannah leaned forward and placed her hands on her knees. "I've got to do something."

"Like what?" Grace asked.

Hannah shook her head, turned her glass round and round in her hand, and announced, "I'm going to buy a greenhouse."

Grace's mouth fell slightly ajar. "A greenhouse?"

"Yes. I'm going to grow and sell ornamental plants."

"Won't there be too much work for you, all that standing, lifting, bending?"

"Hip's perfect. I can stand, walk fine. Can't kneel for too long and sitting on my butt gets uncomfortable, but in a greenhouse the work's at waist level."

"Aren't you a bit too . . ."

"Too what?" Hannah demanded. "Too old? You of all people." Her shoulders stiffened, her jaw tightened. "What's age got to do with it?"

"It's not age. It's how much physical work can you do and not wear yourself out? And you'll be on a schedule."

Hannah relaxed. Grace clucked about their physical well-being like a mother hen over her chicks, of course she'd be concerned about Hannah's physical well-being. "I need to do this, Grace. Working gives me a purpose, gets me out with people." Her eyes searched Grace's face. "You've found work you enjoy at the school. Amelia has her photography. What have I got?"

Grace understood. "Of course you need something challenging to do." She wished Hannah had settled on something of a less strenuous nature. "What will you grow?"

"Anthuriums, chrysanthemums, gardenias. These sell year-round. I'll order two-inch rooted plants from a wholesaler in Florida."

"Won't you have to transplant them?"

"Several times. Keep me busy."

"A lot of work." Grace's eyes clouded. "You won't consider volunteering at the school? Brenda's itching to start a gardening project for fifth graders."

When Hannah drew back, Grace recognized her guarded hurt look. "Why, you're trying to dissuade me," Hannah said.

"I am, aren't I? I'm sorry." She was quiet for a moment, then shrugged. "Why not a greenhouse? If it turns out to be too much for you, you can always sell it, or take in a partner."

"I hoped you'd understand."

"I just worry about your hip and your knees."

Hannah turned away, sipped at her tea.

"Where will you put the greenhouse?" Grace asked.

Hannah eyes brightened. "Out back of the kitchen."

"You sure about this?"

"Yes. I can do it with my hands tied behind my back." She looked hard at Grace.

Stifling the uneasy feeling that this was not going to work out well, Grace said, "I guess I worry too much. You know you can count on me. You've got books and catalogs? Show me."

"Sure, I have them inside. Let's go." They rose and Hannah hooked her arm through Grace's. "You're a blessing of a friend, you know that, Grace?"

"You are to me, too." Then because Grace was never comfortable with compliments, she said, "Remember, we're going with Brenda and Harold to the park for the Fourth of July fireworks."

"And of course you'll introduce me to Tyler's grandfather if we meet up with them?" Hannah spoke lightly. It was difficult for her to imagine Grace having a romance with anyone, much less a retired armed services officer. Hannah stepped back, her hands on her hips, her lips curled in a teasing smile. "Don't look so surprised. You lit up like a firefly when you saw Bob Richardson at Graveyard Fields."

"I didn't."

"You did. And you looked very pretty all aglow like that, I must say." They laughed and slipped their arms about each other's waists as they went into the living room.

♩
Fireworks in the Park

🎇 The Community Park in Covington was inviting, with its picnic tables set under trees, large open green grassy areas, and a play area for smaller children at one end. On this Fourth of July evening fireworks zoomed overhead and exploded in volleys of multicolored radiances. At first Grace held her breath, but then she oohed and aahed along with the rest of the spectators as showers of light illuminated the sky above the park.

Grace, Hannah, and Amelia sat with Brenda and Harold Tate in folding chairs. The fireworks celebration was, in the good-old-fashioned sense of the word, truly a celebration. Like a Norman Rockwell painting. Families were assembled together; they gathered around picnic tables and clustered close on blankets and rows of folding chairs spread across the entire park. Youngsters played, running about with handheld sparklers and joining their families to cheer as every brilliant burst of light and color bombarded the night sky.

The fireworks celebration, organized by Covington's Volunteer Fire Department, culminated a year-long, fund-raising campaign to purchase the fireworks. Everyone contributed. There was a sense of pride-of-ownership, as if it was each person's party, and all the others were welcome.

Hannah leaned toward Grace. "You tell a certain somebody he'd be in for inspection if he showed his face?"

"Heavens, no. I haven't seen him." She looked about. "There are a lot of people here."

Suddenly someone smacked into Hannah's chair, which buckled, toppling her to the ground. Even as she cried out, an unshaven, wiry young man of about thirty was kneeling beside her tugging at her arm. Pushing him hard on the chest, Hannah pulled away. The man reared back, and Harold Tate helped Hannah to her feet.

"Are you drunk or what, Wayne?" he asked the younger man.

Wayne looked sheepish. He removed his cowboy hat. Unkempt, straggly, black hair touched his shoulders and nervously he fingered one end of his handlebar mustache and twisted the rim of his hat. "I'm right sorry, ma'am."

An explosion of fireworks ended their brief exchange. Wayne plopped his hat on his head and hastened away.

"Careless young man." Grace took Hannah's arm. "Are you all right?"

"A bit shaken."

Harold reopened her chair, and with as much composure as she could muster, Hannah sat. "Who was that fellow?"

"Wayne Reynolds," Brenda said. "Lives with his grandfather over the mountain near Tennessee. They grow tobacco, raise pigs, cattle."

"I wouldn't want to meet up with him on a dark street corner," Grace said.

"You wouldn't have to worry," Brenda assured them. "He's not a bad sort, just not very perceptive. Enough about Wayne. Are you all right, Hannah?"

"Yes. Jarred but not hurt."

A blast went off. High above them an umbrella of color flared. Wavering and shimmering, a shower of sparks fell toward the earth. When Hannah saw Wayne again, she drew in her feet and tightened her grasp on the arms of her chair, but he stayed clear of the group, his attention fixed on the pretty, dark-haired girl draped on his arm.

A few more explosions and the fireworks were over. People began to gather up their blankets, fold their chairs, pack up their picnic baskets, and summon their children. Grace excused herself and headed for the rest room. Seeing all these families together reminded her of sweet summer afternoons and picnics in Dentry Park when Roger was little. It wasn't until he tugged on her hand that Grace realized that Tyler was standing alongside her vying with her memories for attention.

"Why, Tyler, I didn't see you. How are you? Did you like the fireworks?" Grace kneeled to talk to him, then rose, almost stepping on Bob Richardson's feet. His hand touched hers, leaving her feeling goose-bumpy.

"Hello, Grace," he said. "I looked for you."

With Ted it had been all comfort: holding hands in the park, short, innocent kisses in his old Chevy. Nothing like this peculiar, twittery sensation up and down her spine. Grace concentrated on Tyler. "How did you like that big one that opened up like a silver umbrella?"

"Neat," he said. Then he yelled, "Billy,

Billy, wait up," and dashed after a friend, leaving her alone with his grandfather.

"I was going to phone you," Bob said, taking her arm and steering her toward a picnic table just vacated by a family. "I won't be bringing Tyler next week."

Grace's heart plummeted. She looked forward to seeing him. "I want to thank you for helping to find Amelia," she said.

He shook his head. "I'm just glad Harold found her. She's doing well, I hope?"

"Yes, she is, thank heaven. But I do appreciate that you took the time to search for her."

"Folks have to help," he said.

Her heart skipped a beat. "We'll miss you. How long will you be gone?"

"Week or so. When I get back I was hoping you'd agree to have dinner with me?" At her hesitation, he said, "How about lunch?"

A date, at her age? How odd she felt, self-conscious, yet she found herself nodding yes, just as Tyler's father, Russell, appeared, and they said their good-byes. With a spring in her step, Grace walked away to join Hannah and the Tates.

On a hot day in July, a nervous and

excited Hannah drove with trepidation to the airport south of Asheville, an hour away, to pick up her grandsons. On that same day Amelia, in a tizzy, sat in the living room trying to decide which one of her photographs to submit for judging to the photographic show that Mike had arranged at a small private gallery in Asheville. None of the twenty photographs propped on the living room couch, on chairs, on the mantel and along the walls seemed good enough. Mike said she was her own worst enemy. In more ways than one, she thought.

Grace bustled about the kitchen baking cherry pies and sugar cookies that she would send to Mike with Amelia, but she was thinking about Bob Richardson. Gone eleven days. It seemed like months. She really liked him. She liked his deep baritone voice, his gentleness with Tyler, his smile, and his big square hands with the tiny spouts of hair on the knuckles. In their brief times together they had chatted about Tyler, but he had also asked where she was from. She had told him a little about Dentry and her family. Still his presence in the library was disorienting; it took concentration to stay focused on Tyler.

Her hands smothered in flour, Grace

stared at the two mounds of dough, one waiting to be rolled into piecrust on the butcher block section of the countertop, the other to be flattened and cut for cookies. Good Lord, she thought, have I got a crush on Bob Richardson? Nonsense. At my age? She poked her hip, leaving a white smudge on her slacks. "Imagine such a thing," she muttered, reaching for the rolling pin. The dough succumbed to the pressure of the rolling pin under her hands, growing rounder, wider, and thinner as she pressed and rolled. Lifting the thin slab of dough, Grace eased it gently into a pie pan and carefully fluted the edge. Then she stamped out cookie dough into giraffe- and cat-shapes and arranged them on a cookie sheet and slipped them into the oven.

Her thoughts returned to Bob. What did she know about him? He was seventy, well preserved, had been career military. A good listener. He had come up from Florida to be with his family. That was all she knew.

Holding the pie pan at eye level, Grace rotated it slowly. The fluted edge must be even all around. As she set the pan down on the table, her elbow hit the rolling pin, which clattered to the floor, spun wildly about before rolling under the round kitchen table. The phone rang while she was on her knees retrieving it, and Grace smacked her head as she struggled out from under the table.

From somewhere in the house Amelia picked up the phone.

"Hello. Is Grace Singleton there?"

The voice was deep, composed, confident, and oddly familiar. It reminded Amelia of someone, but she couldn't place the speaker. "Just a moment," she replied. "I'll get her."

Grace stood at the counter eyeing the leftover pie dough, considering whether there was enough for another pie and rubbing the rising lump on her head when Amelia strode into the room.

"Phone for you. Man with a pleasant voice." She lifted an eyebrow, smiled at Grace, turned and disappeared.

Grace wiped her hands; fine flour drifted to the floor as she walked to the wall phone.

"Grace. Bob Richardson here."

Keep your voice casual, she told herself. Don't fall down. "Hi, Bob, how are you? How was the trip?"

"Fine. Fine." A long pause. "Can I prevail on you to take a ride with me? I'm going to Johnson City in Tennessee tomorrow to pick up the proof of a book my son's writing."

"I didn't know he was a writer." Grace pulled her bandanna from her waist and wiped the beads of perspiration forming above her lip.

"He's a computer program developer, but since Amy died he's been writing his memories of their life together, for Tyler, he says. If it makes it easier for him, like Tyler drawing his mother as an angel, who am I to argue?"

"Of course." Grace swallowed hard.

"Of course what?" he teased. "Russell writing about Amy, or you going over the mountain to Tennessee with me?"

Grace felt like a schoolgirl. "Of course to both things. I'd like to go."

"Well then." His voice relaxed. Was he as nervous as she was?

"I'll pick you up around ten on Saturday, tomorrow?"

"Tomorrow? Fine. Thanks for asking."

"My pleasure, Mrs. Grace." He called her by the name Tyler used, and she smiled, and when they hung up Grace moseyed back to the table to roll the remaining dough and line and flute the edge of another pie pan. The Richardson

318

family might enjoy a homemade cherry pie.

When Hannah and her grandsons returned from the airport, they found Grace rocking on the front porch, a book in her lap, dreamily staring into space.

The tall, sandy-haired, square-jawed young man in tennis shorts, whom Hannah introduced as Sammy, looked at Grace with peevish eyes as he followed his grandmother up the front steps. He carried a small black CD player and wore headphones.

The younger boy trailing them and lugging two duffel bags was strikingly good-looking.

"This is Philip," Hannah said.

With his olive skin, black curly hair, and violet-blue eyes, inherited, Hannah said, from his father, Philip was attractive and engaging. He stepped forward, surprising Grace with an outstretched hand.

"I think your son, Roger, and his friend, Charles, are cool. I've been working at the shop, helping unpack stuff."

Grace, having instantly warmed to him, took Philip's hand.

"Philip's been telling me that at their school they have to do some kind of volunteer work. He's learned to be a clown." Hannah beamed at her grandson.

Grace knew how nervous Hannah was and how important it was for her to have her grandsons here. Hannah was more sensitive than most people knew, and these boys had the power to hurt her. Grace turned her attention to Philip. "A clown. Now that sounds like fun."

"Yep."

"Where do you volunteer as a clown?" Grace asked.

Philip set the duffel bags on the porch. "Kids' ward at our local hospital."

"I bet they love you."

"They're great kids."

"What about you, Sammy?" Grace asked.

From his slouch against the wall of the house he lifted his head for a moment and took off the headphones. "What about me?"

"What volunteer work do you do?"

"I DJ. Rap. Rock and roll." Sammy tossed his head and glared at his grandmother. "We going in?"

Hannah led them inside, leaving Grace to worry about what to wear tomorrow and what she would do or say.

"Well, just look at you, all gussied up." Amelia glanced up from studying the four photographs propped along the railing of the porch. She had reduced the photos to four, had not eaten breakfast, and had been sitting on the porch for the past hour agitating and fussing and trying to select the perfect photograph to submit for judging. Today was the deadline. Of the four, two were striking black-and-whites and two were color. Three were nature scenes. One, a black-and-white, captured a little girl of maybe five, with one grubby fist to her cheek, her mouth puckered to cry and looking utterly bewildered as she sprawled on the sidewalk next to her overturned three-wheeler.

"I like that one," Grace said, pointing to the photograph of the child.

Amelia removed the other three, stepped back, and studied the picture. "This one, really?"

"Yes. It touches me, here." Grace rested a hand over her heart.

"Okay, that's it. I'll take it to Mike's studio right now. Can you drive me?"

"I can't." Heat fanned across Grace's face and neck. "You know Tyler, the little boy I work with? Well, his grandfather,

Bob Richardson, asked me to go with him to Johnson City in Tennessee on an errand for his son."

Amelia's eyebrows arched. A teasing smile spread across her face. "That's why you're all dressed up in new slacks and a jacket. Good color that mauve on you. Left the bandanna off, eh?" Her eyes swept up and down evaluating Grace. "You look very nice. I like your hair back off your face."

Having spent what seemed like forever wetting and combing her hair, then drying it with a curling brush, it pleased Grace that Amelia, whose style she admired, liked the way she looked.

Unexpectedly a look of interest flashed across Amelia's face. "Bob Richardson," she said softly. Something about the way Amelia licked her lips and narrowed her eyes reminded Grace of a cat. It was disconcerting and made her uncomfortable.

"That name sounds familiar. I think I once knew a Bob Richardson. Yes, I remember. After the Korean War, Thomas and I were in Seoul responding to yet another disaster, a typhoon I think. Such a dreary place, Seoul, after the war. As I remember, a Captain Bob Richardson was assigned to us" — she raised an eyebrow, laughed lightly — "to make sure we didn't stumble into a minefield or something. As I recall, he was quite charming." She shrugged and made a dismissive gesture with her hand. "It can't be the same man. Bob Richardson's a rather ordinary name, don't you think?"

Grace nodded, but her excitement at seeing Bob gave way to concern. Amelia looked away, and they were distracted by a pickup truck that rumbled by on the road. Recognizing Harold Tate, they waved. He lifted two fingers from the steering wheel, smiled and nodded in reply.

"I'm going to go inside and call a cab." Amelia gathered her photographs and headed for the front door. "Have a nice time," she called over her shoulder. "One of these days I'm going to take the driver's test and buy a car."

Grace took the cooled cookies from a tray. "Take these to Mike," Grace called after her. Grace remained on the porch staring at nothing, preoccupied with the amazing idea that Amelia might have known Bob Richardson. Bob had been career military and had surely served in Korea. How ironic if they had known one another, liked one another. What if when they met, as they eventually would, they recognized one another, even found one another attractive? Immediately Grace felt overshadowed, dowdy and dull in comparison to the bright lightness that was Amelia. Here you go again, she warned herself, worrying, worrying.

Straightening her shoulders, Grace pulled her chin up. How could she be so upset? After all, there was nothing between herself and Bob. Or was there? The sound of tires crunching on gravel yanked Grace from her internal harangue. Resisting the impulse to call to Amelia, she picked up her purse from the chair and walked down the steps toward the gray Grand Marquis and a smiling Bob.

20

The Date

The road from North Carolina into Tennessee was narrow, a tree-lined tunnel, then a heavily wooded gorge. At the Tennessee border a brand new four-lane-highway opened before them, and the landscape changed from steep and rugged to lush green and rolling with a narrow river winding its way throughout.

"I like the look of this land," Bob said.

"I do, too. It's beautiful."

"Whenever I drive this way I think about the original settlers, the Indians. They had everything here, arable land, open sky spilling over with stars, plenty of water."

Grace nodded.

"You seem glum, not your usual self," Bob said.

"Not glum. Pensive maybe, thinking about how fast things change."

"Like what?"

"Like about how this landscape went

from mountainous and closed in to open and rolling and how your daughter-in-law was killed and how it's changed everything for Tyler, your son, you."

"Believe me, Grace, I've seen a lot of death, but Amy's death, well." He paused, bringing his lips together in a grim line, "Senseless. She was so damned young."

For a moment Grace rested her hand lightly on his arm. "I'm truly sorry."

"When I hung up after talking to Russell that day, I loaded my car and headed for North Carolina." He glanced over at her.

"That's what I meant. In a moment your life changed."

"Well, tell the truth, I'd been molting in a Florida retirement community. I was bored to death with bridge and golf and hustling to get to a restaurant before six in the evening for the early bird dinner specials. I like North Carolina."

Grace clasped her hands too tightly in her lap.

They rode in silence for a few minutes, then he asked, "What did you do when your husband died, Grace?" Momentarily, the question unnerved her, then she said, "I cried all the time. For a long time I was angry at Ted for leaving me. A lot of 'why me' stuff and depression."

"Did you move from your home?"

"No. But the house seemed enormous, full of creaks and sounds I'd never heard before. I left on all the lights at night, had an alarm system installed.

"What about your children?"

"I have one son. He was working as an engineer in Saudi Arabia." She hastened to add, "He came for the funeral, of course. After about a year, I started feeling like myself again, actually began to enjoy living alone. I'd be there still if my son, Roger, hadn't insisted I move."

"Why'd he do that?"

She told him briefly about her "little" heart attack. "Of course if he hadn't insisted I move to Branston, I'd never have met Hannah Parrish and Amelia Declose." She spoke their last names clearly, intentionally, her heart pattering. Would Amelia's name trigger a reaction? When it didn't, she was pleased and felt the weight lift from her heart. She relaxed a bit, musing about the trouble with being interested in someone of the opposite sex. How the uncertainty of it burdens your spirit unless you know up front that it's reciprocated. Infatuation, if that's what she felt for Bob, had thrown her off balance. Almost daily now her normal, easygoing life was vulnerable to roller-coaster clammy hands and a lump that would not dissolve in her throat. No fun at this stage of her life.

"Tyler's birthday's coming up, July twenty-fifth," he said. "His dad wants to give him a party, and I can see his heart's not in it."

"We have a great yard, big oak tree, stream. Let me give Tyler a birthday party."

"I couldn't let you do that. I'll take him and some of his friends to a skating rink."

"I want to do it. Let me."

"Sure you want all those little kids running around? And such short notice?"

"It's fine. Hannah's grandsons are here. One of them's even trained as a clown. I'll ask him to rent a costume and entertain the children. They'll love that."

"If you're sure." He looked at her, and she bobbed her head enthusiastically. His next words both pleased and flustered her. "You're a lovely woman, Grace, and right now you look like a kid yourself." He smiled and his eyes were filled with affection. Blushing, she looked away. As if unaware of her discomfort, he continued, "Tyler, all of us, could use a surrogate family. Amy was an orphan. My wife's been gone ten years now. Tyler's never had a grandma."

"And my son Roger's gay, so I'll never be a grandma." She said it uneasily, concerned that a former Army man might be homophobic.

He spoke casually, as if the news that someone's son was gay were no big deal. "That must be hard on you. You're so good with children."

"I've resigned myself." She smiled. "It'll be fun having a birthday party for Tyler. What will he be, eight?"

Bob nodded. "It's wonderful of you to do this. I'll pay for the boy's clown costume."

"It's hot in late July. We'll set up tables and chairs under the great oak and serve lots of cake and ice cream. I'll need you to give me a list of Tyler's friends and their phone numbers."

"I'll take care of the tables and chairs. Anything else you need me to do, just tell me. It's settled then."

Bob reached over and squeezed her hand gently.

But Amelia's question continued to nag at her. "Did you spend a lot of time overseas?"

"Too much, twice to France, three times to Germany, a stint in Italy, the Philippines, Japan, Korea."

The word Korea burned like a hot coal in Grace's brain. Amelia had said Korea. "How about your family, they go, too?" Unaccustomed and uncomfortable as it was for her to pry, she pushed on. Her palms grew sweaty.

"My wife, Pat, went in the early years. Pat had her own ideas about how she wanted to live, and she hated uprooting. Who could argue?" He shrugged. "I wasn't home most of the time. After Russell came she refused to join me when I was transferred, and that was every couple of years. We bought a house in Atlanta. She had her own business, interior decorating, and a housekeeper who raised the boy.

"I was fifty-two when I got out. Thought I'd fish, catch up on reading, take it easy. Pat wasn't used to having me home. It was hard on her, and me. We both nearly went nuts, so I took a job selling encyclopedias. Hated that. I went back to college, got a master's degree in history so I could teach."

They left the highway and started down the tightly trafficked streets of the old downtown area of Johnson City. Bob swung the car into a parking lot alongside a low, redbrick building with a glass front and signage that read MOUNTAIN MAN PRESS. "Amy was a fine young woman. I miss her," he said, and Grace, sensitive to the crack in his voice, ached for his loss, for all their losses. "Amy would have liked you, Grace."

"Why, thank you," she said, blushing.

After picking up the material from the printer, they lunched in a cheerful Italian restaurant with murals of the Bridge of Sighs in Venice, the church of Santa Maria Novella in Florence, the Baths of Caracalla and another of the Trevi Fountain in Rome painted on the walls. At eleven o'clock they were the only customers, and from speakers centered throughout the room poured the voices of the Three Tenors singing Neapolitan love songs. The restaurant seemed new, the seats in the booths firm and shiny green, and Grace discovered that sitting alongside Bob in the car, not having to cope with the intensity of his gaze, had been easier than sitting across from him at the table. She picked at her chicken Parmesan. He ate meatballs and spaghetti with gusto. She hardly spoke. He ate and talked, ate and talked.

"I have a theory," he said, taking a swallow of wine. "I lay the problems in this country of ours — crime, stress-related illnesses, teenage suicide, divorce — right at the feet of corporate America. They've foisted mobility on families for fifty years now. I taught high school. Insecure kids who didn't belong anywhere, working parents, no grandparents around, no support systems, every two years a new school, new neighborhood. Women work yet they also end up being responsible for finding the new doctor, dentist, shoe stores, all those necessities that bolster life in the new suburb." His brow furrowed as he leaned toward her, elbows on the table. "We've got major problems in this country, and I say it's because of the demise of the extended family and all this grueling mobility."

"Ted was classified 4-F. A childhood accident left one of his legs an inch shorter than the other. It never occurred to either of us to ever leave Dentry." She looked up at him quizzically. "Doesn't the Army move people all the time?"

"They share the blame, of course, but Army brats as we call them have some advantages. There's a shared mystique you might say. Army families meet up with others they've known on other bases, they have the PX, military hospitals, spoken and unspoken social rules. Seems to me they bond more easily." He stopped, his eyes somber now, and beckoned the waiter for another glass of wine.

"I'm an anomaly then," she said. The waiter brought his wine and another bread basket, and Grace reached for a hot, crusty garlic stick.

"How so?"

She held up four fingers, one by one. "Born in Dentry, Ohio. Met and married Ted there. Raised my son there. Expected to die there."

"What did it feel like being rooted in one place all your life?"

"I never thought about it. Good, I guess. I certainly felt at home."

He sat back in his chair. "How'd I get on this topic? It's a pet peeve of mine. Sorry." He finished his wine and leaned toward her. One glass of wine was her absolute limit, and she felt warm and tingly, or was it more than the wine?

"How do you like living in Covington?" he asked. "It's quite a small town, more of a village."

"Small yes, but close enough to Mars Hill and Asheville. Covington's beautiful. People care about their neighbors. You saw how many came to help search for Amelia." She fingered the stem of her empty wineglass. "When I lived in Branston, I used to pine for Dentry. Here in North Carolina it's different. I love sharing the house with Hannah and Amelia. They're wonderful friends, and I have my work at the school."

His next question stunned her. "What did you say Amelia's last name was?"

"Declose."

"Declose. Why does that name ring a bell?" His brows knitted and for a moment his eyes clouded.

Hannah had been encouraging Grace to speak up, to say what she thought and ask for what she wanted. She was getting better at it but in no way felt secure doing so. Now she took a deep breath and hardly recognized her own voice when she spoke. "When I mentioned you to Amelia, she said she'd known a Bob Richardson long ago in Korea. Her husband, Thomas, was with the Red Cross. Did you know them?" She sat there waiting to exhale. Ted came to mind. He always said that men disliked talking about feelings or having people ask too many questions. If she asked Ted, "How was your day?" he'd grunt, "Same as usual," from behind the newspaper. If she asked him his opinion on some matter, social or political, he'd say, "Gosh, Grace, we've lived together so long you know everything I'm thinking." With a swish she breathed out.

Bob's fingers tapped the table. "I knew some people by that name once. I doubt if I'd know them if I ran into them in the street."

"Thomas is dead, but Amelia's very much alive and still very attractive." Grace was amazed at her description of Amelia. Why had she said such a thing?

"Be that as it may. I don't care one way or the other. You're blushing," he said, reaching over and touching her cheek with his fingers. "It's charming that you blush."

"I never," she blurted, bringing her palms to her cheeks.

"Never what?"

One thing she was sure of, she could never compete with Amelia. She ached to ask him how well he had known Amelia and Thomas, and if Amelia had been anything special to him, but that would be going too far.

"I'm sorry I pried. Maybe we should be getting back." She folded her napkin and laid it on the table.

"I hardly call your questions prying. There's so much we don't know about one another. I want to know more about you, and you can ask me anything you'd like."

The restaurant was now filled with people and noisy conversations; the Three Tenors were now replaced with music that galloped to a drumbeat. Grace's neck and shoulders tightened. All she could think of was getting out of there.

Bob paid the bill, and they walked into the warm summer afternoon. He reached for her hand, and without thinking she wrapped her fingers about his. Ted was embarrassed by any public display of affection. It felt wonderful to hold Bob's hand, and she didn't care who saw them, or perhaps she didn't care because there was no one here who knew them?

In the car Bob stared at the windshield, turned on the engine and the air-conditioning, but made no move to shift into gear. Heaving a sigh, he turned to her. "Grace. Let's clear this up, shall we? It's been a lifetime since I knew this Amelia Declose woman, if that's her at all. Her husband was a big shot with the Red Cross, organized huge relief efforts. A fine man, as I recall, considerably older than his wife. He was quite sick when I knew them, gout or something." His tone was detached and unemotional. "I was waiting for orders to go home. Suddenly I'm assigned to escort Declose's wife to official functions. Maybe I should have been happy for a soft assignment, but I didn't have patience baby-sitting a spoiled woman." He sighed. "Anyhow, we ended up friends, probably out of sheer boredom." He cleared his throat. "My orders came and I was out of there. I never heard from either of them again. Never wanted to." He lifted Grace's hand and kissed it, a long slow kiss. "Satisfied?"

"Yes." How good friends were you? she ached to ask, and didn't. Instead she said, "You'll meet her again at Tyler's birthday party."

"I haven't the slightest interest in the woman. I'm interested in you."

She wanted to believe him, but Amelia was pretty and charming. "Amelia's a lovely-looking woman." Again she couldn't believe what she was saying.

His eyes gleamed, intense and seductive. "I repeat, I'm interested in you."

"Let's wait and see how you feel when you meet her."

"You're worrying about nothing. I say we forget it and enjoy the ride back."

21

Going to Pieces

✿ "What's your favorite color?" Grace asked Tyler.

The boy's big black eyes sparkled. "You mean like for T-shirts, stuff like that?"

"Or like for walls or towels and yes, T-shirts." Grace tousled his hair.

"Blue and yellow." He knew, she could read it in his eyes, but he would pretend that his party was a surprise. She hugged him.

When July 25 arrived, bright blue and yellow streamers and helium balloons festooned the porch of the farmhouse. Under the big oak blue and yellow balloons floated to almost the top branches and on one of the tables, presents were stacked high. The cake Grace made was rectangular, frosted in white with blue soldiers marching along the sides and tall yellow candles in the center and *Happy Birthday Tyler* across the top.

A dozen children, their parents, and

Brenda Tate had arrived and the adults chatted on the porch while their youngsters pranced behind Philip, who was dressed as a clown. Earlier that day, Hannah had taken Philip to Asheville and returned with huge, floppy purple shoes, baggy electric-blue pants, a big red nose, enormous, wire-rimmed spectacles, and a yellow mop of a wig. Now Philip plopped pointed hats onto the heads of boys and girls, handed each child a small wooden flute, and with much laughter and skipping led them, Pied Piper–style, down one side of the stream, around the big oak, and up the other side of the stream.

Tyler and his family were late, a flat tire Russell had phoned to say. An edgy Grace checked the ice cream in a cooler under the oak. Was it staying frozen? No. The ice creams: strawberry, Tyler's favorite, and the chocolate and vanilla were softening. Nearby Sammy leaned indifferently against the tree, his hands shoved into his jeans, a blade of grass between his teeth. Periodically he looked with disdain at his brother frolicking with the children. That boy's unhappy, Grace thought. "Sammy. Give me a hand will you? This ice cream needs to go in the house, into the freezer in the pantry."

Sammy appeared not to hear her, then, as if he had weighed the pros and cons and decided in her favor, he ambled over to where she stood. "Do what?"

"Help me get this ice cream back into the freezer in the pantry before it melts, please." His breath smelled of liquor and not for the first time.

"Can do." He swung the ice chest, which she could hardly pull along the ground, onto his shoulder and swaggered toward the house. Grace watched him go, strong and sleek as a tiger. Then, out of the corner of her eye, she saw the white sedan pull in behind a red station wagon parked on the road. Tyler dashed from the car and raced across the grass toward his friends and the clown.

Russell Richardson, a short, stocky man with sad, dark eyes and a slow smile, bent to examine one of the car's tires, then he and his father walked toward the house.

Greet him, Grace urged herself, but her feet were leaden. She watched from the shade of the oak as Bob and Russell reached the porch. Brenda Tate stood chatting with Hannah. Grace could not hear their conversation.

"Grace," Hannah called. "Grace."

Finally, Grace started forward, but at the

very same moment the front door swung wide. Sleek, slender, and regal and with a deep blue scarf arranged smartly about her neck, Amelia stepped onto the porch. With a thudding heart, Grace watched Bob extend his hand to Amelia. Then Hannah, Brenda Tate, and Russell closed about them, obliterating her view. Grace squared her shoulders, plastered a smile on her face, and walked rapidly toward the house.

"Grace. It is the same Bob Richardson, isn't that amazing?"

Grace's heart plunged. Who could resist such an attractive woman? "Amazing," she replied. Dowdy was how she felt. Just plain dowdy. With her plaid apron covering her dress, she felt like somebody's house-keeper.

Bob moved to Grace's side, took her elbow, and propelled her into the circle. His tone was casual when he spoke to Amelia. "What year was that, 1954–55?"

Amelia glowed like a bright white daisy facing the sun. Grace envied her.

Children's shrieks of pleasure came from the lawn, drawing Bob's eyes to Philip and the children. "I'm sorry we're late. Flat tire and no jack in Russell's car. We had to wait for AAA. What can I do to help?"

"Grace is a fantastic organizer, she's

planned this party to the smallest detail." Amelia hooked her arm possessively through Bob's. "You don't mind, do you, Grace, if I show Bob about the property?"

Grace minded. She was so upset she never noticed Bob's hesitation, the way his apologetic eyes sought hers. Awash in emotions, Grace's ability to reason lessened the moment Amelia fastened her arm in Bob's and led him down the steps and around the corner. Shy, unsophisticated, courted by only one man, Ted Singleton, Grace felt diminished by Amelia's worldliness and vivacity. Amelia would capture Bob's imagination and interest, and she had to admit, it mattered terribly.

"Excuse me," Grace said to the others. "I've got to get back to the tent." Occasionally the sound of Amelia's gay laughter reached her, and when it did, Grace wallowed in self-pity and an intensifying sense of loneliness. Then the full weight of the party was upon her. Philip led the children under the big oak, and for the next half hour Grace and Russell served cake and ice cream. With a swoosh, Tyler blew out all eight candles. When Susan Prentiss, a girl he liked from his class, dripped ice cream down the front of her dress and cried, Tyler borrowed Grace's bandanna, wet it, and handed it to Susan to wipe her dress. "Keep it," he said to Susan. "Mrs. Grace has lots and lots of them."

Bobbie Franklin, the oldest and biggest boy at the party, overturned his lemonade, wetting another child, who screamed loudly for his mother.

Russell passed Tyler his gifts, and Tyler beamed with pleasure and remembered to thank each giver and then, somewhat reluctantly, passed everything around. Two children fought and had to be separated, then all the children ran back out onto the lawn to play. Russell helped Grace return the gifts to their boxes.

"Where's Dad?" Russell asked.

Grace could hardly hide the sarcasm in her voice. "Off with Amelia. They knew each other years ago in Korea, didn't you know?"

He gave her a puzzled look. "Why no, I didn't know." Russell left the tent to distribute kites to all the children, who then raced about the lawn hefting kites into the air and screaming with delight when the wind captured one and swooped it off the ground.

A half hour later as Grace, Russell, and Hannah were cleaning up, Amelia breezed around the corner of the house, her arm still fastened in Bob's. Grace turned away, missing the look of relief on Bob's face as he disengaged from Amelia and walked briskly toward the tent, his eyes fixed on Grace.

Hannah watched and said nothing.

As Bob strode up to her, Grace turned from him and crumpled the paper birthday tablecloth and dumped it into a trash barrel. "How can I help?" he asked.

"You're too late." Grabbing a plastic sack of unused party plates and cups, Grace loped toward the house unaware that Russell had intercepted Bob as he started to follow her. She did not hear Russell ask his father for help folding the rented chairs and tables. Bob stayed behind, and that was her answer. She was devastated. He had led her on. She cared for this man, and he had betrayed her trust. Self-pity consumed her. I'll never be able to look him, or Amelia, in the eye again she told herself.

When Russell left the tent with Tyler in tow, Bob again headed for the house, but was intercepted by Philip, whose arms were loaded with Tyler's gifts. And when Grace heard the front door slam, her heart lifted, then fell, as Tyler's voice called, "Mrs. Grace, I've come to kiss you good-bye." She wiped her eyes and responded, "In here, honey." Moments later he threw his arms about her.

"I love you, Mrs. Grace. Thanks for my party. I love the clown. I love strawberry ice cream. Thank you." Another wet kiss and he was gone.

When Bob called to her from the porch, Grace chose not to reply. He had come to make excuses, to let her down gently.

"Grace," Bob called again and again; then turning, he walked slowly down the steps, looking back twice, as if hoping she would appear in the doorway.

Car doors slammed. Peeping from the kitchen window, Grace saw Hannah's grandsons helping to load Russell's car. Hannah had mentioned taking them to Mars Hill to some concert later. She watched Russell's car drive away. Blind with humiliation and a deep sense of betrayal and certain that she stood no chance against Amelia, Grace ground the tears away with the heel of her fist. And when Amelia's light step and Hannah's voice sounded from the front porch, Grace staggered to her feet, too agitated and teary to face her rival. Rushing from the kitchen, she managed the stairs two at a time, locked her bedroom door, and threw herself face down on her bed. Had she been a fly on the kitchen wall she could have saved herself days of misery.

"Isn't Bob a nice man?" Amelia asked as she leaned against the kitchen doorjamb.

"Quite a reunion, you two had." Hannah turned from washing glasses, raised an eyebrow, and looked with skepticism into Amelia's eyes.

"Why the look? Did I do something wrong?"

"You two were gone a long time."

"Sorry about that." Amelia waved her hand in a dismissive manner. "It was a chance to talk about my life and about Thomas. Bob's a tiny bit of my past, someone who knew me when I was young." She loosened her scarf as if she would pull it off and stopped, her hand in the air, her eyes far away. "We talked about Thomas." She shrugged, shook her head, and moving away from the door came closer to Hannah.

"Why tell me?" Hannah asked. "Tell Grace."

"I will tell her. Where is she, upstairs?"

Hannah shrugged.

Amelia's voice was soft yet urgent. "When I was a little girl I had a family:

Thanksgiving dinners at Aunt Clea's, Christmas with my grandparents, summers at the beach. Thomas was a man with a mission, a worldwide mission. I lived in his shadow. All those years we never owned a home, until Silver Lake. I have no family left, no roots like Grace has in Dentry. I have no children or grandchildren." A haunted look crept into her eyes. "Bob and I, long ago, our lives touched." She bit her lower lip and looked past Hannah. "For a brief moment this afternoon when Bob Richardson walked up those steps, I actually felt young again."

"I wouldn't mention that to Grace."

"Does she think I'm after Bob Richardson?" Her voice cracked. She turned away. "Well, I'm not." She tossed her head. "It's just that I've been so alone these past years." Amelia focused her eyes on Hannah. "Bob Richardson's got no interest in me. I dragged him to see the orchard and up to the spring." Her pose turned defiant, hands on hips, head thrown back. Her enormous blue eyes confronted Hannah, as if daring her to argue. "I told him about Caroline, about Thomas, but not about this." Her hand went to her neck. "He talked about Grace, how kind and good she is, how much Tyler loves her.

Grace. Grace. Grace." Suddenly contrite and childlike, Amelia's eyes pleaded for understanding. "Nice for Grace, don't you think?" Her voice turned melancholy. "He was itching to get away from me, to be with Grace."

It was clear to Hannah that Amelia vacillated between wounded pride and contriteness. Noticing a tremor in Amelia's hand, Hannah felt a momentary empathy for this pale, slight woman. It threatened to override the clarity of her irritation at Amelia's self-centeredness. Amelia had hurt Grace and disturbed the harmony of their household.

"Is Grace terribly mad at me?" She did not wait for Hannah's reply, but opened her eyes wide as if experiencing a revelation, and grinned. "She'll forgive me. Grace is too kindhearted, too generous not to."

Will it be so easily solved? Hannah wondered as she studied the wood grain of the kitchen table.

"I'll talk to Grace." Amelia circled the table and kneeled beside Hannah. "I've got a two-day photography field trip. We leave early tomorrow. It's late now. I'll clear this up with Grace in the morning before I leave." Resting her hands on Hannah's knees, Amelia looked up into her eyes. "You're so self-contained, Hannah. Don't you ever feel alone and frightened?" Running her hand across her forehead, Amelia covered her eyes for a moment. "I envy Grace. Bob really cares about her. No one will ever love me or want me in that special way again." Her voice brimmed with longing and regret, and she sat back on her heels. "I'm very tired. Life's odd, isn't it? I nearly died from hypothermia in a forest and now this." She rose and headed for the door. "Good night, Hannah."

Amelia did not say it to Hannah but Bob's unexpected reappearance had jolted her, lifted her spirits, then dashed them, leaving her pining for her husband and child, certain once more that the best of her life was over.

Alone in the kitchen Hannah brooded about the situation in their household. "Bob really cares about Grace," Amelia had said. Hannah suspected as much and the sense of abandonment she herself felt at the thought that Bob and Grace might marry returned. Hannah shook her head and lowered her face into her arms on the table. She was no stranger to loneliness. Many nights at Olive Pruitt's she had lain awake worrying about how she would die and where? Would she be alone? And if she lived a long time, what would she do with the rest of her life? Since Grace had been seeing Bob, she often awakened at two or three in the morning worrying about how life would change, how she would ward off the emptiness and sadness should Grace marry Bob and move away. What Amelia had said in the kitchen made that seem more possible than ever.

Hannah blew her nose and sat straight. Amelia brought whimsy, laughter to the household. She, Hannah offered stability and clarity. But it was Grace, thoughtful caring Grace, who was the heart of their home.

Hannah had intuited almost from the start, though Grace had not yet verbalized it, that Grace loved Bob. This was obvious, first by her crestfallen face when Amelia traipsed off with Bob and then by her display of irrational impetuous behavior upon their return. On Grace's behalf, Hannah's anger flared. Grace was her dearest friend, a boon to her existence. Unconscionable for Amelia to distract and detain Bob so long. And now, sitting in the kitchen, she realized that Amelia's brief and failed flirtation with Bob Richardson, plus Grace's insecurity about herself as a woman, threatened to tear their gently crafted world apart.

The phone rang five times before Hannah set down a wet bowl, wiped her hands, and picked it up. "Bob. It's late. I don't know. Let me call her."

"I'm in the bathroom," came Grace's muffled reply from upstairs.

Bob phoned three times, and each time Grace fudged. "She's exhausted," Hannah told Bob. "Call her tomorrow." I'll talk to her tomorrow, Hannah promised herself as she turned off the kitchen light and, by the hall light they always left on, began to climb the stairs to her bedroom. But before she had a chance to fix things between Grace and Bob, Hannah found herself having to fix things in her own life.

22

The Car Auction

✿ Hannah had pushed the limits of her strength to show her grandsons a good time. The week before Tyler's party, she had taken them to the Biltmore House.

"Who wants to walk around an old place like this?" Sammy asked as they joined a tour of the house.

Touring the Biltmore House was expensive, but Hannah would have done anything at all to make them happy, to see them smile. Neither of them smiled much that day.

Hannah reserved a river raft for them at Hot Springs. It was a forty-minute drive down a winding gorge to the French Broad River. There she rolled up her pant legs, took off her shoes, and stepped gingerly into the cold rushing water at the edge of the bank to climb into the raft with the boys. At first the river was fairly calm. Wonderful trees hung far over the banks. The sky was blue. "Partly a number-two river, partly a number three," their guide said, and although there were few seriously swirling rapids, those they encountered tossed them about like corn being popped and when they reached their destination, five miles down the river, and climbed from the raft, they were wet and cold. But she had survived it, even enjoyed it, and so it seemed had the boys, until Sammy said, "I've been on cooler white water," and Philip had nodded agreement.

"But this was good too, Grandma," Philip said, then grew quiet as Sammy gave him a disgusted look.

She had thought perhaps the Antique Car Museum down behind the Grove Park Inn or the day they spent at Cherokee for a performance of *Unto These Hills* — the story of the expulsion of the Cherokee people from their homeland — might please them, but no matter how they seemed to be enjoying it, following Sammy's lead, they had maintained a sullen silence on the way home. Philip at least sneaked a smile at her now and then when his brother wasn't watching.

Yesterday, she had found beer can caps and an empty liquor bottle under Sammy's bed when she was cleaning. She was appalled. Knew she must question them on this. Adding to her stress, she had not even had time to relax over tea with Amelia and Grace in the afternoons. A meeting with the builder of the greenhouse was postponed, letters from a wholesaler in Florida remained unanswered. Her exhaustion, from all the driving and walking, was compounded by her disappointment that it was all for naught.

And now Miranda had sent a check for three thousand dollars to buy a used car in North Carolina for the boys, one Sammy could drive home.

"Let's go get my car," he demanded the day the check arrived.

"Not today," Hannah had said, firmly. "Your mother's check has to clear the bank, and I've asked my friend, Harold Tate, to help us find a good used car for you."

"What do I need some old guy from around here for? What does he know about cars?"

"More than I do," Hannah replied.

"Well, I know what I want." Clearly annoyed, Sammy sulked all day.

Her grandsons had been in Covington ten days at the time of Tyler's party, yet Hannah felt utterly drained. They were virtual strangers. She fished the depths of memory and could not recall spending an entire day with them since they were three and five and Miranda had asked her to baby-sit one afternoon. Immediately Sammy had kicked, then tripped, Philip, who'd screamed in response and promptly pitched a plastic car at his brother's head. The battle had been joined.

"God, Miranda I can't take the noise and all that anger and hitting. I can relate to them only one at a time," she said when her daughter arrived to pick them up.

"They're brothers," Miranda said. "They have to learn to get along."

"Not on my time." Hannah had been adamant, and Miranda stopped bringing the boys. Now at sixteen and almost eighteen they were joined at the hip, conspiratorial, secretive, rejecting her every overture.

"Don't worry, Hannah. It takes time. This is how teenagers act," Grace had said.

Now, the morning after Tyler's party, as Hannah waited for Grace to come down, she mixed pancake batter in a yellow pottery bowl and counted the days to her grandsons' departure. Then the phone rang, and Harold Tate's familiar drawl came over the line.

"Hannah, a car dealer friend of mine's

arranged for us to go down to the car auction. Think we can find the boys a good used car."

"Thanks, Harold," she said, all the while thinking about Grace. She's usually down by now. Got to get her to listen to me, talk about this. No time now. Later when I get home.

"Harold Tate's coming to take us to an auction to look for a car for you," Hannah announced as Philip and Sammy shuffled into the kitchen.

"That's super," Philip said.

"About time," Sammy muttered as he stacked pancakes on his plate and doused them with syrup. They don't talk much, Hannah thought, but they sure can eat.

An hour later, they were on their way with Harold in Brenda's Ford Explorer. The auction house, located about a half mile past the airport, turned out to be as long as a football field, a gray, rectangular, metal building with three garage-like entrances. In a large field of stubby grass and dirt, hundreds of cars and trucks were lined up, all with numbers painted in white on their windshields along with the make, year, mileage.

With Hannah and the boys in tow, Harold elbowed his way through a cluster of people chatting near a blue Nissan hatchback. The number on the windshield was fifty-three.

"This here's the one my friend, Gus, spotted for you." He walked around the car, bent to check the tires. "Tread's fine." He opened the hood and leaned into the car. "Gus says it rides like a charm."

Sammy opened the front driver's-side door. "Cool. Leather seats."

"It's a noisy place, isn't it?" Hannah said, holding tight to her purse. She was decidedly out of her element among the cigar-smoking, tobacco-chewing men milling about in their overalls and boots. A weatherworn old man with shoulder-length gray hair stomped by, his hand resting easily on a gun in the holster strapped to his thigh. He wore a cowboy hat and boots with spurs. Hannah instinctively drew back.

"That's Rodeo Man. He's harmless," Harold Tate said. "Spends his days wanderin' about the auction grounds. Gun's empty. Guard checks it every time he comes into the place."

"Come on, Grandma." Philip took her arm. "Let's go inside."

If only Philip had come alone, Hannah

thought, she could talk with him, get to know him.

Noise exploded about them as they stepped into the big building through one of the bays. The huge space was hot and dusty and bristled with animated, chattering men, women and children of all ages; the air in the room quivered with the bluish haze of tobacco smoke.

"Come on over here, Hannah, boys," Harold Tate said, easing sideways past people into another bay. "This is where we're going to bid on number fifty-three."

The place was Grand Central Station — a fairground, a playground for children, yelling and screaming and running helter-skelter. People laughed and joked and lined up in one area to buy hot dogs, corn dogs, cheese-doused nachos, chili, doughnuts, popcorn, and candy from vendors' counters. Another section of the huge space provided fenced-off child care. From a loudspeaker, Johnny Cash's voice could be heard belting out "I Walk the Line," one of the few country western songs Hannah recognized. The noise deafened and offended Hannah. Boys and cars! She grimaced, wishing she could just walk out and the boys were subdued.

The blue Nissan, number fifty-three, was

lined up, fourth car down, between the bays. Suddenly, in the midst of the din a short, lean man in a plaid shirt stepped onto a podium on the platform and the bidding began.

"Open at two thousand five hundred dollars for number fifty. Do I hear three thousand? Three thousand five hundred? Four thousand?" A bang startled Hannah as the auctioneer brought his gavel down. "Sold, number fifty at four thousand dollars." Words erupted so fast that Hannah was totally lost. Then another bang of the gavel and the auctioneer called, "Sold, number fifty-two at four thousand, two hundred and fifty dollars." What about number fifty-one? Hannah wondered. Then she noticed a white Buick, number fifty-two, being driven out of the place. And now the blue Nissan was the first car in line.

"Do I hear fifteen hundred for number fifty-three? A Nissan." A hand shot up. "A steal at two thousand." More sales pitch as his momentum picked up. His words became unintelligible to Hannah as he kept up a steady litany of she knew not what. "Do I hear two thousand five hundred?"

Next to her Harold Tate, his face immobile, scratched his shoulder.

"Two thousand, five hundred, going, going, sold at two thousand five hundred dollars."

The Nissan was being driven away, replaced by a Grand Am, and the auctioneer was off again. It was over. The Nissan had been sold for two thousand five hundred dollars. Why hadn't Harold bid? She was totally confused and astonished when Harold rose, took her by the arm, and squired her, followed by Sammy and Philip, to a table where a woman sat before a pile of papers.

"Whose name's this Nissan goin' in?" the woman asked. Her florid face was circled by a beehive of stiffly sprayed blond hair. She chewed gum furiously, but she was obviously efficient, and moments later Sammy had the necessary papers in hand. Hair lady instructed them to take the papers to the office and pointed to the left. The next minute, they were on their way to pay for the Nissan and to get insurance.

"How ever did you do that, Harold? Never saw you raise your hand."

"Scratched my shoulder. That's my sign."

"Scratched your shoulder?"

"Some folks wink, wiggle their nose, lift

their finger." He wiggled his pinkie. "I've come with Gus a time or two. I scratch. Auctioneer knows."

"Thanks lots, Mr. Tate," Philip said. There was admiration in his eyes.

Harold went with Sammy to make the payment.

"It's a cool car," Philip said, patting the hood.

"Tomorrow we burn rubber," Sammy said when he rejoined them at the car.

"No burning rubber, young man," Hannah said sternly.

"Just kidding," he said, but a conspiratorial look passed between him and Philip.

23

Waiting and Worrying

Grace spent an interminable, sleepless night questioning her assumptions and expectations about friendship, love, and trust. She felt as if she had tumbled into a giant clothes dryer and been pitched and tossed up, down, and sideways.

What hurt the most was that she had loved Amelia and trusted her. Hard as it was to admit, she loved Bob. He was the first, the only, man she had ever entertained as a possible companion other than Ted, and he had deceived her.

Her emotions, twisted and gnarled, oscillated from hate to love, hate to love, and hate again. She wanted to wish them well, but couldn't. She wanted them to be happy, but begrudged them happiness. The range of emotions she felt exhausted her. She appalled herself with the recurring thought that her life would be happy had Amelia not been rescued from the forest. Such malevolent musings, she shuddered to think, tapped a dark, unacceptable, evil part of herself, the evil her father had insisted lurked in the corners of every man's smile.

The philosophy that the less she wanted the less disappointed she would be in life had been instilled from childhood, and as Grace swept her hair off of her face she fumed at herself for lowering her guard and welcoming Bob into her life. Suddenly the sense of her father's critical presence loomed all about her.

"You're old, Grace. Act your age," he would surely say.

He would be right. She was too fat, too old, too late for love. It was presumptuous of her to dream, yet, even now, remembering Bob kissing her hand, his seductive voice and eyes indicating his interest in her, her heart beat faster, her whole body weakened. Lies! Her hairbrush clattered to the floor.

Voices below drew Grace to the window, from where she watched as Harold held the front passenger-side door of his wife's Explorer open for Hannah. The boys were already in the back. "Don't leave me here alone today, Hannah," Grace whispered as she watched them drive away.

The phone rang, loud and insistent.

Grace froze. Why didn't Amelia answer it? The she remembered. Amelia had won first prize for her picture of the little girl and her bicycle, the one Grace had selected. This morning, she had ignored Amelia's knock on her door, closed her ears to the thump when Amelia dropped something on the landing, recoiled from the sound of Amelia's laughter mingled with Mike's in the drive below, heard his van door slam, and the van drive away. The woman had gone off on yet another photography workshop.

The desperate need to talk to Hannah mounted in her, but Hannah might be gone for hours. "I can't sit here and stare at the walls," Grace mumbled. Desperate to divert herself, Grace raced downstairs and to the station wagon. She would go to Malaprop's Bookstore/Café in Asheville where she could always find a good book, where she could relax with a cup of tea, read the newspaper. Maybe there'd be a speaker or an author's book signing. Or she would go to a movie, maybe two movies, anything to blot out the thoughts and feelings she was having. Only when she was exhausted would she return.

Later that afternoon, Hannah rode home

from the auction with Harold, and when Sammy zoomed past them on the highway, a monsoon of uneasiness swept over her. Not only was she worried about the boys and the car but there was Grace. Perhaps she and Bob had already patched it all up. If not, she must talk to her. But when Hannah entered the house and called, "Grace," there was no answer, and Grace's door was ajar, her room empty. A note from Amelia posted on the refrigerator reminded her that Amelia would be gone for two days.

Hannah wandered about. She dusted the top of the mantel in the living room, straightened the floral print hanging above it. Outside she picked a bright bouquet of flowers and set them in a vase on the kitchen table. Leftovers would do for herself and the boys. After watching the news, *Wheel of Fortune*, and *Jeopardy*, she showered and retreated to her bed, relieved to be off her feet at last. Even a long day in the garden did not tire her as much as these days with her grandsons. When Sammy knocked at her door, Hannah had just drifted off into a light sleep while watching a mindless sitcom on television.

"We're going into Asheville," Sammy said, sticking his head in the door.

"It's nine o'clock." Hannah was suddenly alert. "You won't get to Asheville before nine-thirty. Where are you going at this hour?"

"Nowhere."

"Nowhere? Where's nowhere, young man?"

"Meeting up with some of the guys we met in the soda shop in Mars Hill, Grandma," Philip said, stepping into the room.

"What guys?"

"One of them's Mr. Tate's nephew. He says they just drive about, or hang out at some dance place in Asheville."

"Everyone goes," Sammy muttered, "that's what guys do here." He shrugged his shoulders and took a small step back toward the door.

Slipping on a bathrobe, Hannah forced herself up and out of bed. In a prone position she felt at a disadvantage. She meant to question them about the empty liquor bottle. "If I say you can't go?"

Sammy leaned against the doorjamb, his arms crossed, his eyes dark and challenging. "Why would you do that? Mom would let us go. Look, we've been shut up out here in the middle of nowhere."

It was the longest sentence he'd said

since his arrival. Hannah reconsidered. They were young. Covington was fine for her and her friends. She was being ridiculous not to trust them. "All right, go. Just be careful driving and be back by midnight."

"She's worse than my dorm proctor," Sammy grunted as they closed her door behind them.

Hannah heard them as they thumped down the stairs and she hated the way she felt: defeated, irritable, out-of-control, apprehensive. Why hadn't she brought up the bottle, the beer caps?

She had determined to stay awake until the boys were home, but now the phone alongside her bed jangled loudly, jerking her awake. It was three in the morning.

"Hello." She heard Grace's groggy voice as she too picked up the phone.

"Hannah Parrish?" A man's voice, gruff and efficient.

"This is Hannah Parrish."

"Officer Benson here, ma'am. I got two young fellers here, your kin, ma'am."

"Sammy? Philip? Where are they?" She was wide awake.

"Hospital emergency room. Car accident. Drunk drivin'. Busted the car up pretty bad."

"Oh my God. What about my grandsons?"

"You'll have to talk to the doctor."

"Just tell me," she pleaded, "are they badly hurt? Broken bones? Burns? Internal injuries?" She was dizzy and confused and needed to ground herself.

"Ma'am, I gotta go," he said.

"Thank you, Officer." The phone went dead, then rang again. Her heart pounded with relief when she heard Philip's voice.

"Grandma. We ran off the road. Doc's gonna set my shoulder." He sounded shaken to the core. "Can you come? Sammy's hurt bad. They wheeled him to surgery, I think. Will you come?"

She wanted to ask who was driving? Had anyone else been involved, another car, other people? Where had it happened? Who was the doctor taking care of them? "Hang in there, boy," she said grimly. "Be there as soon as I can."

There was a light under Grace's door. Hannah knocked. "Grace, you up? The boys were in an accident. They're at the hospital."

Grace, fully dressed, opened the door. "I'm coming with you."

The drive to the hospital seemed to take forever, and they made no attempt to talk.

Bristling with tension, the emergency room looked inhospitable in the glare of bright lights and white-coated doctors and nurses intent on their tasks. A large black-rimmed clock said 3:40. Someone led them to a bank of elevators and gave them a floor number. At the nurses' station a soft-spoken nurse with kind eyes, M. Majors, her nameplate said, put her fingers to her lips indicating silence and led them to a waiting area. "Dr. Milman had another emergency in the hospital," she said. "I'll let him know you're here."

"I want to see my grandsons."

"They're sedated, sleeping," Nurse Majors said. Fifteen minutes later she returned. "Dr. Milman will be up as soon as he can. Help yourselves to coffee." She pointed to a coffeemaker on a table in the corner, then she was gone.

Deeply creased green and brown leather recliners and several green leather couches were set about the room. Tables strewn with magazines also boasted Bibles. Hannah paced.

Dr. Richard Milman, middle-aged, pleasant, balding, with pouches under his eyes, bustled in an hour later and patiently answered Hannah's questions.

"Philip has a broken collarbone and nose and many bruises. He's banged up, but he'll be all right." He flipped over a page on his chart. "We thought the older brother, Sammy, would lose his spleen, but the MRI indicates surgery isn't necessary. He's had a blow to the head, no concussion, several deep gashes, lots of stitches."

"Sammy was drinking, Doctor?"

"I'm afraid so." Dr. Milman flipped the papers on the chart with finality.

"When can they travel, Doctor?"

He raised an eyebrow, looked at her, she thought, as if she'd asked if he was on his way to Mars. "Travel? Week or so."

"Tomorrow?"

Lips pursed, he studied the chart, shook his head. "Might be rough on them; they're pretty banged up."

"Would a plane trip endanger their lives?"

"Well, no."

"Could you give them pain medication for the trip back to their home?"

"Where's that?"

"Philadelphia."

"Yes, I suppose I could."

She nodded, satisfied. "Thank you, Doctor. Can I see them?"

He gave her a curious look. "Yes, for a moment."

Hannah followed Dr. Milman into the hallway. He beckoned Nurse Majors. "Their grandmother can see them." He nodded, threw her one last quizzical look, and walked briskly away.

The shades were drawn. An antiseptic odor cloyed the air. In the dim light Hannah distinguished two beds, their occupants obscured by bandages. A nurse's aide stood by Philip's bed taking his pulse. She turned to Hannah, put her finger to her lips.

A shock ran through Hannah when she saw them, and she reached a hand to the wall to steady herself. A thick wide bandage covered an area near Sammy's eye and spread to his temple. What she could see of his eyes and cheeks were black and blue with bruises. Taped to his arm, a needle infused a clear liquid that dripped steadily from a plastic bag suspended from a pole. Nurse Majors appeared in the doorway. "Lucky young man, gash missed his eyes by a fraction. Dr. Stone, the plastic surgeon, is a genius with stitches; your grandson's lucky he was on call. Twenty stitches, and he'll probably have little if any scarring."

Philip's arm was secured in a sling. A small patch of hair had been shaved above his right ear where a crisscross of black lines identified stitches. Straddling the bridge of his nose ran a long, wide tape. He moaned and turned his head to the wall.

Now that she knew they had no internal injuries and that they had not killed or injured anyone, Hannah's emotions see-sawed between genuine concern for them and anger. She wanted to hug them; she wanted to shake them.

A scene she would have preferred never to revisit invaded her memory — bailing Bill Parrish out of jail again. He had crashed their car while driving drunk. Once out of his cell, he had swaggered about the police station, humiliated her by swatting her on the butt, and had patted the policeman on the back when they left as if they were old friends. She had hated him then, hated the smell of him, his hand touching her. She had been a youthful forty, and coping with a drunk had been grueling then. She couldn't, wouldn't, do it again even if it was her grandson. "Must call Miranda," she muttered.

Philip stirred, opened his eyes. Though glazed, they lit up at the sight of her.

Hannah's heart melted. Philip was not, after all, the drunk driver. Moving to his bedside, she leaned down, patted his hand gently, and smiled. "I'm phoning your mother." That seemed to soothe him, and Hannah stepped back and walked from the room.

Thumbing through a magazine, Grace sat on a sofa in the lounge and looked up as Hannah strode into the room, emptied her purse of change, picked up a pay phone, and placed a call. It was five in the morning.

"Miranda? Sorry to wake you." In a calm, firm voice that belied her agitation, Hannah told her daughter everything she knew about the accident. "No internal injuries. They're going to be fine. It's just that Miranda, my dear, I'm at my wit's end. It's been very difficult having them here, especially Sammy, and now . . . to find out he's been drinking. I can't handle this." She drew a deep breath. "I want you to come and take them home."

Silence on both ends.

"Miranda? Are you there? Can they stay here? No, they can't. I'm worn out. Oh, heavens, I forgot about the business opening. Can Paul come. He's sick? Flu? I'm sorry." She listened, all the while eyes looking down and tapping her foot. Then Hannah looked over at Grace. "Opening so soon? I forgot. Still, if you took an early flight down today, you'd have time to talk to the local police, pay tickets, whatever, and still leave before dark." Hannah's shoulders slumped. She ran her free hand across her forehead and down across her eyes. Her voice grew soft yet urgent. It was a stance and mood Grace had never seen in Hannah. "It's the alcohol. Surely you understand. I just can't have them here any longer. Please, the doctor says they can travel, he'd be sending them home later today anyhow. Please come. I know it's hard, and I sound mean." She shifted position, looked at Grace and shook her head, then focused on the phone. "It's you they need now. They need their mother."

Silence.

"Yes, the doctor said they can travel with medication. Their injuries aren't serious, just well, not very comfortable."

Silence again. Hannah shifted from one leg to the other. "I agree. Life's like that sometimes. Everything gets dumped on you at once." She shrugged, raised an eyebrow, then ran her palm against her left cheek. "They need you now, Miranda, not me. They don't much like me." Another pause. Hannah tapped her foot, held her palm over the receiver. "Miranda's talking to Paul," she said, looking at Grace.

Then Hannah shifted positions, lifted her head, straightened her shoulder, nodded. "I appreciate this. Let me know when, Miranda. I'll meet your plane."

One last peek into their room assured Hannah that her grandsons were asleep. Much as she wanted them to go home, a wave of disappointment coursed through her. All her hopes and plans. She had hoped she'd have a chance to explain and apologize for her distance through the years, but there had been no right moment to talk and no understanding, no possibility of growing closer. Perhaps it was too late. Sadness and a deep regret lingered. She should have gotten to know them. She would have picked up the signs long ago. Maybe Sammy inherited the tendency to drink from his grandfather. She would have told them about Bill and that his drinking was a terrible sickness, but one that could be overcome.

As she and Grace walked through the hospital parking lot toward the car, Hannah said, "Think I was too hard on Miranda?"

"I probably couldn't have done it."

"When you don't have a relationship with your grandchildren from the time they're little, you can't just make it happen overnight. Not so much Philip. I think he'd like to be friends. It's Sammy. Hostile boy." She shook her head. "And he drinks."

"You tried," Grace said.

"I feel like a failure."

"Don't we all at times?" Grace mumbled.

Hannah knew Grace had not talked to Bob. She reminded herself that she must discuss this matter with Grace right now but she was too weary and on the verge of tears. They were silent all the way back to Covington.

The next morning at eight Hannah awakened Grace to say that she was leaving. "I'm off to the hospital. From there, I'm going to pick up Miranda. I'll be gone all day I imagine."

"Okay," Grace mumbled.

"Grace, can we talk when I get back?"

"Sure."

24

Grace Takes the Easy Way Out

✿ When the phone rang Grace considered not answering it. Hannah would get it. No, Hannah had gone to the hospital. Maybe it was Hannah calling her. Maybe the boys were worse and Hannah needed her. Grace, uncharacteristically, flopped onto the delicate, antique quilted bedspread she had chosen with such care and picked up the phone.

"Mother, how are you?" Roger's voice brimmed with enthusiasm. "We're opening the shop next Saturday. Charles and I would like you to be here."

The unaccustomed gentleness of Roger's tone touched her, and her eyes grew misty.

"Mother? Are you there? What's wrong? Are you ill?"

Grace heard the concern in his voice. "I'm fine. Getting over a cold."

Roger persisted. "Sounds like you're

upset. Problem with the ladies?"

She was silent. He continued.

"I know you've never flown, but if you can drive the interstate then you can take the plane and come here, spend as long as you'd like with us. We want you to see the cottage, picket fence and all, that we bought. Charles found it. You'll have a comfortable room. I know you'll love it."

Perspiration rolled down her sides from under her arms. How, if they needed her money so urgently to start a business, were they able to buy a home?

"Mother. Please come." His voice had that old familiar, slightly plaintive little-boy quality that for years had successfully wrangled whatever he wanted from her. "What I wouldn't give for a plate of your meatballs and prunes."

"Fly? I don't know." Yet as he talked, some of the debilitating sadness lifted from her chest. She must get away from Covington, from Bob and Amelia. Roger missed her cooking. There were other favorites she could make: chicken soup with vegetables and rice, and she would treat them to her sugar cookies. It would be like old times. Suddenly aware that she was sitting on the fragile quilt, Grace rose and with one hand smoothed out the wrinkles.

"I think, maybe, I can do it," she said.

"I know you can. Just say the word, Mother, and I'll get you a reservation, see if I can fly you out of there this afternoon, okay? Take a cab to the airport, unless Hannah can drive you. Just pick up the ticket at the airport, at the US Air counter."

"I'll come." How she would step foot on a plane she didn't know, but somehow she would.

His voice lightened. "Wonderful, Mother. Charles and I'll meet you at the gate. We'll be there with open arms."

When she hung up the phone, Grace walked to the mirror and studied her face, then reached for a tube of pale pink lipstick. Her head was bursting with thoughts of moving back to Branston, where she wouldn't have to see Amelia and Bob together, ever.

Excited now, Grace spread a towel to protect her bedspread, then pulled a new soft-sided carry-on bag from the closet and set it on the towel. My goodness, Tyler. She would have to phone Brenda before she left. Hannah. She would leave a note. Hannah would miss her. She would miss Hannah. Having seen the gentler more vulnerable side of Hannah, Grace had come to love this woman who, in a different way, was essentially as vulnerable as she was, though she seemed to have it all together. Grace admired Hannah's deep-seated reverence for the earth. She identified with Hannah's struggle to reach out to her grandsons. Grace would see Hannah when she came to Branston to visit Miranda. Downstairs in the kitchen Grace poured herself a glass of orange juice. Then feeling nervous but excited, she phoned Brenda.

Roger's call came at 11 A.M., confirming her reservations for two that afternoon. Grace's stomach churned. Rapidly and with mounting anxiety she tossed a few items of clothing in the carry-on, then removed everything and laid it all out on the bed. She returned a dress to a hanger in the closet and added a pair of soft, comfortable cotton slacks with a drawstring waist. Hairbrush, shampoo, medication, what was she forgetting? Where was that toothbrush? Wasn't it here a minute ago?

Grace called a cab. Once downstairs, she stood in the foyer, felt the silence of the house, remembered the past months and how she had felt she owned the world. Now she felt empty, as if she had nothing.

A shrill car horn blew several times, yanking her from her musings, and she hastened down the steps and into the taxi. The drive out of Covington seemed endless as the cab wound its way to Mars Hill but then they turned onto Highway 19–23, past Barnardsville, Weaverville, and New Stock Road to Highway 26. Inside the cab she was insulated from the roar of commercial trucks barreling past. Was this trip a mistake? No, she assured herself, she was fine. She would be all right. Time with Roger and Charles would be good for her. She could sort things out. Outside her window the peaks of mountains rose above the low-lying haze. Leaning back against the firm seat, Grace watched the city of Asheville loom ahead then vanish as they swung right and right again and south to the airport.

When they pulled up to the US Air dropoff, the driver turned to look at her. "That'll be fifty dollars."

"What? That's outrageous." Clasping her purse, Grace made no move to open it.

"You can see the meter, ma'am. That's the fare." His face was pockmarked and scowling. Grudgingly she paid him and stepped from the cab carrying her purse and an umbrella and dragging her blue canvas carry-on.

One of the porters disengaged from the

cluster of porters who stood chatting nearby. He smiled at her, took her carry-on, and guided her through the empty airport to the US Air counter where she picked up her ticket and decided to check her carry-on. She tipped the porter, then joined several men looking up at a television screen that announced incoming and outgoing flights. Still berating herself for the expensive cab ride, she settled into a seat outside her gate and waited anxiously for them to announce her flight. When they did Grace ignored her tossing stomach, gritted her teeth, and joined the line of travelers moving slowly down the boarding ramp to the 737 that would take her from Asheville to Charlotte.

With a roar and a shudder the plane lifted from the tarmac. Grace gripped the arms of her seat through the entire flight. When the plane finally touched down safely, she uttered a gasp of relief that drew stares from her seat partner.

"Scared?" the man asked, smiling.

"Terrified. My first flight ever."

"Well," he said, rising to claim his luggage from the overhead rack, "glad it was a good one."

The second leg of the flight, from Charlotte to Philadelphia, was a bit less terrifying. Once they landed, Grace walked up the narrow passage into the noise and bustle of a huge airport. Roger and Charles were hastening toward her, arms wide, all smiles. Charles seemed less ebullient than usual, and Roger more solicitous as he retrieved her bag and guided her past people and traffic to the crowded parking garage.

"I'm terribly excited about our opening," Charles said. He insisted that Grace sit in the front passenger seat, then poked his head close to hers from the backseat and chattered about the much anticipated event. "Trudi Alstead is the star of the musical *Doing It Right* that's been running on Broadway for three years. She lives in Branston, and I literally bumped into her at the bookstore. Imagine we both were holding copies of *Conversations with God*. Our meeting was ordained. Next thing Roger and I were having dinner at her house, a divine mansion on Hyde Boulevard. Corinthian columns, antiques, Florentine marble floors." Charles's voice faded. He coughed, deep rasping coughs.

"Use the inhaler, Charles." Roger looked back briefly.

"I know," Charles answered with soft assertiveness.

Grace heard the wheezing as Charles inhaled. "You don't have asthma, do you, Charles?" Grace asked, turning her body so that she could see him.

"Just a chest cold thing."

Charles coughed again, then collapsed against the seat. A few minutes later, obviously feeling better, he leaned forward. "Trudi and the two of us have become great friends, like we've known each other for years and years."

"Just sit back and rest, Charles," Roger said, and Grace detected a firm but caring note in his voice. "I'll tell Mother." Roger glanced at her briefly and smiled. "Trudi offered to sing at our opening. Her show's going on the road, starting with Philadelphia in a couple of weeks."

"Isn't that nice of her."

"It is. She's a big name. Due to her, we've attracted a lot of press, been written up in the *Philadelphia Inquirer*, and everyone who's anyone's been calling for an invitation."

"Tell her the name of the business, Roger."

"Gracious Entertaining Shop. You made this possible for us, Mother, the gracious is for Grace."

Grace's hand flew to her chest. Overwhelmed with pleasure she fought back tears. When was she ever going to stop being so weepy? "I'm truly flattered," she said, and she was. This was a different Roger than the one she had come to expect and she was glad that she had come.

The eight-lane highway they had been driving on was heavy trafficked, and now they exited onto a busy two-lane. For several minutes they drove in silence. "Recognize where we are?" Roger asked.

"Frankly, no." She had been so happy in Covington that she had relegated Branston to the category of a bad dream.

"See over there?" Charles's hand pushed forward, and her eyes followed his pointing finger. In the distance the top floors of the Isaac Branston General Hospital rose above the trees.

"I recognize the hospital."

Roger slowed, turned the car onto a residential street, and again onto a tree-lined street with charming, well-kept, cottage-type houses, many with white picket fences and dreamy porches furnished with swings and rocking chairs and potted plants.

"Heavens. I had no idea anything like this existed in Branston." Grace felt a twinge of annoyance. Where had the money come from for this charming cottage? Then the quiet pleasant street, the winsome houses, piqued a nostalgia in Grace and a memory of a wintry night: the stillness of a first snowfall, a fire crackling in the living room, Roger lying on his stomach on the rug doing homework, Ted smoking his pipe, reading the newspaper. What had she been doing? Why, watching her loved ones of course and feeling peaceful. The lightness that came with the loving memory was a relief from what she had been going through.

"We found this place two months ago. I wanted to tell you about it straight away, but your son wanted to surprise you, Mother Singleton." As Charles spoke, his eyes shone with excitement. "Our new home is amazingly like Granny's bungalow at Freshwater Bay on the Isle of Wight. Just a few minutes walk from the Farrington Hotel."

"The Farrington Hotel?"

"Very popular these days, smashing views of the bay and downs. Granny left me the bungalow when she died last year, wanted me to have a place to retire. But I sold it, to buy our home here." He rubbed Roger's shoulder gently. "Life's so uncertain." He smiled at Grace. "Don't you agree, we need to make our lives as comfortable as possible today?"

"I guess I do, Charles." She understood now and felt relieved.

"This is it." Roger maneuvered the car between twin maples and into a narrow driveway.

The white picket fence surrounding the property was freshly painted. A wooden gate capped with an arbor festooned with clusters of tiny pink roses opened onto a redbrick path. Painted white with yellow shutters and a yellow front entrance door, the house welcomed them. White wicker furniture on the diminutive front porch caused a slight squeezing of her heart as the farmhouse porch flashed through her mind. The image of the porch was followed by one thought: Amelia. Concentrated as she had been on Roger and Charles, she had, briefly, forgotten her unhappiness, but now like an unwanted guest the sadness returned.

"Get the bag from the boot, Roger, will you?" Charles opened the door of the car and reached for her hand. His skin felt dry, his fingers cool in hers. "Come, Mother Singleton, let's go in through the garden. It's a traditional cottage garden," he said, escorting her to the gate and swinging it wide. "The brick paths run in all four directions. That's a fake well in the center, but I ignore that and I throw in a pence or two and pretend it's a wishing well." His eyes clouded for a moment. Then, as if he had thrown open an opaque window to let in the sunshine, his eyes brightened. "The yellow Welsh poppies and the orange geums were spectacular when we first looked at the place several months ago."

The old familiar wave of Charles's hand comforted Grace, helped mollify her sense that something was wrong. "How beautiful it must have been." She looked about. "It's beautiful now."

Charles guided her along the flower beds. "Don't you just love these pink and white petunias in front of these purple coneflowers? *Echinachea* is the Latin name. Everyone's taking it in pill form these days to ward off colds, flu. Pity I didn't remember about it until it was too late."

They walked past beds of bright blooms, marigolds, petunias, and cosmos and shrubs of bright evergreen holly and maroon-leafed barberry and others that Grace could not identify. Circling the well, they continued toward the steps leading up to the porch. Charles turned from her, coughed several times, and waved his hand, indicating it was nothing, really. A purple clematis vine twisted and squirmed its way in and out of the white trellis alongside the steps.

"That gate leads out back to our courtyard garden," Charles explained, pointing to the end of the porch.

Roger had disappeared around a corner of the house with Grace's bag. Now he stood looking down at them from the porch. "Charles loves this garden. Every week he adds whatever's blooming in the nurseries, and Miranda's no help. They shop together. She eggs him on."

Charles placed his hands on his hips and pivoted slowly around, his eyes combing every inch of the garden. " 'Ah, make the most of what we yet may spend,' " Charles said softly.

Grace recognized the quote from *The Rubaiyat of Omar Khayyam*. "Before we too into the Dust descend" was the line that followed. What was going on here? About to mount the steps, she turned back to look at Charles. A shaft of late afternoon sunlight sliced through the garden and girdled Charles. A vein pulsated in his neck, and suddenly he seemed less robust, less resolute than she remembered him. Grace felt the hairs rise on her arms. Her mind framed a single word, *cancer*. Did Charles have cancer? A horrifying thought. Heaven forbid. A wave of disquietude washed over her.

Before she could speak, Roger started down the steps. Walking rapidly to Charles, Roger put his arm about his shoulder and in so doing pulled Charles out of a seemingly trancelike state and back to them. Charles smiled at Grace, and when they neared her he took her hand and they moved up the steps and into the house.

"You'll love inside," Charles said. "It's been a huge venture, but we've been decorating, almost been right through the cottage. All the wall fitments — the bookcases — every bit done by myself."

And she did love it. Flowered chintz-covered couches, soft beige and pink striped wallpaper, a glass-fronted mahogany bookcase, and a wide, upholstered antique rocking chair gave the cozy room an air of permanence, as if it had been lived in for years, not months. A richly decorated antique cabinet on a stand near the fireplace captured her attention.

"Seventeenth century," Roger said, coming to stand behind her. "The walnut background's oyster veneer." He ran the palm of his hand in a rectangle surrounding the face of the cabinet. "See this contrasting band of pale wood? It encloses these four marquetry panels. See the way the ebony background inside the panels sets off the light brown and green colors of the birds, foliage, and flowers? Lovely, don't you think? We bought it in Morocco a while back. One of those delicious, affordable finds you happen upon once in a lifetime. We use it as a safe, keep wills and other important papers inside."

The walls of her room, their guest room, were a pale dove gray. A deep peach-and-white checkered comforter over a matching dust ruffle covered a four-poster bed. Above the bed hung a white lace canopy. Lending an air of sophistication to the room, an oriental rug in hues of teal and orange and red covered most of the hardwood floor.

"This is your loo," Charles said, opening the bathroom door. "Ours has a Jacuzzi, and you're welcome to use it. We doubled the size of it, tearing out walls and incorporating a small room."

The tour of the house continued. The kitchen startled her, for it was totally out of character with the rest of the house. The room was all tile and glass: tile walls and floor, glass cabinet fronts, tile countertops, and a cheerless, glass-topped kitchen table.

"It's absurd. The former owners were crazy about this decor," Roger said. "If we hadn't bought the place, they'd have torn out every bit of charm, tiled and glassed the whole house."

"We've got our eyes on a cherrywood table and plan to have the oak cabinet doors put back on," Charles said, turning to face her. "You must see the backyard. Come with me." He gestured in the old familiar manner.

Grace turned to Roger to see if he would follow.

"You go ahead. I've just got to put a finishing touch or two on our dinner." She smelled the richness of a thick nourishing soup as Roger lifted the top off the Dutch oven.

From the back porch Grace and Charles stepped down into a walled garden. A circular paved courtyard filled the central area and was surrounded, on every side, by a bank of greenery. Shaded as it was by tall maples, the cool dimness of the area suggested a time just before dawn or at twilight. Three redwood lounge chairs with pink-and-white-striped cushions and two small redwood tables were arranged, conversation distance from one another, near pots of ferns. Suddenly Charles was racked by coughing. There was something wrong, she knew it. Would they tell her?

In an effort to stave off her concern, Grace chattered. "It's a delightful space. So cool, quiet, and peaceful. How did you do it? Whose idea was it?"

"Yes, it's peaceful. Inspired by Italian piazzas." Charles moved unhurriedly about the courtyard, pointing out individual plants. "Hostas, maidenhair ferns, azaleas, rhododendrons. There's a touch of sun in the afternoons over here." Ambling over to one of the lounges, he placed both hands firmly on the back of it. "After the spring, when the shade flowers, the irises, the hesperus, the astilbe are done, we get summer color over there" — he pointed — "from impatiens."

Grace moved close to Charles, surprised at how the possibility of his being ill touched her, upset her. She wanted to put her arms about him and hold him as she had her own child long ago. Was his mother alive? Where did she live? Grace had never asked, and Roger and Charles had never spoken of his family until today.

"I can see it's a very special place. Do you sit out here much?" she asked.

"We've only been in this house since late

May, but yes, we try to sit here every chance we get and every day." Charles leaned against a lounge. "It's like entering a secret world where nothing can reach us."

"We could all use a secret place to go to."

Obviously pleased, Charles smiled. "I buy the plants. I weed. Roger plants and fertilizes. It's a joint venture."

It touched Grace, the love and devotion between them. There was no doubt in her mind that these two men loved one another. Theirs was as good and solid a love as any that a man and woman might share. Compatibility and lasting love were to be treasured wherever found, and obviously her son and his companion shared a deep and true affection, the kind she had begun to hope she could share with Bob. It hurt to think about Bob.

"Dinner's ready," Roger called from inside. "We made a pot of seven-bean soup, and I'm starving." Charles hastened to take the pot of soup from Roger, who carried a tray with bowls and silverware and glasses out into the garden.

They sat around a rustic picnic table lovingly adorned with freshly cut flowers and shimmering in candlelight. The soup was thick, hearty, and filling.

"Where did you learn to make such good soup?" she asked.

"Believe it or not by watching you, when I was growing up. It always smelled so good. Remember how I'd do homework in the kitchen whenever you were making soup?"

Grace cocked her head and studied him. "Why yes," she said, "I do remember. I remember being so pleased to have you there." She took another spoonful of the rich soup. "You certainly learned well."

"Thank you," he replied, looking pleased.

They chatted about food and restaurants and about how they'd found the cottage, after weeks of house hunting. Then Grace excused herself.

"I'm quite tired. It's been a long day for me. Think I'll soak in that nice big tub and go to bed." She kissed each of the men on the cheek. "Thank you for asking me to come, and for the ticket. I'm glad I came."

"We're glad you're here," Charles said, squeezing her hand.

"Enjoy your bath," Roger said.

For a half hour Grace luxuriated in the deep, claw-footed, freestanding tub. Then she stretched out on the big bed and listened to the sounds of the house: the back door closing, the clink of dishes being stacked in the dishwasher, the sloshing of water as the dishwasher was turned on, something dropped and retrieved, the click of a lock, the muffled voices of the men in the hallway as they went to their room.

For Grace the unfamiliar bed, coupled with a long, tiring day, ensured a restless night, that, plus thoughts of Bob. When she thought of him she couldn't help but berate herself for being so gullible. Obviously she had misunderstood his words, misconstrued his attentiveness on their trip to Johnson City. "Dear God," she prayed aloud, "take away this terrible sinking feeling, this sense of meaninglessness. I can't bear it. I feel lost, the way I did after Ted died."

Grace punched the pillows, turned over and shut her eyes, but sleep evaded her. Soon she was sitting up in bed with her light on and a book in her lap, reading the same sentence over and over. Okay she conceded, I'll think this out.

She thought of how Bob had brought excitement and hope into her life. It embarrassed her now thinking how she had preened in the mirror before setting off to tutor Tyler each week, just because she would see Bob. It embarrassed her to even think that along with her innocent 1950s romantic imaginings had come distressingly sensual dreams — from which she awakened drenched with perspiration — that caused her to spring from the bed to douse her face and arms with cold water.

Ted and she had been young and ignorant when they married. All those years fumbling through sex, pretending that she enjoyed it. Maybe Ted pretended too, for as time passed the frequency had diminished.

So different, Bob and Ted. Ted, provincial, set in his ways. Bob, sophisticated, well traveled, well educated. There had been something special between herself and Bob. She was sure of it, for besides the disturbing sexual impulses he sparked in her, Bob had listened to her, treated her as an equal, insisted he was interested only in her. She could see him, see the tiny bridge of freckles that spanned his nose and cheeks. It hurt to think of him, yet with him she had felt intelligent and appreciated.

Grace smoothed the front of her cotton

nightgown. Compared to Amelia she looked and felt frumpy and old-ladyish. It hurt when she pummeled her thigh with her fist. "Look at me," she whispered to no one. "Amelia's slim. Why wouldn't he prefer her?"

Then Grace launched into a conversation with Ted. "So here I am and there's this man I like, but he prefers someone else. Doesn't speak too well for your old girl, Grace." She shook her head resolutely. "Well, I can handle it." Her chin tilted upward. "I drove all the way to North Carolina on an interstate. I've been living far from Dentry in a tiny town named Covington, and I like it, like the people." Then with a flash of determination, "Somehow, I'm going to work this out and not let anyone drive me away from a friend like Hannah and a place I want to be."

Grace sighed. Life would be different now in Covington. Maybe she and Hannah could take a house together, and she could visit Charles and Roger in the summer. Well, it wouldn't be decided tonight. For now, she'd stay here, maybe help in the shop. Feeling a trifle calmer and easier in her mind, Grace turned off the light, pulled the covers to her chin, and lay for a long while talking to herself in the comfortless dark and listening to the creaks and strains of her new surroundings.

25

Mothering — Or the Lack of It

Back in North Carolina the ongoing saga of Hannah and her family was unfolding. Bristling with anger, wound tight as a spring, and with 7 P.M. return reservations for herself and her sons, Miranda arrived in Asheville. Miranda was all business, settling matters with the police, consulting with Dr. Milman, with nary a tear and no fuss made about the accident or its consequences. Again Hannah regretted knowing so little about them as a family.

Dr. Milman, his jaw tight, his eyes disapproving, arranged a 6 P.M. discharge for Philip and Sammy and provided sedatives. In crushing silence Hannah drove them to the airport. Periodically Philip glanced at her, seeming to want to speak, but did not.

"You needn't wait, Mother," Miranda said coolly as she tipped the porter.

But she did, and the wait seemed interminable. The mix of relief and sadness that she experienced when their jet rose into the air lingered on the drive home. It was dusk now, and in the lowering fog the road to Covington seemed to go on forever, offering time to rehash the events of the day.

Miranda had stepped off the plane, stony-faced, and hardly said a word all the way to the hospital or after her visit to the police station. Braced as she was for Miranda's anger, Hannah was unprepared for the overwhelming sense of failure and loneliness that clamped about her torso like an iron vest. Why were family relationships so complicated? As she had so many times, Hannah tried to reconstruct her life with her daughters.

She had tried so hard not to be like her parents: not silent, distant, depressed, and complaining like her mother and certainly not shiftless and irresponsible like her father. Yet she had managed to alienate both her daughters. What could she have done differently? Perhaps she had functioned too much like a hardworking, responsible father rather than a mother. But supporting them financially had been an all-encompassing task. How exhausted she had been at the end of her working day, hardly able to fix a decent meal for the girls, too depleted to ask about their lives or to listen. Their hearts, their minds, even their souls: she had neglected them.

Sammy's drinking had stunned her, roused her old anger toward Bill Parrish. All she could think of when the call had come last night was Sammy drunk and out of control, like his grandfather, yet she could not share her exasperation, her frustration, her sadness with Miranda. In these onerous and exhausting circumstances, they were as strangers unable to talk, to comfort one another, to discuss the event, its outcome, or even the possibilities for the boys' futures.

Watching *Oprah* and other talk shows had opened Hannah's mind to the benefits of counseling. Laura had once told her that she was in counseling, but as far as Hannah could tell, it had changed nothing between them. Should she have asked to be included, flown to Maine? Yes, she should have. Old wounds needed special treatment if they were to heal, and perhaps that treatment was indeed talking therapy. Perhaps with counseling she would not have reacted so violently to Sammy, to the accident, or made the demand on her hardworking daughter to drop everything and fly to Asheville immediately.

"If I'd gone to Alanon maybe I'd have learned to cope with alcoholism, be able to find solutions instead of blindly rejecting," she said aloud to herself.

To relieve her tension as she drove, Hannah continued to talk out loud to the image of Miranda that loomed large in her mind. "I'm sorry. I'm not so smart as I sometimes think I am. I've been derelict as a grandmother, a mother. I hoped to make things right with the boys on this visit of theirs, explain things, tell them I love them but somehow we couldn't connect. I'm frightened by alcoholism. I lost control. I'm so sorry."

Things had appeared to improve between them since the day of their talk at Olive's when Hannah had agreed to sell the nursery. But now, it seemed they were back to square one. Miranda had asked no questions of her and had focused on her sons, which was appropriate, of course, but after listening to the boys grunt and moan as they eased in and out of wheelchairs pushed first by a hospital, then by an airport attendant, Hannah was convinced that she had flunked as a grandmother and, yet again, as a mother.

★ ★ ★

Why is the house so dark? Hannah wondered as she pulled into the driveway and switched off old Nelly's engine. On the unlit porch a mountain of a man rose from a chair and moved to the top of the stairs. Hannah's chest tightened. Nausea made her dizzy. As the figure started down the steps, Hannah punched down the door lock, gripped the steering wheel with her left hand, and fumbled with her right hand to reinsert the key in the ignition.

"Hannah. It's me, Bob Richardson."

The blood rushed back into Hannah's fingers and toes. Her heartbeat slowed. Bottled-up air whooshed from her lungs. She opened the car door, swung her still trembling legs out onto the gravel path, and lighting her way with her flashlight walked carefully toward him. Bob reached out his hand to assist her up the steps.

"You gave me quite a start. Why is everything so dark?" She beamed the flashlight at the entrance door. "Where is everyone?"

"I'm sorry I scared you. No one's here. I've been calling. I came to see Grace yesterday and again today, but she's not here, and I have to talk to her."

"You don't know about the boys, then?"

404

With a little grunt Hannah sank into a chair. She handed Bob the front door keys. He opened the door and reached inside and flipped on the porch light. He looked frazzled. His thick white hair strung out in grooves, as if by running his fingers through it he had worn pathways along his scalp.

"No. What's happened?"

Her long arms dangled loosely over the sides of her chair. "Sammy got a car at the auction. Had it less than twelve hours before he wrecked it driving drunk."

"Good Lord. Are the boys all right?"

"Philip broke his nose and collarbone, but he'll be fine. They thought at first that Sammy would have to have his spleen removed. Turned out he didn't have to. He's badly bruised, cuts, stitches. Miranda, their mother, came and took them home."

"So soon?"

"Yes." Guilt swirled all about her. "I just couldn't handle it." A great weariness settled over her. "Miranda's new business — she's in business, you know, with Grace's son and his friend — opens next Saturday. Terrible timing, but . . ." She shrugged and fanned herself with her purse. "Why am I so hot? Been a long day."

"You push yourself too hard, Hannah."

Bob took the rocker alongside hers and crossed his arms about his chest. "Your grandsons will be fine, I'm sure. Boys are resilient. They're just so darn tough to raise. My son, Russell, went missing at a camp he was at when his mother and I were vacationing in Florida. He was ten. He paddled off in a canoe. No one could find him. The Park Service helped search. They were four of the longest hours of my life before we found him in the Everglades."

"What they put us through, eh?" Hannah started up. "How thoughtless of me. I'm used to Grace offering everyone tea. Join me for a cup?"

Hannah took Bob's arm and they went into the living room, where she switched on two of the low shiny brass lamps, and moved a pottery urn and a candlestick from the coffee table. "Make yourself comfortable. We'll have tea in here."

Hannah headed for the kitchen and soon the kettle whistled on the stove. Then Hannah brought in a tea tray, and with a sigh eased herself into her favorite wing back chair. Most days she could walk, bend, move easily and fairly quickly, but there were times like these last few days when she overdid it. Her mind sped along fast and sharp as ever, but her body refused to keep pace. Dammit. "I'm afraid Grace's gone to visit her son. I found this note, Bob, on the refrigerator." She handed him a piece of pink paper.

"A note?" He reached for it eagerly. "From Grace." His face sobered as he read it. "She's gone to Branston for her son's, Roger's, new business opening. Doesn't know when she'll be back. Darn it." He slapped his knee. "I should never have let Amelia drag me off. I should have been in that tent cutting Tyler's cake with Grace. I shouldn't have let Grace put me off that first night. I should have hung around here and cleared up this whole misunderstanding."

Hannah longed to go upstairs, slip off her clothes, and flop into bed. Not a drop of energy was left in her for a hot shower. She sighed. "I believe Grace thinks she's lost you to Amelia. It's not her nature to fight for what she wants, and in this case she probably feels she can't compete with the elegant A-meel-ia."

"Compete? Grace thinks she's competing? There's no competition. Grace is special to me." He stood abruptly, hitting the coffee table with his knee and jiggling the teacup in its saucer. He reached down to steady it. "What's her son's, Roger's, phone number?"

Hannah copied Roger's number from Grace's note to a piece of paper and handed it to Bob.

"I'll call her."

They spoke a bit further about the boys' accident and the weather, but her drawn pale face, her hair, usually neat but now in disarray, and the slump of her shoulders told him that she was exhausted, and Bob himself was tired and eager to be off. "You look worn out, Hannah. Appreciate the tea . . ." He rose, waved the paper. "And the phone number." He gave her a hug and left her standing in the doorway waving.

"He's really a good man," Hannah said to herself. Expecting Amelia to return, Hannah left the lights on on the front porch as well as in the hall. Then with a Herculean effort, she climbed the stairs and without undressing tumbled onto her bed.

26

The Painful Truth

✿✿ Waking to the reassuring sounds of children's voices drifting from the street, for a moment Grace imagined that she was home in Dentry and that Roger was little. What was he doing playing in the street? She hadn't given him breakfast.

A knock on the door snapped her back to reality. "Would you like breakfast in bed?" Charles's voice sounded bright and cheery.

"Heavens no. I'll be right out."

It was nine in the morning. Concerned that she might be keeping them from the shop at a time when there was still so much to be done, Grace hastened to dress. Within minutes she was sitting across from them at the kitchen table. The sun streamed through the window over the sink, casting pools of light on the black-and-white tile floor. They sat at the glass kitchen table, that Roger had softened with a blue and white cloth and

Rosenthal china. In the center a thick Lalique vase stood, filled with sprays of white and lavender orchids.

For a time they ate in silence. Then Roger placed his hand over Charles's hand. "Mother, we have something to tell you."

Her heart skipped wildly and her fingers trembled around the handle of the teacup as she set it back in its saucer and tried to brace for the blow: Charles had cancer.

"There's no easy way to say this." Roger's eyes were dark-circled, as if he had not slept. He cleared his throat. "Charles is HIV positive."

Time, whole and simple and seamless as an egg, stopped. Grace knew that HIV led to AIDS. Roger's words stunned her, left her stricken, cold, and almost anesthetized. She felt caught up in some unseen force that somehow bound the three of them together. "My God," she said softly.

Charles's hand covered hers. "I'm quite used to the idea now. At first I was terrified." He shrugged. "But it's not the eighties. I could die of a heart attack, like my father did, or a car crash like my mother, and never get AIDS. When I feel especially anxious, I read *Conversations with God* at night; whether it's right or wrong, I find it soothes me, helps me cope."

My God. Dear Charles. He's an orphan, Grace thought, trying to focus on his words while caught up in her emotions.

"HIV isn't a death sentence any longer," Charles continued, "just have to stay healthy, keep the T count high, and there are so many new treatments these days."

That's what the doctor had said to Ted and herself that blustery winter afternoon in Dentry. "Cancer isn't a death sentence any longer." Six months later Ted died. A half gasp, half cry caught in Grace's throat. "Oh, Charles, my dear . . . I'm so sorry." She struggled to make her chin stop quivering. "How long have you known?"

"Charles had a routine physical in Saudi Arabia. The blood work came back HIV positive."

"But my T-cell count has stayed well above five hundred. Five hundred's normal," Charles said.

"That bastard in Saudi Arabia would hear of nothing but chemical treatments, a cocktail of drugs, he called it." Roger slipped his arm about Charles's shoulder and, as one would soothe a baby, made circular motions with his palm. "AZT makes some people horribly nauseated; other drugs can give you diarrhea or a disgusting rash. We decided to try alternatives like

411

homeopathy, acupuncture, exercise, vitamins, diet herbs."

"Roger keeps a keen eye on what I eat, everything I do. Except for this flu, I'm doing just fine," Charles said. "The worst time was with that awful doctor in Saudi Arabia. When we refused traditional treatments, he said, 'You're a walking dead man.' We came home so we could do alternative therapies."

Grace wiped her hands on her bandanna in an unconscious movement of nervousness. A jumble of thoughts raced about in her head. How long could a person test HIV positive without getting full-blown AIDS? Then she caught her breath. What about Roger? When and how had Charles become infected? He and Roger had been together more than ten years. Hadn't she heard that ten years was the longest incubation period? She wanted to scream questions at them, but could not. Roger had not asked her here to cook. How could she help them? What could she say? What should she say? She felt so ignorant about AIDS. Praying suddenly seemed imperative and utterly right. Help me do, say the right thing now, dear God, she said silently.

"I am so sorry." Reaching across the

table, Grace cradled Charles's cold hand in her warm palms, then brought it to her cheek and kissed the pale blue-veined back of his hand. "Why, the best way to handle anxiety and worry, I believe, is to keep busy. Take your mind off yourself." She looked intently at Charles. "The business will be a success, and you'll have many healthy happy years ahead of you, I'm sure." She hoped that her smile and words concealed her fears.

Grace had seen a TV special recently that talked about the fact that some partners of AIDS victims never developed HIV. And some HIV victims never developed AIDS, and that some AIDS victims now lived longer than previously thought possible. There are many theories about why, the reporter had said, but he had added, no one knows for sure. Please, God, let Roger not be infected. But was he? She had to know. This was hardly the moment for niceties or euphemisms. "Roger?"

He crossed his arms. "HIV positive? No." He rubbed his forehead. "We're careful."

She tried hard to remember everything and anything about the TV program. "I've heard that people can live with a diagnosis of HIV positive for years, way past what used to be considered life expectancy for the disease."

In a gesture that seemed like a sigh of relief, Roger stretched his arms above his head. "Now that we're back in the States we feel quite hopeful. We ride bikes, walk every day, eat properly, no fats, meat. We're optimistic."

The anxiety in her son's eyes belied his words. Grace's teeth scraped her lower lip. Meatballs with prunes. Unless they were veggie burgers they were out of the question. "I'm glad you told me."

Charles leaned toward her and murmured, "I don't want Roger to be alone, Mother Singleton."

"I understand." Grace covered each man's hand with one of her own. "I love you both." With that statement she drew Charles into her heart, solidifying his place as family. She would, when needed, do whatever she could for him, for them.

Outside the kitchen, the normal life of the day went on: a horn sounded, the front door of a house slammed, laughing voices drifted from the street. The sun continued its round across the sky. An enormous sadness shifted and slid deep within her, overshadowing her own unhappiness of the last few days.

Roger smoothed and folded his napkin, then carried his cup to the sink. "Want to come to the shop with us? We only have five days before the opening."

"This afternoon maybe, Roger dear. I'll stay here and rest, sit in the garden."

27

Reconciliation

When Roger and Charles had gone, Grace changed into her most comfortable slacks. Impossible to sit still, to stop worrying about Charles and Roger as well as her own situation. She needed to do something.

The worn pair of gloves she ferreted out from behind a can of slug bait on a shelf in the mudroom were almost threadbare and sagged on her hands, but she yanked them high over her wrists. Selecting a hand spade and a long narrow weed digger, she crossed the front porch and stepped down into the front garden. There were always patches to be weeded in any garden.

Grace ambled along the garden path to the front gate. She had never seen a front lawn in an American suburb converted into a garden. Roses spilled from the arbor and along the picket fence.

"Old-fashioned roses," Charles had told her; "they're wonderfully fragrant, like their ancestors." He explained that this type of rose had fallen out of use in favor of hybrid teas, from which, with the exception of a few like Hannah's beloved Chrysler Imperial red rose, the fragrance had been bred away. "But I'm pleased to say that old-fashioned roses are being reintroduced in nursery catalogs and shops." He had cupped a cluster of roses gently in his hands and bent to smell their fragrance. "Here, Grace, smell this," he'd said. "They may not hold their blooms as long or boast the most idealized flower form," Charles said, "but they blanket their bushes with color and fragrance and they live for years and years virtually pest-free."

The rose had smelled delicious, and now Grace again bent to the pink blooms and took a long deep sniff. Lovely. Someone driving by in a dark sedan waved. Warmed by the gesture, she waved back. Walking back along the pathway, Grace spotted slender green leaves, weeds she was sure, sprouting among a well-ordered row of marigolds. Kneeling beside the bed, she inserted the long narrow weed digger, and being careful not to disturb the marigolds, she eased out root after scraggly root.

Concentrating as she was on weeding,

Grace lost all sense of time and place. She ignored the perspiration dribbling down her face and the strong pungent odor of the marigolds that caused her to sneeze occasionally. Then suddenly voices from beyond the gate, out of her line of vision, drew her back to the hard path and her now aching back.

"It's gorgeous, don't you think?" a female voice said.

Then another woman's voice. "Very lovely, but different. I'd never have the nerve to tear up my front yard."

"Me neither," the first voice said. "But I sure would like to."

The voices dimmed as the women walked past the garden.

From inside the house Grace heard the phone ringing. She looked up from her weeding and brushed back her hair from her forehead with her arm. I'm not going to dash in there to get that call, she thought, and then stared down at her work to find a bright yellow marigold, stems, roots, and all, which she had inadvertently yanked from the soil. Unexpected tears snaked a path down her cheeks. She had killed the marigold. The desecrated plant, roots dripping soil, lay in her lap. Cradling it tenderly in both hands, she went inside, murmuring, "I didn't mean to hurt you."

In the kitchen Grace trimmed away the roots and lower leaves and turning the marigold so as to display its sunshiny bloom, set it in a glass of water on the windowsill above the sink. So bright and cheery. It reminded her of her childhood friend, Linda Smiley. Linda's marvelous garden has been on the local garden tour every year. A section of that garden was dedicated to cutting flowers, and Linda had kept Grace supplied with fresh bouquets until the first frost. For Christmas one year, and with the help of Linda's husband, Frank, Grace had secreted Linda's five blue ribbons from their home and had them mounted against pale yellow velvet and framed. Linda cried when Grace presented it to her. But Linda, dear person, had died two years ago while recovering from a stroke, and she was no longer here to comfort, to help.

A rush of anger followed by self-pity overwhelmed Grace. Standing in her son's kitchen with the sun warming her shoulders and back, old fears and anxieties and a crushing sense of loss threatened to engulf her. It was Ted's fault and Roger's. Damn Ted for dying and leaving her so sheltered and too afraid to board a plane or drive eight hours to Dentry, and damn Roger for moving her from her home. Lowering her head on her arms on the kitchen counter, Grace cried. Minutes later, drained and calmer, the ache in her throat finally subsiding, her rage at Ted and at her son gave way to compassion. Poor Ted. He had done his best. They had had good years together. And Roger, well, she would find out about Roger.

Grace splashed water on her face and dried it with a clean kitchen towel. It's all about fear, consuming and debilitating fear that stifles desire, creativity, even love, she reasoned. And who's free of fear? Her inflexible father had ground out each boring day at a job he hated for fear he could not make it in the wider world. His austerity and rigidity were cover-ups for his insecurities. She pitied him.

With a sudden clarity Grace realized how she had grown in self-confidence this last year. Success built on success, just as Hannah had said. And her friends had given her the courage, the push she needed to take that first frightening step. Since overcoming her fear of driving over forty miles an hour, she had begun to speak her mind, had gone on a date, though it hurt her now to think about it, and had managed to get on two airplanes. She addressed the marigold. "Incredible, don't you think? The other day I hung up on an unsolicited phone call, and now when I go to the bank I don't feel as if they're doing me a favor to cash my check." And all because Hannah and Amelia accepted her, encouraged her to try new things, and when, tentatively, she tried a new behavior they applauded her.

Hannah loved her, and Amelia had, too. How then could she begrudge Amelia happiness? It was Amelia's willingness to share Arthur's gift and Hannah's spunk, her derring-do that screamed, grab it tight, that had bolstered Grace's nerve and precipitated these changes. Her eyes burned. Maybe the strong scent of the marigold had affected them and crying had not helped. Opening the freezer door, Grace placed ice in the towel, folded it, and pressed it against her eyes, and counted to sixty, the way her mother had done for her when she had complained of burning eyes as a child.

She did not move away then, but stood at the sink. Talking to the flower was oddly soothing. "I should have told Hannah how I felt about Bob, and all the things he said to me. She'd have helped me get a perspective on everything, helped me keep my feet on the ground." A soft breeze stirred the flower head. "Silly, imagining you understand." Yet she murmured, "Thanks for listening."

The phone rang again. Instinctively Grace walked to the wall near the doorway, picked up the receiver, and offered a tentative, "Hello."

"Grace. This is Bob."

Goose bumps followed the shock. "Bob?" The long cord on the phone extended to the table and she slipped weak-kneed into a chair.

"Don't hang up, please. I want to apologize. I never meant to disappear. I'd looked forward so much to being with you at Tyler's party. I'm sorry. Amelia went on and on telling me about losing her child, her husband. I didn't know how to extricate myself without being cruel."

Of course he wouldn't. She waited, her heart skipping beats. He continued.

"Amelia means nothing to me. She never did. I phoned you and phoned you. Finally I went over. Hannah said you'd gone to Branston. We need to talk. Will you forgive me? I've been going nuts."

As if in a dream she listened to him speak, determined to memorize the caring in his voice and his welcome words. The kitchen glowed with sunshine. Relief and joy coursed through every fiber of her being.

"When are you coming home?"

Home. Was Covington home? "I don't know when I'm coming back."

"I miss you," he said, his voice soft, seductive.

"My son's opening his new business on Saturday. I want to be here."

"Hannah told me. Wish him well for me." A pause. "You have obligations there. I'd like to talk to you while you're up there, is that okay?"

"Why, yes, I'd like that." Hot and flushed but happy beyond words, Grace finally said, "It's good to hear your voice."

"I miss you," he said again. "We've got a lot to talk about."

"I miss you." For a moment, in the heat of longing for him, she considered taking a plane home right after the opening, but reason prevailed. She would not leave without talking to Roger, alone and frankly. "I have things to take care of with my son. I'll be here maybe another week."

"I'll call. At least we can talk."

"I'll look forward to that."

The opening of the Gracious Entertaining Shop was a resounding success and by early Monday morning inquiries were coming in and appointments being set up. Grace found she was ready to leave, but was determined to stay until she had cleared the air with Roger about their years of estrangement. She had to tell him how hurt she had been at the way he had ignored her needs and insisted she give up her home and life in Dentry.

"You need to clear the air with Roger and bring closure to that situation," Hannah had said.

And she would do exactly that. Not even for Bob would she leave the matter of Roger's behavior after Ted's death unresolved.

Then Charles went off to discuss an upcoming dinner party with the mayor's wife, and Grace found herself alone in the kitchen with Roger.

"Charles's been on edge for weeks. He's worried he might not be able to hold up his end." Roger brushed crumbs from the table, from which he had just removed their lunch dishes.

Grace stood at the kitchen counter securing plastic wrap over leftover ham and deli cheeses. This was the time. How to begin?

"Charles acts as if he's confident about maintaining good health, but he — we're both scared to death." Roger's shoulders slumped. Reaching for a dish towel, he wiped his hands. "I wish we could really be honest with one another." He placed the last glass in the dishwasher and looked at her. "He sold his granny's bungalow for me really. I couldn't dissuade him. Something to remember him by, he said. As if I need a house to remember Charles." He clenched his fists. "He doesn't need all the stress a business brings. How do you run a business without stress? It's all my fault. We never should have started this." Turning from Grace, he leaned heavily over the sink, swaying slightly. "I can't bear the thought of losing him."

"The business is something Charles has obviously wanted to do for a long time. As I see it, that's happy stress. Don't go spoiling your life worrying. Enjoy one another, enjoy the business. Charles will be around for a long time."

"But when? What if?"

Grace moved close to her son and placed both hands on his quivering shoulders. "In time, unless we go first, we all lose someone we cherish. If that happens, you'll do what every man or woman does who loses a loved one, from whatever cause. You'll hurt, you'll be angry, you'll cry, you'll be bitterly lonely. There'll be times when it seems there's no light at the end of the tunnel, but you'll go on. Eventually you'll take up your life again." She had never spoken openly to him, never offered her views on such a serious matter.

Roger's face was drawn, his eyes dark-circled, sunken. It pierced her heart to see him looking so serious and aged. "Was it like that for you when Dad died?" he asked.

She hesitated a moment. "I was furious with the doctor, with your father, with God, and depressed, very depressed for months. Fortunately I had good friends who dragged me out to a movie, invited me for dinner, insisted I shop with them for birthday presents, wedding presents. They included me and made me feel loved and needed."

What he said next surprised her. "I've thought a lot about how I behaved, keeping distance between us, insisting you move from Dentry." Roger sank into a chair at the table. "Please, sit with me, Mother." He indicated the chair across from him. Amazed at his sudden candor, Grace sat and waited for him to continue.

"I want to apologize. It's taken this for me to realize how much you needed the support of your friends, the stability of your life in Dentry. And I tore you away from all that."

"I was, to put it bluntly, devastated and very angry with you."

"Why didn't you send me to the devil?" Two bright spots burned on his cheeks.

Blood throbbed in tiny pulses at Grace's temples. "Why? Pick one: Because the male voice of authority had spoken? Because I couldn't risk losing you? Because I didn't know how to say no? Probably all of them."

A hint of a smile creased Roger's lips. "I wish you'd told me off. But then, I used to wish you'd tell Dad off and Grandpa. They dictated what you did, when, how."

Grace reached over and touched his cheek. Bristles of his neatly trimmed beard tickled her fingers. "Your wimpy mother. I'm sorry, Roger." She looked away, shook her head remembering how, even as an adult woman with a husband, a child, a home of her own, her knees had trembled in her father's presence.

Roger squeezed her hand.

"I never got over being afraid of your grandfather," she said. "When you came to Dentry, so cold, unapproachable, uncompromising, you reminded me of him."

"I'm ashamed of myself. I'm truly sorry. If it helps any, we'd just found out about Charles. I was scared out of my mind that I had it, too." Roger's eyes narrowed, his lips tightened. "Pardon the pun but he really screwed up. Once. That's all it took. Once." One fist struck the palm of his other hand. "An unexpected visit from an old lover. I was devastated by Charles's, what shall I call it, betrayal? Infidelity? I hadn't worked it out yet, or forgiven him. Obviously it still makes me angry to think about it. I thought I'd die of the hurt and pain and I was scared like hell for him, for me. My first instinct was to walk out." His face softened. "But I love Charles. We've been good together."

Grace nodded.

"In the middle of it all your letter came, ten days after your heart attack, not even a call, a cable from you or a friend or your doctor. It was all more than I could handle. That made me furious. I guess I transferred my rage at Charles to you." His pain was palpable.

"I wish I had religion. Life without religion, without a belief in a God seems suddenly intolerable." He sighed deeply. "When Charles was diagnosed it felt like someone punched me in the gut. I left Charles in Saudi Arabia with nothing resolved between us. I just needed to make sure you'd be someplace where I wouldn't have to worry about you. I had nothing left over for anyone. I'm sorry."

Grace's voice was soft. "I wish you'd told me, son."

He shook his head. "I couldn't. Shame, I guess."

"*I'm* sorry . . . about Charles, for you, for us all." Her eyes could no longer contain the tears. They rolled steadily down her cheeks even as she dabbed at them with her bandanna.

"Nice to see that old bandanna," he said, breaking the tension. The warmth in his voice eased the ache in her heart. There had been a time when he had teased her mercilessly about the bandanna. Grace lifted her head, and now the determined expression on her face and the set of her chin, indicated that she was through with tears and ready to move on. "I understand now. Thank God, you don't have it." But for how long?

Charles had been unfaithful to her son,

once, only once. She wondered about their intimate life but would never ask. Instead she thought about Ted and how, when he became ill, he had become impotent and rejected all physical contact, thus condemning her to crushing loneliness and disappointment. All she had wanted was to hold and comfort him and to be held and comforted by him. "People survive, my son."

Roger's eyes were anguished. "Stay with us."

"I can't, Roger," she said softly, calmly, knowing that she would return to Covington, to Bob and Tyler, to Hannah, and even to Amelia and to the life she was building there.

His eyes registered bewilderment, then dismay. "Why?"

"I'm happy in Covington. It's a good life with Hannah and" — she hesitated briefly — "and Amelia. I enjoy my work at the school with the children. I'm a small-town person. Covington suits me."

"If we need you?"

"Of course I'll come. I promise."

Roger leaned over and kissed her cheek.

"I'd like it very much if you and Charles would come down for Christmas."

"That might be hard. Our busiest

season, I suspect. Could we come after New Year's? Maybe Miranda would want to visit her mother, and we could have our own celebration, say about January tenth?"

A car pulled into the driveway, the front door opened. Suddenly street sounds filled the room: cars passing by, the tinkle of the ice cream truck's bell. Charles burst into the kitchen, a big grin on his face. "Got the job. Hey, you two, what are you talking about?"

"Mother's going home soon, and she wants us to come in January for a shindig in Covington."

Charles was all smiles. "Don't go so soon, Mother Singleton. We adore having you."

"I need to get home, but it won't be long. You'll come see my new home."

"Love to come, love to, love to," Charles said. "Is there skiing nearby?"

"At Wolf Laurel, not far."

"Wonderful."

Charles noticed a flashing light on the answering machine and punched a button. "Grace. Bob here. Let me know when you're coming home. I'll pick you up at the airport. Can't wait, sweetheart. Miss you."

"Bob?" Roger's eyebrows shot up.

"Sweetheart?" Charles eyed her coyly.

"Grandfather of Tyler, the child I've been working with. He lost his mother in a car accident, Tyler that is. Bob's a friend." She felt like a bumbling fool making light of her feelings for Bob, yet it was still too good to be true and she didn't want to jinx it by blabbing.

"Oh no. It's more than that. Sweetheart?" Charles giggled.

Grace held up both palms. "Don't get any ideas. We're friends, that's all. Don't tell me neither one of you ever casually called anyone honey or sweetheart?"

Charles grinned ear to ear. "Absolutely never." He winked, poked Roger on the shoulder. "Will we meet Bob in January?" When she nodded, he said, "Now I want to know all about your life in Covington. We've done nothing but talk about us since you arrived. I'll fix a pot of tea."

Charles bustled about the kitchen, put a kettle to boil, set out a teapot. Fresh tea leaves spilled from the measuring spoon into the pot. "Tell us about the farmhouse. Does it have a huge porch and rocking chairs? Are there wonderful nooks and crannies and an attic with cobwebs and old chests and a ghost or two?" He set three china teacups on the table.

She laughed and told them about the

house, the land, the stream. She told them about Hannah's surgery and her plans to invest in a greenhouse, about Brenda's and Harold's many kindnesses, about how Covington got its name and Amelia was lost in the forest, and finally about Tyler and her work at the school and meeting Bob. In spirit she was already in Covington.

On her last night in Branston, unable to sleep, Grace wandered alone into the back courtyard and searched the sky for stars, but the city lights erased the stars. It would be hard for me, she thought, to ever again live in a place where I can't, on a clear crisp night like this, locate the constellations. Well, I won't have to. Soon, I'll be back in Covington.

28

To Forgive and Forget

✽ Without Amelia or Grace, Hannah found the big empty farmhouse lonely. When Amelia finally breezed in the door and dumped her camera bag and overnight bag on the foyer floor, Hannah was greatly relieved and stifled her anger at her housemate for not making peace with Grace before going off.

"*Allo*," Amelia called cheerily, then asked, "Where's Grace? The boys? Why's it so quiet?"

"The boys were in a car accident. Miranda flew down and took them home."

"Were they hurt?"

"Bruised, broken nose, cuts that had to be stitched. They'll be all right." Hannah was not in the mood to go into the story with Amelia.

Amelia peered into the hall mirror, removed and reinserted the tortoise-shell comb that held the bun secure at the nape of her neck, then studied her face and nodded, obviously pleased, before turning to Hannah. "Where's Grace? I've had her on my mind the whole time I was away." She stood in the doorway of the kitchen. "What's the matter? Grace still angry?"

"Grace is in Branston."

"Why, for goodness' sake?" Amelia joined Hannah in the kitchen. "What's happened?"

"Roger invited her for the opening of their new business, you know, the one Miranda's a partner in. Grace was in such a state, she just picked up and went."

"How?"

"She flew."

Amelia's eyes widened. "Grace took a plane?"

"Yes."

"Well, I'll be darned." Amelia put a kettle of water on for tea.

"She and Bob talked. Everything's fine now, no thanks to you."

"I'm really sorry, but Grace wouldn't open her door or answer me, what was I supposed to do?"

"Leave her a note? Call in a message on the answering machine?"

"I didn't think of either of those things. I'm sorry. I still can't see why my talking to Bob was such a big deal." Her voice was petulant, as if she, not Grace, was the injured party. Her brows tightened.

Hannah's annoyance surfaced. "Well, it was. You hurt Grace." Hannah leaned against a counter, hands on hips. "Were you always so self-involved, Amelia, and I didn't see it?" Hannah's stinging words were said coolly. They were designed to hurt.

Amelia bristled. Her sapphire eyes registered wounded pride. "Self-involved? Me? No one's ever called me that. I never meant any harm, you know that, Hannah. I care about Grace, about you." Her shoulders slumped. "All my life I've been like a marionette on a stage with someone manipulating me, feeding me my lines with everything laid out for me: what to say, what to do, how to dress. In the last few months I've felt free for the first time." Her eyes challenged Hannah. "I didn't realize I was coming off as, what did you call me, self-involved?"

The kettle screeched. Amelia stared into space. Hannah strode forward, shut off the flame, poured steaming water into her mug and Amelia's cup, and carried them and two tea bags to the table. They sat.

The corners of Amelia's mouth drooped. Her chin trembled. "I acted impulsively

436

with Bob, satisfied a whim, that's all. I guess Grace hates me." She dunked the tea bag repeatedly, then reached for a clear plastic Teddy Bear filled with honey, poured too much into the cup, stirred it, and sat back in her chair. Hannah could see she was on the verge of tears.

"I doubt Grace hates anyone," Hannah said.

"And you're right, photography has consumed me. I've neglected everything, everyone." Amelia appeared disconsolate.

Tight-lipped, Hannah poured milk into her tea. Amelia's just grasping for a little happiness, Hannah sympathized, still she refused to break down. She can have all the happiness she wants, but not at Grace's expense. "It's not your photography. We're all happy you've found something you enjoy so much. It was thoughtless going off for so long with Bob at Tyler's birthday party."

"Didn't Bob explain?"

Amelia looked so forlorn that Hannah's heart softened. "He tried. Grace was so hurt she wouldn't talk to him."

"I'll call her, right now." Amelia headed for the phone on the wall, hesitated and turned back to Hannah. "Or, should I wait until she comes back?"

"She'll be back soon. Call her . . ." Hannah shrugged. This was Amelia's decision to make, ". . . or wait until she comes home." Making a tent of her fingers, she brought them to her lips.

"I'd rather talk to her face-to-face." Amelia brightened.

Hannah nodded. She couldn't worry about it anymore.

Amelia poured herself another cup of tea, offered Hannah another, and they sat in silence for a time before Amelia said, "Imagine, of the three of us, little Grace of all people finds someone to love her."

"I didn't say he loves her," Hannah snapped. Heavens, she thought, I've grown as dependent on Grace as women generally are on men. The idea dumbfounded her. Had she been mollycoddled by Grace's kindness?

Amelia's light laughter snapped her out of her reverie. "Maybe they'll marry," she said.

Hannah stared at her. What a mobile face Amelia has, capricious one moment, contrite the next, glowing with what appears to be pleasure for Grace, she thought.

Amelia bent over her cup, blew to cool it, and when she looked up her eyes were clouded. "But if they get married, Hannah, Grace will leave us. We've been so good together, the three of us, haven't we? Haven't we?" Amelia jiggled Hannah's hands, forcing her attention.

"We have," Hannah said grimly, "but things change. Still, just because they like one another doesn't mean they have to get married. I've never wanted to marry again. Maybe they'll be friends, companions. These days you don't have to be married to have sex." It sounded odd talking about Grace and sex, especially since sexual innuendoes and jokes seemed to plunge Grace into embarrassed silence. Yet Hannah knew, without anyone having to tell her, that Grace was attracted to Bob.

Amelia drew back. "Grace would never have an affair, sex without being married." In response to Hannah's raised eyebrow, she flipped her head. "I bet they'll get married. Men like being taken care of, fussed over. They don't like living alone, and Grace is basically a caregiver."

It's true, Hannah thought. Grace is a caregiver, feeding us, asking if we need another cushion, or a better light for reading, or worrying if we're warm or cool enough. Why wouldn't Bob want that?

Amelia continued. "I'll miss her sitting

at this table, all of us on the porch. Grace makes me feel good."

Hannah chose not to share her own stunning sense of loss with Amelia. Thinking back on her own life, it was clear that she had had few if any meaningful friendships, nothing really but a ragtag collection of relationships patched together through the years. Except for that one time. Do not start thinking of the past, she admonished herself.

Indeed, Grace's mothering was comforting and comfortable, but it was so much more than that. It was Grace herself, her optimism and kindness. It was the way she listened. Hannah realized that she had lowered her guard and had woven both women, but especially Grace, into the woof and weft of her life.

"I assumed at our ages things wouldn't change drastically, that only death would part us," Amelia said.

Hannah sighed. "We can agree on that."

Amelia placed her cup and Hannah's in the dishwasher. It was then that Hannah remembered the time capsule. "Amelia, do you realize we haven't done anything about burying that time capsule, our ceremony?"

"Let's do it as a symbol of our friendship first thing when Grace gets back, after we hug and make up."

Certain that she had permanently damaged her coveted new relationship with Miranda, it pleased Hannah tremendously when her daughter phoned.

"I thought you'd like to know we complied with the police directive, confronted Sammy, and he's entering a rehab program. Philip's working with us at the shop. He's fine."

"Was Sammy willing to go, or did you have to make him?" Her words sounded accusatory, and instantly Hannah regretted them. "I'm sorry, Miranda, that was unkind of me. I'm glad he's getting help."

"He wanted to go. Drinking with friends was one thing, smashing a car, realizing he could have killed them both, or someone else, had a major impact. The cops were tough on him, and your unremitting anger helped to really sober him."

"Can you forgive me for putting such pressure on you? When it comes to alcohol I go crazy, don't I?"

"I understand. I remember Dad, when he'd come in drunk. We were scared what he'd do to you, to us. I don't blame you. If Sammy wasted his life as an alcoholic, I'd go berserk. I was furious with you at first, you knew that, but on the way home I did a lot of thinking. I've been closing my eyes to certain things for too long."

"Well, I'm glad Sammy's getting help, and I'm so glad you called." They talked then about the opening of the Gracious Entertaining Shop, which Miranda described as absolutely wonderful. "Grace, as Charles said, looked smashing. We shopped for a dress, a blue silk skirt with a soft loose jacket. Grace, can she dance, a regular merry widow. Everyone loved her."

It didn't take much for Hannah to imagine Grace greeting people, welcoming them, smiling, and dancing. "She's lovable."

After that, Hannah talked to Grace almost daily about how busy Charles and Roger were, how efficient Miranda was, and about Paul's clever radio ads and Charles's streetside garden, and about Charles's HIV and of course a great deal about Bob. Hannah was convinced that soon Grace would announce her engagement. Hannah would feign happiness at the news, of course. But there were moments, especially when she worked in the yard, when she would find herself, trowel or shovel resting in her lap, thinking about why women, even at their age, were still so dependent on a man's opinion, attention, affection.

She thought too about her mother, and how after her father left, her mother had sulked and pouted and whined. She could not, she mewled to Hannah, cope without a man. And Hannah, struggling and unhappy at low-wage jobs, had tried to support them both, all the while resenting and hating her mother for her dependency and weakness.

Bill Parrish had been her meal ticket, her way up and out of poverty. Fearful always that he would desert her and the girls as her own father had deserted his family, Hannah catered to him, deferred to him for years. She put his wants first, tolerated his abuse, first verbal, then physical. Once free of him, she had determined not to let her girls grow up dependent on a man. For starters, she had educated them.

Hannah pushed herself up from the annual bed she was weeding, pulled off her gloves, walked to the porch, sat in her rocker, and stared at nothing. Miranda caters to Paul, she thought. Well, actually Paul caters to Miranda, too. Laura? Not sure about Laura. Marvin is Laura's *fifth* serious relationship. Where did Laura ever learn about boats? They had separate bank accounts; Laura had mentioned that once. Maybe all those lectures she had given her girls about standing on one's own feet had burrowed through their yawning boredom. Perhaps she had succeeded after all.

Two weeks after Grace's departure, she returned to North Carolina. Bob waited eagerly for her at the arrival section of the Asheville airport. His heart flip-flopped when she appeared in the doorway of the plane holding her oversize purse and walking slightly lopsided under the weight of a blue carry-on bag. Repressing his impulse to snatch her and hug her, he bent to kiss her lightly on the cheek and took the carry-on. Then he apologized again. "I'm so sorry about everything. I'd never hurt you intentionally."

"I overreacted," she said. "I feel idiotic."

"Don't be upset. It's over."

They walked from the terminal: Grace woozy from her trip, Bob bursting with his plans for them. "I've got us tickets for a play over in Abingdon, Virginia, for next Saturday."

"Isn't that a long trip?"

"Hour and a half drive. Pretty country. Fine playhouse. The town's old and charming. It's a matinee. We'll have dinner at this lovely inn and be back by nine or ten at the latest."

"Okay."

He was disappointed that she didn't sound more enthusiastic, but she was probably tired. "Sunday, we'll take a drive to Sliding Rock down by Brevard, have a picnic. Tyler's asked some of his friends from school."

She nodded, but her nod was reserved.

He was planning so much, and that made Grace uneasy. After years of putting Ted and Roger first she didn't know if she wanted to be accountable to any man, no matter how much she liked, loved, him. She and Amelia and Hannah came and went as they pleased. This sense of freedom was so new to her, and it felt wonderful not to have to report to anyone. Now it sounded as if Bob wanted her with him all the time, especially when he said, "I have to make one last trip to Florida. I hope you'll come with me."

Grace the pleaser struggled with the new more independent Grace. "To Florida?" She was bone-tired, hadn't even had a chance to recover from her trip to Branston. Go to Florida with him? Florida was the last place she wanted to go. Now, she mused, if he'd ask her to check in to the nearest motel with him? Nonsense. She couldn't. What would he think of her? Grace chose to change the subject, dramatically, and told him about Charles being HIV positive. "But he doesn't have full-blown AIDS," she finished, and explained the difference as best she could. Unless it struck their own families or closest friends, most people had no interest and knew little about the disease.

They were on I-26 now, heading for Asheville, and no longer sitting thigh to thigh. "God, I'm sorry to hear that," Bob said, his voice genuinely caring. "Must be awful for them. You must be worried sick about your son."

"Roger doesn't have it, thank heavens," she explained. "Charles has no parents or siblings, and I've come to think of him as a son."

"If you like him that much he must be a fine man. I just hope he's one of those who is able to stave off AIDS indefinitely." Then he changed the subject back. "I'm taking you out for dinner tonight so we can be alone and catch up on everything."

"We are alone," she replied, "and we're catching up. I'm really sorry, but I promised Hannah. She's made the one dish she's famous for, sauerbraten. I don't want to disappoint her." She almost said, "Why not come for dinner," but didn't. She knew she needed time to clear the air with Amelia.

"You're right. Sorry. I should have asked. We can go for dinner another evening."

He didn't pout or seem upset, didn't try to make her feel guilty. That was a relief and it endeared him to her.

He twisted his neck to look at her. "I missed you. Can't get enough of you now that you're back."

His look, his words, flooded her with warmth and clouded her thinking. Isn't this what she had secretly dreamed of — to be loved and accepted for herself.

Bob carried her bag inside, exchanged pleasantries with Hannah, and left with a reminder about next Saturday, saying he would call tomorrow. That evening he took Russell out for dinner.

"I believe she really cares for you, but I don't think you can rush her," Russell said when Bob told him how perplexed he was.

"I assumed Grace and I had a deep commitment, was I wrong assuming that she's an old-fashioned woman? That she'd want me to handle things, take the responsibility off her?"

"I think you're dealing with a new breed of woman, a liberated, 1990s type grandmother."

"I can't believe that," Bob protested.

"Remember Mother? You married an independent woman. Now you want someone dependent?"

He ignored that. "This woman's special. I don't want to lose her."

"Then don't press her, Dad. She's as much as told you to slow down."

Back at the farmhouse Grace was greeted like a conquering hero. Hannah hugged her. Amelia burst into tears when Grace hugged her.

"I'm sorry, Grace. It was stupid and selfish, thoughtless of me. Please forgive me. I have no designs on Bob. It was just, well, I could talk to him about Thomas and everything."

"Of course, you're forgiven. I made such a fuss. Forgive me, both of you."

Two days later, at the school, Brenda Tate welcomed Grace with open arms, and when Tyler saw her he rushed to her and flung himself at her. "Mrs. Grace, you're back, you're back." Taking her hand, he announced in a proud voice, "See, Mrs. Grace is home." And with that

Grace was swept back into her life in Covington.

When Bob called and asked if she would help him pick out a birthday present for Russell, she was happy to go with him. They strolled the mall hand in hand. He bought them ice cream cones and she dripped vanilla ice cream down the front of her blouse. Somehow Grace had left her bandanna at home, and Bob loaned her his plaid handkerchief to wipe the stain. They looked at computer games for Russell's new PC.

Bob hesitated. "I think he's spending too much time at that computer. It's an escape from thinking or feeling about Amy."

"Maybe it's what he needs now to help him get through this."

They bought a game and had it gift-wrapped.

The restaurant they went to for lunch was crowded and noisy, and Grace tried to ignore the air-conditioning streaming from an overhead vent and chilling her neck, shoulder, and arm.

Bob spoke of Tyler and beamed. "Tyler reads to us every night now."

"Tyler's bright. He's reading way above third-grade level."

It felt so right, so peaceful being with

Bob. He reached across the table and covered her hands with his. "You're freezing," he said, looking up at the vent. "Let's get out of here."

"But we've ordered."

"We'll cancel it." He waved his arm for the waiter.

They found a quiet restaurant on the west side of the city, and she relaxed in a booth across from him. When he placed his hands over hers she found herself quiet, at a loss for words. Who would imagine that at this age she would love a man, want a man? Maybe she was making too much of her newfound independence.

His foot nudged hers under the table. "I'm going to teach *America Between the Wars, 1945–1951*, at the Center for Creative Retirement at the university in Asheville."

"That's wonderful." She couldn't stop weighing the possibilities before her. He's considerate and generous of spirit. I think I'll marry him if he asks me. That decided, Grace felt amazingly hungry. She ate a club sandwich, drank two glasses of sweetened tea, and finished off lunch by sharing apple pie topped with ice cream.

"Watch the blouse," he kidded her. But this time she was careful and no ice cream dripped on her.

Lunch was about over when Bob said, "So what are we doing tomorrow?"

"Hannah's greenhouse is being set up, and I want to be there." Her eyes clouded. "I'm concerned she's taking on more than she can handle."

"You're very close to her, aren't you?"

"Yes, we're very close, Hannah and Amelia, too. When we met at Olive Pruitt's boardinghouse for retired ladies we were all just biding time. Then Amelia inherited this property." She sat back, laughed lightly. "I was such a coward, so frightened of anything new. I had a million excuses for not wanting to come to see this place." She leaned forward, grew serious. "Hannah's so self-sufficient, Amelia so worldly, and there I was, a cookie grandma-type from Ohio."

He interrupted her. "None of them can hold a candle to my Grace."

Grace ran her finger gently down his cheek. "You're sweet, but that's not how I saw it. They prevailed on me, gave me the gumption to drive and tackle our first trip down. And see," she spread her arms wide. "I'm not nearly the scaredy-cat I was."

He raised an eyebrow. "I can't imagine you . . ."

451

"Oh, but I was so insecure, so full of misgivings, and now, well everything's changing for me. I'm different and I'm happy."

"Are you trying to tell me something?"

"Just that, I guess I'm saying living with women is different. I'm confused. I like my life the way it is now."

Bob's eyes grew serious. "I love you, Grace."

"I love you too, Bob."

His girth and height expanded, reflecting the joy in his face. Their hands reached for each other's across the table.

"Well, then," Bob said, "we can just leave it as is for now."

Suddenly, in one of those unexpected flashbacks that memory springs on us at times, Grace saw herself standing in the utility room in the Dentry house. Ted had dumped his dirty work clothes on the floor near, but not in, the washing machine and walked out. Picking them up, distributing them in the machine, turning it on, was her job. He led. She followed. Although the smoke stung her eyes and she coughed all night from the smoke at the bowling alley, every Saturday night they had bowled, and once a month she'd prepared a gourmet meal for Ted's supervisor and his wife, though Grace found them boring. What would another man ask her to give up? What might she feel she had to do to please him? Was she getting into something with Bob that she would regret?

It startled her to see Bob's hand waving back and forth across her face. "Grace? A penny for your thoughts."

"My goodness. Sorry."

"Happy thoughts?"

Grace nodded, folded her napkin, laid it on the table, and collected her purse. Bob offered his hand and she took it, and they walked out into a bright sunny afternoon, her smile masking the anxiety that suddenly hovered above her.

29

The Interlopers

When the doorbell rang, Grace answered it. Even before the couple standing there registered in her mind, she saw the red pickup in the driveway, saw the gun rack on the window behind the front seat.

"Yes?" Grace said.

"This house here's ours," the man blurted.

"I beg your pardon?"

"You heard me right 'nough. This here property belongs to me and the missus." He motioned with his head toward the woman standing next to him. She wore a nondescript wide-brimmed hat and a yellow print cotton dress and her arms were clutched tight about her concave chest. She seemed to Grace like a woman worn out with years of hard work, who trusted no one, maybe even a woman who had known abuse.

"I'm sorry," Grace said, filling the doorway. "There's some mistake. This house and land were left to Amelia Declose by her cousin, Arthur Furrior."

"Cousin, my foot," the man said. "Old man Furrior done promised us this place and we come to claim it." There was a rim, a line of white skin just below the place where his worn felt hat was pushed back from his forehead. The rest of his face was rough and weathered.

"I'm sorry, but there has to be a misunderstanding —" She froze as the man spit onto the porch, staining the wood with tobacco juice.

Then grabbing his wife's arm he walked down the steps. "Y'all ain't seen the end of Jeb Madison yet, Yankee lady."

At the same moment, Grace smelled gingersnap cookies burning and rushed to the kitchen, where she burned her fingers on the hot cookie sheet. Her heart thudded and she felt wobbly on her legs as she sliced a piece of Aloe plant she kept by the sink and smeared its cool healing jell on her fingers. Then she crumbled into a chair to think.

Jeb Madison? She had never heard the name. What claim could he and his wife have on Amelia's inheritance? She took several deep slow breaths to still her quivering insides. Could they have a valid claim to the property? Could they take this land, this house, away from Amelia? Grace would be homeless. They would all be homeless. Grace's throat tightened. Rising, she went to the sink, ran the tap. Filling a cup with cool, pure water from their stream, she stood there sipping slowly. Stay calm, she admonished. Yet the crafty face of that man floated before her eyes.

Grace pried each burnt cookie from the sheet, scraped the black bottoms, and set the best of the lot on a plate. The rest she dumped. She scoured the cookie sheet cleaner than it had been in weeks and set it to drain. A moment of intense anxiety followed. Had she locked the front door? The back door? She checked both. The front door was locked. Grace double-locked the back door. Where were Amelia and Hannah? Then she remembered, Amelia was at the beauty parlor in Mars Hill. Hannah had dropped her there and would pick her up on the way back from buying plants. Grace would have to wait.

Grace was busy cleaning the second bathroom when the others returned late in the afternoon. "My God, I'm glad to see you two," she said, plopping down on the closed toilet seat.

"Here, you're glad to see us here in the

bathroom?" Amelia was feeling happy. She looked lovely, her hair back in a loose bun.

"Something's happened." Grace beckoned them to her room, where Amelia joined her on the bed while Hannah settled into the rocking chair near the window. Then she told them about the Madisons and their claim.

"Maybe they're cranks. Let's wait and see what happens," Amelia said.

"No, I don't think we should wait. I think you should ask Margaret Olsen to recommend an attorney," Grace said.

"Well, now we know who the red pickup truck belongs to," Hannah said.

Days passed. They did nothing and made light of it in their talk, yet every time a pickup seemed to slow as it passed on Cove Road, or they heard the crunch of gravel in the driveway, Grace started and ran to the window. A week later, Amelia received a letter from an attorney, Jake Herrington, who informed her that the Madisons had been devoted cook and caretaker for Arthur Furrior and in an earlier will, which Madison had in his possession, the land and house in question had been left to Mary and Jeb Madison of Fletcher, North Carolina.

"What I don't get," Harold Tate said when they showed him the letter, "is why that pair waited this long to make a claim."

"You know them?"

"Seen her a couple a times when I'd go down to Saluda to visit old Arthur. Woman'd slink about, try to hear every bit of chat we had. I sure never saw her husband, never knew old Arthur had a caretaker. Only had a quarter acre round his bungalow down there."

Margaret Olsen recommended an attorney, Samuel Tolent, a clean-cut man who looked about forty with hazel eyes, quick-thinking and seemingly efficient. "What they're claiming, Mrs. Declose," he said after phoning the Madisons' attorney, "is that they have a will dated June of 1994 in which your cousin bequeathed them this property. They claim that Mr. Furrior came under undue pressure from you and, being not of sound mind, was persuaded by you to change his will."

Amelia raged. "Not of sound mind? Why, he found me. I have letters —" She stopped, her hand went to her throat, "I never even met Cousin Arthur."

Samuel Tolent leaned forward. "You have letters?"

"Of course she has letters," Grace said.

"Hannah and I've read them and they were clear as a bell. I can't tell you how many times we read those letters . . . they changed our lives."

"Oh dear . . ."

"What's the matter?" Hannah asked.

Amelia fidgeted. "I don't know where they are, if I have them. There was so much stuff to pack when we moved. Oh dear, Hannah."

"Well." Tolent leaned back. "Of course we'll deposition your cousin's doctors, attorneys, friends, anyone he had sustained contact with in the last year of his life. But those letters are what will clinch this in your favor. Try and find them."

Finding them was not easy. The search began frantically with Amelia hauling and dragging boxes about in the hot stuffy attic. Sitting crosslegged, she would rip off the tape sealing a box, then plow through crumbled newspaper and stored items before slamming it shut and shoving the box away with her foot, even as she reached for the next one. The next day Grace and Hannah found her sitting on the attic floor immobilized and crying.

"You're stressing yourself too much. It's going to be all right," Hannah assured

Amelia at supper that evening. "Ease up. When you're looking too hard, you can't find anything. Legal matters take time."

"Why can't I remember where I put them? Did I throw them out when we moved?"

"I don't believe you'd have thrown out Arthur's letters, Amelia. He meant too much to you," Grace said. "You've tucked them away somewhere for safety."

"Tell you what," Hannah suggested. "We'll help you. You're so upset those letters could stare at you and you wouldn't see them. Let's just go slow, set aside a time each day to open one, two boxes. We'll take everything out, then repack and label every container. If they're not there, we'll take it drawer by drawer, nook and cranny by nook and cranny. We'll find them. No one's going to turn us out. It's months, maybe years, from a court date or anything like that. Meanwhile we've got to go on living sanely, normally. We can't put our lives on hold, stay up all night worrying. Agreed?"

"Agreed." Amelia gave her a grateful look. "We need some comfort food."

Grace nodded, then brought them all chamomile tea to settle their stomachs and fresh-baked sugar cookies. She nibbled at a cookie and rolled her eyes. "Yummy. I still like them after all these years. An old friend of mine in Dentry gave me her special recipe. She got me started baking cookies, you know. She died a few years ago, and every time I bake them I think of her. They're the best sugar cookies I ever ate."

"Everyone else who eats them agrees with you," Hannah said.

30

P. J. Prancer's Old-Time Hardware Store

Hannah was determined to proceed with her life, to act as if everything was as it had been before the Madisons had showed up at their door. They had all been deeply touched by Arthur's letters, so open, so honest, and so delighted to have found Amelia, his family. Hannah assumed that she and Grace would testify or give depositions. They had read the letters. Tolent said that, yes, they could do all that, but the other side would scream, vested interest.

Finding the letters had become a great strain on the ladies. Amelia went in and out of denial and was often unavailable to search. Grace bounced back and forth, optimistic one moment, pessimistic the next. Sometimes she agreed with Hannah that all would be well, then she would be glum and depressed, worrying about a negative outcome. Hannah considered Grace's anxiety peculiar since Grace had an alternative and a good one, Bob.

But Hannah chose to live and act as if nothing untoward had occurred. September sulked through hot days, and haze shrouded the mountains. The humidity rose to eighty-nine percent, and the weatherman predicted rain, which did not materialize. The greenhouse, started before the Madisons came, was nearly complete: workbenches, shelves, labeled bins under the counters containing soil, vermiculite, sand, perlite. The sprinkler system would soon be hooked up and boxes of plastic pots of various sizes were neatly stacked on the rear porch waiting to be unpacked. Next week, the wholesaler in Florida would be shipping her first order, one hundred rooted cuttings, fifty anthuriums, fifty gardenia plants. By carrying on, Hannah hoped to bolster Grace's and Amelia's flagging hopes.

"How big is it anyhow?" Amelia's voice in the doorway of the greenhouse startled her.

"Twelve by forty." Ever since that day when she had accused Amelia of being wrapped up in herself, Amelia had bent over backward to prove she was not self-centered.

Hannah rubbed her hands together. "Just closing this up, going over to Prancer's hardware. Want to come?"

Amelia slipped two film canisters from her pocket. "Could you drop this film at the drugstore in Mars Hill for me?"

"Sure." Hannah took the film.

In the silence that followed, Amelia tore at a cuticle on her thumb. "I can barely get my photographic assignments done these days. Right now I'm going down to the basement to check out yet another carton we stored there."

"I thought we agreed we'd do that together?"

"But you see how I am. I've started biting my nails. Look." She extended her hand. Alongside the edge of her nail, the thumb was red and swollen. "Most times, I don't want to open a box. All I want is to be left alone. Sometimes I wake up at night and feel certain I know exactly where they are. I can't wait for you or anyone when it feels right to look."

Hannah nodded. She understood the need to take action, even futile action.

Amelia said, "Then Harold's coming to get me. Hottest day of the year, and we're going to pick out a new car for me."

Every time Hannah stepped onto the lumpy, buckling hardwood floor of P. J. Prancer's Hardware, a landmark in Covington, she began a journey back in time. Tall wooden cabinets faced with wide and narrow drawers lined one wall. Clerks clambered up rickety-looking wooden ladders to reach items five feet or higher above the floor. Besides the usual goods: nails, hammers, paint, cord, etc., P. J. Prancer's stocked three-legged iron cook pots, sickles, scythes, axes, and horse gear, including horseshoes, harnesses, collars, halters, whiffletrees, and traces. If she browsed a bit she would come upon wooden pitchforks, rings for a bull's nose, washtubs and scrub boards, and on and on. And dust. Hannah invariably sneezed, rubbed her eyes, and left P. J. Prancer's with a runny nose.

And the staff was as diverse as the inventory. Hannah had never seen Billie Prancer, old man Prancer's son by his second wife, step from behind the counter. Billie appeared to Hannah to be about forty-five. Affable, ruddy-faced, with elfin ears set close to his head, and big, round eyes, Billie seemed to view all comers with

interest and curiosity and with an inno-
cence that belied his natural shrewdness.

Red, a tall, freckled, energetic, hip-
looking chap with an earring in his left ear,
zipped about the store with droll resignation, it seemed to Hannah, filling orders
given him by Billie. She had the sense that
while climbing the rickety ladder and
chasing from aisle to aisle, Red's mind was
light-years away. Did he fancy himself a
rock singer with rows and rows of girls
screaming approval, desire? Frank Sinatra
had had that effect on her on the one and
only occasion she had sneaked out to see
him in concert. Good luck, Red, she
wished silently. Whatever it is, hold on to
your dream.

Tim was her favorite. He handled paint
and bathroom accessories mostly. Sixtyish
and slightly stooped, his eyes, magnified
behind   thick   wire-rimmed   glasses,
appeared serious and dependable. You
could call in an order, and Tim would fill
it down to the last penny nail, you could be
assured of that. Tim had been among the
men searching for Amelia in the forest.
And then there was Billie's father, old man
Prancer, squirreled away in his office and
rarely seen on the floor.

Today Hannah's list was long: cleaner for

bathroom tile, a window shade that had to be cut to size, a sprinkler nozzle, a one-hundred-foot watering hose, gray deck paint for the concrete stoop that had just been poured outside the greenhouse, a four-inch brush, a watering can, a fifty-foot measuring tape, and a new pair of hand clippers. As she stepped over the threshold into the store, her eyes were fastened on the list in her hand.

A man more lounged than sat on an unopened keg of nails near the door, his long legs extended, a knife in his hand, concentrating hard, whittling.

It was like suspended animation: arms flailing, feet kicking, Hannah toppled headlong across the man's legs.

Casting his knife aside, the man reached down, grasped Hannah by the waist, lifted her, and to her chagrin set her on her feet, then held her about the shoulders to steady her. The hum of conversation and of business ceased. Billie bounded from behind the counter and rushed to her side.

"Are you hurt, Miss Hannah?" He retrieved her purse from behind the keg. Hannah clasped it close. "Get you a chair? Call a doctor?"

Red-faced and humiliated by her situation, Hannah stared back at the customers and staff members who gaped at her with both shock and humor on their faces. Trying to appear self-assured, she smoothed back her hair from about her face, straightened her clothes, and waved a hand at the fidgeting Billie. "No. I'm fine. Back to work. Back to work."

With a relieved look on his face, Billie hastened back to his perch behind the counter. Customers proceeded with whatever business had engaged them prior to her harum-scarum entrance.

Mortified and disheveled, Hannah struggled to collect her wits. The pressure on her arm, she realized, was the hand of the man she had tripped over. Quivering from the shock and angry now, she shook him off.

Her voice was hoarse and self-conscious when she spoke. "Clumsy of me."

"My fault. I'm sorry. You sure you're okay, ma'am? Sit here." Nervously he brushed off the top of the wooden barrel. "Rest a bit. Ain't your fault, ma'am. I got no business shovin' my feet out like that."

"If I'd been using my eyes," she said in a decidedly disgruntled manner. Hannah eyed the man suspiciously. He looked familiar. "Wait. Don't I know you?"

The man stayed close, though he

released his grasp. "I'm Wayne Reynolds. I guess I'm the fellow who knocked you outta your chair at the fireworks."

Speechless, Hannah nodded. I feel like a ridiculous old fool, she thought. Everyone's looking at me. They think I can't stand straight, manage by myself. All she wanted now was to get out of the store, but there was Wayne, looking contrite, hovering, smelling of musky cologne and pungent tobacco. Wayne removed his broadbrimmed brown felt hat with its deep crease in the center. His hair, smashed flat across the top and down the sides of his head, protruded like wing tips below his ears.

"Lemme get your things for you," Wayne said, reaching for her list.

"Do it myself," Hannah said firmly. But her feet wavered when she started toward the counter, more from shock, she was sure, than injury, for she had not actually hit the ground, only gotten a knockout jolt across Wayne's hard, bony legs. Hannah grasped Wayne's right arm.

"Steady, ma'am," he said. "Set yourself down on this here barrel, and I'll carry this list over to Billie. Red'll get everything."

Tim appeared with a chair. "Please sit,

469

ma'am. Likely Mr. P.J. will be here any second."

"Thanks, Tim." Hannah sat. "Billie," Hannah called to the flustered man behind the counter. "Charge my account, will you?" She nodded at Wayne, who headed toward the counter clutching her shopping list as if his very life depended on it.

A flurry of noise from the rear of the store and old P. J. Prancer burst from the back office. For an old man, and stooped as he was, he managed to make his way with amazing agility through the narrow aisles to Hannah's side.

"Terrible. Terrible." He shook his head again and again. "So sorry. Fell, fell, did you, Hannah?" He looked at her intently, circled her.

He's looking me over, Hannah thought, like I'm a bag of flour, making sure I'm not leaking. Her elbow hurt, but she decided not to tell him that.

"You all right? Need, need me to call emergency? Billie, there." P.J. waved his arms in swift, staccato movements. "Call, call nine-one-one." He turned back to Hannah. "How'd it happen?"

"Don't call nine-one-one. I'm fine." Hannah felt battered. She sank into the chair Tim had dragged over. "My fault, P.J.

I wasn't paying attention."

P.J. nodded, looked relieved, wiped his high pasty-white forehead with his hand-kerchief. "Mighty, mighty glad you're not hurt, Hannah."

"Tough old rooster," was the way Hannah had described him to Grace. The first time they had met, she and P.J. had developed a camaraderie based on the fact that at different times each had lived in Santa Fe, New Mexico: a brief stay after the girls had graduated, and for him, a stint at a nearby military installation. Both had loved Santa Fe. Invariably when she was shopping, he materialized from the depths of his office for a chat. They had progressed from a formal Mrs. Parrish and Mr. Prancer to a casual Hannah and P.J. Hannah considered this a mark of his regard.

"Sorry to create such a ruckus, P.J.," she said.

P.J. patted her arm. "Fill, fill your order for you?"

"Wayne Reynolds is doing it, but thanks."

"Wayne, Wayne, eh? Had 'is legs stickin' way out in the passage, Billie tells me. Gonna, gonna give him hell."

The comic nature of the entire episode

struck Hannah, and she struggled not to laugh. When had Billie told P.J.? Billie had never left the room. She smiled. It was common knowledge that old P.J. spent most of his time watching the comings and goings in his store through a one-way mirror in his office. Supposed to be a secret that mirror, but everyone knew. Everyone went along, said that old P.J. had eyes in the back of his head. But they knew.

"I wasn't looking. I'm fine. Nothing to worry about," she said again. "Everything's fine, P.J."

"Glad. Glad to hear that." P.J. reminded Hannah of an ancient steam engine straining to pull other cars along.

P.J.'s face relaxed. He shoved his handkerchief in his pants pocket and seemed satisfied. "Everything, everything, fine. Red," he barked at the frazzled clerk, "get Miss Hannah's order filled right away." P.J. patted her hand and trotted back to his office.

Hannah had calmed considerably by the time Wayne returned with a brown paper bag in one arm and a gallon of paint in the other. "I'm gonna stash this stuff in my pickup. Gonna drive you home and Terry here" — he pointed to a slouching teenager in oversize baggy pants and shirt that hung below his butt — "he's gonna wait for me. When I get back, I'll drive out your car. Terry'll follow in my truck."

It sounded complicated, but at this point Hannah didn't care. It frightened her how much her hip ached. Just a bruise, she tried to reassure herself.

They spoke not a word until they reached the farmhouse. Hannah directed Wayne to drive across the lawn right to the kitchen door.

"That yours?" He indicated the greenhouse.

Lips pressed together, face grim, she nodded.

"What you gonna grow?"

"Ornamentals."

"Ornamentals. Right fine business."

"You know about ornamentals?" She found him irritating. Why was she having this conversation with him?

"Yep. Worked a whole year in a greenhouse that grew 'em down in Georgia. Whatcha' usin' to heat it? We had electric tube heat, but we had way long greenhouses." He spread his arms wide, indicating they were considerably longer, bigger than hers.

"Electric heat. The salesman recommended it." Hannah studied Wayne. The young man had unexpectedly become more interesting.

Wayne nodded, tapped the steering wheel with his fingers and looked at her with skepticism. "Growin' plants to sell. Sure you're up to it, Miss Hannah? Your time of life you should be settin' on the porch rockin'." He laughed, wagged his head. "If you need a hand, just holler."

Was he mocking her? She'd had enough mocking for one day. Her vexation intensified. Sit on the porch rocking? Not Hannah Parrish. Shoving his truck door open, Hannah eased herself down and moved resolutely up the steps and into the kitchen. Wayne followed, carrying the paper bag and paint, to the welcoming smell of Grace's dinner simmering away in an iron pot on the stove. "Smells mighty fine," he said, setting his packages on the kitchen table.

"It's a specialty of Grace's, meatballs with prunes, the celebrated recipe of a woman from her church who had emigrated from, from" — she tapped her forehead — "Lithuania, Belarus, the Ukraine . . . someplace like that." Hannah threw up her hands and laughed lightly. "Somewhere over there."

Wayne shifted from one leg to the other.

"Sounds odd, but meatballs and prunes are amazingly delicious with rice and gravy. Would you like to take some home?" Hannah thought she could pack some meatballs up for him and send him on his way.

He shook his head, but by then she was at the stove, scooping two meatballs, prunes, and lots of gravy into a Tupperware container. She snapped on the lid. "You try this."

He took the container with one hand, lifted his hat. "Now y'all take care of your-self. I'll be lookin' in on you, ma'am." Then he was gone.

31

The Apple Orchard Goes Up in Flames

✿ Hot fall days ushered in a heavy haze that shrouded the mountains. Rain had been scarce all summer. A fine dust, stirred by passing trucks, hovered in the air above the road. It was afternoon and the ladies of Covington, as they had come to think of themselves, sat on the front porch, as usual, but they were uncommonly silent. Samuel Tolent had phoned. Had they found the letters? He was ready to start taking depositions. He asked them to write down everything they could recall from those letters.

Still grateful not to have broken anything in her tumble across Wayne's knees ten days ago, Hannah moved her hand gently over the remains of the bruise that ran from thigh to knee. The blue and black coloration had slowly faded to a murky yellow, and was much less sensitive to touch. What had surprised and pleased her was Miranda's response when she had told her about the fall.

"I'll get the first plane down there," Miranda had said.

With a catch in her throat, she had thanked her daughter. "Nothing's broken, no need to come. I'm just fine." But then the plants arrived, and Hannah had pushed herself, stood on her feet far too long transplanting the tiny four-inch plants from their flats into individual plastic pots. Grace helped, even Bob helped. Amelia did not. Wayne popped in with an offer to help, said he'd come back and didn't. She shook her head. Wayne Reynolds was not anyone she would depend on.

Amelia passed Mike Lester's postcard of Machu Picchu. Mike had taken a photography group to South America, but Amelia had declined to go.

Having a great time. Your presence is missed. You'd adore the native people, so exotic, and such exquisite scenery.

Mike

"There'll be other trips," Grace said,

reaching to take Amelia's hand, but Amelia pushed her rocker back out of reach, and immediately regretted it, feeling guilty. Because she had convinced herself that without the letters, the Madisons would win and it would be her fault, she could hardly bare to think about them. The episode in the forest and now this Madison thing had drained her energy. She was mad, at everyone, at herself. She ought to be in Peru. But how could she justify going? Every day Hannah or Grace nagged her to open and unpack and sort the items in yet another cardboard box. The attic was hot. "I refuse to work up there," she had said.

So, Harold Tate sent a man to bring down twelve boxes, and what had she done? Made appointments, gone to lunch or a movie with Margaret Olsen in Asheville, invited the Tates over for Grace's exotic and delicious meatballs and prunes dinner, feigned a headache and then a backache. In two weeks they had opened just six of the twelve boxes. Nothing but stored and forgotten trivia: bric-a-brac, tiny silver spoons, but no letters tucked under a favorite old high school sweater, not with Thomas's typewriter, not inside a pair of huge snow boots. Where could she have put those letters? Not being able to remember frightened her, and she wondered silently if she were getting Alzheimer's. And Hannah's optimism and Grace's attempts at cheerfulness annoyed her. Why weren't they as insecure, as terrified of losing the house as she was?

Living together had not always been easy. There had been discussions at first about the division of labor, who would wash the dishes if Grace cooked? Who would clean? Were they responsible for leaving a message every time they went anywhere without the others? But they had worked all of that out and now this dreadful strain, this silent stress they were unable to speak openly about. Amelia knew why — they blamed her. All she wanted was to close her eyes and go back to how it was before the Madisons.

Grace was speaking. "Bob called. Says this is his absolutely last trip to Florida. He'll be back tomorrow."

Grace and Bob spent increasing amounts of time together, dinners, lunches, movies, picnics with his family. To many of these functions, Grace invited Hannah and Amelia. Sometimes they went, but more often they declined, not wanting to intrude. Each time Hannah saw them together — the way Bob hovered over Grace and Grace's visible contentment — she felt a deep sense of loneliness, a loneliness that hunkered in the shadows of her life, squeezing her heart at night before she fell asleep and first thing on awakening. Pooling their resources, cooperating with one another, the goodwill among them had created what she considered to be the perfect lifestyle. Where would she, Hannah, be in six months, a year from now, if they lost the house and Grace married Bob?

Grace bubbled on. "Roger called. They catered a stunning black-tie affair last week. I'm so glad things are going well. It's going to be wonderful when they all come in January, don't you think, Hannah?"

January, three months away. Hannah nodded.

"How's Charles?" Amelia asked.

"Says he feels great. He's in his element in the business."

"I'm glad to hear that."

"He's a very sweet and dear man," Grace said. "I've always liked him. I like the way he talks. Took some getting used to at first: boot for the trunk of a car, loo for bathroom, lift for elevator, but now it just sounds right and natural."

The sound, the creak of their rocking chairs on the wooden floor, usually a soothing sound, now irritated Hannah, for it reminded her of time's passage, and in a rare bleak moment she wondered which would come first, Grace's announcement of her engagement, or their loss of the farmhouse. Enough. She stood abruptly. She didn't need anyone. Her happiness, her sense of identity, came from work. Work sustained her. "I'm going down to the apple orchard to rake leaves," she announced. Without waiting for Amelia to say it was too hot, or for Grace to offer help, Hannah strode away.

Under a sprawling apple tree Hannah leaned on her rake and wondered how long the old trees had been here. And planted by whom? Untended for years, many of them no longer bore fruit and the leaves of others, spotted with disease, clung tenuously to their branches.

In early summer Harold Tate had inspected the orchard with her. "Bunch of old trees on their last leg. Best to do is prune 'em, spray and fertilize 'em, and hope you get another year out of 'em." He had wiped his brow and studied the walnut-size, tough little green nuggets struggling to become full-size fruit ready to harvest in the fall. Harold had offered to send some of his tobacco pickers, migrant workers from Mexico whom he housed in a trailer on his land, to pick whatever apples survived. He would take them to the farmer's market. "Might as well try and make a little something to help pay for the fertilizer," he'd said.

Hannah stepped into the orchard, two, three, four rows set ten feet apart, eight trees in each row. Where to start? Returning to the first row, she plunged the rake into the thick layer of leaves and twigs that cluttered the base of a tree. Hannah cleared a circle, then hauled the debris from under the branches and pulled them away into the meadow. "Breathe roots," she said.

The task seemed overwhelming, but not so overwhelming as the depression she felt creeping into her life. Expectations always led to disappointment, she knew that, and she had survived a lifetime of disappointments. If Grace married Bob, well, she'd survive that, too. Hannah shook her head. Stop the crap, she demanded. There's still Amelia. We'll carry on. With all her distractedness, I'm fond of Amelia. I have a new business, and Grace won't stop being my friend. Worst case scenario, we lose the house, so, Amelia and I rent one somewhere near here.

That idea comforted her as she cleared around another and yet another tree. Her watch reminded her that it was six o'clock, suppertime. Sweat glistening on her face, dust and flecks of debris streaking her arms and her back aching, Hannah critiqued her work. Seven trees now had breathing space around their trunks. Standing back, she surveyed the pyramid of nearly waist-high leaves. The back of the farmhouse, plain and tall and sturdy in the open field, lay in shadow, for the sun, having completed its arc in the heavens, was now beating onto the front of the house. She felt a pang of loss and forced it from her mind and heart.

"Grace. Amelia," she called, wanting to show them her handiwork, then realized that her voice would not carry to the front porch. Had Grace been standing looking out of her bedroom window, she would have heard her call. Sometimes in the early morning while she was weeding, she would look up and see Grace standing there gazing out at the stream, the trees, the meadow. If anyone loved this place, it was Grace.

But, she sighed, life's chancy and so darn arbitrary. Totally unexpectedly, Grace had found a man to love in Covington and what was Covington? Less than a speck. They couldn't even find it on the map that day in Olive's kitchen.

Hannah believed that mind, thoughts, preceded feelings. Determined to remain optimistic, she forced herself back to the task at hand. She studied the pile of brown leaves and twigs. "Breeze is up. Can't leave them like that," she said aloud. She drew a pack of matches from her pocket. Later she tried to remember when she had slipped them into her pocket.

A bluebird whisked by. It thrilled her that bluebirds made their homes on this land. Hannah had bought special tall, narrow bluebird houses at P. J. Prancer's and, as instructed, nailed them high on tree trunks. Bluebirds reminded her of an old black-and-white movie with Shirley Temple searching for the bluebird of happiness. There had been a moral to that tale — what was it? Everything you need is right in your own backyard, or was that Dorothy's lesson in the *Wizard of Oz*? Maybe both.

Hannah struck a match. The fragile flame flickered and died. She struck another. It burned bright and strong. "Ouch." The searing flame nipped her fingers. She dropped the match and watched, horrified, as a tinder-dry leaf curled into flames. Spitting and crackling, another leaf and then another crinkled and flamed. The brittle pile erupted into flame. This was not the smoldering fire Hannah had meant to set. In her panic all Hannah could think was to stomp at the edges until, gasping for breath and coughing, she realized the uselessness of her efforts and hobbled back to the farmhouse holding her hip. "Help! Fire! Grace! Amelia! Call nine-one-one." Completely out of breath she collapsed on the porch steps. "Fire!" She pointed in the direction of the meadow.

"Fire. Old Furrior place. One-seventy Cove Road. Hurry." Grace was already inside talking to 911.

Amelia shot from her chair and uttered one hoarse and terrified word, "Fire." Hands clasped at her neck, eyes wild and frightened, Amelia staggered back, until with a jolt she struck the wall of the house.

Hannah stared at Amelia. I'm an arsonist, she thought, as wave after wave of guilt washed over her. She had completely forgotten Amelia's accident, the burning car, her injuries. "I thought I could burn the pile of leaves I raked from under the trees. I never meant . . . my God, I'm so sorry." Uncharacteristically Hannah hastened to Amelia, her arms open wide, and Amelia collapsed against the proffered bosom, shaking and sobbing.

"It's a small fire, just a pile of leaves way down in the meadow, Amelia. The firemen will come and they'll put it out in no time."

Amelia's bun dislodged. Long strands of white hair floated loose about her pale face but her blue eyes held only terror. Keening sounds ushered from her throat. Hannah held and rocked her gently. Behind the farmhouse a thin spiral of smoke curled, twisted, and rose in the hot, dry air.

"The fire's way down in the meadow. The firefighters will be here soon." Grace tried to reassure her. "Hannah and I are here with you. There's no danger." Grace's arms circled both Amelia's and Hannah's trembling shoulders. She looked at Hannah. "Accidents happen."

Accidents happen, yes, Hannah thought, but not this. She had done this. Deliberately? Never. Yet how could she have dared to strike a match with everything so dry? The first line from a poem of Robert Frost's, learned in high school and never forgotten, raced through her mind.

"Some say the world will end in fire, some say in ice."

Hannah's bruise ached. She was suddenly cold and her head hurt. It would be fire, she thought. Fire, not ice. But then her thinking grew fuzzy and she relived her flight from Bill. She stood again in that freezing winter night as Bill Parrish, his face livid with rage, his mouth distorted, his eyes feral, blasted shotgun holes in the radiator of the car. Suddenly Hannah felt herself reach back through the years to feel his impotence, his frustration, his desperate sense of some deep-seated rage as if it were her own. Tears welled in her eyes. Empathy? Understanding? Forgiveness? Hannah felt liberated from and yet connected to her long-detested husband. Then the crackle of curling, burning leaves, the smell of caustic smoke, drew her back to the front porch. Breaking from the others, she rushed down the steps.

"Hannah. No. Stay here. For heaven's sake, don't go back," Grace yelled.

But Hannah was already around the house. Tearing open the door of the toolshed, she grabbed two buckets, filled them from a nearby spigot, and with a strength only possible when driven by adrenaline she staggered down the hill toward the fire. She reached the fire with her legs drenched and water seeping into her shoes. In her panic she had been unaware that firefighters in yellow slickers and hard hats had arrived at the house, dragging hoses, calling to one another.

The fire chief tromped up onto the porch and approached the two women huddled together. "Chief Holbert," he identified himself. "House is safe, ladies. Near's I can tell it's just a brushfire down a piece in the meadow. We'll have it out in an hour tops."

"Hannah's down there," Grace called after the chief as he hastened away. He looked back, raised his hand, and nodded, acknowledging that he heard her.

Lit by the darting orange flames Hannah stood at the edge of the blaze, oblivious to the firefighters. Yet she did not resist when strong, gentle hands pulled her back from the searing heat. The man peered at her from under his hard hat.

"Can you walk, Miss Hannah?"

She could, barely. "Wayne?" He smelled of tobacco and musky cologne and oddly she felt comforted.

"Lemme get you to the house."

"No." She pulled away. "I started it. I must help."

"That's our job. You'll only get in the way."

"My fault, it's my fault," Hannah moaned as she let Wayne guide her faltering steps.

Bob, indistinguishable from the others in his yellow slicker, stepped forward. "You okay, Hannah?" Slipping an arm about her waist, he helped Wayne half carry, half walk her to the house and up onto the porch and into a chair.

Grace knelt beside her. "It's going to be all right."

But Hannah took no comfort. Seeing Amelia, sitting rigid now in her chair, her wide and frightened eyes darting from Hannah's to Grace's face and then from Bob's to Wayne's, stirred unremitting feelings of guilt and deep remorse in her.

"When it's dry like this, we get lots of brushfires 'round here, ma'am," Wayne said. "Our job's to put 'em out." Ready to leave, he turned and motioned to Bob. Bob gave Grace's hand a squeeze, and the two men soon disappeared around the corner of the house.

Fire trucks stood like stanchions in the meadow. Brown water hoses snaked their way down the hillside. An ambulance's siren pierced the air. Pickups ground to a halt on the road, and young and old men in slickers and hard hats raced by, their voices loud and urgent. Everywhere the acrid smell of smoke.

Suddenly Amelia commanded, "Hurry, Hannah, get the station wagon. We've got to escape if the house, if . . ." She buried her face in her hands.

"We won't have to leave, Amelia. It's just a small brushfire. They'll have it out in no time. We can see it from the guest bedroom, way down the slope." Grace extended her hand. "Come upstairs with me. Let's all go."

Amelia shook her head. "I'll wait here." She half rose, then fell back into the chair and tightened her grip on the arms of her rocker. "My camera bag's in my bedroom."

"I'll get it," Grace said.

Utterly exhausted, every bone in her body aching, Hannah stayed with Amelia. Oh God, she thought, if only I could turn back the clock.

During those silent minutes on the porch, Grace ran upstairs and returned with the camera bag. Amelia held it tightly on her lap. Still they did not speak. Grace fidgeted with her bandanna. Finally she could stand the silence and their haggard faces no longer. "I'll go upstairs and have a look, come back and report what's happening."

The orchard was clearly visible from the guest bedroom and Grace drew up a chair and stationed herself at the window, trying to pick out Bob among the firefighters. Shimmering waves of caustic, gray smoke billowed upward. The stinging odor reached as far as the house. Grace coughed, tied her bandanna bank robber-style over her nose and mouth. In the meadow a fountain of sparks erupted. She watched fascinated and horrified as a golden necklace of fire, sinuous and provocative, slunk along the ground and clasped the trunks of apple trees.

Generators roared. Silhouetted against the brightness, firefighters directed streams of water beyond the orchard to the tree line at the edge of the woods. Seeing this action, Grace realized that the real danger lay in the woods bursting into flames. She rubbed her chest, then retrieved several tiny pellets from a vial in her dresser. She slipped them under her tongue. She had not needed any pills since leaving Branston, not even when piqued and miserable about Amelia and Bob, not even with this Madison thing, not until now.

The thunder of a bulldozer drowned out anxious, male voices. Grace watched the huge machine, its purpose clear, swagger over the lawn and meadow, trampling everything in its path. A tall, dark figure, at first she thought it was Bob, but it was not, separated himself from the group and darted toward the machine, waving it on. "Plow 'em under," he yelled. The smoldering apple trees began to topple, and Grace leaned against the window frame and wept.

From the porch Hannah heard the crunch of falling trees and her own heart scrunched. The apple trees were dying, and she was responsible. She, who so loved the trees, had struck the fatal match. Her face was bathed in tears which she made no effort to wipe away until Amelia, drawn out of herself by Hannah's grief, set her camera bag on the floor, stood, and with faltering steps came to stand by Hannah's chair. Putting her arms about Hannah's shoulders, she tried, unsuccessfully, to comfort her. "You'll plant another orchard," she whispered, handing her a handkerchief.

But the tears kept coming. Hannah shook her head and looked beyond Amelia into her past, to the unendurable yet endured misery that had been her marriage to Bill and remembered another man, the only man she had ever truly loved, and lost. And so, although Amelia pulled her chair close to Hannah's, they sat in silence, each nursing their private hells.

An hour later, the men rolled up their hoses and began to back their trucks off the lawn. They had halted the fire at a deep trench ten feet from the edge of the woods. Of the apple orchard all that remained were black, twisted half-buried stumps and the cloying odor of ashes and charred wood.

Later, after the others had gone to bed, Amelia sat at the window of the guest bedroom watching, making certain that no unnoticed spark flared back to life. It would be weeks until she would be able to sleep through the night and not hesitate while doing some routine task to sniff the air with a worried expression.

32

Old Man

✿ Wearing his best, freshly starched coveralls and twisting his wide-brimmed felt hat in his hands, Wayne returned the day after the fire. "I've come to see how Miss Hannah's feelin'."

"It's been too much for her," Grace said as she opened the door for him. "Surgery, then that tumble over your legs, plus all that work in the greenhouse, and now this. She's completely frazzled. She insists she killed the trees."

He shook his head. "Trees gone up too fast. No sap. They was all dried out. Year or two they'd a been gone anyhow."

"You tell her that."

Wayne followed Grace into the kitchen, where Hannah sat mindlessly dipping her spoon in and out of the mug of tea.

"Mornin,' ma'am."

Hannah looked up. "Wayne. You and the other men did a great job last night. Thank you." There was a decided catch in her voice. She looked away, lowered her head.

"That's our job. We saved the woods, ma'am. That's what counts. About 'em trees, they were old, real old. Wouldn't a lasted but a year or so."

Hannah's head snapped up. "How do you know that?"

"Way they burned, weren't no sap, no fight left in 'em. Popped like you'd busted a balloon."

"Really?"

"Yep. Healthy trees give off somethin' like a sigh when fire gets 'em. Sure am sorry though, ma'am. Way you attacked that fire, you'd of thought those trees were young'uns of yours. Something fierce." He grinned and looked at her with respect. "Just like my grandma woulda done."

"It feels like a part of me died with them." Hannah, usually so confident, looked abject now, and Grace worried about her.

Wayne shifted from leg to leg. "You ain't been here more than a few months." He shook his head, fingered the edge of the hat. "You sure get stuck on things fast, Miss Hannah."

His simple statement unsettled her. She hardly saw herself as someone who got stuck or attached to things. Hannah Parrish had never put down roots, never owned a home until a few years before moving to Olive Pruitt's, never gotten too close to people — *not after* — she couldn't finish the thought. All this emotional stuff was getting to her. Turning into a sentimental old fool, she was. It was a relief when Wayne's voice scattered her thoughts.

"You remind me of my grandma. 'Fore she passed on, I brought her one of those red Christmas plants. Never could say its name right."

"Poinsettia?"

"Yes. Poin— Whatever you said. Loved that plant, she did. Talked to it, she did. And she took a yen to me, wanted me about her all the time." He looked away, then back at Hannah and smiled. "Tell you what, Miss Hannah. My grandpa's got him a right fine apple tree or two. I've got me a bunch of trees comin' up. Another day or so, if you're feelin' better, you and me can go up that mountain and get you some apple trees. Start you a new grove, and I'll get some help to take out the stumps and dig up that soil, turn the ash under. Good for the earth."

The fatigue that had taken up residence

496

in her brain eased a little. "Plant a new grove?"

"Oh yes, Hannah, yes," Grace said. Anything to pull Hannah out of the doldrums.

"Not yet, feels like I've been run over by a tractor."

"That feelin' will pass, ma'am." He nodded sagely and for a moment looked twice his years.

His suggestion seemed too formidable an undertaking. Hannah's weary mind anchored on autopilot, and though she appeared to be listening to Wayne, the whole of her attention was riveted to the nerve endings in her back and legs. "Thanks, Wayne. Just can't."

"And I figured you'd be needin' some help right about now with all those new plants you got out back." He nodded toward the rear window of the kitchen, from where the greenhouse was clearly visible.

"I can't . . ." She shook her head, stared at the wall.

"You fixin to quit, ma'am?"

His words jolted her. She straightened and scowled at him. "I never quit." Her reaction was as much a response to his challenge as it was the realization that enthusiastic as she had been about the greenhouse, once it arrived, coupled with the Madison ordeal, she had lost the will to get on with it. The sense of pressure, of hurry, that usually drove her was gone. In fact, she felt downright lazy. "Could use help out there." She nodded, sighed, lifted her head. "Well, all right, I'll go with you, see about those trees."

"Bravo, spoken like the Hannah I know and love," Grace said.

Wayne's face broke into a wide grin. "I'll come get you, Miss Hannah. Roads are real rutted though, better take my old truck."

Hannah merely nodded.

"Be seein' you then in a week or so, Miss Hannah. Ladies." Wayne nodded to each, put on his hat, and took his leave.

"He's not as bad as he looks," Hannah said.

"He's not bad at all, a character maybe, but basically a good person." Grace smiled at Hannah. "I think he's going to adopt you to replace his grandmother." For the first time since the fire, a smile formed at the corners of Hannah's lips.

At the insistence of Grace and Amelia, Hannah spent most of the week with her legs up and offered unsolicited advice when Amelia agreed to open three boxes one afternoon. "Don't yank the stuff out like that," and, "Tray's too heavy to be on top. Take everything out. Put it on the bottom." Amelia humored her.

Then, on a day so clear and fresh that Hannah could no longer bear to remain tucked away in the house, she cajoled Grace and Bob into helping her in the greenhouse to transplant the new plants. Bob moved clumsily in the confined space set aside for potting, but Grace deftly set plants into their new and bigger plastic pots. Hannah was impressed by Bob's noncompetitiveness and the way he praised her and Grace for their dexterity with plants.

A week later, on a muggy, cloudy day that could have won first prize for being the most oppressive day of fall, Hannah heard the crunch of Wayne's tires on the gravel driveway, and moments later they were on their way. Ten miles later after they got to the four-lane highway, Wayne turned onto a two-lane road that soon devolved into an unpaved road and then a narrow rutted road that made Hannah nervous. She focused on the thick under-growth that grazed the sides of Wayne's truck and tried somewhat haphazardly to identify the flora: mountain laurels, oaks, poplars, tall straggly pines.

When Wayne gave a yell and slammed on the brakes, but for her seat belt she would have slammed into the windshield. "What's wrong?"

Wayne leaned forward, rocked back and forth, and almost jumped out of his seat all at the same time it seemed to Hannah. This venture, she thought, was a huge mistake. "What's the matter?" she asked.

Wayne pointed. Hannah squinted. The sinuous, copper-colored, coiled creature sunning itself smack in the center of the road repulsed her.

"Snake." Reaching behind him, Wayne grabbed a long thick stick and leaped from the truck. Hannah watched dumbfounded as he crept up on the snake, and yelling unintelligible words pushed and prodded it until he enraged the creature, which hissed, recoiled, then rebounded as if to strike before wrapping itself around the stick. Wayne lifted it and calmly approached the truck.

"Get that thing away from me," Hannah yelled, winding up first her window, then stretching across his seat to wind up his.

In the mirror she could see Wayne at the rear of the truck. He pulled a wooden crate out from the back and in one deft movement slammed the stick hard against the top edge. The snake slid into the crate. Wayne shut the cover and a second later was back behind the wheel. "That should hold him."

"Won't he push off the lid?"

"He'll thrash about a bit, but he can't get out." Wayne started the truck. "Snake's worth money alive."

Both the snake and Wayne's perverse interest in trapping it gave Hannah goose bumps. "Alive?" she asked.

"Yes, ma'am. Snake preacher's always tryin' to get their hands on them."

"Really?"

"Yep. They believe it's God-given to handle snakes. They dance around, pray, talk in tongues. Sometimes snakes bite 'em."

"You've seen this?"

"Once when I was a kid, like to scared the devil out of me."

"If the snake bites them, don't they die, these preachers?"

"Sometimes. Some of 'em are tough. If the venom don't kill 'em, folks say, it's 'cause they've built up a resistance, but their followers think it's God's will. I hear tell those preachers don't even feel the bite."

They were silent as the truck lurched and jerked across the deeply rutted tracks. It was more than she wanted to know, and Hannah asked no further questions even though Wayne kept talking about snakes. Proudly he told her about the first snake he had caught and brought home alive.

"I was about thirteen, drivin' my pa's old Chevrolet. Come on two boys about nine, ten years standin' watchin' a rattler. Said to myself, 'Those there boys lookin' for trouble.' So I run 'em off."

Hannah glanced over at him. Shivered. His face was rapturous, as if he were speaking of a lover. "My head was workin' like lightnin'," he said. "I took off my heavy winter jacket, dumped it over that critter, wrapped it up real tight." Wayne rolled his hands one over the other to illustrate.

The truck lurched toward a tree trunk. Hannah grabbed the wheel and Wayne dropped his hands back onto it. They started down a twisting, rutted one-lane road, much like the road they had been on.

"Dumped that critter in the trunk of that car and headed home. Asked Old Man, that's my grandpa, 'How we gonna' get that critter out of there?'

"Old Man just opened that old rusty

trunk. He got him two sticks and he run one under that snake and the other atop of it and squeezed. Lord a mercy, Miss Hannah, you should have seen how he lifted that snake right out, dumped it in a box, and slammed the lid. That was my first one. Sold it to a snake preacher. Used the money to get me a motor scooter." Wayne pointed. "Look ahead, Miss Hannah, there's Old Man."

A swirl of dust and the crank and clatter of a tractor greeted Hannah before she saw the driver, and even then he looked absurdly small sitting on that huge machine in the open pasture. Wayne waved his hat. The tractor turned and started in their direction.

A tree-shaded winding dirt road had brought them down to a valley where a rushing stream divided deep verdant pastures. Soft hills cradled the valley. On the far side of the stream a faded, gray livestock barn leaned slightly toward a faded, gray tobacco barn. Nearby, sheds housed tractors, small farm equipment, chickens and other animals. Brown-and-white Jersey cows nibbled at the soft grass in a fenced area. Close by stood a mare with her foal.

Two faded yellow mobile homes, planted into concrete blocks, were side by side on a slight rise about thirty feet from the stream behind where Hannah and Wayne now stood. "Old Man and me, we just couldn't live together," Wayne said, laughing. "Old Man's too darn messy."

Old Man, as Wayne affectionately called his grandfather, was just that. Skin darkened and thickened by a lifetime of weather, his face deeply furrowed, his work-stained overalls hanging loose on his hunched frame, Old Man looked as old as Methuselah. His hands were tough and thick as rawhide, but his eyes twinkled. There were gaps in his teeth and a hiss in his speech, yet he smiled, laughed, and talked unself-consciously. His hair, cut in a flattop, was littered with bits of grass and dust. He brushed at it vigorously.

"Howdy. Howdy," he said.

"Old Man, this here's Miss Hannah, lady I told you about that's buildin' that greenhouse to grow them inside bloomin' flowers."

"Howdy, lady." Old Man waved them toward a metal folding table and chairs under a faded green awning suspended from the side of one of the trailers. "Get a jug of lemonade fer the lady, boy," he said. He peered intently at Hannah through blue eyes sunk deep under drooping eyelids. "Heard about yer fire."

A weight settled over Hannah. "We lost the apple orchard."

"Wayne's got him a couple apple trees he's been a growin'."

It suddenly occurred to Hannah that Wayne had offered her trees he had grown, probably for several years, to start his own orchard. She couldn't take his saplings.

"Mighty hot weather we been havin'," Old Man said.

Hannah agreed. They spoke of the weather, how cold last winter had been, how dry the summer had been. Old Man predicted a mild winter. "These old bones know, and squirrels 'er leavin' plenty nuts on the ground. Cold weather comin' you can't find a nut nowhere. Woolly worms ain't puttin' on heavy coats."

"Good year to plant apple trees, Miss Hannah," Wayne said. "They get a chance to settle." Wayne placed a heavy glass pitcher and three green plastic glasses on the metal table. "Old Man likes it sweet. Hope that's okay, Miss Hannah?" Wayne poured them each a glass of lemonade, slung himself into a folding chair next to Hannah, his legs stretched out.

"Old Man's ma and pa brung him up here from the flatlands, near the coast, when he was two. Been here ever since," Wayne said with obvious pride.

Old Man grinned. His eyes scanned the hills about them. The sky was blue, nearly cloudless and seemingly limitless. "Wouldn't trade this here land fer nothin'. You oughtta see them hills come a summer's evenin'. Purple like, wouldn't you say, boy?"

Wayne nodded, his eyes dreamy.

Old Man held up his hand. "Worked in a factory over in town. Machine got these fingers."

Hannah gasped, shocked to see one finger missing at the first joint from his left hand and a stump where a finger ought to be on his right. "I'm sorry."

"Quit that old factory. Been farmin' here for nigh on fifty years." He downed his glass of lemonade and poured a refill.

"Old Man's got the biggest, fattest porkers this side of the Mississippi," Wayne said.

What are porkers? Hannah wondered, even as she heard the grunts and got a whiff of the enormous pigs shuffling and snuffing inside a pen near the barn across the stream. *To market, to market to buy a fat pig.* Hannah wanted to sing the old nursery song aloud but didn't. She smiled at the idea of Old Man, poking and prodding those enormous creatures into a truck. *Home again, home again jiggity-jig.* Surely Wayne helped him.

"Smell pretty raw." Wayne nodded toward the barn.

Old Man launched into family history. "Buried two wives, three sons. Got me sixteen grandkids," he chuckled. "This here boy" — he pounded Wayne's knee — "Wayne's the only one stayed. Ain't that right, boy?" Old Man poked at Wayne's ribs.

The solidity of connection, the depth of affection between Wayne and his grandfather was obvious; a chilling loneliness swept over Hannah. She belonged nowhere. This kind of thinking's going to get me a big fat zero, she reminded herself. Covington's my last stop, no matter what house I live in. She lifted her chin. She would accept their generous offer of the saplings, and she would plant a new orchard, not so much for herself, but for future generations. She might never eat its apples but someone would, and someday maybe someone would stand in the orchard as she had done and wonder who the orchard planter had been and appreciate her efforts.

Old Man stood up slowly from his chair. Then, inch by inch he stretched his arms, legs, torso before taking a few steps. "Gotta keep movin'. Stoppin' turns the joints stiff. Well, lady, got plowin' to do." At the narrow footbridge that forded the stream Old Man stopped and waved at them. Then he shuffled across the narrow wooden bridge to the pasture.

"Ninety years and still plowin' and plant'. Won't have it no other way," Wayne said proudly.

"The man's got the health to work. It's his life. We should all be so lucky."

"You got no kin, Miss Hannah?" Wayne held up the pitcher, offered her another drink. Hannah set her palm over her glass and nodded.

"Two daughters, two grandsons up North. Don't see much of them."

"Right sorry to hear that. Once a year we Reynolds get us a great old picnic up at that old graveyard over yonder on that hill." He pointed, and Hannah saw, for the first time, a stone archway with REYNOLDS CEMETERY carved in bold letters across the top. Gravestones, white, gray, tall, short, ornate, simple, dotted the hillside. "Got us shade, picnic tables, benches. Come Labor Day a whole bunch of kin come. Got me three sisters and a brother." Wayne shaded his eyes and stared at the hillside graveyard. "See 'em once a year, regular. Take my nephews huntin'." He grew pensive. "Day Old Man passes, I don't know what I'll do. Marry me up maybe." He laughed, heaved to his feet. "Miss Hannah, before we get the apple trees, lemme show you my guns."

It seemed important to him, and so Hannah accepted his offer to help her up the steps into his home. The neatness of the place surprised her: kitchen countertops clear, sink clean and empty, faux leather recliner worn smooth with use, huge TV, overstuffed faux leather couch. No books, no pictures, no mess. The walls teemed with guns, fifteen she counted, and one crossbow. "For deer huntin'," he told her with satisfaction. "Old Man loves venison. Every deer huntin' season I gets him one big buck to cut into steaks and roasts so's he can freeze 'um for winter eatin'."

Hannah, who put the guns in the same category as snake preachers, saw the pride in Wayne's face when he spoke of provisioning his grandfather's larder, but she asked no further questions about snake handling or guns or hunting.

33

Capturing the Magic

✿ Amelia set her portfolio on the highly polished mahogany hall table and removed the eleven by eight black-and-white, prize-winning copy of the framed photograph that would soon be hanging in the Asheville Art Museum. Photographers from all of western North Carolina had competed at the photography fair held each year at the Civic Center in Asheville. To her amazement, she had walked away with a blue ribbon and had been written up in the newspaper along with a picture of her photograph.

Amelia took the photograph into the living room and propped it on the mantel. She trained a spotlight lamp on it and stepped back to study the print she had shot lying flat on her belly in Harold Tate's tobacco field.

She had shot the picture at the end of summer and Harold, as usual, had been immeasurably helpful, clearing an area for her, patiently helping her down and up, and convincing one of his men to agree to be photographed. The problem had been how to take the picture without showing the man's face but capturing his pathos and his strength. Amelia had been frustrated by this restriction until she remembered a field in Indonesia, and how, following Thomas, she had stumbled into the soft mud near a rice paddy and looking up had seen a man, naked to the waist, straining over the green stalks. She remembered how his sleek, sweat-covered muscles rippled in the sunlight. She had never seen his face, yet the man's image, so earthbound and timeless, could still be conjured up at will. "From below," Amelia had said to herself. "I'll shoot my picture of him cutting tobacco stalks from below."

The outcome was the prize-winning photograph that pleased her so enormously. It had been taken in the late afternoon when the sun, the defining element in daytime photography, cast long shadows across the tobacco field. The man had agreed to remove his shirt, and as he cut the stalks of tobacco and hung them on poles to dry, a nearby fence cast long dark lines, suggestive of prison bars, across the oblique line of his powerful back. The sheen of sweat coated his muscles. One hand, hard and knotty, grasped the knife and prepared to cut the heavy leaf-laden stems. The other hand, fixed firmly on the stalk, waited for the blow. A quivering globule of his sweat glistened on a leaf. It spoke volumes and was the focal point of the photograph.

One of the delights of black-and-white photography for Amelia was anticipating the outcome of each new print. First a vague outline, then the entire print would materialize as if by magic through the shimmering bath of developing fluid. Many prints merited discarding: a tiny bit of a leaf in a corner, too much sky, not quite the right exposure, an unsatisfactory composition. But then that special print would emerge with just the right combination of light and dark and a pleasing composition. It was the element of uncertainty, the gap between her vision of a shot and the developed results, that challenged her to compete with herself and others to create better photographs, the best photograph even, a flawless composition boasting the precise light, creative composition, arresting subject. Ah! That made it worth lying on the hard ground, the long walks, the brambles, stepping in holes, the morning or evening chill, even the leg cramps.

Pushing forward a hassock, Amelia flopped onto it and leaned forward with her elbows on her knees, chin on her hands, relishing her accomplishment. My heavens, she thought, I'm good. Thomas would be proud of me. Immediately a question came to mind. Would he really? She then recalled a recent disturbing dream of Thomas.

In the dream Thomas was dressed in black pants, a black Nehru shirt, and a black beret. In what appeared to be an art gallery, he coldly ordered men to remove her photographs from the walls.

"But they're mine, Thomas. Let me take them home," she begged, circling him as she pleaded.

"No, they must be disposed of," he replied disdainfully, waving her away.

Amelia found herself unable to move as strange men carted off her precious photographs. She had awakened in tears, disconsolate, feeling betrayed and at the same time guilty for hanging her photograph in an art gallery, and she slept not another wink that night.

Now as she sat on the hassock and scrutinized her winning photograph, Amelia shook her head. Thomas would look at it, and he would ignore the aesthetics of it and instead talk about the wages this man earned, or what his living conditions were. "He'd say my work was frivolous, of no redeeming social value," she muttered.

"Who thinks that about your work? That's a wonderful picture."

Startled, Amelia looked up.

Flushed from exertion, hair limp from the humidity in the greenhouse, Hannah strode into the living room with Grace behind her. Grace's face and hands were smudged with dirt, or soil, as Hannah called it. "We got every last plant potted. Wayne and Grace helped," Hannah said.

Grace moved closer to the photograph, and folding her arms over her chest stepped back to study it. "It's beautiful. It would make a great picture for the cover of a book. Ever thought about doing a book, Amelia?" Grace slipped rather inelegantly onto the floor next to where Amelia sat on the hassock.

Even when she's sweaty, Grace smells like her toilet water — fruity, Amelia thought. "A book? I've never thought about that, but why not?" She nodded and smiled at Grace. "I'll talk to Mike about it." Then she looked up at the photograph again. "I won first prize."

"Did you? Terrific. I'm so proud of you." Grace made no attempt to get up, but instead crossed her knees and settled back as if prepared to stay right where she was for a long time.

"Powerful picture. Not surprised you won," Hannah said.

"Do you really think I could do a book?" Amelia was off and running. "Would you two help me?"

Hannah nodded. "Should either be all black-and-white or all color."

"It should have a theme, like winter, or spring or something, right?" Amelia asked.

Now she had another excuse to avoid searching for the letters. Always a late sleeper, Amelia's internal clock had changed and she now started her day before the sun scattered the morning mist. The otherworldly quality of the mist, so eerie and mystical, drew her out morning after morning. On this day in early November she rose at six, in the still dark, dressed hastily, slung her camera bag over her shoulder, and by six-thirty moved softly down the stairs. Low-lying fog, endemic to the Blue Ridge Mountains, lallygagged in tiers across the hills. Cove Road, seen through a scrim of nacreous light, seemed a ghostly ribbon and far away.

Photographing rivers, trees, empty streets, streams, and graveyards, anything shrouded in hovering fog became her passion. The swirling, silent mist seduced her. There were moments when she thought she heard a child giggle, or sensed a serious-eyed man with gray hair watching. Caroline. Thomas. At those moments, she would stop and think about her dream. Surely Thomas must know what this work meant to her. He would never remove her pictures from a gallery. Then Amelia would set all thoughts of Thomas aside and concentrate on the work she had come to love.

A dark irregular watermark across a weathered gravestone, a glistening spider-web stretched taut between leaves, dew on a blade of grass, rounded black boulders, their tops visible above morning mist; all of these Amelia captured on film.

The weather this morning had a heavy feel to it. Amelia climbed into her car. The fog was nearly opaque in spots and as Amelia drove slowly along, she thought of Grace and how she had driven, for years, as slowly as Amelia was driving now. Within twenty minutes, Amelia unwittingly found herself on Reems Creek road in Weaverville.

Responding to an instinct, she turned off the paved road onto Oxbow Road, which was mostly unpaved and winding up toward the Blue Ridge Parkway. The hardwood forest, thick with fog, dripped with dew. Shafts of light angled their way through the trees to the puckered earth. Amelia stopped the car and sat staring into the forest. Mysterious. Otherworldly. The kind of place where elves and fairies lived and frolicked. It would be marvelous if she could see them. Amelia squinted, then sighed. No such luck.

It took only minutes to set up her tripod, then Amelia bent to her task with a sense of awe and urgency. Click. Click. Change exposure. Click again, change lens, click again until she had shot three rolls of color slide film and three rolls of black-and-white. By 9:30 A.M., satisfied and peaceful, Amelia was home.

A week later, Grace found Amelia scrunched over her light box at the kitchen table examining contact sheets and color slides.

"Look at these, Grace. Usually if I get two good shots out of a roll of thirty-six, I'm lucky. Something's different here. I shot all of these up on Oxbow Road a week ago. Am I imagining so many of them are good? Tell me what you think." Making room for Grace, she handed her the magnifying eyepiece.

"They're good, all right. They draw me in. I love them. How do you ever choose only one?"

"Weeding out, going over them again and again, but with these black-and-whites, well, I'll have to narrow them down to about seven shots and go ahead and print them all. I'll show them in class and ask the other students and Mike, of course, to evaluate them."

"You must show them to Hannah, and Bob. He'd love seeing them."

"You wouldn't mind?"

"Don't let that one incident hang over us, Amelia, or make you uncomfortable with Bob. He's not angry with you and I'm not, either. Bob's got so many interests, I think he'd find your photos lovely."

"Grace, will you marry Bob, leave us?"

"I'm in no rush to do anything but find those letters of yours." She set down the magnifying eyepiece. "You don't seem to care about finding them, do you?"

Amelia did not look at Grace. "I care. I don't know where else to look. I'm afraid we'll never find them, and then what?"

34

Their Wildest Dreams

On a balmy Saturday, Grace and Bob took Tyler to the Nature Center in Asheville.

"A bear, a bear," he screamed, hiding behind Grace. His fascination with the bear quickly overrode his fear and soon Tyler peeked around her waist, then pushed as close as he could to the protective fencing. Bob pointed out a baby bear, the first Grace had ever seen up close.

Fuddruckers, noisy and crowded at one-thirty in the afternoon, was Tyler's choice for lunch. They had hot dogs, and Tyler spent two dollars in quarters killing monsters on the video game machines. When they took him home Tyler planted a wet kiss on her cheek, then scooted up the steps to his father, who stood waiting in the doorway.

As they started back to Cove Road, Bob asked her, it seemed out of the blue, "Would you consider remarrying?"

"Remarry? I don't know," she said, realizing that her voice sounded cool and indifferent, belying her deep caring for him. As a young woman she would have equated passion with commitment, but not anymore. Lying in bed at night Grace had questioned what she really wanted. Scene by scene, she had replayed life with Ted: the sense of obligation she felt to get up early and prepare a hot breakfast for him, even if some days he had wanted only coffee. Never had she gone anywhere without reporting where, what for, and when. The dicta of the wedding ceremony, love, honor, obey, for better or worse, she had taken to heart, and Ted's needs and interests had superseded her own.

Her emotions had become a seesaw, up, she wanted Bob, down, she preferred her life as it was. Was this really love, she wondered, or admiration for his intelligence and his kindness? Was this gratitude for his attention and interest or plain, simple physical attraction? It rather tickled Grace to think it was physical attraction, at her age. Would he think her loose and lose respect for her if she indicated that she was open to their being lovers and not getting married?

"Why is it so important to get married?"

she asked. "Why can't people our age, just, well, you know, be together, without having to get married?"

Just last night Bob had said to Russell, "I used to think if I ever remarried it would probably be a younger woman with a career. Then along came Grace. Not at all the kind of woman I'd imagined or even been attracted to in the past. Independent, dependent, it hardly matters now. Grace is a rare woman without guile. She's generous of spirit, doesn't play games with other people's emotions."

"I like her," Russell replied. "Grace listens. You can tell she cares about people, especially you. It shows in her eyes when she looks at you."

"And," Bob had replied, "she's got a life of her own, just as I do. No clinging vine here."

"Why, if you care so much, don't you two just become lovers?" Russell had asked and that had brought the issue to the front of his mind. And now Grace was implying the same thing.

"I'm sorry," she whispered, breaking into his reverie. "Are you dissatisfied with the way things are?"

"In some ways." He raised an eyebrow,

looked at her suggestively. "I'd like us to be more, how shall I say, intimate." He held his breath. "I hope I haven't offended you." But Grace just nodded, took his face in her hands, and gave him a long passionate kiss.

"I'd like that too, very much," she said softly, nudging close to him.

Imagining them together quite took her breath away, until the old anxiety, the sense of inadequacy she had always felt with Ted, kicked in. It never occurred to Grace that Ted might have had his own problems, or a low sex drive, or that Ted would ignore foreplay and ejaculate quickly with any woman. How would it be with Bob? If she were only thinner, prettier, sexier, more like Amelia. But Bob didn't want Amelia, and he had never suggested that she "take off a few pounds." He complimented her clothes, her hair, her eyes, and seemed to like her just the way she was. Oddly this took some getting used to.

They said nothing more about such matters that evening, and when Bob kissed her good night with increased ardor, Grace did not pull away but allowed herself to relish the sexual stirrings he roused in her, stirrings she had felt with Ted only when they were young, just married.

35

The Greenhouse

✤ Outside the thermometer read seventy-two degrees and it was late November. Hannah wiped the perspiration from her face. Breathing heavily, she leaned against the worktable in the greenhouse, then walked over to the thermostat and peered at the numbers. Sixty degrees. "Couldn't be. Too darn hot." She ran the back of her hand across her forehead, tapped the glass cover with her fingertips, ambled back to the worktable, and stared in increasing consternation at the larger pots waiting for soil and plants, waiting to tax her ability to lift and carry. "This constant transplanting is killing me," she muttered, and yet she knew that three quarters of the nursery business was about planting and transplanting two, sometimes three times before ten-inch containers brimming with sturdy stems and leaves and flowers finally made their way to the retailer.

The greenhouse smelled of dampness

and freshly mixed soil. Bubbles of water had accumulated on the glass roof. She would have to call the distributor. He'd probably instruct her to call the manufacturer, and it could be days until someone came out to check it. "Heaven give me strength," she muttered as she emptied yet another pot and inspected the fine silvery roots slivering from the root ball. A plant's needs don't wait, and she had overestimated her ability to keep up with the work. She needed the help of a good strong back and capable hands.

Wayne came to mind, and as usual she resisted the idea. He was inconsistent. He arrived and departed at whim. True, he did copious amounts of work when he was here, but Hannah sensed Wayne hated commitment, and she needed reliability, knowing that he would be there on such and such a day and time.

Grace dashed into the greenhouse. "Roger called. They've made reservations, Miranda, Paul, Philip, even Sammy, for January eleventh." She stopped. "You look awful. You've got to get some help. I'll help you." Reaching for a pair of gloves on a nearby shelf, Grace pulled them on. Working with Hannah, as she did some afternoons, was pleasurable, but she preferred weeding outdoors and not being confined to the space and humidity of the greenhouse. When she and Hannah worked side by side on a flower bed, trimming, deadheading fading blooms or weeding, she was at peace. Now, as she mushed and pressed soil around the plant she placed in the container, she thought about Bob and felt a twinge of disappointment. It was four days since she had hinted at sex, and he had neither said nor done anything about it.

"You're an answer to a prayer." Hannah put an end to her musing. "You warned me it might be too much for me." With a large blue handkerchief Hannah wiped her brow and upper lip. "Can you believe I didn't calculate how much more space ten-inch pots take up than four- or six-inch pots? Look at those shelves." She motioned behind her to the rows of shelves that ran from ceiling to floor and extended the length of the greenhouse. Black plastic pots squeezed together on every shelf. "I overordered."

"Wayne any help?"

"He drifts in and out." The plant in her hand dangled upside down. She cocked her head, speculating. "It goes better, faster when he's here. I rather like the boy.

I'd like it better if he'd show up when he says he's going to. Different work ethic than mine. Amelia says since I'm living in the South now, I need to relax and go with the flow, easy like."

"I agree."

Hannah righted the plant in her hand and delivered it into its new home. Next she dribbled a small scoop of pellet fertilizer, Osmocote, around the stem, and used her finger to stir the pellets into the loose soil. Grace held the watering can and doused the soil until water oozed from drainage holes in the bottom of the pot.

"Shame about Wayne. You've mentioned getting rid of the greenhouse several times lately. Do that, Hannah, or get yourself a working partner."

"Want the job?"

"No thanks. I know my limits."

Hannah knew Grace was right. She had ignored the possibility of having to move the greenhouse, downplayed and overstepped her physical limits, so determined had she been to prove herself as able as she had been when she was fifty. Hannah carried another filled and planted pot to a shelf and unsuccessfully tried to squeeze it among the others. Bending carefully, she set it on the ground. Water dribbled along her arms.

"There's no more room. Why not just give Wayne the rest of those plants in the smaller containers? He could transplant them and grow them to maturity for you at his place. Maybe make a deal with him, split the profits on those he raises."

Hannah's brow furrowed. Placing her hands on her hips, she took a hard look around. "Going to have to just get rid of the whole darn thing."

"Is that what you really want, Hannah? Deep inside, is it?" Then in exasperation, "Why does it have to be all or nothing?"

"You're right, of course. I'll do it. I'll take the rest of these to Wayne's place. Drive with me?"

"Sure. I'd like to see where Wayne lives, meet that amazing grandfather of his."

As they stepped from the greenhouse, they saw it again, the red pickup truck, only this time a hand, probably Jeb Madison's, stuck out from the open window waving a Confederate flag.

"What's the flag about? Those people give me the willies," Grace said.

"Maybe they're saying, Yankee go home."

"Bob asked me if I'd considered remarrying," Grace said as they drove up the thickly wooded, heavily rutted mountain road with its overhanging branches and thick undergrowth.

"He proposed?" It was the news Hannah had been dreading.

"He didn't propose. Just asked me if I'd consider remarrying."

"And you said?"

"I didn't say."

"Maybe?"

"I've thought about it a lot. I'd prefer to keep things as they are."

Hannah let out a long slow breath. She hadn't realized she was holding her breath. "Don't you want a permanent commitment?"

"I have one, with you and Amelia, here, please God."

Hannah tried to keep her voice casual. "I've yet to see a woman stick with women friends when a man comes into the picture."

"Well, see it now. I like the way we live, the three of us, whether it's here in Covington or in Mars Hill or in Caster in another house. I'm happy to sit together in the evenings and enjoy a bit of local gossip, share a joke, have a good belly laugh. I like it that no one expects to be waited on. I'm satisfied with life as it is."

"Do you love Bob?"

Her seat belt strained across her bosom when Grace twisted toward Hannah.

"Yes, but why can't I have a relationship with Bob that's more, well intimate, you know, and not get married?"

"Grace Singleton, you of all people, an affair?" There was a light jesting quality to her voice.

"I'm not such an old stick-in-the-mud anymore, remember, and you and Amelia are responsible." Playfully she poked Hannah's shoulder.

"So, what are you thinking?"

Grace's voice turned serious. "What do you imagine it would be like, you know, at this age and everything?"

Hannah laughed good naturedly. "Sex?"

"Yes." Grace raked her teeth over her lip and looked out the window. "It's been so long, I shut off those kinds of feelings long ago, even before . . ." She stopped, ruddy-faced, embarrassed.

"Before what?" Hannah teased.

Grace drew a deep breath. "Even before Ted died."

"I get it, celibacy. But haven't the old feelings come back with Bob?"

"Yes, but they scare me." Her bandanna came in handy for keeping fidgeting hands busy. "I push them away, tell myself I'll deal with them later, like my mother told me to do the one time I had the courage to bring up that topic. 'Don't think about it,' she said. 'It'll come natural when you get married.' "

"And did it?"

"Ted told me what to do. I did it. Frankly, it was more duty than anything else." Bits and pieces of scenes from her wedding night plowed through her mind: nightgown waist-high, intense pain at penetration, bewilderment, shock, disappointment when it was over. Her sexual education had been vicarious, through books and movies. After a few years she had stopped blaming Ted. He had had no more experience than she and had lacked the drive or curiosity to explore.

Hannah maneuvered the car around an "S" curve, and Grace slid to one side. "Sorry." Hannah turned right down a narrow dirt road that had obviously seen better days. "I've had it both ways. Dull, dutiful as you say, and great, the way sex ought to be."

Grace nudged Hannah's arm. "Great? Tell me, Hannah, please."

"Sex with Bill was good, I thought." She grinned, shrugged. "What could I compare it with?" Her voice went flat. "Less so after the babies, and in time, less and less, until, when he started drinking I'd just lie there and wait for it to be over." She paused and when she spoke again her voice grew stringent. "Most men are so absorbed in their own satisfaction."

Hannah swerved to avoid hitting a turtle. Grace looked back to see the little creature poke its head out from its shell, then proceed on its lingering, perilous journey across the road. "Except sometimes a really special man, sensuous, loving, comes along and sweeps you off your feet."

"You knew someone like that?"

"Late for me. I was forty-seven. Fell head over heels. He was married. Dan Britton, the great love of my life. Dan Britton." His name rolled off her tongue with tenderness, and Grace caught a glimpse of Hannah's flushed face, and her eyes were soft. "Making love with Dan was incredible, wild, impulsive." For an instant Hannah took her hands off the wheel, pressed them against her chest. "And so satisfying."

"Oh," Grace said softly, feeling humble.

"I've heard that a person's sexuality has nothing to do with age. If you've been a *hot tamale* all your life, well, you go on burning tongues. Of course, I never knew I was a hot tamale until Dan." They laughed.

They could see Old Man's fields through the trees. Hannah's voice was barely a whisper. "I *loved* him, Grace." Her voice cracked, hardened. "It's scary to love a man that much."

"What happened to Dan Britton?" Grace asked tentatively.

Hannah's face grew sober. She cleared her throat, straightened her shoulders; when she spoke her manner was oddly reportorial. "He was killed in a boating accident on a lake. Some teenager speeding in a racing boat smashed into Dan's twenty-one-foot sailboat. Dan was pitched into the lake. It was days until they found his body. No one knew about us. He'd been talking about divorcing his wife. Still, I felt it was inappropriate to go to his funeral. Four months later I'd lost thirty-five pounds, got pneumonia, and wanted to die. I hated the doctor who saved my life with his intravenous antibiotics." Tears strained Hannah's voice. "No one knew. I couldn't tell anyone. Unfinished business. Sheer hell."

"Oh, Hannah." Grace wanted to weep for her friend, wanted to throw her arms about her, which was foolish since Hannah was driving. Instead Grace sat quietly, allowing Hannah time to manage her feelings.

They were almost into the valley. Hannah lifted her shoulders, sighed, shook her head. "I'm fine, Grace. Dan was my wildest dream come true. Even with all the pain, I still wouldn't change a minute of it. He was the most special person who ever graced my life." They rolled out of the tree-shaded road into the open, sunlit valley and parked near the stream by the two mobile homes.

"I've never been in love like that," Grace said softly. "I guess I gave up my dreams of being a professor of history at a college or of having a great love a long time ago." Yet, whenever she saw Bob, a thrill followed by anxiety floated up her spine. She knew she was captive to a sexual past spent sucking in her stomach, draping a sheet to cover her ample breasts and hips, concerned always about where Ted would touch her, what he would think. Such uninspiring memories only added to her insecurity and definitely repressed her desires.

There was no time to discuss all this with Hannah now, for suddenly the pasture and barns and mobile homes swept into view. Hannah pointed to a bent old man on horseback. "That's Old Man, Wayne's grandfather."

Old Man waved and turned the fawn-colored horse that moved rhythmically, relaxed and uninterrupted, toward the stream. "Wayne got this new kindda horse fer me." Leaning forward, he stroked the horse's mane. "Paso Fino they calls 'em, real smooth ride. You ladies wanna try 'er?"

"No thank you," they said at the same time. Then Hannah said, "This is my friend and housemate, Grace Singleton."

He nodded. "Mighty glad you dropped in. Go on up to the house. I'll be jest a minute."

They were unloading boxes of large empty pots and boxes of smaller pots filled with thriving green plants when Old Man ambled up to his home. "Wayne here?" Hannah asked. "I've brought him anthuriums and begonias. Ran out of space in the greenhouse. Thought maybe he'd like to grow these on."

"Well good. Ain't that nice." Old Man poked his head into one of the boxes Grace and Hannah had set on the ground under the awning. "Mighty good-lookin' plants you got there, lady."

Hannah was used to his calling her lady. Suddenly chilled, she rubbed her shoulders. "Think it's going to get cold tonight?"

"Could get a hard freeze any night now." He shuffled around the boxes of plants. "You grow'd 'em yourself?"

"Ordered rooted cuttings from Florida."

"Well, well," he said. "Florida's a far piece south." Unself-consciously, Old Man turned from them and spat a wad of tobacco from the side of his mouth. "Went there one time with my cousin Fred fishin'." He chuckled, shook his head. "All the way down there fishin'." Old Man removed his Braves baseball cap, fanned his face, and scratched his head. "Fall sure's been pretty this year." He watched as they unloaded a second box of plants. "Boy's gonna be mighty surprised." He scratched his head again, smiled. "Mighty pleased."

Grace looked about. The land was well tended, hay rolled into neat golden bales waiting to be moved to storage in the barn, fences freshly painted the maroon/red color of barns, a new bridge across the stream. "Wayne's not here?" She thought of Wayne as a trickster. He might be playing hide-and-seek, might burst out of his door any moment.

Old Man waved his hand out toward the road. "Gone to pick up his sister Emily

536

and her husband, Parson Jackson, down in Young Harris, little town in Georgia." He sounded pleased. "Primitive Baptist Church he's pastorin' down there. They're comin' up fer our church. Pastor Jackson's gonna lead an old-time, foot washin' come Sunday."

"Foot washing?" the ladies both wondered aloud.

Old Man eased himself onto a chair with a sagging, webbed bottom. He sighed, brought his hands together in prayer fashion, and cast his eyes to the sky. "Christ teached it Himself. Humbled Himself. Washed his disciples' feet." He nodded vigorously, with assurance. "Says so in all four gospels, Pastor Jackson says."

"I thought someone named Mary washed Jesus' feet, dried them with her hair?" Grace asked.

Old Man's head bobbed up and down. "You knows your Bible, young lady. All 'bout humility." He chuckled. "Reckon we could all use a touch more humility, eh?" He shook his head. "Always did have a hankerin' to be a pastor. Lived a far piece out from the schoolhouse."

Grace felt sad for him, wondered what his life had been like. Had he been happy with his wives, his children, his work? If she asked, he would probably brush it all aside and say something like her father might say, "A man's gotta do what a man's gotta do." Grace noticed the empty spaces in his mouth, more empty spaces than teeth. If he'd been a pastor his appearance would have mattered, but as it was Old Man didn't give a hoot about how he looked.

"We'll leave these for Wayne. He can stop by anytime, let me know if he needs more fertilizer or anything." Hannah accepted the bandanna from Grace and wiped her hands.

"Boy'll be mighty pleased." He nodded. "Thank ye, ladies. Y'all come back."

They left him standing in the shade taking pots out of a box and stacking them on the table.

The following day Wayne's rackety truck tore across the lawn and braked near the greenhouse. Hannah stepped out and wagged her finger at him.

"Hello, Miss Hannah. Come to say I'll grow those plants on for you."

"No, Wayne. Not for me. They're for you to grow and sell."

"I can't take your plants, Miss Hannah."

Wiping her hands on her apron, Hannah walked to the truck. "As a favor to me,

Wayne. I've run out of space. They'll all die if you don't take them."

"I won't take 'em. I'll grow 'em for you."

"Then let's split the profits when they sell, how would that be?"

"I won't just take 'em, Miss Hannah, so I guess you got you a partner." He grinned.

She did not want Wayne for a partner and here she was, shaking his hand, nodding and smiling as if it was the greatest thing in the world. Hannah changed the subject. "Old Man looked happy as a kid riding that horse you got him."

Wayne grinned, shoved back his hat, chewed on a toothpick protruding from between his teeth. "Yep. He sure likes Firebrand. That's her name. Small horse, fourteen hands high. Just right for him. Moves gentle like. Don't shake him up."

Hannah smiled. Wayne could infuriate her one minute, charm her the next. "You're a good grandson, Wayne." Partner, eh? If only she could depend on him with his zero sense of time.

Wayne turned the key and the motor coughed, sputtered, and sprang to life. "Shucks, I about forgot. Old Man says he'd be real glad if you'd come to church with us Sunday. Old Man says he told you about the foot washin'." Wayne grinned ear to ear. "Feels real good, gettin' your feet washed. Ain't had mine washed since I was fifteen." He touched his chest. "Gives a person a right fine feelin' in here, people so lovin' and all. Y'all come. Bring Miss Grace, Miss Amelia, too. Y'all welcome. Won't have another foot washin' in these parts not ever again maybe. Parson Jackson and my sister Emily are movin' to Louisiana. You think on it, Miss Hannah." He revved the engine. "Just leave a message for me with Tim at Prancer's. Tim's comin'. His momma used to belong to a church in Georgia, and they'd have foot washin' every fourth Thursday." He was off then, and Hannah grimaced to hear him burning rubber down the street.

Hannah leaned against the edge of the greenhouse. She hadn't set foot in any church for maybe thirty years. After Dan's death she had sworn off God. She wasn't sure she wanted to start back with some antiquated custom. She'd never heard of it. Later, when she asked Brenda Tate about it, Brenda said she'd heard it was a nice ceremony, but as far as she knew, they didn't do it at any of the area churches anymore.

36

A Visit to Abingdon, Virginia

.ᢞ Bob read from a brochure as they strolled down historic Main Street in Abingdon, Virginia. This was their first trip to the Barter Theater. "Says here Abingdon's named for Abingdon Parrish, the English home of Martha Washington. And the Martha Washington Inn, where we're having dinner, was built as a private residence in 1832, used as a hospital during the Civil War before it became Martha Washington College for Women."

"I thought you said it was a boarding-house for actors from Barter Theater across the street?"

"Oh, it was, it was. But it was renovated as an inn and reopened in 1935." He folded the brochure and stuck it into his jacket pocket, then tucked her arm through his.

They both loved history and had come

early in order to meander the streets of the historic district. Many of the buildings dated from the 1800s and early 1900s and had been converted from homes to shops or offices. A plaque at The Tavern proclaimed it to be the oldest building in town.

ABINGDON'S OLDEST BUILDING
FAITHFULLY RESTORED TO
ITS 1779 CONDITION.
PRESIDENT ANDREW JACKSON AND
KING LOUIS PHILIPPE OF FRANCE
ATE HERE.

At the Cave House, built in 1858, and now a charming craft shop, Bob bought Grace a pewter vase. "For flowers, so you can talk to them this winter," he said. She selected a silver tie clip with a tiny book on it and insisted he wear it. A sign explained the name, Cave House.

THIS BUILDING IS NAMED FOR THE CAVERNOUS LIMESTONE GROTTO LOCATED DIRECTLY UNDERNEATH THE SHOP.

There was no time to explore the grotto. "We'll save it for another time." he said.

The old classic *Arsenic and Old Lace* was the play. Though they had both seen it years before, they enjoyed it and exited the playhouse into the chill afternoon air, laughing. They walked on cobbled sidewalks. Grace pulled her coat close about her, and Bob drew her to him, bent and kissed her cheek. "You laugh good," he said.

"You smell good," she replied, snuggling against him. Being close to Bob made her warm and goose-bumpy, and she could feel the sense of sexual frustration as they made small talk and ate a leisurely early dinner at the Martha Washington Inn in an elegant room with crystal chandeliers, oriental carpets, and beautiful antiques.

"It's been a lovely day, the drive, the play was well done, and now dinner's delicious," she said.

"Couldn't have said it better."

Grace felt relaxed, cozy, chatty. "About laughter," she said. "Once my cousin Sally and I, she was eighteen, I was fourteen, took a dinghy out on the lake in Dentry. We rowed to the middle of the lake and started singing off-key, giggled and laughed so hard we capsized the dinghy. We couldn't stop laughing. Couldn't even swim to shore. Just clung to that overturned dinghy and tread water."

He laughed and leaned forward, his eyes

soft and caring. "Who rescued you?"

"My father, raging mad. He rowed out in another dingy, and we held on to it while he rowed us to where we could touch bottom. I was grounded for a month." She frowned and her eyes grew serious, sad. "He lectured me every day for weeks about my irresponsible, attention-getting, immature behavior." Grace pushed her chair back a bit and crossed her legs. "I haven't seen cousin Sally in twenty years, but I'll always remember how much fun we had that day, even with the punishment."

Bob pulled out the brochure from the inn from his pocket and leaned forward. "The inn is furnished with antiques. There are brick fireplaces and canopy beds in many of the rooms." He turned the color brochure so she could see it.

Grace smiled. "They do look lovely." Was he asking her to stay overnight here? She wasn't sure she was ready to do that. But then Bob drew back from the table, folded his napkin, took a sip of water, and said nothing more about it.

On the drive home they sat close to one another, their thighs and shoulders touching. "What's happening with the attorney and the Madisons?"

"Seems that Arthur Furrior's attorney

passed away five months ago. He was the one who drew that last will, where Arthur bequeathed the property to Amelia. No one else in that firm had much contact with Arthur, and they can't find a letter he sent Amelia telling her of her inheritance. One more piece of paper we can't locate."

"What about friends?"

"Not many. Harold Tate gave a deposition. He told the lawyer Arthur was the same as he ever knew him, but then, he hadn't seen him the last eight months of his life."

"His doctor?"

"Seems Arthur hated doctors. His was in Greenville and he hadn't been to him in a year."

"Ever find the letters you told me about?"

"Nope. We've looked in every box and drawer."

"Hell of a thing," Bob said, shaking his head.

"Yes. We could lose the place."

Neither spoke much after that, and when they reached the farmhouse and he turned off the motor Bob wrapped Grace in his arms and whispered endearments that set his blood racing, and he hoped her blood racing as well.

37

The Foot Washing

✻ The freshly painted, boxy white church with its slender steeple sat in a grove of walnut trees a hundred feet from the bank of the Trout River, so named for the abundant trout that had drawn anglers from around the country until Grand's Paper Mill upstream polluted the water. Two years ago, local fishermen and the Trout Fishermen's Association of America made enough of a stink that the mill was forced to clean up the river. But the fish, even when restocked by the Fish and Wildlife Service, repeatedly disappeared. Trout River Primitive Baptist Church, as it was called, was as devoid of ornamentation as the river was of trout.

Whether drawn by curiosity, or by a genuine interest, people jammed the church, sitting shoulder to shoulder in the plain, scrubbed wooden pews. Brenda Tate, Amelia, Hannah, and Grace sat on one side of the church with the preacher's wife,

Emily, a slim pretty woman with clear blue eyes, and several other women in white that they did not know, but who nodded and smiled at them.

Erect and stiff as their freshly starched white shirts, Wayne and Old Man sat with the men on the other side of the room. Wood benches without backs had been set up below the pulpit, and empty basins, jugs of water, and towels placed on them. There was no organ, no piano. Off to one side of the pulpit the choir, eight women, one of whom held a child of perhaps six months in her arms, stood ready to sing, a cappella. A communion table covered with a white linen cloth waited in front of the pulpit. Later, after the pastor had blessed the wine and bread, three deacons would serve communion.

As they drove over the mountain to Trout River in Tennessee, Brenda shared information gotten from a friend who had been a member of a Primitive Baptist Church. "My best girlfriend in high school was a Primitive Baptist," Brenda said. "Her church held services only once a month. They didn't do missionary work, or have revivals, or Sunday School, or take up offerings. Women couldn't talk in church. My friend's mother told me once that in their church people never claimed to be saved. She said one couldn't really know if they had been saved until they got to heaven."

"Makes sense to me," Hannah said.

Service began when Old Man rose and faced the congregation. "We're mighty blessed havin' Pastor Frank Jackson leadin' us in prayer and worship this evenin'. If you've never had yer feet washed, I say, shed yer shoes and socks and git 'em washed this here evenin'. Ain't nothin' better."

He sat, and the choir lifted their song sheets. "Rock of Ages" was followed by "Hide Thou Me." Voices sweet, vibrant, and in perfect harmony filled the room.

Pastor Jackson's voice was rich and mellow, fit for revivals. "Welcome y'all," he said, smiling down at the upturned faces. "It is with joy and humility that I stand before y'all this evening." He spoke of God's love and God's healing powers, then read from Corinthians 1 about the foundation on which communion was built. He spoke of the Last Supper, the sharing of bread and wine, then urged the assembled to search their hearts, to expel all sinful thoughts, all hate, anger, pride, arrogance, covetousness, and to place the burden of their lives into the hands of Jesus Christ. Pastor Jackson turned to the thirteenth chapter of the gospel of John. " 'And after supper Jesus girded a towel about Him, took a basin and began to wash the disciples' feet.' " He stopped, looked out at the assembled, and even though he spoke in a softer, more intimate way his voice still filled the room. "In my whole life I never felt caught up with spirit like I did when I sat for my first foot washing. The Holy Spirit washed my soul that very day."

A great silence, a huge sense of expectation filled the church. Hannah could hear her heart beat.

" 'Jesus,' " he continued, " 'admonished his disciples to act in love and serve with humility and wash each other's feet, for no man is better than another.' " Pastor Jackson's eyes gazed down at the congregation. His tone changed, became less oratorical. Leaning forward, he grasped the sides of the pulpit. "We call down a special blessing this evening on Jethro Reynolds, my grandfather-in-law, a God-fearing man, who made this evening possible. And to all of you, I say, listen for God's voice calling y'all to walk up and partake in the foot washing. Amen."

"Amen." The congregation intoned.

There followed a time of silent prayer and reflection. Except for those in the choir, Hannah noted only a few young people in the church. She thought about what it meant to listen for God's voice. She had never heard it. It was impossible for her to imagine an anthropomorphic entity, who might look like anyone of the assembled, sitting in some heaven communing with each and every person. Far more likely, she thought, if there is a God, He has given His creation free will, and like a producer He sits back watching the total play unfold. God must be pretty disappointed with the results.

Memories of Dan Britton, stirred by her talk with Grace, haunted Hannah. A Catholic, he had been remembered with special masses offered for the repose of his soul. On a raw January morning, out of love and respect for Dan, she had attended a service and had sat shivering, more from anguish than from cold, at the rear of St. Anthony's Cathedral. That day in the cathedral Hannah challenged God for answers and having received none had withdrawn from God. She took her life entirely into her own hands, for good or ill. As if aware of Hannah's thoughts, Grace's small hand covered hers. Amelia sat on the other side of her, her eyes closed, swaying slightly. Hannah fixed her attention on the minister.

Pastor Jackson descended from the pulpit and said a blessing over the communion table, where several deacons of the church stood waiting before passing trays of wafers and tiny cups of wine to each pew. Amelia and Grace accepted a wafer. Amelia, remembering her experience at the Church of Our Lady, prayed silently, "The letters, please help me find them."

Hannah declined communion.

Finally, the minister administered communion to the deacons, who then took their seats.

Anticipation was palpable, like smoke in the air. People shuffled their feet, squirmed on the hard benches, and coughed. Emily and several women in the front pew rose. Old Man, Wayne, and others rose. They walked to the benches in front and poured water into the basins. Then Wayne motioned to his grandfather. Old Man sat, removed his shoes and socks, and his grandson knelt before him, head bent, and tenderly, lovingly washed first one then the other of his callused feet. Old Man laid his hands on Wayne's head in the manner of a blessing. They changed places and Old

Man, assisted to his knees by Pastor Jackson, washed his grandson's feet.

Silently, reverently, others moved forward, sat, removed their shoes, socks, or stockings and placed their feet in basins. Women ministered to women on one side of the church, men ministered to men on the other. After washing another woman's feet and having hers washed, Brenda returned to their pew, a peaceful look on her face. She gave Hannah an encouraging nod toward the pulpit. Pew after pew, people stepped forward and took their places. All seemed entranced. Many returned to their seats with radiant faces. Some wept. And so it went, until almost every person in the church had been moved to partake in the blessing tendered by the act of foot washing.

It was at this point that Brenda took Amelia's hand, led her forward, and knelt to wash Amelia's feet. Hannah and Grace had not intended to participate in the foot washing but now, as if compelled, they came to the front. Grace and Hannah washed one another's feet, unselfconsciously, and with great care and affection.

Later that night, Hannah came into Grace's bedroom. Her chenille bathrobe, worn over her pajamas, was tied at the waist with a piece of curtain cord. Somewhere, she had lost the original chenille belt. She flopped alongside Grace on the bed and accepted the pillow Grace handed her to prop behind her back.

"I get goose bumps thinking about tonight. Seeing Wayne and his grandfather wash each other's feet really touched me," Hannah said.

"It was special."

"Something odd happened for me. When you were washing my feet," Hannah began, but then hesitated and made a motion with her hand as if to brush the idea away.

"Out with it, tell me," Grace said.

"Well, it sounds crazy, but I felt as if you and I connected on some very deep level. You feel anything like that?"

Grace looked squarely into Hannah's eyes. "Yes. I felt it. Our spirits, if you can call them that, somehow joined." She sat back in her bed and drew her knees up close to her chest. "How lucky I feel knowing you and Amelia."

Amelia appeared in the doorway. "Couldn't help hearing. I agree tonight was special. I'm glad we went."

"So am I," Grace said.

"Yes," Hannah said.

Amelia's face lit. "*Mes amies,* each thing that's happened to us since we've come to Covington has been a square in a patchwork quilt, a friendship quilt."

"How close we've become, the three of us," Grace said.

Then Amelia said, "If we don't find the letters, what will we do?"

"We'll find them. I feel it in my bones," Hannah said.

"Worst case scenario, we could rent a house together, someplace near here, couldn't we?" Grace asked.

"But we've invested so much of ourselves into making this our home. I love this old farmhouse."

"Remember our first night, the flood?" Grace leaned forward, still hugging her knees.

"I wondered how we'd ever be able to live here, the three of us alone." Amelia smiled.

"Managed, didn't we? Solved every darn problem that's come along. Three of us living together, working out our differences. We're remarkable women."

"Indeed we are, Hannah." Grace spoke with determination. "This is our home. We'll find a way."

38

Responding to Change

November 29, 1997

Dear Grandma,

Mom told us about Grandpa Bill's alcohol problem. She wanted us to know why you sent us home like that. Sammy's sobered up, let me tell you. We're not together so much anymore, and I'm glad. He used to boss me around a lot. I want to thank you for all you did for us when we were in Covington. I had a great time river rafting, and the Car Museum was interesting.

I'm really sorry about the accident. We caused you a lot of worry. I'm all healed. Sammy went to a rehab center for six weeks. He's finishing his last year at prep school. Not me. I'm going to Branston High. Cool. I think I owe you for this. Well, can't think of anything else to say. Hi to Grace and Amelia. See you in January.

Love,
Philip

Hannah closed her eyes. The letter from Philip slipped to the ground beside her porch chair. During their chat on the phone last week, Miranda had said that Philip's teachers were willing to assign him work and he could come with them to Covington in January. Life, fate, whatever, in its own backhanded way was providing the opportunity for her to repair her damaged relationships, even as prospects of home here, in this place, were slipping away.

Was fate offering her the opportunity to go back to live in Branston? She had found that in life when you made a major decision to change something, often the opportunity to return to it was presented to you, and you had to really listen to your heart and instincts and choose again. She felt closer to Miranda, tolerant of her son-in-law, loving toward Philip, and forgiving of Sammy. She shuddered. No. She would enjoy visiting with them in Branston next year, seeing the new shop, but she had made her choice, thrown in her lot with Grace and Amelia, and here she would remain.

Miranda wrote enthusiastically about the business. She reported regularly on Charles's T count, and Hannah of course relayed the information to Grace. "Well over five hundred."

"Miranda's so caring of Charles, as if she's got a personal stake in his well-being."

"Well, maybe she feels she does. A partnership's like a marriage." Hannah's tone changed. "Lately, Grace, I've been seriously thinking of selling the greenhouse." She clenched her fists and brought them up to chest level. "Goes against my grain."

"I see how you drag yourself to bed and wake up so tired like the dancing princesses in Andrew Lang's fairy tale, remember?"

"I remember the story."

By late January, the plants would be grown on sufficiently and Hannah expected to deliver her first orders to local nurseries, and to a large flower shop. "Why keep it anyway? I'll only have the expense of moving it."

"You giving up hope?" Grace nudged.

"I've been thinking about going up to see Miranda, see the new business, maybe go on to Laura in Maine." She had been collecting newspaper articles and travel magazines with stories and pictures of Maine and could see herself sitting stolidly on a craggy cliff overlooking a rugged stretch of coastline. It made her mouth water thinking about gorging on Maine lobster in a quaint weather-beaten restaurant on a quiet bay, and she had begun to anticipate shopping for winter clothes at L.L. Bean. "Too much work anyway, that greenhouse. If I go away, who would look after it, check the temperature, keep the glass free of moisture, spray for insects, wipe mildew, do general cleanup, maintenance?"

"I'd try . . ."

"No." She held up her palm. "Selling it's best, regardless, even if we found those confounded letters tomorrow."

Lately Hannah worried about her judgment, first the fire, then investing her money in this project. She understood that her fear of meaninglessness, her obsession with work, and being a stickler for routine and a daily schedule had created the problem in the first place. "Grace, you've got volunteer work at the school and Bob, and Amelia has her photography. I've always looked down my nose at volunteering, considered it a frivolous playtime for rich ladies without meaning in their lives. You've opened my mind. Maybe I could do something with you at the school, or at some retirement home."

"I've always volunteered. Seen it as a way of giving something back to the world," Grace said. She had said this to Hannah before, urging her to set up a gardening class for kids at Caster Elementary.

"What if I sold the greenhouse to Wayne? Let him pay it off over time. Move it to his place, yet retain part ownership? He's young, strong. I could market the plants." As she waited for Grace's reply, she thought: my feelings about him have completely reversed. I like Wayne, have come to respect his reading of the weather, the way he can pick up a handful of soil, sniff it, and know what it does or doesn't need. He certainly has a green thumb. But if he says he'll be here Monday, maybe he'll show up on Thursday. Yet, the way he takes care of Old Man touches me; it redeems Wayne. "He's a good person, a prodigious worker, when he works," she said.

"Can you ease up on this time thing?"

Grace asked. "Not care when he does it so long as he meets a deadline? Do you think he can meet a deadline?"

"Actually yes, I think he can. He'll work all day and night, just not when you specifically insist he work."

Their conversation was interrupted by Amelia's Taurus crunching gravel in the driveway. They watched her walk lightly up the steps and onto the porch.

"Hi," Amelia said, all smiles. "I'm glad you're home. I need some advice." Straggles of hair clung to her flushed cheeks. She flopped into her accustomed rocking chair. "Mike says, since my book is a North Carolina book, it'll have a local and tourist market. He thinks I should self-publish. What do you think?"

"I don't know anything about the publishing business," Hannah said.

"Mike arranged for me to talk to several local authors, and they agree. Seems that publishers often don't invest much in marketing. For most books it's like they throw a handful of spaghetti against the wall and, you know, most of it falls off."

"Tell me about self-publishing," Grace said.

Amelia spread her legs, tucked her khaki skirt — a new venture into style for her —

into the well between them and leaned toward Hannah. "It'll be a coffee-table book, photos on one side, captions, poems maybe, on the opposite page. I have two recommendations, a printer in Tennessee and one in Nebraska."

"Tennessee's closer," Hannah said.

"So you think I should self-publish?"

"I wouldn't want to give up control. But how will you market it?"

Amelia rubbed her chin and bit the side of her lip. "Local TV, radio, talks. Local bookstores would carry it. I'd start by sending a copy to the *Asheville Citizen Times*. They review books. There are small distributors around who sell self-published books."

"I heard of an author who piled his books in a station wagon and went across the country selling them. His book got to be a bestseller," Grace said.

"What's it cost to publish?" Hannah asked.

"That's what I need to find out. Mike thinks eight to ten dollars a book." She looked off into the distance, smiled. "A book's a kind of immortality. You're gone, but your work lives on."

"A kind of immortality," Hannah said. "Of course."

"I'd be dead, and people would remember me, my name at least." She traced the letters in the air with a long slim finger, A-M-E-L-I-A D-E-C-L-O-S-E. "A legacy you might say, right?"

Hannah nodded, then said, "Amelia, I need help with the greenhouse."

"Hannah, don't ask me to do that." Skinning up her nose, Amelia spread her fingers wide. "I hate dirt in my nails, my hands."

"I didn't mean that kind of help. I've a big decision to make."

"What?"

"Should I work a deal with Wayne, let him pay me off and move it up to his place?"

"You've invested so much in it, can you get that back from him?"

"Too much work for me." She poked her chest. "Voices inside say, 'Be strong, Hannah. Never quit. You're not going to let a little thing like age get the best of you?' What was I thinking, Amelia? Hip operation would turn back the clock?" She looked away. "Dammit. Always been a workaholic." She was suddenly struck with regret remembering all those Saturdays she had said no to Dan and worked instead, needing to prove again and again her competence, her reliability, how indefatigable she was. "Three hours in the greenhouse these days, I'm so tuckered out I can't make it upstairs to lie down."

"Why do you need a big career now? Can't you relax and putter in your greenhouse?"

"Putter?" The word offended her. "Maybe the same reason you need immortality?"

Amelia was silent. Finally, Grace spoke. "Immortality? Workaholic? What does immortality or overworking mean when you're in your grave, anyway? Isn't it meaning you're talking about, having a reason to get up each day, feeling satisfied with your life when you go to bed at night?"

Amelia nodded. Hannah smiled.

"Right of course. I'll make Wayne my partner. Let him stand on his feet all day." Hannah's eyes drifted to the distant mountains, lingered on trees whose autumn peach and rust and yellow and gold leaves had fallen. The Appalachians, she thought. Oldest mountains in the world and growing older every day. Imperceptible change. Why couldn't she grow old graciously like the mountains instead of resenting her wrinkles, her aching legs, back? Aging was the most aggravating part of one's life. What's the point, Hannah often wondered, of struggling to gain wisdom, maturity, to hone your skills, if you simply grow old and frail and can't use them anymore, and then you die? What's the struggle for? Books she had read on the meaning of life, on God and man's relationship, left her unsatisfied and still questioning. Once she had put a poster of a long winding road on her office wall. The caption said, *It's not the goal at the end, but what happens along the way that makes life meaningful.* Maybe it was as simple as that. And she thought, it's a year since we sat under that old oak and made plans to move to Covington.

She lifted her head. Across the road in the pasture, the farmer's young son ran haphazardly after a calf. Was he playing or trying to herd the calf to the barn? Either way he seemed to be having fun. He waved. Hannah, Grace, and Amelia waved back.

Hannah picked up Philip's letter, returned it to its envelope, and tapped the edge of the envelope on her chair. "Miranda wants me to go with her to visit Laura in Maine next summer."

"Then go."

"Can't just walk away from my respon . . ."

Amelia interrupted. "Mike's planning a field trip for our class to Deer Island in Maine this summer. You could plan your trip to meet us there."

Hannah ignored her; her mind wandered. Maybe Philip would take a train trip across Canada, or to Mexico, with her. She had always had a yen to go South of the Border. Hannah rested her head on the back of the chair. "I'd hate to give up gardening."

"I keep telling you. You don't have to. Just come to my school and set up a class for the fifth graders. Brenda would be thrilled."

"Teach gardening classes at AB Tech. You could teach about greenhouses, or about marketing plants, whatever." Amelia smoothed her skirt and picked up her camera. "Travel, indulge your dreams, be good to yourself. It's about time."

"You could develop a whole gardening program for the school, garden plots, flowers, vegetables. I could work with you," Grace said, her eyes glowing. "And we could teach kids how to can or freeze the veggies they grow." Her eyes swept across the front yard. "Look at all the beds you've

565

added, just in front. Why you could stay busy all year just taking care of them."

Amelia rose, and as she moved past Hannah's chair Hannah reached for her hand and squeezed it. "Thanks for your ideas, Amelia." She looked warmly at Grace. "You too, Grace."

"Just decide," Amelia said. "You're making yourself crazy."

Hannah knew that what Amelia really meant was, "You're making us all crazy." She resented that. Who made them crazier than Amelia with her failure to find those letters?

39

Memories and Dreams That Haunt

✱ On this fall morning, as fog mottled the landscape of distant fields and the hills, Amelia's photographic destination was a small family cemetery. Flinging wide the iron gate, the distinct smell of morning dew rose to greet her, to tickle her nose, causing her to sneeze. Moving along, paying no attention to the ground beneath her feet, she scouted the expanse of gravestones like a hawk selecting his target before swooping from the sky.

Within moments Amelia's attention was drawn to a prominent moss-speckled tombstone. A lean, graceful white Queen Anne's Lace flower leaned against the marble marker. Hastening forward, Amelia lost balance, stumbled and fell. Using the solid marble tombstone, damp with morning dew, she pulled herself up, and as she did so, noted the inscription:

CAROLINE HODGKINS.
BELOVED DAUGHTER.
JUNE 5, 1902–FEBRUARY 19, 1911.
DROWNED IN THE POND.

Amelia crumbled to her knees on the dew-dampened grave. Another Caroline. The same age as her daughter. Closing her eyes, she conjured up the fruity smell of Caroline's hair, the pungent odor of Thomas's Sir Walter Raleigh pipe tobacco. They were gone, gone, and the letters were gone, and soon the house and land would be gone. Anguished, all enthusiasm for work gone, Amelia gathered up her equipment and fled from the place.

That day and the next Amelia worked feverishly at the kitchen table selecting photographs for her book, *Memories and Mists: Mornings on the Blue Ridge*. A perfect name, Amelia thought. She had fallen in love with it. The photograph she held up now had a dreamy elusive look utterly at odds with the images from her awful dreams of a Thomas she had come to dread. In those dreams she pleaded with Thomas, who remained aloof, indifferent, and mocking, that her photographs not be destroyed or thrown overboard, or crated and stored in some deep dark vault.

What did it mean? What would make Thomas so hostile that he would want to destroy her work? For years he had been in her thoughts daily, but now she was busy, even happy, and days passed without thinking about him or Caroline. Then she would come across something like the grave marker, and guilt would overwhelm her, and the nightmares would increase from once a week to nearly every night. Was it guilt for being less attentive to their memory? For being happy and successful? For her growing friendship and dependence on Mike Lester?

What should she do? Mike was important to her, not as a lover, never that, but as a friend who encouraged her newfound talent, praised her, and guided her. Once or twice she had started to tell Mike about the dreams; there were moments when she ached to tell Hannah and Grace. But always, she stayed silent. "Keep your problems to yourself. You'll drive your friends, everyone, away." That's what her grandmother would admonish her to do, and her mother reinforced this family rule with, "In our family, we do not hang our dirty laundry on the line," and her father's refrain, "Keep a stiff upper lip."

So Amelia's life, though charged with the excitement of newfound creativity, was nevertheless plundered of satisfaction by fearsome dreams and frequent ruminations on dying. She had come so close to death in the forest and, looking back, it seemed so easy, so painless. Fearful of dreaming, Amelia often lay awake imagining dying. Who would help her die if she was suffering at the end? Hannah? Grace? How would they know her desires if she could not even tell them about her fears of dying, her growing belief that she would have no peace until she died.

The episode with Bob at Tyler's party had left her with a lingering sense of not quite measuring up. Plus, with all the seemingly good things in her life, Hannah and Grace would think her maudlin and definitely self-involved if she came to them mewling about silly dreams. From the kitchen window Amelia could see that it had begun to rain. Laying the mist-shrouded photograph on top of those she intended to include in the book, she closed the portfolio.

Several days later, captions and photographs assembled, Mike drove Amelia to

Tennessee for their first meeting with the printer.

"Can you have it done for me by December thirtieth?" Tolent had told her at their last meeting that a court date would be set soon, perhaps for late January. They would still be in the house at Christmas, and she wanted to give the books as gifts to Mike, Hannah, and Grace and to their families when they came on January 11.

Frank Lancing, the printer, turned the pages slowly. "That's not much time. Can't promise. This time of year's busy."

"Try."

"Be patient," Mike said to her. "We want it well edited and well designed."

He wanted the best for her. She didn't mind his "we."

40

And Life Goes On

The days grew chill. The nights colder. They missed the poplars shimmering gold, the maples decked in majestic reds, the peach tones and rusts that had in late October matted the hillsides. On a dull, windless, and dripping evening, the first night that week that Grace was not off somewhere with Bob, Amelia called a meeting in the living room she had warmed with a homey fire. "The time capsule," she said. "We must do it."

"I agree." Grace had become resigned to leaving, though it hurt. "At least we'll leave our mark, something of ourselves here. I've been thinking," Grace said. "Roger once gave me a silver brush and comb set, engraved, *To my mother, from your loving son, Roger.* I never use it. I'll put that in. I want to be remembered as a loving mother, and as a cook. I'll write out my recipe for meatballs and prunes, and for sugar cookies, put them in."

"One of my scarves. A photograph. It'll have to be laminated. I'll have to think about what else" said Amelia.

"Shovel, spade, my letter of commendation and appreciation from Dr. Hansen, a book I'll paste up of my favorite flowers." Hannah drew a photograph from her pocket and passed it around. "The boys. Miranda sent it. Doesn't Sammy look handsome in his school blazer? And Philip, what a smile that boy has. I'll have a copy made, laminated and framed."

"Who's going to pick up a good solid metal box?" Amelia asked.

"I will," Grace said. "Tomorrow."

On Saturday, a deliciously clear crisp day, Wayne arrived at the greenhouse to help Hannah clean up. They worked silently for a time. "Goin' too fast for you, Miss Hannah?" he asked. "Want me to slow down?"

Winded from bending too often and lifting too heavy pots, she shook her head. Wayne no longer smoked or chewed tobacco in her presence, but the odor permeated his hair, his clothing, and his teeth and fingers were stained an ugly yellowish brown. "Ever think about not chewing tobacco, Wayne?" she asked.

"I broke up with a gal 'cause she poked at me all the time to quit."

"I worry you might get cancer of the mouth or throat."

"We all gotta pass one day, Miss Hannah. Sooner's good as later's what Old Man says. Been smokin' his whole life and he ain't dead yet."

And she let it go at that.

Wayne was in a talkative mood. "You got to get used to enjoyin' your older years, Miss Hannah."

"Work's an enjoyment for me, Wayne."

"Hard for my grandma, too. Wore herself out workin'. Could of lived to be a hundred. Must have been seventy-five, but come plowin' time she had to follow Old Man behind that horse. Lord a mercy if that dern old horse didn't step back hard. Crunched right down on her two feet. Broke 'em." He raked his fingers through his hair and reflected. "Never could walk proper after that. She'd hobble about that house worryin' herself to death. She'd call me. 'Boy,' she'd say. 'Now you get out there and make sure Old Man ain't killin' himself in that field.' Or, 'Boy, I heard a noise out back. Go look. Now, you find a snake, you kill 'em,' and she'd hand me a big old stick."

"Must have been hard on her not getting about like she was used to," Hannah said. She enjoyed Wayne's stories about his family.

"She settled down after a bit, took to knittin' and bakin' pies. Never baked pies before."

Was he telling her, as everyone else had, that she needed to rethink her life?

On a day soon after, Hannah was working in the humid greenhouse and accidentally knocked two pots off the table. Soil splattered in all directions. Hannah sank to the floor and sat staring into space.

That is how Grace found her. "What are you doing on the floor? Are you hurt?"

Hannah patted the dirt-strewn wood-slat floor. "Sit. Chat."

Grace plopped down alongside Hannah. "What are we looking for? Did you drop something, lose something? Why are we on the floor?"

"Dear, dear Grace. I just love you. Darn pots fell." She wiped a smudge of dirt from near her mouth.

"Let me help you up. We'll go inside. Have a nice cup of tea."

"Nope." Turning onto her stomach,

Hannah brushed soil particles down out of sight between the slats of the wooden floor. Grace flipped onto her stomach and did the same. They lay there bottoms up, silent for a moment, scrabbling unsuccessfully for the fallen pots, which rolled out of their reach. They looked at one another and began to laugh, ignoring the fact that their clothes were becoming increasingly smeared with dirt.

Bob, who had been invited for dinner, discovered them laughing on the floor of the greenhouse. He stood in the doorway with a puzzled expression, then he began to laugh. Finally, he helped them to their feet, and with his hands around both their waists urged them, giggling, up the steps into the kitchen.

41

When You Can't Do It All Yourself

✿ Wayne stopped by on Wednesday afternoon. "Had to carry Old Man to St. Joseph's Hospital," he said. "Sure worried it might be his heart, but he had an attack of hiatal hernia's what they said." He shook his head and fingered the edges of his scraggly mustache. He wore a white shirt and a tie with multicolored dots splattered the width and breadth of it. His black shoes were polished to mirror clearness, as if Wayne had painted them with a clear polyurethane finish.

Seeing them, Hannah smiled, remembering her friend in third grade, Irene Lee, telling her, "Boys polish their shoes so they can see up our dresses. They can see our underwear in them." She had actually believed Irene and avoided standing close to boys right through high school. Instinctively she took a step backward.

"I'm sorry about Old Man."

"Doc says not to worry. All he's gotta do is stay away from grease. Fat chance of that, way Old Man loves his fried chittlins, bacon, and pork chops."

"I'm glad it wasn't his heart." Taking Wayne's elbow, Hannah guided him to a chair at the kitchen table. "Grace's sugar cookies?"

He rubbed his palms together. "Sounds mighty good."

A breeze fluttered the sheer lace curtains at the window above the sink. Hannah took down the pink cookie jar and filled a plate with cookies. Grace had prepared her once a month dinner of meatballs and prunes earlier, and their savory smell still permeated the room. Wayne had one, two, three cookies and had lifted another halfway to his mouth, then stopped. "Ain't you gonna have none?"

"Had mine already." She motioned him with her hand to eat however many he wished, then pulled out a chair and sat across from him. "Been wanting to talk to you."

He swallowed a big piece of cookie, reached for the glass of milk she had set beside him, and looked at her quizzically.

"I want you to consider being my

partner in the greenhouse."

He sat back, raised his hands in protest, and she reached over and gently eased them back to the table. "Eat cookies. I'll talk."

"I ain't got no money to buy nothin', Miss Hannah."

"No money involved now. Over time, you'll pay me something. You've already got a share. You're raising a third of the plants."

"I gotta punch a clock?" He stared at her, his mouth slightly ajar, then leaned over and laid his callused hand on hers for a moment. "Miss Hannah. I appreciate your askin' but I ain't never been in business, wouldn't know how to do it."

She shook her head. "No specific days or times. Sleep all day, work all night if you want. You know what needs doing, and I'll teach you whatever you need to know about the business as we go along."

"Well, I donno." He shook his head.

"I'll have to list with a realtor if you say no." She watched him closely, saw his face fall, his eyes cloud. Hannah placed her hands against the edge of the table as if she were about to get up. "Plants are babies. I'm too old for babies." She raised her hands in a gesture of defeat. "At least, thanks to you, there'll be an orchard again."

"Begging your pardon, Miss Hannah, I hear tell you ladies might lose the place. I can move those trees, wherever you settle."

"Bless you, Wayne."

The phone rang. She rose to answer it. It was a realtor asking if she was interested in selling the greenhouse and the plants. "I have an interested buyer," the woman said. Word of mouth in a small town.

Hannah glanced across the room at Wayne. Cookie crumbs lay like specks of sawdust on his dark mustache, rose and fell when he chewed. She had this instinct to go to him and brush away the crumbs.

He was studying her. She pointed to the place above her upper lip, and he took a napkin and wiped above his. She placed her hand over the mouthpiece, lifted her eyebrows, and told him, "Realtor has some folks might be interested in buying the greenhouse. You say no, I'll tell them to come on over."

Wayne's sober face rested on his propped hands for a moment. She imagined his mind working furiously. Then he looked at her and nodded, yes. The tension drained from her shoulders. "I've sold it already," she said. "Thanks anyway."

From the nearby window everything looked peaceful: a lone patch of low, matted blueberry shrubs planted near the house, and across the street cows grazed in the pasture close by a thick windbreak of evergreens that sheltered the neighbor's weathered old farmhouse. It all matched the mood that now settled over her. Hannah walked to the table and sitting down across from Wayne got down to business.

"All the plants are sold. Late January we deliver them to the shops. We could reorder large quantities or cut back, grow smaller amounts, sell them at the tailgate market, the swap meet. That would take a lot of pressure off," she said.

His face grew stony. His eyes clouded with doubt. She was moving too fast. Pushing back her chair, Hannah crossed her legs. "Sorry. We can decide these things later."

Wayne scratched his head, seemed to be struggling with something, then smiled. "Sounds good. Old Man'll be right pleased. He's been after me to do some other kinda work. We grow a lot of tobacco. Old Man says tobacco's on its way outta here. Got a couple of pigs Old Man and I've fattened up to take on over to the county fair in Sylva. After that . . ." He lifted his hands and twisted his wrists in an "I'm all yours" gesture.

It might take years to teach him everything she knew but she had time. "Maybe I'll teach some classes over at Caster school."

He seemed pleased. "Good for you, Miss Hannah."

She extended her hand. "We got a deal then?"

"Yes, ma'am, we got a deal."

After Wayne left, Hannah wandered out to the greenhouse, filled now with dark green foliage. Next they would fertilize with phosphorous to force bloom. Hannah checked the thermostat, brushed soil off a table, hung a shovel on a rack nearby, and went back to the house. Where were Grace and Amelia? They'd be glad she had made a decision. They'd be pleased about her deal with Wayne. Back in the kitchen Hannah spooned herself a fat meatball smothered in gravy heavy with prunes, ate it slowly, then with a strong sense of closure and anticipation went upstairs.

Once in her room Hannah studied her face in the mirror. Clear blue eyes, thick hair, more salt than pepper and badly in need of a cut, stuck out from about her ears. For years she had worn it short, but being so busy she had not had time to go into town to the beauty parlor. She would have time now and that added to her sense of calmness and ease. Gone was her usual drive to act, to accomplish things, to get on with it. It actually felt good.

After a long shower Hannah pulled a pale yellow flannel nightgown over her head, settled into bed, and opened a novel about belonging that Grace had recommended. She must have dozed, for the book lay to the side and her glasses had slipped into her lap when she awakened to a soft rap, rap on the door. "It's me, Grace. May I come in?"

There was an urgency in Grace's voice. Hannah set her glasses and the book on her night table. What was it these days that made everything seem to change so fast? One hardly had time to catch one's breath.

"Well, Grace," Hannah said, noting Grace's radiant face. "You look like the proverbial cat who's swallowed the canary."

"And that's about how I feel." Grace flung herself across the foot of Hannah's bed, rolled over on her back, and hugged herself. She was sixteen. No, sixteen was under age for what she'd spent the night doing. Nineteen, and she was beautiful, desirable — Bob had said so. She felt totally happy with him and with herself.

Pushing herself high against the pillows, Hannah folded her hands. "So tell me."

"It's about Bob and me." Grace's eyes glowed. Her cheeks were pink like Old World roses, and she bubbled with excitement like a schoolgirl. Her gaiety and pleasure were infectious, and Hannah found herself smiling broadly, leaning forward, and demanding to know what was going on.

Sitting up, Grace crossed her legs and looked at Hannah coyly. Her tone was conspiratorial, excited, happy. "We did it, Bob and I."

"Did what?" Hannah teased.

"You know." Grace could not contain her exuberance, and Hannah eased her legs out of the way a bit to make more room for her friend.

"From the look of you, things went well."

"Beyond all expectation. Oh, Hannah, it was wonderful." She was sitting bolt upright on the edge of the bed now.

"Okay, calm down a little and tell me." Hannah raised her hand. "No. You don't have to tell me."

"I'll burst if I don't."

Hannah folded her hands in her lap. "Okay, I'm listening"

"We'd planned to take Tyler to the Boone area to Tweetsie Railroad, but he was running a slight fever. Russell said he'd take good care of him, and if his fever got higher than a hundred and two he'd call the doctor, so Bob and I drove over there, just the two of us. We rode the train, took a tram way up to the children's zoo, ate crap. It was fun. Then the rain started. We got all wet running to the car. After dinner it was still raining and the fog was as thick as a board. Bob suggested we take rooms at a motel. Some kind of convention in town. Hard to find a vacancy, and when we did they had one room left. Two beds. We took it." Grace buried her face in her hands for just a moment, then gave Hannah a mischievous look.

"We didn't stay in two beds." Hannah was silent. Grace grabbed her leg and shook it. "Aren't you going to ask me what happened?"

"What happened?" She's glowing, Hannah thought.

"It was wonderful. Bob's so gentle and loving. He said I'm beautiful, that my skin's so soft he loves touching it, he loves the way I smell, loves my voice, loves me. And guess what? I forgot to worry about being" — she waved her hand along her front — "you know, fat." Grace sat up, wrapped her arms about her shoulders, and rocked back and forth. "I never knew it could be like that." Her face grew serious and her expressive eyes filled with affection and gratitude. "Thank you, dear Hannah, for sharing about your Dan with me. It helped me, well, freed me up."

"What now?" Hannah asked, expecting Grace to announce her engagement.

"Why, more of the same, of course." She pointed at herself. "This hot tamale's sizzling." Her eyes sparkled. "I could get used to all the seasoning." Grace laughed, flung out her arms, twisted her torso from side to side and sang, "If they could see me now." Grace misinterpreted Hannah's puzzled look. "You know," she said, referring to the song. "It's that song Kathy Lee Gifford used to sing on that cruise ship. Now Grace Singleton's really a liberated woman."

"Do I hear wedding bells?"

Grace sobered. "We talked about that. Bob thought if he didn't propose marriage I'd be insulted, he'd lose me. Bob and I agreed that we have the best of both worlds. We can be together whenever we choose and not have to adjust to each others' foibles or accommodate to the humdrum of daily living. You know what it's like with a man, you fall back into the old rut of caretaker." She stretched her arms high above her head.

"But what if we . . . ?"

"Lose this house? I'd hate it, of course, but, you, of all people, the eternal optimist asking such a question." Her eyes clouded. "Worst case scenario? We find another house around here and move into it. Happiness isn't a house, I've learned. It's what your life's about. Is it meaningful? Do you enjoy and love the people you live with?"

"How'd you get so smart?" A paroxysm of laughter shook Hannah.

They giggled like girls.

Hallelujah. Hannah rejoiced silently. Grace would continue to share a home with them. Things had changed; things had not changed.

A knock on the door brought Amelia into the room. "What's going on?"

"You're looking at a wanton, totally satisfied woman," said Grace. She gave Amelia a come-hither look, then told her story again.

Amelia looked genuinely pleased for Grace, then tears clouded her eyes, "Why, why can't I find those letters? I don't know where to look anymore."

Grace put her arm about the woman's frail shoulders. "It's all right, Amelia. None of us want to leave Covington. If we must, we'll rent a house until we can find one we can afford to buy."

"Sam Tolent says if we lose this case, he'll fight to get the money that went into renovations. At least I kept all those receipts for the accountant."

"It's going to be all right. We're going to go over this house again this weekend, inch by inch. We're going to find Arthur's letters," Hannah declared.

42

The Time Capsule

✻ "We'll have to wait until the lights go out over at Hubbard's. Anyone sees us, our sterling reputations will be permanently tarnished," Amelia said. For a moment she wondered why they were doing this, here and now, then decided they had to do it; it was a gesture, a statement, if only to themselves, that their claim on this property was valid.

The metal box was about eighteen inches high by at least two feet wide, waterproof and fireproof, the kind used to store valuable papers away in vaults. They were gathered in the living room and had spread their "artifacts" on the coffee table before the couch and were preparing to fill the container with mementos of their lives.

Amelia handed Grace the box. This desire to honor the land and house and to preserve a part of themselves had developed into a ceremony with Grace officiating.

"We begin by thanking your cousin, Arthur, and this marvelous old house itself for all the blessings we've received," she said. They bowed their heads and stood silent, each giving thanks in her own way. After a moment Grace said, "Amen."

"If you can hear us, Cousin Arthur," Amelia said, turning her head as if expecting him to walk into the room, "help me find your letters."

Hannah dimmed the lights in the living room. On a marble lazy Susan to one side of the table, seven tall white candles waited in their crystal candleholders. Silently, reverently, Amelia lit them now.

Lifting the metal box high above her head, Grace began. "Into this time capsule go bits and pieces of our lives, important moments of our lives." Slowly Grace circled the room. "Bless this house for providing us with shelter. Within its walls we have grown wiser and gained new visions. Our friendships have blossomed. To Arthur Furrior we say again, thank you for altering, expanding, and enriching the lives of Amelia, of Hannah, and of myself, Grace." With deliberate ceremony she placed the container on the table near the candles. "Into this time capsule we now place memorabilia from our lives."

They kneeled, and Grace opened the metal container. Within lay three smaller flat boxes. Each of them took a box, wrote their name on white tape Amelia had secured on their individual boxes. After folding a lovely jade necklace into a square of green satin Amelia placed it carefully into her box. "In memory of Caroline," she whispered, "for green eyes."

A small black jewelry box from Hannah, which Grace knew contained a ring, a ruby ring Dan Britton had given Hannah. Perhaps, if there is a God, we'll meet again, Hannah said silently, blinking back tears.

"My father's Bible." Grace set the frayed-looking book gingerly into her box. "For forgiveness, from you and for you."

Amelia added a scarf, neatly folded and wrapped in plastic, a roll of undeveloped film taken at a lake recently, and several thickly laminated newspaper reviews of her work rolled neatly and secured with blue satin ribbons. A Red Cross badge went last. Her eyes grew tense, and she looked about the room anxiously for a moment, then said, "For you, Thomas."

The look was not lost on Grace, who wondered why this symbol of Thomas's would make Amelia anxious. Moments later Grace included the silver brush and comb set, a miniature bread pan and rolling pin, and a laminated photo of her house in Dentry with Linda Smiley and other friends sitting on the steps. "To the home that sheltered me for so many years and to those good friends," she whispered.

Hannah laid in a child-size hand shovel and rake, one bronzed baby shoe of each of her daughters, and a laminated page of pressed flowers.

Grace looked from one to the other. They nodded, and solemnly she lowered the lid and locked the container. "We're ready."

Slowly then, in single file, bundled in sweaters and jackets against the evening cold, and with only the full-swollen luminous moon to light their way, they stepped out onto the porch, moved lightly down the steps, and walked briskly to the rear of the house.

Hannah had prepared the hole as if for a small tree, two feet deep and three feet wide and lined it with the black plastic builders use to secure basements from water.

Grace placed the box on the ground. Speaking clearly and firmly, she turned to face east. "We thank you for guiding us to this place, Covington, and for the community of caring people who have been so welcoming to us here." To the west. "Gratefully we acknowledge our friendship. We have been blessed." To the south. "We thank you for our health and for our lives and families." And lastly to the north. "Thank you for the joy we have had in this house, in Covington." Her eyes misted, her heart sank. She pressed on. "And for the caring and sharing, the creativity, the overcoming that has taken place here. Help us, if we have to, to find another home we will love as much."

Their joint "Amen" floated on the air.

Then Amelia lowered herself onto her stomach on the frosty grass and, leaning into the hole, placed the box into its niche. The plastic was drawn close about it, and Hannah picked up the shovel.

"To memories," she said. Soil hitting the plastic made a sound like rain. Grace and Amelia took turns with Hannah, and they filled the hole and lay fresh sod over it. Except for a shallow-rooted gardenia bush Hannah would plant above the spot, they had decided against marking the place. The finding of their time capsule would rest with time and accident.

Hannah rested the shovel against the wall of the house and wiped her eyes. They were silent for a long while. Then Amelia spoke. "It was a wonderful ceremony. I felt Arthur's presence close by."

"And the lady in the moon's watching us." Grace's looked up at the celestial orb.

"Lady? I thought it was a man in the moon," Amelia said.

"Look up." Grasping Amelia's shoulders, Grace turned her about. "She's tall, like Hannah, and slim like you, and her hair flies behind her in the wind. She carries a bundle of sticks across her shoulder."

"I don't see her," Amelia protested.

"Let your mind go free, Amelia. Stop thinking man in the moon. Follow the dark jagged lines upward."

Amelia made a tube of her thumb and fingers to isolate the moon. After peering through it for a moment, she grew excited. "I see her now. Yes, a woman, how wonderful." She hugged Grace.

"Shining light on others, just like you two do." Hannah would have liked to hug them both, but that was not her way.

"Ladies," Grace said, "I'll make us some hot spiced cider."

The moment was special, joyous, and Amelia slipped her arms through those of both Grace and Hannah.

43

The Snow Storm

⚘ Amelia smoothed the comforter, fluffed the pillows on her bed, and, turning slowly, scanned her room. She had searched everywhere for the letters. She had lifted her mattress and emptied, for the third time, every single drawer in her dresser. She had stared at the hatbox, and shaken her head. She remembered using the hat for a picture and returning it to the box. Definitely not in the hatbox. Her eyes roamed slowly about her room, lingering on the comfortable armchair in whose embrace she often sat relaxing, enjoying the view of pastures and mountains. On her night table was the photograph of her family, and she realized that she no longer felt a pang of anguish when she looked at it. Then Amelia moved to her door, pulled it open, and stepped into the hall.

It was early morning buffeted by haze and a chilly wind. To the west a leaden sky hovered, while in the east the sky was a washed-out blue. She was restless. For weeks now she had been thinking about a small red barn she had discovered during her wanderings. Barns here were usually large and weathered gray with age and sometimes lopsided as if about to topple, but this barn was neat and painted red and alongside it a wooden plank fence suggested a pasture beyond for cows or horses, though she had seen none on the days when she had passed it by. Perhaps one hundred feet to the left of the barn stood a traditional two-story white clapboard farmhouse with a covered porch on two sides, and to the right of the barn on a gentle slope of meadow a cleft in a cluster of tall trees offered a doorway onto a path that hinted of somewhere magical.

The several times Amelia had driven by, the angle of light was never right. She needed the early morning light with the sun's rays streaming through the mist in order to lift the scene to the level of the sublime. Perhaps this morning. She could drive to Barnardsville, a small town nearby, follow the gravel road up to the barn, and be back before the others were up and about.

Shoes in hand, Amelia slipped downstairs, poured herself a glass of orange juice, and posted a note on the refrigerator.

I'm off to Barnardsville to shoot that little red barn off Sugar Creek Road. Be back in an hour or two.

Amelia

It was colder than she expected. A biting wind seared her face. Amelia set the camera bag and tripod on the porch and went back inside to put on a cashmere sweater under her coat and jam a wool cap over the skiers' band that covered her ears. Better, she thought, hastening down the steps.

Once off the highway, on the two-lane Barnardsville road, traffic slowed behind a school bus. Annoyed by the delay, Amelia fumed. She would miss the moment when the sun crested the hills to the east. The bus came to yet another halt. Five boys and girls hastened from the small wooden shelter on the side of the road.

Amelia sat there, fingers tapping the steering wheel, brooding on her recurring dream of Thomas and the museum that had in its repetition become even more elaborate. She saw him standing with his back to her in the huge, well-lit space imperiously ordering that her photographs be stripped from the walls of the art gallery. Brushing past her, short men in gray jackets ignored her pleas and moved swiftly to carry out his commands. Then Thomas glowered at her and said, "Silly, foolish woman, your work's just a flash in the pan." She would jerk awake, heart racing, her body drowning in perspiration, stricken by the memory of those stinging words.

As the weeks passed Amelia came increasingly to regard the dream as prophetic, defining her and chronicling the demise of her work. The unexpectedly wonderful career she had stumbled upon and found so satisfying was, as Thomas said in the dreams, a flash in the pan, a fluke. She was a fake and soon would be found out, derided, rejected, humiliated. It was stupid of her to want to publish a book. Yesterday, sitting on the porch, she had come close to sharing her nightmare and her increasingly frequent bouts of depression with Grace and Hannah.

"Everyone's looking forward to your book," Hannah had said. "Margaret Olsen can't wait to buy an autographed copy."

"I'm so proud of you, Amelia. Look at

what you've accomplished," Grace said.

"We're all so proud of you," Hannah agreed.

"You don't think I'm a flash in the pan?"

"Flash in the pan? Heavens no," Grace said.

"Just a late bloomer." Hannah's brows had furrowed. "All those years being Thomas Declose's shadow, a second pair of hands and feet to further his work, and I say *his* work, not yours." Her fingers had tapped the arm of her chair for emphasis. "A lot of women of our generation put their husbands first. Their creativity went by the wayside."

Hannah had not said she had been Thomas's brains, or eyes, or ears, just hands and feet. "Are you saying I had no mind of my own?"

"I'm saying you were programmed to live his agenda, not your own."

Amelia had resented that. "Thomas's work was very important," she snapped at Hannah. "And I was a small part of it. I traveled, saw the world." And then it hit her. She had seen the world mostly from behind a table handing out blankets or food. In India, for example, they had been too busy, Thomas said, to visit the Taj Mahal. He had dismissed it as "just another old tomb." It made her angry remembering that. She had so wanted to go inside the magnificent building. Yet being critical of Thomas, even in her thoughts, deepened her confusion and stirred her guilt. She defended her life to Hannah. "When Caroline came I took care of her all by myself without a nanny. I was a good mother."

"I'm sure you were." Amelia had seen Grace give Hannah a quick warning look.

In the process of adjusting to living together, the three of them had determined not to pry into one another's business, accepting that when each was ready, she would share with the others. But that day, sitting there on the porch, Amelia wished they would pry, question her sadness and ask about the guilt she felt for not finding the letters.

"I had thought years ago about taking photography lessons," Amelia had said, looking off into the distance. "I bought a nice camera once, but it got lost some-where in our travels." Then she had looked deep into Hannah's eyes. "Maybe you're right about Thomas and me. Our marriage would never have survived if I'd been at cross purposes with him."

"You did the best you could," Hannah

said in a conciliatory tone.

"We can't redo the past, Amelia. We've all made mistakes, done the best we could. Your relationship with your husband was what mattered," Grace said. "But now you've got years of marvelous photographs to take: children, buildings, scenery. It's really quite wonderful what's happened." She smiled. "To all of us."

Grace's smile had warmed Amelia's heart. And still she had not told them about the dreams that crushed her spirit and made a pariah of sleep. How could she have told them? Hannah had accused her of being self-involved. They would have laughed at her, labeled her self-indulgent, and she thought again, what could be more self-involved than brooding on Thomas or something as ridiculous as her dreams?

Ahead of her, the bus groaned to life and crawled along, then to her relief it turned off the main road, and her foot hit the accelerator.

Sunlight spilled across the hillside. Tree trunks cast long shadows. It was freezing cold and it hurt to breathe. When she pulled off her gloves and tried to set up the tripod, her fingers began to ache and stiffen with cold and she stopped and returned the tripod to the backseat of the

601

car. Then, shivering, Amelia took the camera from the bag and shot frame after frame before the deadly cold and draconian wind drove her back to the car. Then the sun disappeared, the world dimmed, and the sleet began.

Amelia turned on the motor and started down the hillside. Spiked pellets of sleet hammered the windshield. She was almost to the main, paved road when the snow came, each fat flake racing to overtake another, crowding against the windshield, hindering her sight and stopping the windshield wipers in their tracks. She snapped on 1310 on her radio and caught part of the report.

". . . are under a severe storm warning," the reporter was saying. "Temperature has plunged to twenty degrees. Secondary roads are freezing over. All Madison and Buncombe county schools are closed. Anyone who doesn't have to go out is advised to stay inside."

Folks in Covington spoke about weather like this: unpredictable, dangerous, terrifying. "One minute I had perfect visibility," she remembered Harold saying, "next minute my wipers froze up, stuck, couldn't see a thing."

It hadn't seemed real when he'd talked

about it, but it was real now. Amelia could not see two feet ahead of her. The side of the road and its ditch were invisible. Then the car began to slide. Amelia lost the ability to think clearly. She lifted both hands from the wheel. The Taurus skidded left, then right, and left again until it stopped short, and Amelia felt the thud against her door as the car slid off the road and hit something hard, probably a tree on the driver's side.

Amelia lifted each shoulder, rotated her head, extended her arms. Everything worked. Then control gave way to loud moans and gasping sobs. When she stopped crying it occurred to her that on this isolated road, she might not be found for hours. She would have to crawl over to the passenger side, push that door open, and slug her way down to the main road, not far, but just how far she was uncertain. Boots. Thank God she had listened to Mike and kept them in the car. Where were they? She unlatched her seat belt, twisted about, and her hands searched the floor behind her until they struck the hard slick rubber of the fur-lined boots. She hauled them over the back of the seat and into the front, then grunting she struggled, in the limited space between her seat and the steering wheel, to remove her shoes. By the time she pulled on the heavy socks that were tucked in the boots and squeezed into them and the boots, she was out of breath and a cold sweat trickled down her sides.

Pushing the camera bag before her, Amelia eased herself over to the passenger side of the car, then shoved and shoved until that door opened. Gingerly, she stepped out into a white and silent world. Snow instantly layered her coat and hair.

Lifting one heavy booted foot, and then the other, Amelia wove through the deepening snow. The camera bag pulled at her shoulder. Her mind drifted back to her childhood: to her father, a busy attorney, and her beautiful mother dashing out to yet another meeting for her charities. They hardly noticed her except to issue some truism she was expected to obey. When she was twelve, they had told her she had been an accident, and they had laughed lightly and ogled one another in a special, private way, then looked at her as if waiting for her to see the joke in it. She'd understood. It wasn't funny.

Clutching the camera bag as if it were a child and she its only protector, Amelia trudged along, breathing heavily and thinking about her childhood. When had she not felt guilty: for being alive, for catching chicken pox, for having a birthday and a party that took her parents from other more important matters?

Amelia stumbled, righted herself, raised her boot, and took yet one more laborious step. Early on she had learned not to make waves, not to be seen, and certainly not heard. But now, at this stage of her life, why should she feel such guilt over her success? A branch broke and fell, scattering snow, frightening her. Another step. The camera bag grew heavier by the moment. Then suddenly it was very clear. The nightmares, Thomas's rejection of her work . . . they were machinations of her own mind fed by her own sense of guilt that for days, sometimes a week or longer at a time, she did not think about Thomas.

Her life had changed so much. Now she had Mike's friendship and her confidence was bolstered by his support, and there were Hannah and Grace, who took her seriously, loved her. In general her life was satisfying in ways it had never been. Amelia brushed the snow from her face.

"No more guilt." In the deep silence her whispered words seemed like shouts. Dear Thomas, she thought, we had a good, satisfying life. We did it your way. Now it's my turn.

A car drove by, so close and so far away on the main road. Amelia tried to quicken her pace, an impossibility in the soft deepening snow. "It's my turn, Thomas," she muttered, lifting a boot high to take the next step. The wind rose, moaning, restless, shifting. Finally, Amelia reached the main road. No tracks remained from the car she had seen go by. Her back and chest ached from the cold. She hardly felt her toes. Every breath seared her lungs as she stood there shivering, teeth chattering uncontrollably. Small and helpless, in this too lonely a place, Amelia stomped her feet, rubbed her hands together, and prayed. "Dear God, please send a car, a truck. Don't let it end like this."

Wayne called Hannah at seven-thirty in the morning, waking her.

"Can't get off this here mountain," he said. "Snowin' heavy. You got snow yet?"

Hannah peered outside. "East is still blue."

"Well, it's a-comin' believe me."

She believed him. Hannah brushed her teeth, slapped water on her face, then sauntered downstairs and put on a pot of coffee for herself, a kettle of water for tea. She set the table, turned on the oven to heat a tray of blueberry muffins Grace had made last night.

"Smells good." Grace, in her terry cloth bathrobe, stood over the table and stretched, yawned, rubbed her eyes. "Where's Amelia?"

"Don't know." Then Hannah saw the note on the refrigerator. "She's gone to take sunrise photographs in Barnardsville. Weatherman's calling for a major storm, maybe twelve inches of snow. Says the power might go out. Wayne's snowed in."

"God, I hope Amelia's okay." Grace turned to look out the window.

"She must have heard the reports on the radio, and turned back."

"I don't know, Hannah. Sometimes, especially with all the worry about losing the house, she gets so wrapped up in her photography, she doesn't know what's going on about her."

"Muffins are hot. Sit."

"Bob and I were driving to Asheville for dinner last night and we had the most frightening experience."

"What happened?"

"We nearly hit a kid on a bicycle, no helmet, dark clothes, no bike lights. Missed

him by a hair. Shook us both up terribly."
She looked at Hannah. "I'm worried about
Amelia driving in this weather."

They ate in silence, Grace getting up
several times to look out of the window. "If
Amelia doesn't come in five minutes, I'm
calling nine-one-one. Did she say where
she was going in Barnardsville?"

Hannah picked up the note. "Someplace
called Sugar Creek Road."

Grace apologized to the operator for
calling 911, then explained her concerns.

"What kind of car, license plate
number?"

"Taurus, white. License plate number?"
Grave looked dumbly at Hannah, who
closed her eyes for a moment.

"PRR seven-nine-four-two." Hannah
said each letter slowly, as if hauling them
up in an old bucket from a deep well.

"Thank you," Grace said, and hung up.
"I feel better. They're going to send
someone to search for her."

To stand and freeze, to walk and maybe
survive. The effort to lift her heavy boots
out of the snow was inexpressibly difficult
yet Amelia moved, taking one hesitant step
after the other until she stopped,
exhausted. Looking back, she counted the

holes in the snow, six, seven, eight. She had worked so hard for only eight steps. It had seemed like one hundred. "If I make it," she spoke aloud, "I promise I'll never waste my time being guilty about anything ever again. I'll fight to keep the property Cousin Arthur wanted me to have, and if I lose, we'll find a nice house and we'll live in it. What matters is that Grace and Hannah and I'll be together agreeing and disagreeing and listening and caring for one another."

With enormous effort Amelia slung the camera bag onto her other shoulder, wrested a booted foot from the snow, then set it back into the hole it came from. She couldn't go on.

She never heard the car behind her and was startled to see the flashing lights. Moments later, strong arms gathered her and she was lifted and carried to the police car and settled into the back. She must have slept, for when she opened her eyes, Hannah was there, and Grace was reaching into the car, pulling back the blankets that covered her, helping the policeman walk her to the house.

44

To Life

✻ "We nearly lost you." Grace pulled a chair close to Amelia's bed.

Their family doctor, an angel who made emergency house calls even in bad weather, had examined Amelia and declared her a lucky lady. He prescribed a few days bed rest.

Grace had brought a tray of herbal tea to Amelia's room.

"Thank you, Grace," Amelia said, taking a sip, then blowing into the cup. "I'm so ashamed putting you through this, and all because I paid no attention to the weather."

"We love you, Amelia," Grace said softly. "We were frantic when we found you'd gone out."

"Stupid me."

"Stop with the stupid," Hannah said. "We all make mistakes."

"What do you need with a housemate like me, wandering off scaring everyone?"

"We were afraid you'd freeze out there," Grace said.

"I was, too." Amelia's eyes grew serious and intent as she studied Grace's face. "Do you ever worry about dying?"

Grace hesitated, stirred her tea, tapped the spoon against the cup before looking first at Hannah and then Amelia. "It's not so much dying that worries me, it's how I'll die." She closed her eyes for a moment and shuddered. "I've seen lingering painful deaths, Ted, my parents. I don't want to suffer like they did. I'd want someone to help me end it."

Amelia set her cup in the saucer. "Thomas never knew what hit us that day. The doctor told me if they hadn't found me in the forest at Graveyard Fields, I would have drifted off to sleep and just died. I remembered that today when I thought I couldn't take one more step." With both palms she smoothed her hair back from her face. Her eyes were luminous. "I didn't want to die. My life's . . . well, it's wonderful. There's so much to do, my book and everything . . ."

They were silent for a time, and then Hannah spoke. "Let's agree to help one another if, or when, such a time ever comes."

"Could we? Would you?" The relief in Grace's voice was audible.

"We can draw up living wills stating that we don't want to be kept alive by machines, and we can give one another the power to act on our behalf if we can't make our own medical decisions," Amelia said. "Thomas and I had those things." Amelia took a few more sips of tea, then set her cup on the night table. "Listen you two," she said. "I had so many insights out there in the cold. I realized I've felt guilty about everything all my life, and especially now, being successful. Somehow it seemed a betrayal of Thomas's memory, so I had horrible nightmares that were driving me out of my mind." Finally, she told them about the dreams and about Thomas destroying her photographs.

Grace took Amelia's hand. "It's time to let Thomas go, Amelia. Let him go."

Suddenly Amelia looked up and pointed to her closet. "The hatbox. Oh, get the hatbox will you, Grace, Hannah. I said I'd looked everywhere, but . . . I was sure . . . oh, hurry, will you? Get the hatbox."

Beneath sheets and sheets of tissue paper, under the hat and its burdensome cherries, the letters lay, pressed flat. Amelia clutched them to her chest. Her eyes misted, then tears bathed her cheeks. *"Merci, merci,"* she whispered.

"Oh, dear God, the letters." Grace covered her quivering lips with her fingers.

Hannah looked at each letter. "Arthur's letters. Fantastic."

They did not hear the knock on the door until Bob called, "Grace, what's the matter in there?"

Grace went to the door. "We found the letters, Arthur's letters," she said, beaming. "You got here in this weather?"

"You can do it with a four-wheel drive, and they've been plowing." He made fists and lifted them in a gesture of victory. "The letters. Terrific. Listen, I'll wait downstairs. Here." He handed her a box. "I found this on the porch. Guess you didn't see it. It's for Amelia."

Grace laid the gaily wrapped box on Amelia's lap. "Why it's like a holiday. The letters, now a gift for you."

Tearing away the electric purple bow and the wrapping paper, Amelia gasped with pleasure as she lifted a sinfully gorgeous, sapphire-colored silk bed jacket from the box. The accompanying note read, *Amelia, my dear. Never can remember birth dates. This is for yours, whenever. The color will look absolutely scrumptious with your eyes. Enjoy.* It was signed, *Your friend, Mike.*

"He's a good friend to you, Amelia."

"He surely is."

"You look tired. Rest now."

Amelia slipped on the bed jacket. "Call Sam Tolent, tell him we found the letters."

"With pleasure."

They slipped out, leaving Amelia alone.

Amelia propped herself high on her pillows, pressed her fingers against her eyelids, then opened her eyes and looked out of the window. The snow formed cotton puffs on branches and layered the mountains. Relief, satisfaction, peace came over her. *"Magnifique,"* she murmured, closing her eyes.

In the winter days and weeks that followed, Mike came and went, a welcome guest. His rich hearty laugh, his jokes, the way he mimicked Amelia by sweeping his parakeet-green cashmere scarf about his neck drove them to peals of laughter. He and Amelia spent hours huddled together, critiquing slides, planning field trips.

"We're going to take a group to Ecuador in February to photograph monarch butterflies," Mike said.

"They migrate there in the winter,"

Amelia added, "hundreds of thousands of them."

Grace experimented with new recipes — cauliflower soufflé, spiced fruit, turkey and pineapple meat loaf — and set the table with crystal and china she had stored and which Bob lugged from the attic and helped unpack. Bob and Mike came often for dinner and sometimes Brenda and Harold. When Russell and Tyler joined them, they added a leaf to the table and sat squeezed shoulder to shoulder.

"You cook yummy, Mrs. Grace. Much better than Dad or Grandpa." Tyler insisted on calling her Mrs. Grace. Mrs. Grace, Mother Singleton, what difference did it make? Grace beamed at Tyler, reached over and tousled his hair.

A week before Christmas the three ladies sat on the living room floor before a nurturing fire wrapping gifts. Outside the wind howled although the sky was clear and blue. Any moment they expected Russell, Tyler, and Bob to arrive with the Douglas fir that Tyler with Hannah's and Grace's guidance had chosen and the men had cut.

When the phone rang Amelia set aside a bow she was forming from a wide green

615

ribbon and picked up the portable phone. For a long moment there was silence, then a wide happy smile spread across her face and her eyes sparkled. "Really? Truly?" A pause, then, "That's wonderful. Merry Christmas to you, too." She set down the phone and turned to them. "It's over," she said. "Over. The Madisons dropped the suit and signed off on their claim." She scrambled up, grabbed Grace's hands, and pulled her to her feet and together they did the same to Hannah. Then they danced about in circles singing, "We've won," and then broke into an off-key version of "Home on the Range."

Moments later the men and Tyler arrived with the tree, which they lugged, with Grace and Hannah and Amelia urging them on, into the living room. The furniture had been pushed aside to make room for the tree. When they shared the good news, Bob hugged each of them in turn, as did Russell, and Tyler stripped off his boots and jacket and ran about the room yelling, "Hooray, hooray."

It was several minutes before they all calmed down enough to set the tree in its stand and begin to decorate it. It was then that Amelia lifted from a box a shining angel with gossamer wings, and Tyler's eyes widened into huge round globes.

"Angel." He took it from Hannah and cradled it gently in his hands. "Angel," he cooed as he touched its golden hair and ran his fingers along its fine lace gown. "Like Momma." Tyler handed it to his father, who nodded and smiled and then climbed a ladder and set the angel at the pinnacle of the tree.

Hannah unpacked a collection of rocking horse ornaments. "Thought I'd never use these again," she mumbled. She called to Tyler, and while he placed some of her ornaments low, she placed others high on the tree.

There was further excitement when the package arrived from Roger and Charles with a sticker announcing, OPEN BEFORE CHRISTMAS.

"Oh so pretty," Tyler said, as one by one they unpacked eight exquisitely detailed carolers in Victorian maroon, green, and purple clothes with ornate, gold trim that soon became part of the tree's eclectic finery.

The high spirits continued to soar the following days, and on the twenty-third of December it snowed lightly, frosting branches and fence posts. In the warm, cozy living room, Amelia knelt with Tyler before the tree, arranging the presents according to color, reds here, blues there, greens and whites there, when they heard the crunch of tires in the driveway.

Hannah and Grace sat writing notes. From a window Amelia and Tyler watched Sam Tolent take the porch steps two at a time, and Tyler ran to open the front door for him.

"I've brought you a Christmas present," he said, handing Amelia a brown envelope. "The Madisons signed this abrogation of their claim on your property. I thought you'd like to have a copy."

Amelia hugged the envelope to her chest. "Thank you so much, Sam."

"You found the letters. Once we had them, they couldn't go any further with this." Sam handed her another envelope. "The new deed, in all your names."

Grace looked at Hannah and they walked swiftly to Amelia and hugged her.

Mike stood in the doorway, his hair mussed from the wind, flecks of snow on his jacket and a brown cardboard box in his hands. "Look what I have." He set the box at Amelia's feet.

Amelia did not move, only stared down into the box. Then she clasped both hands over her heart. "Is it? . . . Is . . . ?"

He nodded, bent, picked up a copy of *Memories and Mist: Mornings on the Blue Ridge*, and handed it to her. Reality dawned slowly, and Amelia simply sat there clasping the book as Mike distributed a copy to everyone, even Tyler, who left off counting packages under the tree for the umpteenth time and came to sit quietly between his grandfather and Grace on the couch.

"Isn't it gorgeous?" Mike gushed. "Such an eye. They're almost otherworldly."

Slowly Bob turned each page. "I'm impressed."

"You certainly are a fine photographer, Amelia," Sam Tolent said, and prepared to leave, but Amelia reached for the book he held and signed it, and with thanks and good wishes for the holidays, he took his leave.

"Look at this one." Bathed in light, the forest on Oxbow Road lay spread across both pages.

"Remember this, Grace? You helped me select it," Amelia said.

"I'm so very proud of you." Grace grasped Amelia's hand. Then, she remembered the batch of cookies she had just made. She rose. "I've got to get something, be right back." She returned with a plate of hot cookies and a flat box wrapped in a holiday paper, which she handed to Mike. "For you. This is my present to you, since you won't be with us for Christmas Day."

"Family obligations, you know, darn it. Would rather be here." His eyes misted and he looked like a little boy as he took the box. "Can I open it now?"

"Certainly. You might like to use what's inside over the holidays."

Mike sank cross-legged to the carpet. "What can it be?" In moments he had unwrapped the package and lifted out one box of cookies and another wrapped box. A gold picture frame held a copy of Grace's sugar cookie recipe written in a bold dark script. "Your recipe. Oh, Grace, thank you. All these months I've been nagging you for it."

"I wanted you to have it, but I wanted to have it framed first so you wouldn't get it all smudged like my recipe cards."

"Thank you so much." He jumped to his feet and kissed her on both cheeks. Then he held it before him and passed it around for all to see.

Grace's Sugar Cookies

2/3 cup butter
3/4 cup granulated sugar
1 teaspoon vanilla
1 egg
4 teaspoons milk
2 cups sifted all-purpose flour
1/2 teaspoons baking powder
1/4 teaspoon salt

Roll the dough thin for 2 dozen cookies.

Preheat the oven to 375 degrees. Thoroughly cream the butter, sugar, and vanilla. Add the egg and milk. Beat until light and fluffy. Sift together the dry ingredients. Blend into the creamed mixture. Divide the dough in half. Cover and chill for at least 1 hour.

On a lightly floured surface, roll to 1/8-inch thickness. Cut into the desired shapes with cookie cutters. Bake on an ungreased cookie sheet 8 to 10 minutes. Cool slightly before removing from the cookie sheet.

Amelia smiled up at Mike. "Now we'll have sugar cookies on every field trip, won't we?"

"Betcha we will," he said, smiling as he clasped the framed recipe to his chest.

Then Amelia sank back into the cushions of her chair and proudly traced the title on the glossy cover with her fingertips. *Memories and Mists: Mornings on the Blue Ridge* exceeded her wildest expectations.

She looks beautiful, a woman in her prime, Grace thought as she looked at Amelia and remembered their conversation on the porch. Immortality. Amelia has achieved a kind of immortality. She looked around the room and her heart swelled. We've become a family, Grace thought, feeling thoroughly content as she bent to kiss Tyler's cheek.

45

New Year's Eve

December 31, a miracle of a day. With temperatures hovering near sixty-two it was perfect for sitting out. The ladies, satisfied that Christmas had gone so well, and delighted with the sunshine and blue clear sky overhead, drew their rockers in a semicircle close to the edge of the front porch. Before them on a round wood table Grace placed a bottle of sherry and three small crystal glasses on a shiny silver tray. She poured a round. "To us," she said, tears forming in her gentle eyes.

"To us," Hannah seconded. "For all we've accomplished, starting the day Amelia inherited this place and cajoled us into coming down here."

"To Grace, for courage, for driving us down."

"To Hannah for saving us from a flood, teaching us we could do it."

Turning to Grace, then to Hannah, Amelia looked deep into their eyes and lifted her glass. "To understanding, kindness, and tolerance."

"To your great talent, and to friendship and love," Grace said.

"To a new year in this wonderful old house that's sheltered us," Hannah said. "And again, to your cousin Arthur. I think he'd be proud of all we've accomplished."

"Yes, to Cousin Arthur, who made our new beginnings possible. I bet if he's looking down on us now, he's smiling."

"One more," Hannah said, refilling their glasses. "A toast to tomorrow, to our families coming to visit us. Rain or shine, we'll walk the path together."

"To all of us," Grace chimed in. "To life."